Praise for *New York Times* bestselling author

PENNY JORDAN

"Women everywhere will find pieces
of themselves in Jordan's characters."
—*Publishers Weekly*

"[Penny Jordan's novels] touch every emotion."
—*RT Book Reviews*

"Penny Jordan opens the Royal House of Niroli series
with *The Future King's Pregnant Mistress* (4 stars),
a charming story about who will be the successor
to the throne in Niroli."
—*RT Book Reviews*

"Jordan's record is phenomenal."
—*The Bookseller*

"Their passionate and romantic relationship is indeed
a fairy tale, and *A Royal Bride at the Sheikh's Command*
(4 stars) brings the Royal House of Niroli series to its
happily-ever-after ending."
—*RT Book Reviews*

Penny Jordan, one of Harlequin's most popular authors, sadly passed away on December 31st, 2011. She leaves an outstanding legacy, having sold over 100 million books around the world. Penny wrote a total of 187 novels for Harlequin, including the phenomenally successful *A Perfect Family, To Love, Honor and Betray, The Perfect Sinner* and *Power Play,* which hit the *New York Times* bestseller list. Loved for her distinctive voice, she was successful in part because she continually broke boundaries and evolved her writing to keep up with readers' changing tastes. *Publishers Weekly* said about Jordan, "Women everywhere will find pieces of themselves in Jordan's characters." It is perhaps this gift for sympathetic characterization that helps to explain her enduring appeal.

PENNY JORDAN
Collection

DUTY & DESIRE

HARLEQUIN®

entertain, enrich, inspire™

Special thanks and acknowledgment are given to Penny Jordan for her contribution to The Royal House of Niroli series.

ISBN-13: 978-0-373-24982-4

DUTY & DESIRE

Recycling programs for this product may not exist in your area.

www.Harlequin.com

Printed in U.S.A.

CONTENTS

THE FUTURE KING'S PREGNANT MISTRESS

CHAPTER ONE

MARCO OPENED HIS eyes, and looked at the bedside clock: three o'clock in the morning. He'd been dreaming about Niroli—and his grandfather, the king. His heart was still drumming insistently inside his chest, its beat driven by the adrenalin surges of challenge and excitement that reliving one of his past youthful arguments with his grandfather had brought him.

It had been in the aftermath of one of those arguments that Marco had made his decision to prove to himself, and to his grandfather, that he was capable of achieving success somewhere other than Niroli and without his grandfather's influence and patronage. He had been twenty-two then. Now he was thirty-six, and he and his grandfather had long since made a peace—of a sort—even if the older man had never really understood his grandson's refusal to change his mind about his vow to make his own way in the world. Marco had been determined that his success would come *not* as the grandson of the King of Niroli but via his own hard work. As simple Marco Fierezza, a young European entrepreneur, he had used his shrewd grasp of finance to become one of the City of London's most lauded financiers, and a billionaire.

In the last few years it had caused Marco a certain amount of wry amusement to note how his grandfather had turned to him for financial advice with regard to his own private wealth, whilst claiming that their blood tie absolved him of paying for Marco's services! The truth was, his grandfather was a wily old fox who wasn't above using whatever means he could to coerce others into doing what he wanted, often claiming that what he did was done for the good of Niroli, rather than himself.

Niroli!

Outside, the icy cold rain of London rattled against the windows of his Eaton Square apartment, and Marco felt a sudden sharp pang of longing for the beautiful Mediterranean island his family had ruled for so many generations: a sun-drenched jewel of green and gold in an aquamarine sea, from where dark volcanic mountains rose up wreathed in silvery clouds.

The same sea that had claimed the lives of his parents, he reminded himself sombrely, and which had not just robbed him of them, but also made him heir to the throne.

He had always known that ultimately he would become Niroli's king, but he had also believed that this event lay many years away in the future, something he could safely ignore in favour of enjoying his self-created, self-ruled present. However, the reality was that what he had thought of as his distant duty was now about to become his life.

Was that knowledge the reason for the dream he'd had? After all, when it came to the relationship he would have with his grandfather if he agreed to do as King Giorgio had requested and return to Niroli to become its ruler, wasn't there going to be an element of the prodigal male lion at the height of his powers returning to spar with the ageing pack leader? Marco knew and understood the older man very well. His grandfather might claim that he was ready to hand over the royal reins, but Marco suspected that Giorgio would still want to control whoever was holding them as much as he could. And yet, despite his awareness of this, Marco knew that the challenge of ruling Niroli and making it the country he wanted to see it become—by sweeping away the outdated and over-authoritarian structures his grandfather had put in place during his long reign—was one that excited him.

There had never been any doubt in Marco's mind that when ultimately he came to the throne he would make changes to the government of the island that would bring it into the twenty-first century. But then he had also envisaged succeeding his gentle, mild-mannered father, rather than having his tyrannical grandfather standing at his shoulder.

Marco gave a small dismissive shrug. Unlike his late father, a scholarly, quiet man who, Marco had recognised early in his life, had been bullied unmercifully and held in contempt by the King, Marco had never allowed himself to be overwhelmed by his grandfather, even as a child. They shared a common streak of almost brutally arrogant self-belief, and it had been this that had led to the conflict between them. Now, as a mature and powerful man, there was no way Marco intended to allow *anyone* to question his right to do things his own way. That said, he knew that taking the throne would necessitate certain changes in his own lifestyle; there were certain royal rules he would have to obey, if only to pay lip-service to them.

One of those rules forbade the King of Niroli to marry a divorcée. Marco was in no hurry to wed, but when he did he knew he would be expected to make a suitable dynastic union with some pre-approved royal princess of unimpeachable virtue. Somehow he didn't think that it would go down well with his subjects, or the paparazzi, if he were to be seen openly enjoying the company of a mistress, instead of dutifully finding himself a suitable consort.

He looked towards the bed where Emily lay sleeping, oblivious to what lay ahead and the fast-approaching end of their relationship. Her long blonde hair—naturally blonde, as he had good reason to know—was spread against the pillow. To Marco's surprise, he was suddenly tempted to reach out and twine his fingers through its silken strands, knowing that his touch would wake her, and knowing too that his body was hardening with his immediate need for the intimacy of her body. That he should still desire her so fiercely and so constantly after the length of time they had been together—so very much longer than he'd spent with any woman before—astonished him. But the needs and sexual desires of Marco Fierezza could not be compared with the challenge of becoming the King of Niroli, he acknowledged with his customary arrogance.

King of Niroli.

Emily knew nothing about his connection with Niroli, or his past, and consequently she knew nothing either about his future. Why should she? What reason would there have been for him to tell her, when he had deliberately chosen to live anonymously? He had left Niroli swearing to prove to his grandfather that he could stand on his own feet and make a success of his life without using his royal position, and had quickly discovered that his new anonymity had certain personal advantages; as second in line to Niroli's throne he had grown used to a certain type of predatory woman trying to lure him. His grandfather had warned him when he had been a teenager that he would have to be on his guard, and that he must accept he would never know whether the women who strived to share his bed wanted him for himself, or for who he was. Living in London as Marco Fierezza, rather than Prince Marco of Niroli though he was cynically aware that his combination of wealth and good looks drew the opposite sex to him, he did not attract the kind of feeding frenzy he would have done if he'd been using his royal title. Marco had no objection to rewarding his chosen lovers generously with expensive gifts and a luxurious lifestyle whilst he and they were together. He started to frown. It still irked him that Emily had always so steadfastly—and in his opinion foolishly—refused to accept the presents of jewellery he'd regularly tried to give her.

He'd told her dismissively to think of it as a bonus when she had demanded blankly, 'What's this for?' after he had given her a diamond bracelet to celebrate their first month together.

Her face had gone pale and she'd looked down at the leather box containing the bracelet—a unique piece he'd bought from one of the royal jewellers—her voice as stiff as her body. 'You don't need to bribe me, Marco. I'm with you because I want you, not because I want what you can buy me.'

Now Marco's frown deepened, his reaction to the memory of those words exactly as it had been when Emily had first uttered them. He could feel the same fierce, angry clenching of his muscles and surge of astounded disbelief that the woman who was enjoying the pleasure of his lovemaking and his wealth could dare to suggest that he might need to bribe her to share his bed!

He had soon put Emily in her place though, he reminded himself; his response to her had been a menacingly silky soft, 'No, you've misunderstood. After all, I already know exactly why you are in my bed and just how much you want me. The bribe, if you wish to think of it as that, is not to keep you there, but to ensure that you leave my bed speedily and silently when I've had enough of having you there.'

She hadn't said anything in reply, but he had seen in her expression what she was feeling. Although he'd never been able to get her to admit to it, he was reasonably sure that her subsequent very convenient business trip, which had taken her away from him for the best part of a week, had been something she had conjured up in an attempt to get back at him. And to make him hungry for her? No woman had the power to make herself so important to him that being with her mattered more than his own iron-clad determination never to allow his emotions to control him and so weaken him. He had grown up seeing how easily his strong-willed grandfather had used his own son's deep love for all those who were close to him to coerce, manipulate and, more often than not in Marco's eyes, humiliate him into doing what King Giorgio wanted. Marco had seen too much to have any illusions about the value of male pride, or the strength of will over gentleness and a desire to please others. Not that Marco hadn't loved his father; he had, so much so that as a young boy he had often furiously resented and verbally attacked his grandfather for the way the older man had treated his immediate heir.

That would never happen to him, Marco had decided then. He would allow no one, not even Niroli's king, to dictate to him.

Marco was well aware that, despite the fact that he had often angered his grandfather with his rebellious ways, the older man held a grudging respect for him. Their pride and their tenacity were attributes they had in common, and in many ways they were alike, although Marco knew that once *he* was Niroli's king there were many changes he would make in order to modernise the kingdom. Marco considered that the way his grandfather ruled Niroli was almost feudal; he'd shared his father's belief that it was essential to give people the opportunity to run their own lives, instead of treating them as his grandfather did, like very young, unschooled children who couldn't be trusted to make their own decisions. He had so many plans for Niroli: it was no wonder he was eager to step out of the role he had created for himself here in London to take on the mantle his birth had fated him to wear! The potential sexual frustration of being without a mistress bothered him a little but, after all, he was a mature man whose ambitions went a lot further than having a willing bed-mate with whom he would never risk making an emotional or legal commitment.

No, he wouldn't let himself miss Emily, he assured himself. The only reason he was giving valuable mental time to thinking about the issue was his concern that she might not accept his announcement that their affair was over as calmly as he wished. He had no desire to hurt her—far from it.

He still hadn't decided just how much he needed to tell her. He would be leaving London, of course, but he suspected that the paparazzi were bound to get wind of what was happening on Niroli, since it was ruled by the wealthiest royal family in the world.

For her own sake, Emily needed to have it made clear to her that nothing they had shared could impinge on his future as Niroli's king. He had never really understood her steadfast refusal to accept his expensive gifts, or to allow him to help her either financially or in any other way with her small interior design business. Because he couldn't understand it, despite the fact that they had been lovers for almost three years, Marco, being the man he was, had inwardly wondered what she might be hoping to gain from him that was worth more to her than his money. It was second nature to him not to trust anyone. Plus, he had learned from observing his grandfather and members of his court what happened to those whose natures allowed others to take advantage of them, as his own father had done.

Marco tensed, automatically shying away from the unwanted pain that thinking about his parents and their deaths could still cause him. He didn't want to acknowledge that pain, and he certainly didn't want to acknowledge the confused feelings he had buried so deeply: pain on his father's behalf, guilt because he could see what his grandfather had been doing to his father and yet he hadn't been able to prevent it, anger with his father for having been so weak, anger with his grandfather for having taken advantage of that weakness, and himself for having seen what he hadn't wanted to see.

He and his grandfather had made their peace, his father was gone, he himself was a man and not a boy any more. It was only in his dreams now that he sometimes revisited the pain of his past. When he did, that pain could be quickly extinguished in the raw passion of satisfying his physical desire for Emily.

But what about the time when Emily would no longer be there? Why was he wasting his time asking himself such foolish questions? Ultimately he would find himself another mistress, no doubt via a discreet liaison with the right kind of woman, perhaps a young wife married to an older husband, though not so young that she didn't understand the rules, of course. He might even, if Emily had been sensible enough, have thought about providing her with the respectability of marriage to some willing courtier in order that they carry on their affair, once he became King of Niroli. But, Marco acknowledged, the very passion that made her such a responsive lover also meant she was not the type who would adapt to the traditional role of royal mistress.

Emily would love Niroli, an island so beautiful and fruitful that ancient lore had said Prometheus himself caused it to rise up from the sea bed so that he could bestow it on mankind.

When Marco thought of the place of his birth, his mental image was one of an island bathed in sunlight, an island so richly gifted by the gods that it was little wonder some legends had referred to it as an earthly paradise.

But where there was great beauty there was also terrible cruelty, as was true of so many legends. The gods had often exacted a terrible price from Niroli for their gifts.

He pushed back the duvet, knowing that he wouldn't be able to sleep now. His body was lean and powerful, magnificently drawn, as though etched by one of the great masters, in the charcoal shadows of the moonlight as he left the bed and padded silently toward the window.

The wind had picked up and was lashing rain against the windows, bending the bare branches of the trees on the street outside. Marco was again transported back to Niroli, where violent storms often swept over the island, whipping up its surrounding seas. The people of Niroli knew not to venture out during the high tides that battered the volcanic rock cliffs of a mountain range so high and so inaccessible in parts that even today it still protected and concealed the bandit descendants of Barbary pirates who long ago had invaded the island. In fact, the fierce seas sucking deep beneath the cliffs had honeycombed them into underwater caves and weakened the rock so that whole sections of it had fallen away. The gales that stirred the seas also tore and ripped at the ancient olive trees and the grapevines on the island, as though to punish them because their harvest had already been plucked to safety.

As a boy Marco had loved to watch the wind savage the land far below the high turrets of the royal castle. He would kneel on the soft padded seating beneath an ancient stone window embrasure, excited by the danger of the storm, wanting to go out and accept the challenge it threw at him. But he had never been allowed to go outside and play as other children did. Instead, at his grandfather's insistence, he'd had to remain within the castle walls, learning about his family's past and his own future role as the island's ultimate ruler.

Inside Marco's head, images he couldn't control were starting to form, curling wraithlike from his childhood memories. It had always been his grandfather and not his parents who had dictated the rules of his childhood, and who'd seen that they were imposed on him...

'Marco, come back to bed. It's cold without you.' Emily's voice was soft and slow, warm, full and sweet with promise, like the fruit of Niroli's vines at the time of harvest, when the grapes lay heavily beneath the sun swollen with ripe readiness and with implicit invitation.

He turned round. He had woken her after all. Emily ran her small interior design business from a small shop-cum-office just off London's Sloane Street. Marco had known from the moment he first saw her at a PR cocktail party that he'd wanted her, and that he'd intended to have her. And he'd made sure that she'd known it too. Marco was used to getting his own way, to claiming his right to direct the course of his own life, even if that meant imposing his will on those who would oppose him. This was an imperative for him, one he refused to be swayed from. He had quickly elucidated that Emily was a divorced woman with no children, and that had made her pattern-card perfect for the role of his mistress. If he had known then her real emotional and sexual history, he knew that he would not have pursued her. But, by the time he had discovered the truth, his physical desire for her had been such that it had been impossible for him to reject her.

He looked towards her now, feeling that desire gripping him again and fighting against it as he had fought all his life against anything or anyone who threatened to control him.

'Marco, something's wrong. What is it?'

Where had it come from, this unwanted ability she

seemed to possess of sensing what she could not possibly be able to know? The year his parents died, the storms had come early to Niroli. Marco could remember how when he had first received the news, even before he had said anything, she had somehow guessed that something was wrong. However, whilst she might be intuitive where his feelings were concerned, Emily hadn't yet been shrewd or suspicious enough to make the connection between the announcement of his parents' deaths and the news in the media about the demise of the next in line to the Niroli throne. He remembered how hurt she had looked when he'd informed her that he would be attending his mother and father's funeral without her, but she hadn't said a word. Maybe because she hadn't wanted to provoke a row that might have led to him ending their affair, the reason she didn't want it to end being that, for all her apparent lack of interest in his money, she had to be well aware of what she would lose financially if their relationship came to a close. It was, in Marco's opinion, impossible for any woman to be as unconcerned about the financial benefits of being his mistress as Emily affected to be. It was as his grandfather had warned him: the women who thronged around him expected to be lavishly rewarded with expensive gifts and had no compunction about making that plain.

Under cover of the room's darkness, Emily grimaced to hear the note of pleading in her own voice. Why, when she despised herself so much for what she was becoming, couldn't she stop herself? Was she destined always to have relationships that resulted in her feeling insecure?

'Nothing's wrong,' Marco told her. There was a note in his voice that made her body tense and her emotions flinch despite everything she was trying to do not to let that happen. The trouble was that once you started lying to yourself on an almost hourly, never mind daily, basis about the reality of your relationship, once you started pretending not to notice or care about being the 'lesser' partner, about not being valued or respected enough, you entered a place where the strongest incentive was not to seek out the truth but rather to hide from it. But she had no one but herself to blame for her current situation, she reminded herself.

She had known right from the start what kind of man Marco was, and the type of relationship he wanted with her. The problem was that she had obviously known Marco's agenda rather better than she had understood her own. Although she tried not to do so, sometimes when she was feeling at her lowest—times like now—she couldn't stop herself from giving in to the temptation of fantasising about how Marco could be different: he would not be so fabulously wealthy or arrogantly sexy that he could have any woman he wanted, but instead he'd be just an ordinary man with ordinary goals—a happy marriage, a wife... Her heart kicked heavily, turning over in a slow grind of pain. She thought of children—theirs—and it turned over again, the pain growing more intense.

Why, why, *why* had she been such a fool and fallen in love with Marco? He had made it plain from the start what he wanted from her and what he would give her back in return, and love had never been part of the deal. But then, way back when, she had never imagined that she would fall for him. At the beginning, she had wanted Marco so much, she had been happy to go along with a purely sexual relationship, for as long as he wanted her.

No, she had no one but herself to blame for the constant pain she was now having to endure, the deceit she was having to practise and the fear that haunted her: one day soon Marco would sense that deceit and leave her. She loathed herself so much for her own weakness and for not having the guts to acknowledge her love or take the consequences of walking away from him, through the inevitable fiery consuming pain. But, who knew? Maybe walking away from Marco would have a phoenix-like effect on her and allow her to find freedom as a new person. She was such a coward, though, that she couldn't take that step. Hadn't someone once said that a brave man died only once but a coward died a thousand times? So it was for her. She knew that she ought to leave and deal with her feelings, but instead she stayed and suffered a thousand hurtful recognitions every day of Marco's lack of love for her.

But he desired her, and she couldn't bring herself to give up the fragile hope that maybe, just maybe, things would change, and one day he would look at her and know that he loved her, that one day he would allow her to access that part of himself he guarded with such ferocity and tell her that he wanted them to be together for ever…

CHAPTER TWO

THAT WAS EMILY'S dream. But the reality was, recently, she'd felt as if they were growing further apart rather than closer. She'd told herself yesterday morning she would face her fear. She took a deep breath.

'Marco, I've always been open and…and honest with you…' It was no good, she couldn't do it. She couldn't make herself ask him that all-important question: 'Do you want to end our relationship?' And, besides, she hadn't always been honest with him, had she? She hadn't told him, for instance, that she had fallen in love with him. Her heart gave another painful lurch.

Marco was watching her, his head inclined towards her. He wore his thick dark hair cut short, but not so short that she couldn't run her fingers through it, shaping the hard bone beneath it as she held him to her when they made love. There was just enough light for her to see the gleam in his eyes, as though he'd guessed the direction her thoughts had taken and knew how much she wanted him. Marco had the most piercingly direct look she'd ever known. He'd focused it on her the night they'd met, when she had tried to cling to reason and rationality, instead of letting herself be blatantly seduced by a pair of tawny-brown predator's eyes…

Emily knew she should make her stand now and demand an explanation for the change she could sense in Marco, but her childhood made it difficult for her to talk openly about her emotions. Instead she hid them away behind locked doors of calm control and self-possession. Was it because she was afraid of what might happen if she allowed her real feelings to get out of control? Because she was afraid of bringing the truth out into the open? Something *was* wrong. Marco *had* changed: he had become withdrawn and preoccupied. There was no way she could pretend otherwise. Had he grown tired of her? Did he want to end their relationship? Wouldn't it be better, wiser, more self-respecting, if she challenged him to tell her the truth? Did she really think that if she ignored her fears they would simply disappear?

'You say that you've always been open and honest with me, Emily, but that isn't the truth, is it?'

Emily's heart somersaulted with slow, sickening despair. He knew? Somehow he had guessed what she was thinking and—almost as bad—she could see he was spoiling for an argument...because that would give him an excuse to end things.

'Remember the night I took you to dinner and you told me about your marriage? Remember how "open" you were with me then—and what you didn't tell me?' Marco recalled sarcastically.

Emily couldn't speak. A mixture of relief and anguish filled her. Her marriage! All this time she had thought—believed—that Marco had understood the scars her past had inflicted on her, but now she realised that she had been wrong. 'It wasn't deliberate, you know that,' she told him, fighting not to let her voice tremble. 'I didn't deliberately hold back anything.' Why was he bringing that up now? she wondered. Surely he wasn't planning to use it as an excuse to get rid of her? He wasn't the kind of man who needed an excuse to do anything, she told herself. He was too arrogant to feel he needed to soften any blows he had to deliver.

Marco looked away from Emily, irritated with himself for saying what he had. Why had he brought up her marriage now, when the last thing he wanted was the danger involved in the sentimentality of looking back to the beginning of their relationship? But it was too late, he *was* already remembering…

He had taken Emily to dinner, setting the scene for how he had hoped the evening would end by telling her coolly how much he wanted to make love to her and how pleased he was that she was a woman of the world, with a marriage behind her and no children to worry about.

'Just out of interest,' he'd quizzed her, 'what was the reason for your divorce?' If there was anything in her past, he wanted to know about it before things went any further.

For a moment he thought that she was going to refuse to answer him. But then her eyes widened slightly and he knew that she had correctly interpreted his question, without him having to spell it out to her. She clearly knew that if she did refuse, their relationship would be over before it had properly begun.

When she finally began to speak, she surprised him with the halting, almost stammering way in which she hesitated and then fiddled nervously with her cutlery, suddenly looking far less calm and in control than he had previously seen her. Her face was shadowed with anxiety and he assumed that the cause of the breakdown in her marriage must have been related to something she had done—such as being unfaithful to her husband. The last thing he expected to hear was what she actually told him. So much so, in fact, that he was tempted to accuse her of lying, but something he saw in her eyes stopped him…

Now Marco shifted his weight from one foot to the other, remembering how shocked he'd been by the unexpected and unwilling compassion he had felt for her as she'd struggled to overcome her reluctance to talk about what was obviously a painful subject…

'I lost my parents in a car accident when I was seven and I was brought up by my widowed paternal grandfather,' she told him.

'He wasn't unkind to me, but he wasn't a man who was comfortable around young children, especially not emotional young girls. He was a retired Cambridge University academic, very gentle and very unworldly. He read the classics to me as bedtime stories. He knew so much about literature but, although I didn't realise it at the time, very little about life. My upbringing with him was very sheltered and protected, very restricted in some ways, especially when I reached my early teens and his health started to deteriorate.

'Gramps' circle of friends was very small, a handful of elderly fellow academics, and…and Victor.'

'Victor?' Marco probed, hearing the hesitation in her voice.

'Yes. Victor Lewisham, my ex-husband. He had been one of Gramps' students, before becoming a university lecturer himself.'

'He must have been considerably older than you?' Marco guessed.

'Twenty years older,' Emily agreed, nodding her head. 'When it became obvious that my grandfather's health was deteriorating, he told me that Victor had agreed to look after me after…in his place. Gramps died a few weeks after that. I was in my first year at university then, and, even though I'd known how frail he was, somehow I hadn't…I wasn't prepared. Losing him was such a shock. He was all I had, you see, and so when Victor proposed to me and told me that it was what Gramps would have wanted, I…' She ducked her head and looked away from Marco and then said in a low voice, 'I should have refused, but somehow I just couldn't imagine how I would manage on my own. I was so afraid…such a coward.'

'So it was a marriage of necessity?' Marco shrugged dismissively. 'Was he good in bed?'

It continued to irk Marco to have to admit that his direct and unsubtle challenge to Emily had sprung from a sudden surge of physical jealousy that the thought of her with another man had aroused. But then sexual jealousy wasn't an emotion he'd ever previously had to deal with. Sex was sex, a physical appetite satisfied by a physical act. Emotions didn't come into it and he had never seen why they should. He still didn't. And he still had no idea what had made him confront her like that, or what had driven such an out-of-character fury at the thought of her with another man, even though she had had yet to become his. It had caught him totally off guard when he had seen the sudden shimmer of suppressed tears in her eyes. At first he'd wanted to believe they were caused by her grief at the breakdown of her marriage, but to his shock, she had told him quietly:

'Our marriage…our relationship, in fact, was never physically consummated.'

Marco remembered how he had struggled not to show his astonishment, perhaps for the first time in his life recognising that what he had needed to show wasn't the arrogant disbelief so often evinced by his grandfather, but instead restraint and patience, to give her time to explain. Which was exactly what she had done, once she had silently checked that he wasn't going to refuse to believe her.

'I was too naïve to realise at first that Victor making no attempt to approach me sexually might not be a…because of gentlemanly consideration for my inexperience,' she continued. 'And then even after we were married—I didn't want him, you see, so it was easy for me not to question why he didn't want to make love to me. If I hadn't lived such a sheltered life, and I'd spent more time with people my own age, things would probably have been different, and I'd certainly have been more aware that something wasn't right. But as it was, it wasn't until I…I found him in bed with someone else that I realised—'

'He had a mistress,' Marco interrupted her, his normal instinct to question and probe reasserting itself.

There was just the merest pause before she told him quietly, 'He had a lover, yes. A *male* lover,' she emphasised shakily.

'I should have guessed, of course, and I suspect poor Victor thought that I had. He treated me very much as a junior partner in our relationship, like a child whom he expected to revere him and accept his superiority. For me to find him in bed with one of his young students was a terrible blow to his pride. He couldn't forgive me for blundering in on them, and the only way I could forgive myself for being so foolish was to insist that we divorce. At first he was reluctant to agree. He belonged more to my grandfather's generation than to his own, I suspect. He couldn't come to terms with his sexuality, which was why he had tried to conceal it within a fake marriage. He refused to say why he couldn't be open about his sexual nature. He got very angry when I tried to talk to him about it and suggested that, for his own sake, he should accept himself. The truth was, as I quickly learned, that to others his sexuality was not the secret he liked to think. There was no valid reason why he should have hidden it, but he was just that kind of man.

'I'd been left a bit of money by my grandfather, so I came to London and got a job. I'd always been interested in interior design, so I went back to college to get my qualifications and then a couple of years ago, after working for someone else's studio, I set up in business on my own. I wanted a fresh start and to get away from people who had known…about Victor. They must have thought me such a fool for not realising. I felt almost as though I was some kind of freak… Married, but not married.'

'And a virgin?' Marco added.

'Yes,' Emily agreed, before continuing, 'I wanted to be somewhere where no one was going to make assumptions about me because of my marriage.'

Their food arrived before Marco had the chance to ask her about the man whom he assumed must have eventually taken her virginity. But he wondered about him. And envied him?

Marco frowned now, not wanting to remember the fierce sense of urgency to make Emily totally his that had filled him then and that had continued to hold him in its grip even when he had ultimately possessed her.

He walked back to the bed whilst Emily watched him, her heart thumping unsteadily into her ribs. They had been lovers for almost three years, but Marco still had the same effect on her as he had done the first time she had seen him; the impact of his male sexuality was such that it both enthralled and overwhelmed her, even now when she could feel the pain of the emotional gulf between them almost as strongly as she felt her own desire. When they had first met, she had immediately craved him, though she hadn't known then that her desire for him would enslave her emotionally as well as physically. And if she had, would she have behaved differently? Would she still have turned on the heels of those expensive Gina shoes she'd been wearing and have tip-tapped away from him as fast as she could?

Emily was glad of the night's shadows to conceal the pain in her eyes—a pain that would betray her if Marco

saw it. It had been just before Christmas when she had
first noticed that he'd seemed irritated and preoccupied,
retreating into himself and excluding her. She had thought
at first he must have some big business deal going down,
but now she was beginning to fear that the source of his
discontent might be her and their relationship. If his with-
drawal had begun in the months immediately after the accident in which Marco had lost both his parents, she might
have been able to tell herself that it was his grief that was
responsible. After all, even a man who prided himself on
being as unemotional as Marco did was bound to suffer
after such a traumatic event. However, the first thing he
had done on his return was take her to bed, without saying a word about either the funeral or his family, making
love to her fiercely and almost compulsively.

Marco had rarely talked to her about his childhood, and
never about his family. That had suited her perfectly at first.
She had looked on her relationship with him initially as
a necessary transition for her from naïveté to experience,
a much-needed bridge across the chasm dividing her past
from her future, her passport to a new life and womanhood. Because even then she had hoped that, one day, she
would find a true partner: a man with whom she could
share her life; a man to whom she could give her love as
freely as he would give his to her; a man with whom she
could have children.

But how foolish she had been, how recklessly unaware
of the danger she had been placing herself in. It had simply
never occurred to her then that she might fall in love with
Marco! He had been totally open with her about the way
he lived his life and what he looked for in his relationships:
whilst they were together she could rely on his total fidelity, but once their relationship was over, it would be over,
full stop. He wanted no emotional commitment from her

nor should she expect one from him. And most important of all, she must not get pregnant.

'But what if there's an accident and…?' she asked him uncertainly.

He stopped her immediately.

'There will not be any accidents,' he told her bluntly. 'With modern methods of contraception, there is no reason why there should be an accident—if you have any reason to suspect there may have been, then you must ensure that the situation is rectified without any delay.'

She wanted him too much to allow herself to admit how shocked she was by his cold-hearted attitude. Instead, she told herself that it didn't really matter, since she wanted to wait to have her children until she had found the right father for them and the right man for her.

Marco had pursued her so relentlessly and determinedly and she had wanted him so badly that the truth was whatever doubts she might have had had been totally overwhelmed by the sexual excitement they generated between them. For the first time in her life she knew the true meaning of the word 'lust'. Her every waking thought—and most of her dreams too—were of him and what it was going to be like when he took her to bed.

Thanks to the kindness of her first employer, who had passed on to her some of his clients when she had started up on her own, she had established a good and profitable business, which earned her enough to enable her to visit one of London's more exclusive lingerie shops in search of the kind of discreetly provocative underwear her fevered imagination hoped would delight and excite Marco. Within a week of meeting him, she had taken to wearing the seductively skimpy bits of silk and lace to work, just in case Marco appeared and insisted on taking her to his apartment to consummate their relationship. It made her smile now to remember how sensually brave she had felt. And the things she had imagined might happen...

Her fevered imaginings had come nowhere near to matching the reality of her reaction to Marco's skilled love-making. He had undressed her slowly and expertly, in her pretty bedroom in her small Chelsea house, almost teasing her by making her quivering body wait for his touch. And then, even when he had finally touched her, his caresses had been tantalisingly—tormentingly—light, the merest brush of fingertips and lips, which had fed her longing for something darker and far more intimate. Just thinking about it now was enough to make her heart turn over inside her chest and make her go weak with longing for him. She remembered how she had tried to show him her impatience, but Marco had refused to be hurried. His lips had teased the tight flesh of her nipples, and his fingers had brushed her belly and then stroked lightly against her thighs whilst she had sighed with arousal. His hand had parted her thighs, his fingers stroking over her sex, his touch making her want to moan out loud with hunger.

He had just begun to kiss her more passionately when the telephone beside her bed had begun to ring. Idiotically she had answered it, only to discover that the caller was one of her more difficult clients who wanted to discuss her idea for a new makeover. By the time she had got rid of the client, Marco had got dressed, smiling urbanely at her, but making it clear that he was *not* going to take second place to her business.

The incident had shown her that he would always have it his way and she had not made the same mistake again. Or had her mistake been in tailoring her working life around him? That hadn't been just for his benefit though; she had wanted to make room in her life for him. Something deep inside her, which she had only recently begun to recognise, was showing her that she was the kind of woman who secretly longed to be the hub of her family, both as a wife and a mother. She didn't want to be on the other side of the world helping a client to choose the right paint shade for her new décor, leaving her partner to come home from work to an empty house and an empty bed. When she did marry and have children, she wanted to be the one those children ran to with their small everyday triumphs and hurts. She enjoyed her work, and she was proud of the ways in which she had built up her business, but she knew that it was the pleasure of creating a happy environment for those she loved that truly motivated her, rather than the excitement of a large bank balance.

Nonetheless, Marco was the kind of man who enjoyed a challenge, and it had made her feel a bit better when, later, he'd admitted how much he had ached for her that night. It could not have been any more than she had ached for him, she knew. Less than three months after they had first met he had asked her to move in with him. And then they'd had their first quarrel, when she had discovered that he'd expected her to give up her business, saying imperiously that he would give her an allowance that would more than compensate her for any loss of income.

'I want to be with you,' she told him fiercely. 'But I will not give up my financial independence, Marco. I don't want your money.'

'So what do you want?' he demanded, almost suspiciously.

'You,' she told him simply, and their quarrel was forgotten, as he was appeased by her bold request—or so she had thought. It was only later she had learned that, far from respecting her for refusing his money and his expensive gifts, he was both suspicious of her and slightly contemptuous. Perhaps if she had heeded the warning that knowledge had given her, she would not be in the situation she was now.

CHAPTER THREE

THEY HAD SHARED such wonderful months. Marco worked hard, but he believed in enjoying the good things in life as well. He had the air of someone who was used to the best of everything. But whilst sometimes she had deplored his inbuilt arrogance, and had teased him gently about it, Emily admitted that she'd enjoyed the new experiences to which he'd introduced her. Marco had taken her out several times a week but, best of all, as a lover he hadn't just fulfilled her fantasies, he had exceeded them and then taken her with him to realms of sexual discovery and delight she had never imagined existed.

Within weeks of them becoming lovers she had been so exquisitely sensually aware of him that just the touch of his hand on her arm, or the look in his eyes when he'd needed her to know that he wanted her, had been enough to have her answering with a look of her own that said, 'Please take me to bed.' Not that they had always made it to a bed. Marco was a demanding and masterful lover who enjoyed leading the way and introducing her to new pleasures, sometimes taking her quickly and erotically in venues so nearly public that she blushed guiltily afterwards when she remembered, sometimes ensuring their lovemaking lasted all night—or most of the day. And she had been an eager pupil, wanting him more as time went by, rather than less, as her own sexuality and confidence grew under his expert guidance.

The first Christmas they had shared together, Marco had given her a beautiful three-carat diamond, which he had told her she could have set in the ring design of her choice. Emily knew that it had surprised him when she'd asked him instead to make a donation to her favourite children's charity.

Marco hadn't said anything, but on her birthday he had taken her away to a romantic hideaway and made love to her until she had cried with joy. He had then presented her with a pair of two-carat diamond ear-studs, telling her, 'I have sent a cheque of equivalent value to your charity.'

It had been then that she had realised that she had done the unforgivable and fallen in love with him!

Yes, how very foolish she had been to do that. He was back in their bed now, but lying with his back to her. Outside, the gale that had begun to blow earlier last evening hurled itself against the windows as the storm increased in force.

Normally, the knowledge that she was safe and warm inside whilst outside ice-cold rain sleeted down would have given her a feeling of delicious security, especially if she was wrapped up tightly in Marco's arms. But of course she wasn't. *Was* he tiring of her?

MARCO COULD HEAR Emily breathing softly behind her. His body craved the release physically possessing her would bring, and why shouldn't he have it? he asked himself. He had already decided on the financial amount he was prepared to give Emily in recognition of the time they had spent together—a very generous one. So generous that he felt justified now in thinking that he might as well continue to enjoy her. He couldn't entirely get his head around the fact that he wanted Emily still, when other women who had shared his bed before her—women who had been so

much more experienced and sexually enterprising—had
bored him so quickly. It surprised him even more that he
had actually grown to want her company away from bed,
to the extent of talking to her about his business, and allowing her to persuade him to make donations to her precious charity. He had scarcely even been able to believe
it at first when he had found out how much of her modest income she gave to helping a foundation set up to help
London's deprived children and teenagers. Emily would
not approve of his grandfather's refusal to do anything to
help the least wealthy of Niroli's people; King Giorgio did
not see the sense of educating the poor to expect more out
of life than he felt the island could give them.

No, Emily was definitely not suitable material as the
King of Niroli's mistress. But, of course, he was not yet
King. Purposefully Marco moved, swiftly reaching for
her, briefly studying the outline of her figure, the curve of
her breast making him remember how perfectly its softness fitted into his cupped hand. As always, the strongly
sensual core of his nature reacted to Emily's nearness. He
might have already made love with her a thousand times
and more during their relationship, but that couldn't dim
the fierce desire he felt now. Somewhere deep down within
himself he registered the potential danger of such a com-
pulsion and then dismissed it. He intended to end his affair with her before he left for Niroli. He'd make sure that
no vestige of longing for her would cling to his memory
or his senses; he was determined she would be easily replaced in his bed. If his body recognised something in her
that was particularly enjoyable, that did not mean that he
was in danger of craving her for ever. He relaxed as he dismissed as ludicrous the notion that he was at any kind of
risk from his desire for her.

The moment Marco touched her, Emily could feel her

body becoming softly compliant, outwardly and inwardly, where it tightened and ached, the desire for him that never left her ramping up with a swift familiarity. Marco pushed back the bedclothes; a thin beam of moonlight silvered her breast, plucking sensually at her nipple and tightening it for his visual appreciation and enjoyment. He traced its circle of light, making her shiver with pleasure whilst her back began to arch in an age-old symbolic female gesture of enticement in offering her flesh to her lover.

Marco's hands tightened on Emily's slender form. She looked up at him, her eyes wide with arousal and excitement as she reached up to him. All that mattered to him right now was his possession of her, his pleasure found in witnessing her ecstasy as he took her and filled her, losing himself in her and taking her with him. His need pounded through him, obliterating everything else. He pushed aside her hair and kissed the side of her neck where he knew his touch reduced her to quivering delight, his hands cupping her breasts, kneading them erotically, his erection already stiff against her thigh where he had locked her to him with one out-flung leg.

Emily smiled to herself. Sex to Marco meant physically claiming every bit of her. Even when he kissed her casually, he liked to have her body in full contact with his. Not that she minded. Not one little bit! She loved the possessive sensuality of his desire for her. It was only in his arms, here like this, that she was truly able to let her real feelings have their head, instead of fighting to preserve the protective air of calm control she normally used to conceal them. When he made love to her, Marco never held back from showing her his passion for her, which, in turn, allowed her to set free her equally passionate longing for him. There was sometimes something almost pagan in the way they made love that secretly sometimes half shocked her. Always attuned to Marco's moods, tonight she sensed an urgency about him that added an extra edge to her own growing sexual tension. She gave a soft whimper as his mouth took the silvered ache of her nipple and his hand accepted the invitation of her open legs.

Once in their early days as lovers, sensing her uncertainty and slight awkwardness with her own sexuality, he had relaxed her with an evening of champagne and slow lovemaking, before coaxing her to let him position both of them where she could see the reflection of their naked bodies in a mirror. Then carefully, and with breathtakingly deliberate sensuality, he had revealed to her the mysteries of her own sex, showing her its desire-swollen and flushed outer lips, caressing them so that she could see her body's reaction to his touch, sliding his fingertip the whole length of her wetness before focusing on the tight, excited and oh-so-sexually-sensitive flesh of her clitoris. He had brought her to orgasm there in full view of her own half-shocked, half-excited gaze.

But she'd had her own sweet revenge later, turning the tables on him by exploring him with shamelessly avid hands and lips, spreading apart his heavily muscled male thighs so that she could know the reality of his sex with every one of her senses.

Now, as his fingers probed her wetness, she rose up eager to accept their gift of pleasure. But, for once, he didn't seem inclined to draw out their love-play, instead suddenly groaning and reaching for her, covering her and thrusting powerfully and compulsively into her, as though he couldn't get enough of her, driving them both higher, deeper, closer to the sanctuary that waited for them.

Instinctively Emily clung to him, riding the storm with him, welcoming him and sharing its turbulence.

Marco could feel an unfamiliar urgency possessing him

and compelling him, demanding that he thrust harder and deeper. Emily shuddered beneath the intensity of his passion, immediately responsive to it. Her nails raked his back where his flesh lay tightly against his muscles, inciting him to fill her and complete her. The sensation of the tight heat of her wetness as it gripped and caressed him flooded everything but his ability to respond to her sensual urging from his mind. A primitive need surged through him. It had been some time since he'd last used a condom when they had sex; their relationship was of a long enough duration for him to know that there were no health reasons for him to do so, and that Emily was on the pill. Also, he knew how much she herself loved the skin-on-skin contact of their meshing bodies.

Was Marco aware of how deeply he was penetrating her, Emily wondered dizzily, or how intense and primeval a pleasure it was for her, as surges of sensation built, promising her orgasm? Did he know that when he came he would spill so very close to her womb? Did he know how much she wanted him; how much she ached now, right now, for him? She gave a low, soft, almost tormented cry as her orgasm began, clutching at Marco, her head thrown back in pagan ecstasy as her pleasure shuddered through her, only to intensify into a second spiral of even greater intensity that shook her in its grip and melted her bones as Marco came hotly inside her.

Emily blinked fiercely. What they had just shared had been incredibly close and physically satisfying. Emotional tears slid down her face. Surely it wasn't possible for Marco to make love to her like this and not be in love with her? Perhaps the change she had sensed in him was because he *was* falling in love with her and he was reluctant to admit it? Tenderness for him, and for the vulnerability she knew he would never admit to, stole through her. She snuggled closer to him, warmed by his body and the intimacy they had shared, and most of all by the glow of the hope growing inside her. She would teach him that their love would make him stronger, not weaker; she would show him, as she'd tried to do all along, that *he* was what mattered to her and not the things he could give her. Marco had never told her why he was so adamant that love wasn't something he believed in or wanted, and she assumed that it must be because as a very young man he had been badly hurt and had vowed never to fall in love again. In a man as proud as Marco, such a wound would go very deep. Although people had been quick to gossip to her about him when she'd first met him, and about the stream of glamorous women who'd graced his arm and his bed before her, no one seemed to know much about his life before he had come to London. Marco was fiercely protective of his past and his privacy, and Emily had learned very early on in their relationship how shuttered he could be when she tried to get him to open up to her. So, it had to mean something that they were still together, Emily told herself sleepily. Why shouldn't that something be that he had fallen in love with her without even realising it?

CHAPTER FOUR

'AND I WANT the whole place to—y'know—like be totally me. So there'll have to be plenty of pink and loads of open-plan storage for my shoes. All my fans know that I'm a total shoe-freak.'

Emily was finding it a struggle to focus on what her latest client was saying, and not just because the reality-TV star's views on how she wanted her apartment designed and decorated were depressingly banal, she admitted.

The truth was that her normal professionalism and love of her work had in recent weeks become shadowed by her almost constant tiredness and bouts of sickness that had to be the legacy of a virus that she didn't seem to have entirely thrown off.

The reality-TV star was pouting and looking impatiently at her watch.

'Do we have to do this?' she asked the PR executive who was 'minding' her. 'I thought you said that I'd be doing a TV documentary about me designing my new apartment, not doing boring stuff like listening to some decorator.'

Whilst the PR girl attempted to soothe her charge, Emily moved discreetly out of earshot. Marco had left early this morning for his office whilst she had still been asleep, leaving her a scrawled note on the kitchen counter to say that he had some work he needed to catch up on. There was nothing particularly unusual in his early start. As an entrepreneur he often needed to be at his desk while the

Far-Eastern financial markets were dealing. But today, for some reason, Emily was conscious of a deep-rooted emotional need to see him, be with him. Why? Surely not just because he had left without waking her to give her a good-morning kiss? A little rueful, she shook her head over her own neediness, determined to dismiss it. But it refused to go away, if anything sharpening so that it became a fierce ache of anxious longing. She looked at her watch. It was almost lunchtime. In the early stages of their relationship before Marco had told her that he wanted her to move in with him, she had, with some trepidation, and with what she had considered to be great daring, taken him up on what she had believed to be a casual invitation to drop in on him if she was ever passing by his office. Emily's heart started to go faster in a sudden flurry of excited little beats, the grating sound of the TV star's voice fading, as she recalled how she had taken him up on his offer...

Marco's initial greeting of her had not been welcoming. 'You were beginning to annoy me with the way you've been deliberately keeping me waiting,' he told her flatly, after his secretary had shown her into his office and then discreetly left them alone together. 'In fact you were beginning to annoy me so much that if you left it another day to visit, you wouldn't have got past my receptionist,' he added arrogantly.

His verbal attack stunned her into a bewildered silence, which had her shaking her head in mute protest.

'If you think that by holding me off, and making me wait, you'll—'

'Why on earth should I do that?' Emily interrupted him, too shocked by his accusations to recognise what she was giving away until she saw the satisfaction gleaming in his eyes.

He came towards her saying softly, 'Well, in that case,

we've got some catching up to do, haven't we?' When he took hold of her hands and drew her towards him, she was trembling so much with arousal and excitement that he smiled again. Not that he wasn't equally turned on; he told her with sexy intent in between his kisses how much he wanted her and what that wanting was doing to him.

If his telephone hadn't rung, Emily suspected that she would have let him make love to her there and then in his office. She certainly hadn't tried to stop him when he had unfastened her blouse and peeled back the lace of her bra, exposing her breast to his glitteringly erotic gaze and the skilled touch of his hand. His lips had been on its creamy slope when his phone had rung. She had tried to straighten her clothes as he'd answered the call, but he had stopped her, very deliberately tracing the tight excitement of her nipple with one lazy fingertip whilst he'd spoken to his caller. Emily could feel her body tightening now as she remembered the effect the highly charged atmosphere between them had had on her, and the contrast between the calm, businesslike tone of his voice and the deliberately sensual way in which he had been touching her. By the time he had finished his call she had been aching with longing for him to take their intimacy to its natural conclusion, but instead he had released her, fastening her top and then saying calmly, 'Come on, let's go out and have some lunch.'

She hadn't known him well enough then, of course, to realise that his deliberate arousal of her had been his way of punishing her for what he believed had been her attempt to control their relationship, and him.

Those had been such achingly sweet times, when they had first met. Suddenly she yearned to recapture them. Impulsively, she went over to the PR girl and told her firmly, 'I'm afraid I have to go. You've got my e-mail address if you need to contact me.' Emily suspected from the look the TV star was giving her that she wasn't going to get any commission for this project. But then, she told herself, right now being with Marco was more important to her than anything.

MARCO STOOD BESIDE his desk in the sleek modern office suite where he conducted his global financial affairs. When he had left Niroli vowing to make his own mark in the world without his royal status, his grandfather had laughed at him and warned him that he would be back within six months with his tail between his legs. He could have been, Marco admitted: at twenty-two, his belief in his own abilities had been far greater than his financial astuteness; initially he had lost money as he'd played the international stock markets. But, just when he had begun to fear the worst, his mother's great aunt had died in Italy, leaving him a substantial amount of money. A second stroke of luck had led him to come to the attention of one of the city's richest entrepreneurs, who had taken Marco under his wing, teaching him to use his skills and hone his killer financial instincts. Within a year, Marco had doubled his inheritance, and within five years he had become a billionaire in his own right.

Emily had designed Marco's office for him. On the traditional partners' desk she had given him as a birthday gift, there was a silver-framed photograph of the two of them, taken on the anniversary of their first year together, before the death of his parents. Marco now studied it: he saw Emily looking up at him, her expression filled with laughter and desire, whilst his own was shadowed and half hidden. But then, Marco knew, his eyes reflected the physical hunger he had seen in hers, just as the positioning of their bodies mirrored one another. Emily was gazing at him with open happiness in her eyes, because she knew he was a wealthy man and a skilled lover.

'Niroli's kings receive love, Marco,' his grandfather had told him when he was a young adolescent, 'they do not give it. They are above other, weaker men, and they do not try to turn physical desire into mawkish sentiment like other, lesser men. They do not need to. You are maturing fast and you will discover very soon that your royal status will draw to you your pick of the world's most beautiful and predatory women. They will give you their bodies but, in return, they will try to demand that you give them money and status. They will try to scheme, lie and cheat their way into your bed, and if you are foolish enough to let them they will present you with bastard sons who will become permanent reminders of your own folly and permanent dangers to Niroli's throne. It is not so many centuries ago that a newly crowned sultan would order the death or the castration of all his many male half-siblings in order to prevent them from trying to take his place. You're welcome to taste the pleasure of the women who offer themselves to you as much as you wish, but remember what I have told you. Ultimately you will make a necessary dynastic marriage with a young woman of royal and unimpeachable moral virtue, and she will give you your legitimate heirs. Your only heirs, if you are wise, Marco.'

Well, he had been wise, hadn't he? Marco told himself grimly. And he intended to continue to be so. He looked down at the letter on the desk in front of him. It had arrived the previous day, its royal crest and the Nirolean stamp immediately marking it out as the reason why he was in the office so early this morning. It was from his grandfather, setting out the final details of his abdication plans. The people of Niroli, King Giorgio had written, were already being encouraged to expect Marco's return and to welcome him as their new ruler. He needed to speak with his grandfather. But protocol meant that, yesterday, Marco had patiently followed an archaic, convoluted procedure, which had ensured that none of the ancient statesmen who surrounded his grandfather would have their pride dented, before finally arranging to speak directly to the king. Marco intended to make a clean sweep of these elderly statesmen once he was on the throne. His plan was to bring a forward-thinking modern mindset to the way Niroli was ruled, via courtiers of his own generation who shared his way of thinking. In fact, this new regime was something he already had in hand after a few discreet one-to-one telephone calls.

HE LOOKED AT his watch: in another twenty minutes exactly, the telephone on his desk would ring and the Groom of the Chamber would announce in his quavering voice that he was going to connect him to his grandfather. Marco sighed. The elderly courtier was hard of hearing, as indeed was his grandfather, although King Giorgio denied it! Marco had a rueful fondness for his older relative, and he knew that Giorgio had a grudging respect for him, but he also knew that both of them were far too similar to ever be willing to be open about those feelings. Instead they tended to conform to the roles they had adopted in Marco's teenage years, when his grandfather had been the disapproving disciplinarian and he had been the rebellious black sheep. He checked the time again. All this simply so that he could assure his grandfather that he would be returning to Niroli just as soon as he had dealt with his outstanding business in London, something that should have been a simple matter of a quick phone call rather than this long-drawn-out ceremonial.

The part of Marco's outstanding business that concerned

Emily was of course something he did not intend to discuss with the old king. He estimated that it would be a few weeks yet before he would be ready to leave, and he had already decided that there would be no sense in telling Emily their relationship had to end until then. One single clean cut, with no possibility of any come-backs, was the best way to deal with the situation. He would tell her they were finished and that he was leaving the country—and that was all. He had taken her to his bed as plain Marco Fierezza and he saw no point in revealing his royal status to her now. She had known him as her lover and a wealthy entrepreneur, not as the future King of Niroli. It was true that she might at some future point come to discover who he was—the paparazzi took a keen interest in the Royal House of Niroli—but by then their lives would be entirely separate. Their relationship had never been intended to end in commitment. He had told her that right from the start. But they had been together for almost three years, when previously he had become bored with his girlfriends within three months. Marco shrugged away the dry inner voice pointing out things to him he didn't want to acknowledge. So, sexually they might have been well suited, or maybe at thirty-six the raw heat of his sex drive was cooling and he demanded less stimulation and variety, which made him content to accept a familiar physical diet? It would do him good to get out of that kind of sexual rut, he told himself coolly.

It would do them both good. Marco started as, out of nowhere, a sharply savage spear of sexual jealousy stabbed through him. What was this? Why on earth should he feel such a gut-wrenching surge of fury at the thought of Emily moving on to another man? His mouth compressed. His concern was for Emily, and not for himself. She was after all the vulnerable one, not him. Emily's sexual past was very different from his own, and because of that—and only that, he assured himself—he was now experiencing a completely natural concern that she was not equipped to deal with a lover who might not treat her as well as he had done.

Marco looked at her picture, reluctantly remembering the first time he had possessed her. He'd planned to surprise her, but in the end she had been the one who had surprised him...

He had seen how excited she'd been when he'd walked into her shop and told her that he was taking her away for a few days, and that she would need her passport. When he'd picked her up later that day, he had seen quite plainly in her expression how much she'd wanted him. As he had wanted her.

He had been totally—almost brutally, some might have said—honest with her about the fact that he had no time for the emotional foolishness of falling in love. He had informed her calmly that he had ended previous relationships for no other reason than that his girlfriends had told him that they were falling in love with him. Emily had greeted his announcement with equal calm. Falling in love with him wasn't something she planned to do, she had assured him firmly. She was as committed to their relationship being based on their sexual need for one another as he was himself. She had smiled, adding that this suited her perfectly, and Marco had felt she was speaking the truth.

He had booked the two of them into a complex on a small private island that catered exclusively for the rich and the childfree. Everything about the location was designed to appeal to lovers and to cocoon them in privacy, whilst providing a discreet service.

The individual villas that housed the guests were set apart from the main hotel block, each with its own private pool. Meals could be taken in the villas or in the Michelin-starred restaurant of the hotel, where there was also an elegant bar and nightclub.

Amongst the facilities included for the guests' entertainment were diving and sailing, and visits to the larger, more built-up neighbouring islands could be arranged by helicopter if guests wished.

They had arrived late in the afternoon, and had walked through the stunningly beautiful gardens. Marco recalled now how Emily had reached out to hold his hand, her eyes shining with awed wonder as they had paused to watch the breathtaking swiftness of the sunset. He remembered, too, how he had been unable to resist taking her in his arms and kissing her, and how that kiss had become so intimate it had left Emily trembling.

They had returned to their villa, undressing one another eagerly and speedily, sharing the shower in the luxuriously equipped bathroom. Emily's physical response to him had been everything Marco had hoped it would be and more. She had held nothing back, matching him touch for touch and in intimacy until he had started to penetrate her. It had caught him off guard to have her tensing as he thrust fully into her, believing she was as eager to feel the driving surge of his body within hers as he was to feel her hot, wet flesh tightening around him.

At first he had assumed she was playing some kind of coy game with him, mistakenly thinking that it would excite him if she assumed a mock-innocent hesitancy. His frustration had made him less perceptive than he might otherwise have been, and more impatient, so he had ignored the warning her body had been giving him and had thrust strongly again. This time it had taken the small muffled sound that had escaped past her rigid throat muscles to make him realise the truth: she was still a virgin.

His first reaction had been one of savage anger, fuelled

by the toxic mingling of male frustration and the blow to his own pride that was caused by the fact that he hadn't guessed the truth. Sex with an inexperienced virgin—and the potential burden of responsibility that carried, both physical and emotional—was something he just had not wanted.

'What the hell is this?' he swore. 'Okay, I know about your marriage, but I would have thought that…if only because of that…'

'That *what?* That I'd jump on the first man I could find?' Emily retaliated sharply. But beneath that sharpness he caught the quiver of uncertainty in her voice, and his anger softened into something that caught at his throat, startling him with its intensity.

'Well, it did cross my mind,' she told him. 'But in the end I was too much of a moral coward to go through with it. Blame my grandfather, if you wish, but the thought of having sex with a man I didn't truly want, just to get rid of my virginity, has made it harder rather than easier for me to find a man I did want enough.'

Marco shrugged dismissively, not wanting to have to deal with his own unfamiliar feelings, never mind hers!

'If you're expecting me to be pleased about this, then let me tell you—'

'You don't need to tell me anything, Marco,' she had stopped him determinedly. 'It's rather obvious what you feel.'

'I don't know what you're thinking, or hoping for,' he told her, ignoring her comment, 'but, despite what you may want to believe, the majority of sexually mature men do not fantasise about initiating a virgin! I certainly don't. The reason I brought you here was so that we could indulge our need for one another as two people starting from the same baseline. For me, that means we share matching physical desires for one another and awareness of our own sexual wants and expectations.'

'I'm sorry if you feel that I've let you bring me here under false pretences,' Emily told him, admitting, 'Maybe I should have said something to warn you?'

'Maybe?'

The scorn in his voice made her flinch visibly. 'I didn't want to play the I'm-still-a-virgin card for the reasons you've just mentioned yourself,' she defended. 'I didn't want it to be an issue and, besides, I wasn't even sure that you'd notice.'

Marco remembered how she had coloured up hotly when he had looked at her in disbelief.

'I really am sorry,' she told him apologetically.

'*You're* sorry? I'm so damn frustrated...' he began.

'Me, too,' Emily interrupted him with such candour that he felt his earlier irritation evaporating.

'Frustrated, but virginal and apprehensive?' he felt bound to point out.

'Yes, but not one of those has to remain a permanent state, does it?' she responded.

'You trust me to deal effectively with all three?'

'I trust you to make it possible for *us* to deal with all three,' she corrected him softly. 'I'm a woman who believes that participation in a shared event makes for mutual enjoyment, even if right now in this particular venture I am the junior partner.'

He wasn't used to being teased, or to sharing laughter in an intimate relationship and, as he quickly discovered, shared laughter had its own aphrodisiacal qualities.

He made love to her with a slow intimacy which, he was the first to admit, had its own reward when in the end she showed him such a passionate response. It was she who urged him to move faster and deeper, until he was as lost in the pleasure they were sharing as she was. But not so lost that he couldn't witness the shocked look of delight widening her eyes as her orgasm gripped her...

What the hell was he doing, thinking about that now? It was over; they were over; or rather they soon would be.

Someone was knocking gently on his office door. Marco frowned. He wasn't expecting anyone and he had expressly told his PA not to disturb him. He was still frowning when the door opened and Emily stepped through, smiling at him. It wasn't often that Marco was caught off guard by anything or anyone, but on this occasion...

'My meeting finished early,' he could hear Emily saying breezily, 'so I thought I'd come over and see if you were free for lunch?'

When he didn't answer her she closed the office door and came towards him, dropping her voice to a playfully soft tone as she told him, 'Or maybe we could forget the going-out and the lunch. Remember, Marco, how we used to... What's wrong?' she asked him uncertainly.

Her smile disappeared and Marco recognised that he had left it several seconds too late to respond appropriately to her arrival.

Normally, the fact that his timing was at fault would have been his main concern. But, for some reason, he found that, not only was he acutely aware that he had hurt and upset Emily, he was also suppressing an immediate desire to go to her and apologise. Apologise? Him? Marco was astounded by his own uncharacteristic impulse. He never apologised to anyone, for anything.

'Nothing's wrong,' he told her flatly, knowing that something was very wrong indeed for him to have felt like that. It couldn't be that he was feeling guilty, could it? a traitorous, critical inner voice suddenly challenged, pointing out: *After all, you've lied to her and you're about to leave her...*

She knew the ground rules, Marco answered it inwardly. That his own conscience should turn on him like this increased his irritation and, man-like, he focused that irritation on Emily, rather than deal with its real cause.

'Yes, there is,' Emily persisted. 'You were looking at me as though I'm the last person you want to see.'

'Don't be ridiculous. I just wasn't expecting to see you.' He flicked back the sleeve of his suit—handmade, it fitted him in such a way that its subtle outlining of his superb physique was a whispered suggestion caught only by those who understood. 'Look, I can't do lunch, I've got an important call coming through any time now, and after that I've got an appointment.' That wasn't entirely true, but there was no way he wanted Emily to suggest she wait around for him whilst he spoke with his grandfather. For one thing, he had no idea just how long the call would last and, for another... For another, he wasn't ready yet to tell Emily what she had to be told.

Because he wasn't ready yet to deny himself the pleasure of making love to her, his inner tormentor piped up, adding mockingly, *Are you sure that you will ever be ready?* He dismissed that unwanted thought immediately but its existence increased his ire. 'Mrs Lawson should have told you that I'd said I didn't want to be disturbed,' he informed Emily curtly.

She heard the impatience in his voice and wished she hadn't bothered coming. Marco's arrogance made him forget sometimes how easily he could hurt her, and she certainly had too much pride to stay here and let him see that pain.

'Mrs Lawson wasn't there when I came in.'

'Not there? She's my PA, for heaven's sake. Where the hell is she?'

'She'd probably just slipped off to the cloakroom, Marco.

It isn't her fault,' Emily pointed out quietly. 'Look, I'm sorry if this isn't a good time.' She gave a small resigned sigh. 'I suppose I should have checked with you first before coming over.'

'Yes, you should have,' Marco agreed grimly. Any minute now the phone was going to ring and if he picked it up she was going to hear his grandfather's most senior aide's voice booming out as he tried to compensate for his own deafness, 'Is that you, Your Highness?' The Comte had never really accustomed himself to the effectiveness of modern communication systems and still thought his voice could only travel down the telephone line if he spoke as loudly as he possibly could.

Emily's eyes widened as she registered Marco's rejection and then she stood still staring blankly at him, the colour leaving her face. He was treating her as though she were some casual and not very welcome acquaintance.

'Don't worry about it. I'm sorry I disturbed you,' she managed to say, but she could hear the brittle hurt in her own voice. Right now, she wanted to be as far away from Marco and his damn office as she could get! She was perilously close to tears and the last thing she wanted was the humiliation of Marco seeing how much he'd wounded her. To her relief, she could hear sounds from the outer office suggesting that his PA had returned, enabling her to use the face-saving fib that she didn't want to have Mrs Lawson coming in to shoo her out. Emily opened the door and left, barely pausing to acknowledge the PA's surprise at seeing her, Emily hurried out of the office, her head down and her throat thick with unshed tears.

What was it with her? she asked herself wretchedly, five minutes later as she hailed a taxi. She wasn't a young girl with emotions so new and raw that she overreacted to every sucked-in breath! She was in her twenties and divorced, and she and Marco had been together for nearly three years, the intimacy of their sex life having given her an outward patina of radiant sensuality. It had been so palpable in the first year they'd been together, one of her clients had told her semi-jokingly, 'Now that you're with Marco you're going to start losing clients if you aren't careful.'

'Why?' Emily had asked.

'Jealousy,' had been the client's succinct answer.

Emily remembered how she had smiled with rueful acknowledgement. 'You mean, because I'm with Marco and they'd like to change places with me?' she had guessed.

'They may very well want to do that, but I was thinking more of their concerns that their husbands might be tempted by the creamy glow of sexual completion you're carrying around with you right now, Emily.'

Emily remembered she had blushed and made some confused denial, but the client had shaken her head and told her wisely, 'You can't deny or ignore it. That glow shimmers round you like a force-field and men are going to be drawn to you because of it. There is nothing more likely to make a man want a woman than her confident wearing of another man's sexual interest in her.'

She doubted that she still wore that magnetic sexual aura now, Emily admitted sadly. That was the trouble: when you broke the rules, it didn't only make you ache for what you didn't have, it also damaged what you did.

The taxi driver was waiting for her to tell him where she wanted to go. She leaned forward and gave him the address of Marco's apartment. *Marco's apartment*, she noted— for that was how she thought of it. Not as *their* apartment, even though he had invited her to make it over to suit her own tastes and had given her a lavish budget for its renovation. Material possessions, even for one's home that evoked deep-rooted attachments, were nothing without the right kind of emotions to surround them. Why had it had to happen? Why had she fallen in love with Marco? Why couldn't she have stayed as she was, thrillingly aware of him on the most intimate kind of sexual level, buoyed up by the intensity of their desire for one another, overwhelmed by relief and joy because he had brought her from the dark, wretched nowhere she'd inhabited after her divorce to the brilliant glittering landscape of unimaginable beauty that was the intimacy they shared together? Why, why, why couldn't that have been enough? Why had she had to go and fall for him?

Emily shivered, sinking deeper into the seat of the taxi. And why, having fallen for him, did she have to torment herself by hoping that one day things would change, that one day he would look at her and in his eyes she would see his love for her? The hope that, one day, it would happen sometimes felt so fragile and so unrealistic that she was afraid for herself, afraid of her vulnerability as a woman who needed one particular man so badly she was prepared to cling to such a fine thread. But what else could she do? She could tell him, honestly, how she felt. Emily bit her lip, guiltily aware that she wasn't being open with him. Because she was afraid in case she lost him... Why was she letting herself be dragged down by these uncomfortable, painful thoughts and questions? Why did they keep on escaping from the place where she tried to incarcerate and conceal them? What kind of woman was she to live a lie with the man she loved? What kind of relationship was it when that man stated openly that there was no place for love in the life he wanted to live?

The taxi stopped abruptly, catching her off guard. She didn't really want to go up to the apartment, not feeling the way she was right now, but another person was already hurrying purposefully towards the taxi, wanting to lay claim to it.

Emily got out and paid her fare to the driver, shivering as she waited for her change. Her stomach had already begun its familiar nauseous churning—this time, it had to be a result of Marco's rejection of her appeal to him, though she had to admit she had also felt too nauseous to want any breakfast this morning. She was definitely beginning to feel slightly dizzy and faint as well as unwell now.

Psychosomatic, she told herself unsympathetically as she headed up to the apartment.

It had started to rain while Emily was getting out of the taxi. Yes, the miserable weather was adding to her feelings of lowness. Why couldn't she talk to Marco? They were lovers, after all, sharing the closest of physical intimacy. Physical intimacy—but they did not share any emotional intimacy. Emily's experiences as a child had made her wary of appearing needy. It was now second nature to her to hide the most vulnerable part of her true self. Only in Marco's arms, at the height of their shared passion, did she feel safe enough to allow her body to show him what was in her heart, knowing that he wasn't likely to be able to recognise it.

She let herself into the apartment, mutely aware of how empty and impersonal it felt, for all her attempts to turn it into a shared home.

'YES, GRANDFATHER, I do understand, but I cannot work miracles. It is impossible for me to return to Niroli before the end of the month as we had already tentatively agreed.' Marco managed to hold onto his temper as his grandfather's complaints grew louder, before finally interrupting to say dryly, 'Very well, then, I accept that whilst I had talked about the end of the month, you had not agreed to it. But that doesn't alter the fact that I cannot return sooner.'

The sound of his grandfather slamming down the receiver reverberated in Marco's eardrum. Replacing his own handset, he stood up and turned to look out of the window of his office. It was raining. In Niroli, the sun would be shining. Marco's grandfather was obviously furious that he had refused to give in and alter the timing of his return and bring his arrival on Niroli forward. But his grandfather's rage did not worry Marco. He was used to it and unaffected by it, apart from the fact that he too didn't like having his plans challenged. He looked irritably at his watch. He was hungry and very much in need of the gentle calm of Emily's company. That, plus the natural reserve that made her the kind of woman who was never going to court the attention of the paparazzi, or expose their relationship to the avid curiosity of others, were two other major plus-points about her. But not quite as major as the sensuality that spilled from her like sweetness from a honeycomb, even if she didn't realise it.

The direction his thoughts were taking surprised him. It was nonsense for him to be thinking about Emily like this when he was about to end their relationship! Far better that he focused on the things he didn't like about her, such as… Such as the way she insisted on keeping professional commitments even when he had made other plans. *Is that the only criticism you can make of her?* an increasingly voluble and irritating inner voice demanded sardonically. Marco sighed, mentally acknowledging the irony of his own thoughts. Yes, it was true that, in many ways, Emily was the perfect mistress for the man he had been whilst he'd lived in London. But he wasn't going to be that man for much longer.

When the time came for him to take a royal mistress,

she would have to have qualities that Emily did not possess. Chief amongst those would be an accepting, possibly older husband. This was an example of the kind of protocol at the royal court of Niroli which, in Marco's opinion, kept it in the Edwardian era. He certainly planned to bring about changes that would benefit the people of Niroli rather than its king. But perhaps there were certain traditions that were better retained. No, Emily could not continue to be his lover, but even so he could have responded better to her arrival in his office earlier, Marco admitted. He could, for instance, have suggested that she go ahead to one of their favourite restaurants and wait there for him. It had, after all, been predictable that his grandfather would lose his temper and end their conversation so abruptly, once he realised that he wasn't going to get everything that he wanted.

Marco toyed with the idea of calling Emily now and suggesting that she meet him for a late lunch, but then decided against it. She wasn't the kind of woman who sulked or played silly games. But honesty compelled him to accept that some measure of compensatory behaviour on his part would be a good investment. Ridiculously in many ways, given the length of time they had been together, just thinking about her triggered that familiar sharp ache of his desire for her. He picked up the phone and rang the number of her shop.

Her assistant answered his call, telling him, 'She isn't here, Marco. She rang a couple of minutes ago to say that she's going to spend the rest of the day working at the apartment. Poor Emily, she still isn't properly over that wretched virus, is she?'

Marco made a noncommittal reply. He himself was never in anything other than the very best of health, but right now his mood was very much in need of the soothing touch that only Emily could give. She had an unexpectedly dry sense of humour, which, allied to her intelligence and acute perception, gave her the ability to make him laugh, sometimes when he least felt like doing so. Not that her sense of humour or his laughter had been very much in evidence these last few weeks, he recognised, frowning a little over this recognition. It surprised him how sharp the need he suddenly felt to be with her was. It was amazing what a bit of guilt could do, he decided as he told his PA that he, too, would be spending the afternoon working at home.

The best way to smooth over any upsets, so far as Marco was concerned, was in bed, where he knew he could quickly make Emily forget about everything other than his desire for her and hers for him…

Emily scowled as she worried over the message she had just picked up from one of her clients. The lady in question was a good customer, but Emily had still felt slightly wary when she'd been asked a while ago to take on the complete renovation of a property in Chelsea.

'Darling, darling, Emily,' Carla Mainwearing had trilled, 'I am so in love with your perfect sense of style that I want you to choose everything and I am going to put the house totally in your hands.'

Knowing Carla as she did, Emily had taken this with a pinch of salt and had therefore insisted on having her work approved at every single stage. Now Carla had left her a message saying that she hated the colour Emily had chosen for the walls of the property's pretty drawing room, and that she wanted it completely redone—at Emily's expense. Emily recalled that Carla had previously sanctioned the colour of the paint. But discretion was called for in telling her this, so rather than phone Carla back she decided to e-mail instead. Her laptop was in the study she shared with Marco, as were her files, so she made her way there, firmly ignoring the leaden weight of her earlier disappointment at Marco's refusal to join her for lunch.

Five minutes later, she was standing immobile in front of the study's window, her laptop and original purpose of coming to the study forgotten, as she stared in shocked horror at the vellum envelope she was holding. Her hand, actually not just her hand but her whole body, was trembling violently, as she felt unable to move. Waves of heat followed by icy chill surged through her body and somewhere some part of her mind managed to register the fact that what she was suffering was a classic reaction to extreme shock. She could hardly see the address on the envelope now through her blurred vision, but the crest on its left-hand front corner stood out, its *royal* crest, followed by the address: *HRH Prince Marco of Niroli*…

She didn't hear Marco's key in the apartment door, she didn't even hear him calling out her name. Her shock was so great that nothing could penetrate it. It encased her in a kind of bubble, which only concentrated the torment of what she was suffering and branded it on her brain so that it could never be forgotten. It was only finally pierced by the sudden opening of the study door as Marco walked in, but of course there was no way his arrival could ease her pain. Instead she gripped the envelope even tighter, her voice high and tight as she said thinly, 'Welcome home, *Your Highness*. I suppose I ought to curtsey to you.'

She waited, praying that he would laugh and tell her that she had got it all wrong, that the envelope she was holding, addressing him as Prince Marco of Niroli, was some silly mistake.

CHAPTER FIVE

LIKE A TINY candle flame shivering vulnerably in the dark, her hope trembled fearfully. And then the look in Marco's eyes extinguished it as cruelly as a hand placed callously over the face of a dying person to stem their last breath. It was over. Now, in this minute, this breath of time, they were finished. Emily knew that without the need for any words, the pain of that knowledge slamming a crippling body-blow into her. Her stomach felt as though she had plunged down a hundred floors in a high-speed lift.

'Give that to me,' Marco demanded, taking the envelope from her.

'It's too late to destroy the evidence, Marco,' Emily told him brokenly. 'I know the truth now. And I know how you've lied to me all this time, pretending to be something you aren't, letting me think…' She dug her teeth in her lower lip to try to force back her own pain. 'Do you think I haven't read the newspapers? Do you think the people of Niroli know that their prince is a liar? Or doesn't lying matter when you're a member of the Royal House?' she challenged him wildly.

'You had no right to go through my desk,' Marco shot back at her furiously, his male loathing at being caught off guard and forced into a position in which he was in the wrong making him determined to find something he could accuse Emily of. 'I thought we had an understanding that our private papers were our personal property and out of bounds,' he told her savagely. 'I trusted you…'

Emily could hardly believe what she was hearing.

'Did you? Is that why you hid this envelope under everything else?' she challenged him, shaking her head in answer to her own question. 'No, you didn't trust me, Marco, and you didn't trust me because you knew that I couldn't trust you. And you knew that because you are a liar, and liars don't trust people because they know that they themselves cannot be trusted.' She not only felt sick, she also felt as though she could hardly breathe. 'Everything I thought I knew about you is based on lies, everything. You aren't just Marco Fierezza, you are Prince Marco of Niroli. You yourself are a lie, Marco…'

'You are taking this far too personally. The reason I concealed my royal status had nothing whatsoever to do with you. It was a decision I made before I met you. My identity as plain Marco Fierezza is as real to me as though I were not a prince. It has nothing to do with you,' he repeated.

'How can you say that? It has everything to do with me, and if you had any shred of decency or morals you would know that. How could you lie about who you are and still live with me as intimately as we have lived together?' she demanded brokenly. 'How could you live with yourself, knowing that others, not just me, believed you, accepted and gave you their trust, when all the time—'

'Stop being so ridiculously dramatic,' Marco demanded fiercely. 'You are making too much of the situation.'

'Too much?' Emily almost screamed the words at him. 'Too much, when I have discovered that you have deceived me for the whole time we've been together? When did you plan to tell me, Marco? Perhaps you just planned to walk away without telling me anything? After all, what do my feelings matter to you?'

'Of course they matter,' Marco stopped her sharply. 'And it was in part to protect them, and you, that I decided not to inform you of the change in my circumstances when my grandfather first announced that he intended to step down from the throne and hand it on to me.'

'To protect me?' Emily almost choked on her fury. 'Hand on the throne? Don't bother continuing, Marco. No wonder you told me when you first took me to bed that all you wanted was sex. You *knew* that was the only kind of relationship there could ever be between us! You *knew* that one day you would be Niroli's king. No doubt you are expected to marry a princess. Is she picked out for you already, your *royal* bride?'

'No.'

Emily shrugged disdainfully. 'There's no point in replying because, whatever you say, I can't believe you, not now.'

'Emily, listen to me. This has gone far enough. You are being ridiculous. I know you have had a bit of a shock, but…'

'A bit of a shock? *A bit of a shock?*'

When she whirled round and headed for the door, Marco demanded, 'Where are you going?'

'To pack my things,' Emily told him fiercely. 'I'm leaving, Marco, right now. I can't and won't stay here with you. I feel I don't know you any more, and right now I don't really want to.'

'Don't be stupid. Where will you go? This is your home.'

'No, this is *your* apartment, it has never been my home. As to where I will go, I have a home of my own—remember?' she challenged him.

Marco frowned. 'Your house in Chelsea? But your assistant is living there.'

'She was living there, but she moved in with her new partner at the weekend, not that it or anything else in my life is any business of yours, Your Highness. Or should it be Your Majesty?'

'Emily.' He reached for her but she started to pull away from him, a look of angry contempt in her eyes that infuriated him. She had accused him of deceit and duplicity, but what about her actions? What about the fact that she had gone through his private papers behind his back? Her accusations had stung his pride, and now suddenly recognising that control of the situation had been taken from him and that she was about to walk out on him awakened all his most deeply held, atavistic male feelings about her. She was his—his until he chose to end their relationship.

Emily's eyes widened in mute shock as his fingers closed round her wrist, imprisoning her, and she saw the familiar look of arousal darkening his eyes. 'Let go of me,' she snapped. 'You can't really expect…'

'I can't really expect what?'

He wasn't going to let her go, Emily realised. She felt a quiver of sensation run down her spine—and it wasn't fear.

'What is it that I can't expect, Emily?' he repeated silkily. 'Is it that I can't expect to take you to bed any more— is that what you were going to say? That I can't expect to touch you or hold you?'

She had edged towards the study door as he'd advanced, but before she could open it and escape Marco reached past her, kicking it shut. Then, he placed his hands on it either side of her so that she was caught between the door and him. A tell-tale spiral of excitement was sizzling through her, its presence within her reminding her of the early days of their affair, when just to know that Marco wanted her and intended to have her was enough to leave her quivering on the edges of erotic need and surrender. Just as she was doing now. She tried to vocalise her denial, not just of her own arousal but also of Marco's intentions, but the words were locked in her throat. Beneath the soft wool of her sweater she could feel the growing hardening of her nipples and the desire-heavy weight of her breasts. How long had it been since she had felt like this? How long had it been since Marco had shown her this side of himself? So long that she couldn't remember? So long that, because it was happening now, she couldn't resist his allure?

Her heart jerked around inside her chest as though it were suspended on a piece of elastic. The ache in her breasts curled down through her belly to taunt her sex and tease from it a throbbing pulse of excitement and longing. She realised that she should be horrified by the way she was reacting to him, in view of what she had now discovered, horrified and determined not to let him touch her, sickened by the thought of him touching her. But she also knew that she wasn't; instead she wanted him with a physical intensity that held her fast in an unfamiliar, almost violent grip.

'Is that what you wanted to say to me, Emily—that I can't make you want me any more, that I can't arouse you, that I can't do this…?' He lifted his hand and stroked a fingertip down the side of her neck and along her collarbone, making her shudder in violent erotic delight. He had moved closer to her, so close that she could smell the familiar scent of his cologne and the aroused heat of his body. Was it *that,* with its powerful but subtle message of male sexuality, that was turning her boneless with aching longing for him, even while her mind was telling her that she should resist him, and that this was no way for her to behave if she truly wanted him to believe what she had said?

She should say something, tell him to stop; tell him that there was no point in this for either of them. But she knew that she wouldn't, just as she knew that some deep-rooted female part of her wanted this show of male dominance from him, wanted her own sense of fierce surging excitement, wanted and needed the pure, fierce searing heat of the mutual lust they had conjured up out of nowhere. She could quite easily have pushed past him, Emily knew, and she knew too that Marco would not try to stop her if she did. But the reality was that she didn't want to... The reality was that her body was possessed by an incendiary mix of anger and desire that took fire from Marco's determination to confront her with her own acceptance of his power to arouse her.

'But that would be a lie, wouldn't it?' Marco challenged her softly as he continued his relentless sensual assault, his lips brushing the bare flesh of her throat in between each word, imprisoning her in her own wild arousal.

'Wouldn't it?' he insisted as he slid his hand beneath her sweater and freed her breasts from the constriction of her bra. A low moan of unappeased longing bubbled in her throat as he fed her craving for his possession.

'You want more?' he demanded, his voice thickening and softening.

'No!' Emily lied. She could feel his hand cupping her breast and his fingertips stroking deliberately against her nipple again. She knew she couldn't hold out much longer against the dammed-up force of her own need. With a low sound of surrender, she reached blindly for him, drawing his head down towards her own, her lips parting for his kiss and the swift, exultant victory of his tongue.

She could feel the thick hardness of his manhood pressing against her body. In her mind's eye she visualised his naked body, familiar now after their years together, seeing behind her closed eyes the thick sheathing of smooth flesh over rigid muscle, where it rose from the dark silky thickness of hair. She could almost feel the smooth warmth of him, so enticingly supple to her touch, and so responsive to the caress of her fingers and her mouth. Fresh longing seized her. Impetuously she reached down between their bodies to touch him, spanning his length with the spread of her fingertips, and then stroking his thickness. A deep purr of satisfaction gathered in her throat as she felt him stiffen further and then pulse, becoming a moan of out-of-control urgency when she felt him tugging at the fastening of her skirt.

Not even in their early days together had she experienced this degree of intense need, she recognised. It was so much bolder than anything she remembered feeling before; bolder, and fiercer and hungrier—the sexual desire of a woman who must be satisfied.

The demoralising fear that had in recent weeks sucked from her any delight in their intimacy was as easily sloughed off by their shared passion as were their clothes, unwanted encumbrances that prevented her from taking all that she could. Marco was driving both of them to that place where they had no choice other than to plunge into the turbulent flood of the maelstrom together.

Emily's fingers trembled over and tugged at his shirt buttons and trouser fastenings, her endeavours deliberately interrupted by him when he raked his teeth against the sensitive thrust of her nipple, causing her to gasp and then moan, unable to do anything other than give in to the intensity of the sensation he was inflicting on her. When pleasure was this intense, she thought frantically, it bordered on the almost unendurable. And yet she wouldn't have wanted it any other way, wouldn't have wanted any other man, wouldn't have been able to reach this lack of inhibition with anyone else.

'You want me to stop?' Marco demanded. His breath cooled the aching flesh that had been tormented by his erotic caress, whilst the subtle touch of his fingertips continued to play on her nipple, increasing its dark, swollen call for the renewed heat of his mouth.

Emily couldn't speak, she could barely stand up any more. But she knew Marco knew she wanted no such thing. She ran her hands along his sweat-dampened naked torso, deliberately bending her head so that she could graze her tongue-tip along his skin and taste the tangy maleness of his flesh, whilst she breathed in his aphrodisiacal Marco-drenched scent. At times like this, just the smell of him was enough to make her go weak with lust.

The ache deep inside her tightened and burned with a heat that could only be slaked by the possession of Marco's hard flesh filling her and completing her. She could feel the small hungry ripples of sensation caused by her muscles as they tightened with the need to have him fill the empty, wanton place inside her.

'Now, Marco,' she urged him fiercely, 'now!'

When he still waited, she looked up at him. She could see the dangerous look in his eyes, the darkness that said he was on the verge of wanting to punish her and that he was challenging her, needing to force her to acknowledge his supremacy, his ability to control her desire, arouse it and then satisfy it. It was too late for her to try to play him at his own game and deny him his triumph by pretending that she didn't want him. Her own need was too great and too immediate. She would have to punish herself later for her weakness. Right now, no price was too high to pay for the satisfaction her body craved. She had tried to resist…

'Now!' she repeated.

For a second, she thought he was going to refuse, but then he was reaching for her, lifting her up so that she could wrap her legs tightly round him whilst he thrust firmly into her in one long, slow, deliberate movement that made her shudder violently. As he withdrew her muscles tightened, protesting around him, not wanting to let him go, and were then rewarded for their adoration by the almost mind-altering sensation of his second, stronger, deeper thrust. The sensitive nerve-endings in her flesh wept with joy at the intensity. Instinctively Emily drew in her muscles around him, savouring the sensation.

She could feel his hot breath in her ear, the tip of his tongue tracing the curls of flesh. She felt his teeth against the sensitive cord in her neck. Her whole body was being possessed by a pleasure so heightened she thought she might die from it.

'Marco...' She moaned his name as a plea, striking a solitary note of female praise as he thrust deeper, harder and faster now.

'Mmm...more. Marco...more!' she urged him, gasping out aloud in delight as he obeyed her and his movements became fast and rhythmic. Then he drove them to their climaxes, and she was left so boneless and weak that she collapsed helplessly against him, trembling in the aftermath.

The heat of the fury that had driven him was cooling on his sweat-slicked skin. Where he should have felt satisfaction and triumph at making Emily acknowledge that he could still arouse her, Marco could only feel a dark sense of stark awareness that he had crossed over a boundary he should not have breached. In forcing Emily to give in to the desire he had summoned in her, he'd also forced himself to acknowledge his need for her. A fleeting need, brought on by his justifiable anger, he assured himself, that was all! It meant nothing in the broader picture of his life.

'I think we both needed that,' he told her coolly, 'and perhaps it was a fitting end to our relationship, a tribute to the mutual attraction that brought us together.'

Emily couldn't believe what she had done—and what she might have betrayed. She couldn't bear the thought of Marco thinking now how stupid she had been, maybe guessing she had dreamed that, one day, he might fall in love with her as she had done with him. A wave of irritation surged through her—not against him, but against herself. What a fool she had been, deliberately blinding herself to reality and fixating on something that her common sense could have warned her wouldn't possibly happen. If Marco had really loved her he would have told her so. But he hadn't, and he never would. She had deceived herself just as much as Marco had deceived her, and if anything her crime against herself was even greater than his. The fierce, turbulent, almost torrid heat of their lovemaking had subsided now, and her anger had burned down into stark bleakness and grinding pain. Her dreams had been swept aside, shown to be pitifully worthless. Marco was a stranger to her, but no more so than she felt at this moment she was to herself.

'Mutual attraction then, but perhaps mutual contempt now,' she answered Marco pointedly. 'I'm not the naïve girl that I was when we first became lovers, Marco.'

'Meaning what?' he challenged her, frowning.

'Meaning that I've learned enough about sex from you to know that it isn't always used as an expression of positive emotions. It's common knowledge these days that couples on the verge of splitting up do sometimes use sex as a way of venting their negative feelings. Some couples say that they had the best sex of their relationship when the emotional side of it was dying. Of course, I know that *we* aren't emotionally intimate with one another.' What she meant of course, Emily admitted, was that Marco had never been emotionally close with her, because he didn't want to be, whilst she had had to struggle not to be close when she'd wanted to be. 'But I think both of us would accept that the break-up of any relationship—even one like ours—does bring things to the surface that aren't easy to accept.'

Marco's frown deepened. She was now being far more matter-of-fact about their relationship ending than he had expected—and he didn't like that! But he was being ridiculous. He should feel very relieved that she was being so sensible, especially after her earlier, uncharacteristic outburst…

CHAPTER SIX

FROM HIS SEAT on the royal jet, Marco looked down onto his family's private runway at Niroli's airport to where a group of formally dressed courtiers and officials were waiting to greet him. The ostrich-feather plumes of their dress hats fluttered in the breeze as they stood straight-backed, ignoring the heat of the sun. Marco's lips twisted with irony at the thought of the heavily gold-braided, be-medalled uniform that his grandfather had sent him, along with strict instructions that he must wear it when he landed and was greeted by the courtly welcoming committee. In fact, the uniform, appropriate for the rank of Lieutenant Colonel in Niroli's ancient Royal Guard, was lying in its leather dress-trunk in the plane's hold, whilst he wore his own handmade Saville Row suit. His grandfather wouldn't be pleased. But Marco intended to let him, and the court, know right from the word go that he would make his own decisions and judgements and he wouldn't allow them to force theirs on him.

Emily would have appreciated and understood his decision, though she would probably have laughed gently, and teased him as well into wearing that undeniably magnificent, beautifully tailored uniform. Emily...he tried to thrust the thought of her away from him, along with the erotic mental image of her alongside him in his bed that was forming inside his head, but it was too late; she was there, smiling at him, wanting him, as he ached for her. What the hell was this?

He stood up so abruptly that the young Niroli air force aide-de-camp, who'd been sent to escort him home, was caught off guard, and his own attempt to get to his feet before Marco was severely hampered by his ceremonial sword. The red-faced young man saluted as he semi-stuttered, 'Highness, if you wish to have more time in order to prepare, then please allow me—'

'No, I am ready,' Marco told the aide shortly and then relented when he saw his anxious expression. It was not the lad's fault—and he was little more than a boy, a scion of one of Niroli's foremost titled families. Marco had chosen to be the man he was, rather than the grandson his grandfather wanted him to be. Damn Emily for pursuing him like this, insinuating herself into his thoughts where she now had no right to be! Her abrupt departure from his apartment had decided him that he should leave London earlier than he had originally planned—much to his grandfather's delight. Marco suspected the old king would not have been so cock-a-hoop over his 'victory' if he had known that it owed less to his own power than to his grandson's loss of his bed-mate.

The aide-de-camp, who was carrying his own plumed hat as protocol demanded, stood beside his king-to-be as the doors to the royal jet were opened. He bowed as Marco walked past him and stepped out onto the gangway steps and into Niroli's sunshine. Just for a few seconds, Marco stood motionless and ramrod-straight at the top of the steps, not because he was the island's future ruler, but because he was one of its returning sons. He had almost forgotten the unique scent of sunshine and sea, mimosa and lemons, all of which hit him on a surge of hot wind. Not even the strong smell of jet fuel and tarmac could detract from them, and Marco felt emotion sting his eyes: this was his home, his country, and the crowds he could see lining the wide straight road that ran from the airport to the main town were his people. Many of them had not had the benefit of being part of a wider, modern world, but he intended to change that. He would give to Niroli's young the opportunities his grandfather's old-fashioned rule had denied them. Determinedly, Marco stepped forward. The waiting military band broke into Niroli's national anthem and the waiting officials removed their hats and bowed their heads. Their faces were familiar to Marco, although more wrinkled and lined than he remembered—the faces of old men.

As he reached his grandfather's most senior minister the elderly gentleman placed his hands on Marco's arms, greeting him with a traditional continental embrace. His voice shook with emotion and Marco could see that beneath his proud, stern expression and the determinedly upright stance there was a very aged, tired man, who probably would have preferred to spend his last years with his grandchildren than doing his king's bidding. Tactfully, Marco adjusted his own walking pace to that of the courtiers surrounding him as they escorted him unsteadily to the waiting open-topped royal limousine.

At least his grandfather hadn't sent the coronation carriage to collect him, Marco reflected ruefully; its motion was sickeningly rocky and its velvet padded seats unpleasantly hard.

This should be his moment of triumph, the public endorsement of the strength he had gained in becoming his own man. Soon the power of the Royal House of Niroli would become his, and he would step into his grandfather's shoes and fulfil his destiny. So why didn't he feel more excited, and why was there this sense of emptiness within him, this sense of loss, of something missing?

The cavalcade started to move, the waiting crowds began to cheer, children clutching Niroli flags and leaning dangerously into the road, the better to see him. Marco lifted his hand and began to wave. The cool air-conditioned luxury of the limo protected him from the midday heat. *But what about the people? They must be feeling the heat, Marco.* As clearly as though she were seated at his side, he could hear Emily's gently reproachful voice. Angrily he banished it. The limousine travelled a few more yards and then Marco reached forward, rapping on the glass separating him from the driver and an armed guard.

'Highness?' the guard queried anxiously.

'Stop the car!' Marco ordered. 'I want to get out and walk.' As he reached to open his door the guard looked horrified. 'Sire,' he protested, 'the king…it may not be safe.'

Marco's eyebrow rose. 'Knowing my grandfather as I do, I cannot imagine he has not had ordered that plain-clothes security men be posted amongst the crowd. Besides, these are our people, not our enemy.'

As they saw Marco stepping out of the limousine the crowd fell silent. At no time in living memory had their ruler done anything so informal as walk amongst them. Marco shook the gnarled hands of working men, his smile causing pretty girls to glow with excitement and older women to feel a reawakening frisson of their youths.

One aged woman pushed her way through the people to reach him. Marco could see from her traditional peasant costume that she came from the mountains of Niroli. Her back was bent from long years spent working in the orange groves and vineyards that covered their lower slopes, her face as brown and lined as a wrinkled walnut. But there was still a fiery flash of pride in her dark eyes and as she held out to him the clumsy leather purse she had obviously made herself Marco felt as though a giant hand were gripping his heart in a tight vice.

'Highness, please take this humble gift,' she begged him. 'May it always be kept full, just like the coffers and the nurseries of the House of Niroli.' It was plain that the old peasant could ill afford to give him anything. Indeed, Marco felt he should be the one to give something to her, so he was not surprised to see the angry, hostile glower on the face of the shabbily dressed youth at her side.

'This is your grandson?' Marco asked her as he thanked her for her gift.

'Aye, he is, sire, and he shames me with his sullen looks and lack of appreciation for all that we have here on our island.'

'That is because we have nothing!' the youth burst out angrily, his face now seemingly on fire with emotion. 'We have nothing, whilst others have everything! We come to the town, and we see foreigners with their expensive yachts and their fancy clothes. Our king bends over backwards to welcome them, whilst we mountain-dwellers do not even have electricity. They look at us as though we are nothing, and that is because, to our king, we *are* nothing!'

Suddenly, like a cloud passing over the sun, the mood of the crowd gathered around Marco had changed. He could see the anger in the faces of the group of rough-looking, poorly dressed young men who had joined the outspoken youth. The first of his grandfather's security guards rushed to protect Marco, but very firmly he stepped between them, saying clearly, 'It is good to know that the people of Niroli are able to speak their minds freely to me. This issue of getting electricity to the more remote parts of our island is one that has, I know, taxed His Majesty's thoughts for a long time.' Marco put his hand on the angry youth's shoulder, drawing him closer to him, whilst he gave the hovering guards a small dismissive shake of his head. He could see the grateful tears in the old peasant woman's eyes.

'My grandson speaks without thinking,' she told him huskily. 'But, at heart, he is a good boy and as devoted to the king as anyone.'

The youth's friends were hurrying him away and Marco allowed himself to be escorted back to his limo. Once inside, he realised that he was still holding the old woman's carefully made purse. There was anger in his heart now, pressing down on him like an unwanted heavy weight. Niroli's royal family was the richest in the world and yet some of its subjects were living lives of utmost poverty. He could well imagine how upset and shocked Emily would have been if she had witnessed what had just happened. The leather purse felt soft and warm to his touch. He was the one who should be giving to his people, not the other way around. His time away from the island had changed him more than he had realised, Marco acknowledged, and somehow he didn't think his grandfather was going to like what he had in mind...

HUDDLED INTO AN armchair in the sitting room of her small Chelsea house, a prettily embroidered throw wrapped around her like a comfort blanket, Emily let the full riptide of her anguish take her over. What was the point in trying to fight it or escape it? The reality was that Marco, no, *Prince Marco, soon to be King Marco*, she corrected herself miserably, had gone, not just from her life, but from Britain itself, to return to his home, his throne and his people. Ultimately her place in his life would be filled by someone else. She gave a small low cry as more pain seized her, and then reminded herself angrily that the man she loved did not exist; he had been a creation of her own imagination and his deceit. Everything they had shared had been based on lies; every time he had held her or touched her she had been giving the whole of herself to him, whilst he had been withholding virtually everything of his true self. But even knowing this, as the numbing shock of her discovery of the truth rose and retreated, she was left with the agonising reality that she still loved him.

As much as she despised herself for not being able to cease wanting him, because she knew just how much he had deceived her, her self-contempt could not drive out her love.

What was he doing now? Was he thinking at all of her? Missing her? *Stop it, stop it,* all her inner protective instincts demanded in agony. She must not do this to herself! She must accept that he had gone, and that she had to find a way of living without him and the comfort of being able to look back and know that they had shared something very special. It was over, they were over, and her pride was demanding that she accept that and get on with her life. She was as much a fool for letting him into her thoughts now as she had been for letting him into her life. There was one thing for sure: he would not be thinking about her. He would not have given her a single thought since she had walked out of his apartment, following that dreadful discovery and the bitterly corrosive row that had ended their relationship.

What a total fool she had been for deluding herself into thinking that he would ever return her love...

CHAPTER SEVEN

'So, MARCO, WHAT is this that the Chief of Police tells me about your welcome parade? About your being threatened by some wretched insurrectionist from the mountains? Probably one of the Viallis. Mind you, you have only yourself to blame. Had you not taken it into your head to so rashly get out of the car, it would not have happened. You must remember that you are my heir and Niroli's next king. It is not wise to court danger.'

'There wasn't any real danger. The boy—for he was little more than that—was simply voicing—'

'His hostility to the throne!' King Giorgio interrupted Marco angrily.

His grandfather had aged since he had last seen him, but the old patriarch still had about him an awesome aura of power, Marco admitted ruefully. The problem was that it no longer particularly impressed Marco—he had power of his own now, power that came from living his life in his own way. He knew that his grandfather sensed this in him and that it irked him. That was why he insisted on taking his grandson to task over the incident at his welcoming parade.

'My feeling was that the boy was more frustrated and resentful than hostile.'

Marco watched his grandfather. There was a larger issue at stake here than the boy's angry words, one which Marco felt was essential, but which he knew wasn't something his grandfather would be happy to discuss.

Nevertheless, Marco had been doing some investigation of his own, and what he had discovered had highlighted potential problems within Niroli that needed addressing before they developed into much more worrying conflicts.

'The boy was complaining about the lack of an electricity supply to his village. He resents the fact that visitors to our country have benefits that some of our own people do not.' Marco held his ground as his grandfather's fist came crashing down on the desk between them.

'I will not listen to this foolish nonsense. Tourists bring money into the country and, naturally, we have to lure them here by providing them with the kind of facilities they are used to.'

'Whilst some amongst our people go without them?' Marco challenged him coolly. 'Angry young men do sometimes behave rashly. But surely it is our duty to equip our subjects with what they need to move into the twenty-first century? Our schoolchildren cannot learn properly without access to computers, and if we deprive them of the ability to do so then we will be maintaining an underclass within the heart of our country.'

'You dare to lecture me on how to rule?' the king bellowed. 'You, who turned your back on Niroli to live a life of your own choosing in London?'

'You're the one who has summoned me back, Nonno,' Marco reminded him, lowering his voice and deliberately using his childhood pet name for his grandfather in an attempt to soften the old man's mood. It was easy sometimes to forget his grandfather was ninety, yet still immoveable about what the right thing was for Niroli and its people. Marco didn't want to upset the king too much.

'Because I had no other choice,' Giorgio growled. 'You are my direct heir, Marco, for all that you choose to behave like a commoner, rather than a member of the ruling House of Niroli. At least you had the sense to leave that…that floozy you were living with behind when you returned home.'

Anger flashed in Marco's eyes. It was typical of his grandfather to have found out as much about his private life in London as he could. It also infuriated him that Giorgio should refer to Emily in that way and dismiss their relationship. Worse, it felt as though, somehow, his grandfather had touched a raw place within him that he didn't want to admit existed, never mind be reminded about. Because, even though he didn't want to own up to it, he was missing Emily. Marco shrugged the thought aside. So what if he was? Wasn't it only natural that his body, deprived of the sexual pleasure it had shared with hers, should ache a little?

'As to what we agreed, it was simply that I should *initially* return to Niroli alone,' Marco pointed out.

Immediately the king's anger returned. 'What do you mean, "initially"?'

When Marco didn't answer him, the old man bellowed, 'You will not bring her here, Marco! I will not allow it. You are my heir, and you have a position to maintain. The people—'

Marco knew that he should reassure his grandfather and tell him he had no intention of bringing Emily to Niroli, but instead he said coolly, 'The people, our people, will, I am sure, have more important things to worry about than the fact that I have a mistress—things like the fact that ten per cent of them do not have electricity.'

'You are trying to meddle in things that are not your concern,' the king told him sharply. 'Take care, Marco, otherwise, you will have people thinking that you are more fitted to be a dissident than a leader. To rule, you must command respect and in order to do that you must show a strong hand. The people are your children and need to look up to you as their father, as someone wiser than them.'

This was an issue on which he and his grandfather would never see eye to eye, Marco knew…

'EMILY, WHY DON'T you call it a day and go home? No one else will come into the shop now and you don't have any more client appointments. I know you hate me keeping on about this, but you really don't look at all well. I can lock up the premises for you.'

Emily forced herself to give her assistant an I'm-all-right smile. Jemma wasn't wrong, though she didn't like the fact that the girl had noticed how unwell she looked, because she didn't want to have to answer questions about the cause. 'It's kind of you to offer to do that, Jemma,' she answered, 'but…'

'But you're missing Marco desperately, and you don't want to go back to an empty house?' Jemma suggested gently, her words slicing through the barriers Emily had tried so desperately to maintain.

She could feel betraying tears burning the backs of her eyes. She had tried so very hard to pretend that she didn't mind that she and Marco had split up, but it was obvious that her assistant hadn't been deceived.

'It had to end, given Marco's royal status,' she told Jemma, trying to keep her voice light. Initially, she had worried about revealing the truth of Marco's real identity. But, in the end, she'd had no need to do so because her assistant had seen one of many articles appearing in the press about Marco's return to Niroli; most of them had been accompanied by photographs of his cavalcade and the crowd waiting to welcome him. 'I just wish that he had told me the truth about himself, Jemma,' Emily said in a low voice, unable to conceal her hurt.

'I can understand that,' Jemma agreed. 'But according to what I've read, Marco came over here incognito because he wanted to prove himself in his own right. He had already done that by the time he met you, yet I suppose he could hardly tell you his real identity—not only would it have been difficult for him to just turn round and say, "Oh, by the way, perhaps I ought to tell you that I'm a prince," he most probably wanted you to value him for himself, not for his title or position.'

Emily could see the logic of Jemma's argument, and she knew it was one that Marco himself would have used—had they ever got to the stage of discussing the issue.

'Marco didn't tell me because he *didn't want* to tell me,' she retorted, trying to harden her heart against its betraying softening. 'To him, I was just a...a...temporary bed-mate—a diversion he could enjoy, before he left me to get on with the really serious business of his life and return to Niroli.'

'I think I know how you must be feeling,' Jemma allowed, 'but I did read in one article that it wasn't until the death of his parents in an accident that Marco became the next in line to the throne. I'm sure he didn't tell you because he assumed he would continue to live in London with you anonymously.'

'I meant nothing to him.'

'I can't believe that, Emily. You always seemed so happy together, and so well suited.'

'It's pointless talking about it, or him, now. It's over.'

'Is it? I can't help thinking that there's a lot of unfinished business between the two of you,' Jemma told her softly. 'I know from what you told me that you left the apartment virtually as soon as you discovered the truth. You must have still been in shock when that happened, and my guess is that Marco must have been equally shocked, although for different reasons.'

'Reasons like being found out, you mean, and resenting me being the one to end our relationship, not him?' Emily asked her bitterly.

'So, you wouldn't be interested if he got in touch with you?' Jemma probed quietly.

'That isn't going to happen.' But she knew from the look in her assistant's eyes that Jemma had guessed her weakness and how much a foolish, treacherous part of her still longed for him.

'Be fair to yourself, Emily,' Jemma told her. 'You and Marco have history together, and there are still loose ends for you that need proper closure, questions you need to ask and answers Marco needs to give you. A poisoned wound can't heal,' she pointed out wisely. 'And until you get that poison of your break-up out of your system, you won't heal.'

'I'm fine,' Emily lied defensively.

'No, you aren't,' Jemma responded firmly. 'Just look at yourself. You aren't eating, you're losing weight and you obviously aren't happy.'

'It's just this virus, that's all. I can't seem to throw it off properly,' Emily told her. But she knew that Jemma wasn't deceived.

EMILY WAS STILL thinking about her conversation with Jemma more than two hours later as she wandered aimlessly round her showroom, pausing to straighten a line of already perfectly straight sample swatches. Jemma had been right about her not wanting to return to her empty house and correct too about how much she was missing Marco.

It had been all very well telling herself that he had lied to her and that she was better off without him. The reality was very different: the empty space he'd left in her life had been taken over by the unending misery of living without him. He had only been gone just a short time, but already she had lost count of the number of times every night she woke up reaching out for him in her bed, only to be filled with anguish when the reality that he wasn't there hit her once more. No matter how hard she worked, she couldn't fill her mind with enough things to block out the knowledge that Marco had left; that she wouldn't be going home to him; that never again would he hold her, or touch her, or kiss her; never ever again. It was over, and somehow she must find a way to rebuild her life, although right now she had no idea how she was going to accomplish that. To make matters worse, as Jemma had already commented, she was losing weight and felt unable to eat properly. Emily had put it down to a flu bug she had picked up earlier in the year. She just couldn't seem to get rid of it.

Allied to which, she had an even nastier heartache bug, Emily recognised. Did Marco think of her at all, now he was living his new life, Emily wondered miserably, or was he far too busy planning his future? A future that was ultimately, and surely, bound to include a wife. Pain seized her, ripping at all her defences, leaving her exposed to the reality of what loving him really meant. Marco…Marco… How could this have happened to her? How could she have avoided falling in love with him? What was he doing right now? Who was he with? His grandfather? His family? She mustn't do this to herself, Emily warned herself tiredly. It served no purpose, other than to reinforce what she already knew, and that was that she loved a man who did not love her. She reached for her coat. She might as well go home.

'WHAT IS THIS I hear about you returning to London? I will not allow you to leave Niroli to go to London. What possible reason could you have for wanting to be there?'

Marco had to struggle to stop himself from responding in kind to his grandfather's angry interrogation.

'You know why I need to return. I have certain business matters to attend to there,' he answered suavely instead.

'I do not permit it.'

'No? That is your choice, Grandfather, but I still intend to go. You see, I do not need your permission.'

Obstinately they eyed each other, two alpha males who knew that, according to the law of the jungle, only one of them could truly hold the reins of power. Marco had no intention of allowing his grandfather to dominate him. He knew well enough that once he let him have the upper hand, the king would treat him with contempt. Giorgio was the kind of man who would rather die with his sword in his hand, so to speak, than allow a younger rival to take it from him. The truth was that Marco could have dealt with the business that was taking him to the UK from the island, and that, in part, his decision to go to London in spite of his grandfather's objections had been made publicly to underline his own determination and status. It was more than two weeks since he had first arrived on Niroli, and there hadn't been a single day when he and his grandfather hadn't clashed like two Titans. Every attempt he had made to talk to Giorgio about doing something to help the poorer inhabitants of the island had been met with a furious tirade about what a waste of money this would be, and a threat to royal rule.

Marco was determined that electricity should be made available to those living in the more remote villages, and his grandfather was equally adamant that he was not prepared to sanction it.

'Very well, then, I shall pay for it myself,' Marco had told him grimly. But the reality was that things were not as simple as that: the topography of the mountain region meant that they would need to bring in expert outside help, and it was of course Vialli country.

Marco suspected that King Giorgio was being difficult for the sake of being difficult, more than anything else. He could also admit to himself that his years in London running his own life and not having to worry about consulting anyone about his decisions was now making it very difficult for him to conform to the role of king-in-waiting. He was very much the junior partner in this new relationship. He started to walk away.

'Marco, I trust that this visit of yours to London does not have anything to do with that woman you were bedding?'

Marco swung round and looked at his grandfather, his voice flattened by the weight of his fury as he demanded, 'And if it does?'

'Then I forbid you to see her,' his grandfather told him fiercely. 'The future King of Niroli does not bed some commoner—a divorcée, with no pedigree and no money.'

'No one tells me who I can and cannot take to my bed, Grandfather, not even you.' Marco didn't wait to hear what the older man might say in reply. Instead he strode out of the room, fighting to dampen down the heat of the fury burning along his veins. The bright sunshine that had warmed the air earlier that day was turning to vivid dusk as he left the palace. He had refused the offer of a suite of rooms within its walls, preferring instead to stay in the nearby villa he had inherited from his parents. His grandfather hadn't been too pleased about that, but Marco had refused to give in. It was very important to him that he retained his privacy and independence. However, right now, it wasn't the villa he was heading for as he climbed into his personal car. He was bound for the airport, and a flight to London, despite his grandfather's opposition. How dared Giorgio attempt to tell him that he couldn't sleep with Emily? He glanced at the clock on the dashboard of his car. It would be early evening in London, just after six o'clock. Emily would most probably have left her shop and be on her way home.

Emily! It hadn't needed his grandfather's mention of her to bring her into his thoughts. Indeed, it had surprised and disconcerted him to discover just how much she had been there since they had parted. It was only because he was discovering that he wasn't enjoying sleeping alone, he assured himself. The fact that Emily was so constantly in his thoughts was simply his mind playing tricks and had no personal relevance for him.

He turned his thoughts back to his grandfather; despite his frustration with the older man's arrogant and domineering attitude, he was very aware that the king was not in the best of health. He must continue to temper his reaction to him as much as he could. But it wasn't easy.

'EMILY, WHY DON'T you go and see your doctor?' Jemma suggested, her face shadowed with concern as she studied Emily's wan complexion.

'There's no need for that. It's as I've said before—it's just that virus hanging around,' Emily explained tiredly. 'The doctor will only tell me to take some paracetamol, and that it's bound to wear off soon.'

'You've been sick every morning this week, and now you've left your lunch. You look exhausted.'

'I need a holiday, some sunshine to perk me up a bit, that's all,' Emily replied lightly. She didn't want to continue this discussion, but she didn't want to hurt Jemma's feelings either; she knew her assistant was genuinely concerned about her.

'You certainly need something—or someone,' Jemma agreed forthrightly, leaving Emily regretting that she had ever allowed her guard to slip and admit that she was missing Marco.

'Why don't I pop across the road and bring you back a sandwich and a cup of coffee?' Jemma suggested.

'Coffee?' Emily shuddered with revulsion. The very thought made her feel nauseous. 'I couldn't face it,' she protested. 'Just thinking about the smell makes me feel sick.'

'I think you're right about you needing a holiday,' Jemma told her firmly.

Emily gave her a forced smile. The truth was, what she needed and wanted more than anything else was Marco—Marco's arms—to hold her close, Marco's body next to hers in bed at night and, most of all, Marco's love, and the knowledge that it would last a lifetime. But she wasn't going to be given any of those. She hadn't realised just how hard it would be for her after their relationship had ended. The emotional pain she was suffering now was almost unendurable; it tore through her emotions like a fever in her blood, burning up her immunity. Every night when she went to bed she told herself that it couldn't get any worse and that soon she would start to feel better. But every morning when she woke up it *was* worse. She hated herself for wanting him like this after the way he had deceived her. However, hating herself couldn't stop her from loving him…

THE BUSINESS THAT had brought Marco to London had been concluded, and the first consignment of the generators he'd bought at his own expense were already on their way to the airport to be flown out by a cargo plane to Niroli. He had been on his way back to his hotel when, for no logical reason he could find, he had leaned forward and told the cab driver he had changed his mind, then given him the address of Emily's small shop in Chelsea. He didn't owe her anything; she had refused to let him fully explain to her that his decision to conceal his real identity had been one he had made long before he had met her. Sleeping dogs were best left to lie and, anyway, their relationship would have had to end sooner or later.

Marco's purchase of the generators would infuriate his grandfather, as would the knowledge that he was seeing Emily, he acknowledged as he paid the cab fare and looked along the pretty Chelsea street basking in afternoon sunshine. So was that why he was here? To infuriate his grandfather? Marco's mouth curled in sardonic awareness. The days when he had been immature enough to need to infuriate the man he had seen as an unwanted authority figure were long gone. No, he didn't want to upset his grandfather at all. But he was not quite ready to let go or move on. Therefore a little reinforcement to him of the fact that Marco wasn't going to be dictated to wouldn't do any harm. Plus, he liked the idea of dealing with two separate issues at a single stroke—Emily had walked out on him without giving him the chance to explain his situation to her rationally. She owed him that opportunity and his pride demanded that she retract the contemptuously angry insults she had thrown at him. That was what had brought him here: his own pride. And no one, not his grandfather, and certainly not Emily herself, was going to stop him from seeing her and demanding that his pride was satisfied. And his body, which needed satisfaction so desperately? Any woman could provide him with that! Marco dismissed the throb that was increasing with every step that took him closer to Emily. No way would he ever allow one woman to dominate his senses to that extent.

He could see into the window of her shop-cum-showroom from where he was standing. The simple elegance of the set Emily had created was both immediately refreshing and soothing on his eye. She had a remarkable, indeed an inspired, gift for transforming the dull and utilitarian. His Niroli villa could certainly do with her skills!

Marco began to frown. Whilst he had to admit how poorly the décor of his villa compared with that of the London apartment Emily had decorated for him, he could well imagine his grandfather's reaction if he were to return to the island with her at his side, claiming that he needed an interior designer. His grandfather wouldn't believe him for one moment and he would think that Marco was deliberately flouting his orders. Perhaps he should flout them in this way, Marco reflected ruefully; it would be a sure and certain way of making his grandfather understand that he wasn't going to be pushed around. And Emily's presence on Niroli and in his life wouldn't directly impact on their subjects.

The more he thought about it, the more Marco could see the benefit to himself of Emily's temporary and brief presence on the island as a sharp warning to his grandfather not to trespass into his privacy. Certainly in the unlikely event of Emily being willing to return to Niroli with him, he would want her to share his bed. He would be a fool not to, given the level of his current sexual hunger. Was that really why he was here now? Not solely because of his pride, but because he still wanted her too?

No!

He was already pushing open the shop door, but then he paused, half inclined to turn round and walk away just to prove how unfounded that motivation was. However, it was too late for him to change his mind: Emily had seen him.

She was sitting behind a desk talking with her assistant, Jemma, and the first thing Marco noticed was how much weight she had lost and how pale and fragile she looked. Because of him? It shocked him to discover that a part of him wanted to believe it was because she was missing him. Why? *Why* should he feel like this when, in the past, with other women, he had been only too pleased to see them move on to a new partner after he had broken up with them. But in the past he hadn't continued to want those other women, had he?

He pushed his thoughts to one side, watching Emily's eyes widen as she looked up and saw him, the blood rushing to her face, turning it a deep pink. He saw her lips frame his name. She pushed back her chair to stand up and then he saw her sway and start to crumple, as though her body were no more than one of the swathes of fabric draped over the back of another chair nearby. That deep pink glow had receded from her cheeks, leaving her so pale that she looked almost bloodless.

He reacted immediately and instinctively, pushing his way through the pieces of furniture, reaching her just in time to hear her saying huskily, 'It's all right, I'm not going to faint,' before she did exactly that.

Through the roaring blur of sick dizziness, Emily could hear voices: Jemma's sharp with anxiety, Marco's harsher than she wanted it to be, their words, moving giddily in and out of one another, weaving through the darkness she was trying to free herself from. Then she felt Marco's arms tightening around her, holding her, and she exhaled on a small sigh of relief, knowing she was safe and that she didn't have to battle on alone any more. Gratefully she let the darkness take her as she slid into a faint.

'What the hell's going on?' Marco asked Jemma abruptly. Any idiotic thought he might have entertained that there was something ego-boosting about Emily's reaction to him had disappeared now, banished by his realisation of just how fragile she was. In all the time they had been together he had never once known her faint, or even say that she thought she might be going to, which made it all the more shocking that she had done so now.

'I wish I knew,' Jemma admitted. 'What I do know is that she hasn't been eating properly. She says it's because of that flu bug she had earlier in the year. She just can't seem to throw it off. She isn't the only one, of course. I read in a newspaper the other day that many people are still suffering from its after-effects. The health authorities say that the best cures are rest and sunshine to build up the immune system. Emily's admitted as much herself, although I can't see her taking a holiday. I'm so glad you're here. I've been really worried about her.'

'Will you both please stop talking about me as though I don't exist? I'm all right…' The blackness was receding and with it her nausea. She was sitting on a chair—Marco must have put her there, and no doubt he was the one who had pushed her head down towards her knees as well. She turned her head slightly and saw that he was standing next to her. So close to her, in fact, that she could easily have reached out and touched him. Weak tears stung her eyes, causing her to make a small anguished sound of protest.

'Emily?' She could feel Marco's hand on her shoulder, her flesh responding to its familiar warmth, weirdly both soothed and excited by it. The hardness of his voice lacerated both her pride and her heart. This was not how she would have wanted them to meet for the first time after their split; she must seem so vulnerable and needy, virtually forcing Marco to step in and manage things. Fate wasn't being very kind to her at the moment, she reflected wearily. She held her breath as Marco crouched down beside her, struggling to lift her head and fight off the swimming sensation within it. She would have given a lot for him not to have seen her like this, not to have witnessed her humiliating loss of consciousness.

'There's no need to fuss. I'm fine,' she repeated, sounding as steady as she could.

'Don't listen to her, Marco. She isn't all right at all. She's hardly eating and when she does, she's sick.'

'Jemma!' Emily warned sharply.

'Jemma is hardly breaking the Official Secrets Act,' Marco defended her assistant dryly. 'After all, she hasn't told me anything I can't see for myself. And, besides, there's no reason why I shouldn't know, is there?'

None, except her pride and her aching heart, Emily admitted inwardly. And, of course, those wouldn't matter to Marco. 'I don't know what you are doing here, *Your Highness*,' she addressed him, deliberately underlining his title.

He couldn't just walk away and leave her like this, Marco decided. So what was he going to do? His return flight was already scheduled for later this evening. Emily wasn't his responsibility. She was an adult. There was no good cause for him to involve himself here. But another voice deep inside him told him it was too late for such arguments. He had already made his decision.

'I came to see you because I've got a business proposition to put to you,' he told Emily levelly. He could see her eyes widening with confusion and disbelief. She was lifting her hand to her head, as though she couldn't take in what he was saying. Seeing her look so thin and unwell touched an unfamiliar chord inside him, which he crushed down the instant he felt it.

Emily's head was aching painfully. She was finding it hard enough to grasp that Marco was actually here, never mind anything else. Her thoughts were in complete disarray. She couldn't really comprehend what he was saying. It was difficult enough for her to focus simply on stopping her heart from spinning and shaking her body with the force of its frantic beats, without having to think logically and calmly as well. It had upset her far more than she wanted to admit that the sight of him should have affected her to such an extent that she had collapsed. Worryingly, even now her senses were still clinging possessively to the memory of being held in his arms as he had caught her. Part of her, the sensible part, she told herself firmly, wanted to put as much distance between them as she could, to protect herself from making it even more obvious just how intensely aware of him she was. Whilst the other part longed to be as intimately close to him as it was possible to be: body to body, skin to skin, mouth to mouth—heart to heart.

'A business proposition?' she repeated uncertainly. 'What exactly does that mean, Marco? I'm an interior designer.'

'Exactly,' Marco agreed, 'and a very good one.'

Marco was praising her? *Flattering her?* Why? she wondered suspiciously. It was totally out of character for him to behave like this.

'Since it could be a while before I formally take over from my grandfather, instead of moving into the palace and being cooped up in a suite of rooms there,' Marco told her, 'I've moved into a villa I inherited from my parents. It's in the old part of the town and it's badly in need of modernisation. I want a designer who knows what she's doing and, just as important, one who knows my taste.'

It took several seconds for the full meaning of what he was saying to sink in. But once it had, Emily could hardly conceal her disbelief.

'Are you saying that you want to commission *me* to be that designer?' she asked Marco faintly.

'Yes, why not?' Marco confirmed.

'Why not?' Emily stared at him as her heart lurched

crazily into her ribs. 'Marco, we were lovers, and now our relationship is over. You must see that I can't just let you commission me as your designer as though everything that took place between us never happened.'

'Of course not, Emily. You never let me explain properly to you why I didn't tell you about Niroli or my role there.' Out of the corner of her eye, Emily could see Jemma discreetly edging out of the room to go into the stock room, closing the door after her to give them some privacy.

Emily waited, feeling helpless and weak. She was her own worst enemy, she knew that. She shouldn't even be thinking of listening to him, instead of sitting here desperate for every second she could spend with him.

'As a boy, I had a very difficult relationship with my grandfather. I suppose I was something of a black sheep in his eyes. I resented the way he treated my father, who was too gentle to stand up to him, and I swore that I would never let him control me the way he did my parents. I came to London determined to prove to him and to myself that I could be a success without the power of the Royal House of Niroli. It was for that reason that I came here and stayed incognito, and no other.'

'But when we met, you had achieved that success, Marco,' Emily forced herself to remind him.

'Yes, but I had also grown used to the freedom of living and proving myself as plain Marco Fierezza. It seemed to me then that there was no need for me to live any other way—at least not for many years. My father was still alive and he would have succeeded my grandfather when the time came.' Marco gave a small shrug. 'I had no expectation of becoming king until I was much older.'

'Maybe not. But you would surely have to marry appropriately and produce a son to whom you can pass on the crown,' Emily couldn't help pointing out quietly.

Marco inclined his head.

'Yes, at some stage. One of the archaic rules that sur-round the Royal House of Niroli is that the king cannot marry a woman who is divorced, or of ill repute. The chal-lenge of finding such a paragon in today's world is such that I was more than happy to remain unmarried until ne-cessity directed otherwise.'

Emily had to blink fast to disperse her threatening tears. Marco obviously had no idea just how hurtful his casual words were. It could never have occurred to him to think of her as someone he might love and want to commit to permanently. She should hate him for showing her how in-different he was to her, Emily told herself, but somehow she felt too sick at heart to do it.

'Look,' Marco told her crisply, 'I don't have much time, and since you obviously need to eat, why don't we discuss this over an early dinner?'

Emily shuddered and shook her head in instant denial, her reaction making him frown. She'd always had a good appetite, having never needed to worry about what she ate. But now the fact that she had not been eating prop-erly was plain to see in the sharp angles of her cheekbones and her jaw.

'Jemma's right, Emily, you aren't looking after yourself properly,' Marco announced firmly. 'You need a break. I don't have time to argue with you. I've made up my mind. You're coming back to Niroli with me.'

Was this giddy, soaring feeling inside her really because she was so weak that she was glad that Marco had made up her mind for her? She was an independent woman, for heaven's sake, not some wilting Victorian heroine. She tried to wrench back some control of what was happening.

'I can't do that, Marco. For one thing, there's the busi-ness—'

'Of course you can, Em. I can take care of things here,' Jemma piped up from the threshold of the storeroom. With Marco's back to her, she mouthed to Emily, Go with him, you know you want to... Before announcing to both of them that time was getting on and she had to catch the post with some invoices.

Emily and Marco were alone in the shop now, and she wished violently that she were not so all-consumingly aware of him.

'You can't take me back with you, Marco. It wouldn't work. We were lovers—'

'And still could be, if that's what you want,' Marco interrupted softly.

Emily didn't dare look at him in case he saw the hope and the longing in her eyes. She struggled between her own helpless awareness of how much she still wanted him and the practicalities of the situation, protesting unsteadily, 'Marco, we can't. Even if I wanted to...to go back, it isn't possible.'

'Why not, if it's what both of us want?

What *both* of them wanted. Her heart lurched, joyously intoxicated by the pleasure of hearing the admission his words contained.

'But what about the rules of the House of Niroli? Surely your grandfather wouldn't approve, or—'

'My grandfather doesn't rule my personal life,' Marco responded with familiar arrogance.

She had no idea how to handle this. She shook her head. 'I don't know what to say,' she admitted. 'How long have I got?'

'To share my bed?' Marco cut her off smoothly. 'I doubt that my grandfather is really ready to step down, for all that he says he is. We could have the summer together and then reassess the situation.'

Emily could feel her face burning.

'That wasn't what I meant. When I said how long have I got, I meant how much time will you give me to think things through before I make up my mind about your business proposition?' she told him primly. 'Nothing else.'

'No time. Because you aren't going to think about it. You are coming back with me, Emily—you don't have a choice about that. What you can choose, though, of course, is in what capacity. My flight leaves at eight, so we've just got time to go back to your house and collect your passport, and anything else you might need. And time for me to show you exactly what both of us will be missing if you don't,' he told her, giving her a look that was so explicitly sexual that her whole body burned with longing. And then, as though he had said nothing remotely outrageous to her, he continued smoothly, 'I should warn you, the villa is going to tax even your creative eye, but I'm sure you'll enjoy the challenge.'

He was handing her her handbag and her coat, and somehow or other she was being ushered out of the door, helpless to stop what was happening and not really caring that she couldn't.

'How many bedrooms does the villa have?' she managed to ask Marco slightly breathlessly, once they were outside on the street.

The look he gave her as he turned to her made her heart thud recklessly.

'Five, but you will be sleeping in mine—with me.'

'You're going to be Niroli's next king, Marco!' Emily felt bound to remind him. 'You can't live openly with me there as your mistress.'

'No?' he challenged her softly.

CHAPTER EIGHT

AT SOME STAGE during the drive from Niroli's airport, into which they had flown by private jet, she must have half fallen asleep, Emily realised as the motion of the car ceased and she heard Marco's voice saying through the darkness of the car's interior, 'We're here.'

But not before she had seen the impressively straight road leading from the airport, with huge placards attached to lampposts bearing a photograph of Marco, a royal crown hovering several centimetres above his head and an ermine-edged cape around his shoulders. Underneath were Italian words, which she could just about translate as, 'Welcome home, Your Highness'.

It made her shiver slightly now to think about them and to remember how she had felt at seeing them, how very aware they had made her of the gulf between her and Marco's royal status.

The emotional roller-coaster ride of the last few hours had taken its toll on her, Emily knew. It had drained her and left her feeling so exhausted that she barely had the energy to get out of the car, even though Marco opened the door for her and reached out his hand to support her. Just for a moment she hesitated and looked back into the car. Wishing she had not come? She pushed the thought aside and focused instead on the fact that the night air had that familiar scent of Mediterranean warmth that she remembered from her many holidays elsewhere in the region with

Marco: a mingling of olfactory textures and tints, ripened by the day's sunlight and then distilled by the soft darkness.

Emily breathed it in slowly, trying to steady her own nerves. She was, she realised, standing in the courtyard of what looked like a haphazard jumble of white stone walls, shuttered, arched windows and delicate iron balconies, illuminated by moonlight and lamplight from the surrounding buildings. The courtyard was shielded from the narrow street outside by a pair of heavy wooden doors, and as Emily's senses adjusted themselves to the darkness she could hear from somewhere the sound of water from a fountain falling into a basin.

'It looks almost Moorish,' she told Marco.

'Yes, it does, doesn't it?' Marco agreed with her. 'History does have it that the Moors *were* here at one time, and it's here in the oldest part of the main town that you can see their architectural influence. Although there were also Nirolians who travelled as traders to and from Andalucia in Spain, as well.' He was guiding her towards an impressive doorway as he spoke. Emily hesitated, knowing it was too late now to change her mind about the wisdom of allowing him to bring her here and yet not totally able to overcome her uncertainty.

'You said that you're living here, instead of at the palace?'

'Yes. Are you disappointed? If so, I am sure I can arrange for us to have a suite of rooms there—'

Us? 'No…' Emily stopped him hurriedly. 'Marco…' She stopped, and shivered slightly despite the warmth of the air. She was a fool to have allowed Marco to steamroller her into coming here so that he could have her back in his bed, when she knew there was no real future for her with him. But why think of the future when she could have the present? an inner voice urged her. Every day she could have with Marco, every hour, were things so precious she should reach out and grab them with both hands. Emily squeezed her eyes tightly closed and then opened them again. She wasn't used to this unfamiliar recklessness she seemed to have developed, with its blinkered refusal to acknowledge anything other than her determination to be with him. She did love him so much, Emily accepted, but it would be far better for her if she did not.

Fine, the reckless voice told her. *So you spend your time trying to stop loving him, and I'll spend mine enjoying being with him. You can't leave—not now.* What *was* this? She felt as though she were being torn in two. The sensible, protective part of her was telling her that it would be better if she spent her time here learning to recognise the huge differences between them; far better if she made herself focus, not on the fact that Marco was her lover and the man she loved, but on the fact that he was Niroli's future king and as such could never be hers. However, this new reckless part of her was insisting that nothing mattered more than squeezing the intimacy and the sweetness out of every extra minute she had with him, regardless of what the future might bring. How could she bring together two such opposing forces? She couldn't.

'Let's go inside,' she heard Marco telling her, 'then I can introduce you to Maria and Pietro, who look after the villa for me.'

Emily still hung back.

'They are bound to talk about my being here.'

'I expect they will, but why should that matter?' Marco knew all too well that they would, and that their talk would very quickly reach his grandfather's ears. There was no need for him to share that knowledge with Emily, though.

'Wouldn't it perhaps be better if…well, you said you

wanted me to restyle the villa. Perhaps I should have my own room, for convention's sake, and then you could…'

'I could what? Sneak you into my bed at dead of night?' Marco shook his head, his mouth tightening. 'I am a man, Emily, not a fearful boy.'

'But if we are going to be lovers…'

'"If" we are?' he mocked her softly. 'There is no "if" about it, Emily. You will be sleeping in my bed and I shall be there with you, make no mistake about that. I know you're tired, so I shall not make love to you, but only for tonight. My people will understand that I am a man, as well as their future king, and they will not expect me to live the life of a monk. They will accept that—'

'That what? That I am your mistress, and that you have brought me here to warm your bed?' When Marco talked like this, she felt as though she were listening to a stranger, Emily recognised in sharpening panic. His casual reference to 'his people' and his position as 'their future king' set him on a different plane from her, and a different life path; already he was someone else from the man she had known…a king-in-waiting…

'Are you saying that you don't want to warm it?' Marco asked her, breaking into her thoughts and then adding so seductively, almost like the old Marco that she used to know, 'Did you know there is something about the smell of your skin that right now is filling my head with the most erotic thoughts—and memories?' His voice had dropped to a whisper that was almost mesmeric. 'Can you remember the first time I tasted you?'

Despite the doubts and fears she was experiencing, his words sent a thrill of sensation through her, making her body quiver with arousal at the images he was conjuring up. She wanted to tell him that she wasn't a naïve virgin

any more and that she wasn't going to play his game, but
instead she heard herself saying thickly, 'Yes.'

'And the first time you tasted me?'

Now she could only nod her head as desire kicked up
violently inside her stomach.

Marco's fingers had encircled her wrist and he was
stroking her bare skin in a rhythmic, beguiling caress.

'You didn't care then about the staff of the hotel knowing that we were lovers.'

'That was different,' she protested.

'Why?'

'Then we were private lovers. But here, Marco, as you
yourself have just said, in the eyes of the people of Niroli
you are their future king, and I will be your mistress.'

'So?'

Could he really not understand how she felt? Was he
really already so far removed from ordinary life that he
couldn't see that she would a thousand times rather be the
lover of plain Marco Fierezza, than the mistress of the future King of Niroli?

'I can assure you that you will be treated with courtesy
and respect, Emily, if that is what is worrying you,' he
continued when she didn't answer him. 'And if it should
come to my ears that you aren't, I will make sure that is
corrected.'

He sounded shockingly, sickeningly, aloof and regal.
The words he had spoken were the kind of statement that
previously she would have laughed openly over and expected him to do the same. But she could tell from his
expression that he meant them seriously. Marco's always
had been a very commanding presence, but now Emily
felt there was a new hauteur to his manner, a coldness and
a disdain that chilled her through. The hardening of his
voice and the arrogance of his stance betrayed his deter-

mination to have his own way. And a belief in his royal right to do so? Emily wasn't sure. But she did feel that the subtle change she could sense in him highlighted her own uncertainties. In London, despite the financial gap between them, they had met and lived as equals. Here, on Niroli, she knew instinctively that things would be different. But right now she was too tired to question how much that difference was going to impact on their new relationship. Right now, all she wanted… Marco was still stroking her arm. She closed her eyes and swayed closer to him. Right now, she admitted, all she wanted was this: the scented darkness, the proximity of their bodies and the promise of pleasure to come…

IT WAS THE single, sharp, shrill, animal cry of the victim of a night predator who had come down from the mountains to hunt, cut off along with its life, that woke Emily from her deep sleep. At first, her unfamiliar surroundings confused her, but then she remembered where she was. She turned over in the large bed, her body as filled with sharp dread as though the dying creature had passed on its fear to her.

'Marco?' She reached out her hand into the darkness and to the other side of the bed, but encountered only emptiness.

She had been so tired when they had arrived that she had gone straight to bed, in the room to which Marco had taken her, leaving him to explain the situation to the couple who looked after the villa for him. She suspected she must have fallen asleep within seconds of her head reaching the pillow. She had assumed though, after what he had said to her, that he would be joining her in it. She hadn't had the energy to argue, even if she had wanted to.

The door to the room's *en suite* bathroom opened. A mixture of relief and sexual tension filled her as she watched Marco walk towards her. He always slept naked and there was enough light coming in through the window to reveal the outline of his body. Her memory did the rest, filling in the shadow-cloaked detail with such powerfully loving strokes that she trembled.

'So, you're awake,' she heard him murmur as she lifted her head from the pillow to watch his approach.

'Yes.' Her response was little more than a terse, exhaled breath, an indication of her impatience at herself at being unable to tear her gaze from his magnificent physique.

'But still tired?' Marco was standing at the side of the bed now, leaning down towards her.

'A little. But not *too* tired,' she whispered daringly. She had known all along, of course, that this would be the outcome of being with him again. How could it not be when you had a man as sexually irresistible as Marco and a woman as desperately in love as she was?

They looked at one another through the semi-darkness; night sounds rustled through the room, mingling with the accelerated sound of their breathing. The darkness had become a velvet embrace, its softness pressing in on them like an intimate caress, stroking shared sensual memories over their minds.

The sudden fiercely intense surge of his own desire caught Marco off guard, as it threatened his self-control. He knew that he had missed their sex, but he hadn't been prepared for this raw, aching hunger that was now consuming him.

Emily's skin smelled of his own shower gel in a way that made him frown as his senses searched eagerly for the familiar night-warm, intimate scent that was hers and hers alone, and which he was only recognising now how much he had missed... She moved, dislodging the bedclothes, and his chest muscles contracted under the pressure of the pounding thud of his heartbeat. His pulse had started to race and he recognised that the ache of need for her, which had begun here in this bed the first night he had spent in it without her, had turned feral and taken away his control.

'Emily.'

The way he said her name turned Emily's insides to liquid heat. He and this yearning beating up through her body were impossible to resist. She sat up in the bed, giving in to her love, pressing her lips to his bare shoulder, closing her eyes with delight as she breathed him into her. She ran the tip of her tongue along his collar-bone, feeling the responsive clench of his muscles and the reverberation of his low groan of pleasure. When he arched his neck, she kissed her way along it, caressing the swell of his Adam's apple, whilst his muscles now corded in mute recognition of his arousal. And his desire fed her own, intoxicating her, empowering her, encouraging her to make their intimacy a slow, sweetly erotic dance spiced with sudden moments of breathless intensity.

It felt good to keep their need on a tight knife-edge, refusing to let him touch her until he couldn't be refused any more, and then giving herself over completely to the touch of his hands and his mouth, crying out her need as he finally covered her and moved into her. But it was his own cry of mingled triumph and release that took them both over the edge, to the sweet place that lay beyond it.

Several minutes later, rolling away from Emily, Marco lay on his back, staring up at the ceiling and waiting for his heartbeat to steady, willing himself not to think about what his body had just told him about the intensity of his need for Emily.

If the way in which Marco was rejecting her in the aftermath of the intimacy they had just shared was hurting her, then it served her right for coming here, Emily told herself.

She must take her pain and hold onto it, use it to remind herself what the reality of being here with Marco meant. It would do her good to see him in his true role, in his true habitat, because it would show her surely that the man she loved simply did not exist any more, and once she knew that her unwanted love would die. How could it not do so?

CHAPTER NINE

KING GIORGIO WAGGED a reproving finger. 'Is it not enough that you have deliberately attempted to undermine the authority of the Crown—an authority which is soon to be your own—with these generators you have brought to Niroli, without this added flouting of my command to end your association with this…this floozy? You know perfectly well that there are channels and protocols to be followed when a member of the royal family takes a mistress. It is unthinkable that you should have brought back with you to Niroli a woman who is a common nothing, and who never can and never will be accepted here at court!'

'You mean, I take it, that I could take my pick from the married women amongst the island's nobility? Her husband would of course be instructed to do his duty and give up his wife to royal pleasure and, in due course, both would be appropriately rewarded—the husband with an important government position, the wife with the title of Royal Mistress and a few expensive baubles.' Marco shook his head. 'I have no intention of adorning some poor courtier with a pair of horns so that I can sleep with his wife.'

'You cannot expect me to believe that you, a prince of Niroli, can be content with a woman who is a nothing—'

'Emily is far from being nothing, and the truth is that you insult her by comparing her with the blue-blooded nonentities you seem to think are so superior to her. There is no comparison. Emily is their superior in every way.' The immediate and heated ferocity of his defence of Emily and his anger against his grandfather had taken hold of Marco before he could think logically about what he was saying. His immediate impulse had been to protect her, and that alone was enough to cause him to wonder at his uncharacteristic behaviour. And yet, even though for practical and diplomatic reasons he knew if he could not bring himself to recall his statement, then at least he should temper it a little. But he couldn't do it. Why not? Was it because by bringing Emily here to Niroli he now felt a far greater sense of responsibility towards her than he had done in London?

His grandfather didn't give him time to ponder. Instead the king pushed his chair back from the table and eased himself up, before demanding regally, 'Do you really think that I am deceived by any of this, Marco? Do you think I don't realise that you have brought those generators and this woman here to Niroli expressly to anger and insult me? You may think that you can win the hearts of my people by giving them access to the technological toys you believe they crave, and that they will accept your mistress, but you are wrong. It is true that there are elements of rebellion and disaffection amongst the mountain-dwellers, the Viallis who will give you their allegiance and sell you their loyalty for the price of a handful of silver, but they are nothing. The hearts of the rest of the Nirolian population lie here with me. They, like me, know that on Niroli the old ways are the best ways, and they will show you in no uncertain terms how they feel about your attempts to win round the Viallis.'

'No, Grandfather, it is you who is wrong,' Marco answered him curtly. 'You may wish to stick with the old ways as you call them, enforcing ignorance and poverty on people, refusing to allow them to make their own choices about the way they want to live, treating them as children.

You try to rule them through fear and power, and some of them rightfully resent that, as I would do in their places. I have brought back the generators because your people, our people, need them, and I have brought Emily back because *I* need *her*.' It wasn't what he had planned to say, and it certainly wasn't what he had been thinking when he had walked into this confrontation, but as soon as he had said the words Marco recognised that they contained a truth that had previously been hidden from him. Or had it been deliberately ignored and denied by him? He had known that he wanted Emily; that he desired her and that he could make use of her presence here to underline his independence to his grandfather, but needing her…that was something else again, and it made Marco stiffen warily, ready to defend himself from what he recognised was his own vulnerability.

'The woman is a commoner, and commoners do not understand what it is to be royal. They cause problems that a woman born into the nobility would never cause.'

'You're speaking from experience?' Marco taunted his grandfather, watching as the older man's face turned a dangerously purple hue.

'You dare to suggest that I would so demean myself?'

Marco looked at him.

'Whilst Emily is here on Niroli she will be treated with respect and courtesy, she will be received at court and she will be treated in every way like the most highly born of royal mistresses,' he told his grandfather evenly. 'I have a long memory and those who do otherwise will be pursued and punished.'

He had spoken loudly enough for everyone else in the chamber to hear him, knowing that the courtiers would know as well as he did that he would soon be in a position to reprimand those who defied him now.

Before this he had never had any intention of bringing Emily to court, but he did not intend to tell his grandfather that. How dared the old man suggest that Emily was somehow less worthwhile as a person than some Nirolian nobleman's wife? He'd back Emily any day if it came to having to prove herself as a person. She possessed intelligence, compassion, wit and kindness, and her natural sweetness was like manna from heaven after the falseness of the courtiers and their wives. He had seen the pleased looks that some of the flunkies had exchanged when his grandfather had flown into a rage over the generators. Of course, they couldn't be expected to like the fact that there were going to be changes, but they were going to have to accept them, Marco decided grimly. Just as they were going to have to accept Emily. He was striding out of the audience chamber before he recognised how much more strongly he felt about protecting Emily than he had actually known...

EMILY STARED AT her watch in disbelief. It was closer to lunchtime than breakfast! How could she have slept so late? The sensual after-ache of the night's pleasure gave her a hint of a reason for her prolonged sleep.

Marco! She sat up in bed and then saw the note he had left for her propped up on the bedside table. She picked it up and read it quickly.

He was going to the palace to see his grandfather, he had written, and since he didn't know when he would be back, he had given Maria instructions to provide her with everything she might need, and had also explained to her that Emily was going to be organising the interior renovation of the villa.

'If you feel up to it, by all means feel free to have a good look around,' he had written, 'but don't overdo things.'

There was no mention of last night, but then there was

hardly likely to be, was there? What had she been hoping for? A love letter? But Marco didn't love her, did he? The starkness of that reality wasn't something she was ready to think about right now, Emily admitted. It was too soon after the traumatic recent see-sawing of her emotions from the depths of despair to the unsteady fragile happiness of Marco's appearance at the shop and their intimacy last night.

But she would have to think about it at some stage, she warned herself. After all, nothing had changed, except that she now knew what living without him felt like. She mustn't let herself forget that all this was nothing more than a small extra interlude of grace; a chance to store up some extra memories for the future.

It wouldn't do her any good to dwell on such depressing thoughts, Emily told herself. Instead, she would get up and then keep herself occupied with an inspection of the villa.

If Maria was curious about her relationship with Marco, she hid it well, Emily decided, an hour later, when she had finished a late breakfast of fresh fruit and homemade rolls, which Maria had offered her when she had come downstairs. She had eaten her light meal sitting in the warm sunlight of a second inner courtyard, and was now ready to explore the villa, which she managed to convey with halting Italian and hand-gestures to Maria, who beamed in response and nodded her head enthusiastically.

Emily had no idea when the villa had first been built, but it was obviously very old and had been constructed at a time when the needs of a household were very different from the requirements of the twenty-first century. In addition to the dark kitchen Maria showed her, there was a positive warren of passages and small rooms, providing what Emily assumed must have been the domestic service area of the house. To suit the needs of a modern family, these would have to be integrated into a much larger, lighter and more modern kitchen, with a dining area, and possibly a family room, opening out onto the courtyard.

The main doors to the villa opened into a square hall-way, flanked by two good-sized salons, although the décor was old-fashioned and dark.

The bedrooms either already had their own bathrooms or were large enough to accommodate *en suites*, although only the room Marco was using was equipped with rela-tively recent sanitary-ware.

On the top floor of the villa, there were more rooms and, by the time she had finished going round the ground and first floors, Emily was beginning to feel tired. But her tiredness wasn't stopping her from feeling excited at the prospect of taking on such a challenging but ultimately worthwhile project. The attic floor alone was large enough to convert into two self-contained units that could provide either semi-separate accommodation for older teenagers, staff quarters, or simply a bolt-hole and working area away from the hubbub of everyday family life. The courtyards to the villa were a real delight, or at least they had the po-tential to be. There were three of them, and the smaller one could easily be adapted to contain a swimming pool.

It was the second courtyard, which Marco's bedroom overlooked, that was her favourite, though. With giant ter-racotta pots filled with shrubs, palms and flowers and a loggia that ran along one wall, it was the perfect spot to sit and enjoy the peaceful sound of its central marble fountain.

Standing in it now, Emily couldn't help thinking what a wonderful holiday home the villa would make for a family. It had room to spare for three generations; with no effort at all she could see them enjoying the refurbished villa's luxurious comfort: the grandparents, retired but still very active, enjoying the company of their great-grandchildren, the kids themselves exuberant, and energetic, the sound of their laughter mingling with that of the fountain; the girls olive-skinned, pretty and dainty, the boys strongly built with their father's dark hair and shrewd gaze, the baby laughing and gurgling as Marco held him, whilst the woman who was their mother and Marco's wife—Niroli's queen—stood watching them.

Don't do this to yourself, an inner voice warned Emily. *Don't go there. Don't think about it, or her; don't imagine what it would be like to be that woman.* In reality, the home she had been busily mentally creating was not that of a king and a queen. It was the home of a couple who loved one another and their children, a home for the kind of family she admitted she had yearned for during her teenage years when she had lived with her grandfather. The kind of home that represented the life, the future, she wished desperately she would be sharing with Marco, right down to the five children. The warmth of the sun spilling into the courtyard filled it with the scent of the lavender that grew there, and Emily knew that, for the rest of her life, she would equate its scent with the pain seeping slowly through her as she acknowledged the impossibility of her dreams. If this were a fantasy, then she could magic away all those things that stood between her and Marco, and imagine a happy ending, a scenario in which he discovered that she loved him and immediately declared his own love for her. But this was real life and there was no way that was going to happen.

One day—maybe—there would be a man with whom she could find some sense of peace, a man who would give her children they could love together and cherish. But that man could not and would not be Marco, and those dark-haired girls and boys she had seen so clearly with her mind's eye, that gorgeous baby, were the children that another woman would bear for him.

And, poor things, their lives would be burdened by the weight of their royal inheritance, just as Marco's was, and that was something Emily knew she could not endure to inflict on her own babies. For them she wanted love and security and the freedom to grow into individuals, instead of being forced into the mould of royal heirs.

It was just as well that Marco had no intentions of wanting to make her his wife, on two counts, Emily told herself determinedly as she battled with her sadness, because the revealing nature of her recent thoughts had shown her what her true feelings were about Marco's royal blood. Plus, of course, as he had already told her, it was not permissible for him to marry a divorced woman.

The sound of crockery rattling on a tray and the smell of coffee brought her back to the present as Maria came into the courtyard carrying a tray of coffee for her, which she put on a table shaded from the heat of the sun by an elegant parchment-coloured sun umbrella.

Thanking her with a smile, Emily decided that she might as well start work.

Within half an hour, she was deeply engrossed in the notes she was making, having moved the coffee-pot out of the way. Although she hadn't felt nauseous this morning, the smell of the coffee had reminded her that her stomach was still queasy and not truly back to normal.

An hour later, when Marco drove into the outer courtyard, Emily was still hard at work. After leaving the palace he had been to the airport, where the generators had already been unloaded. He had already made a list of those villages up in the mountains most in need of their own source of power and whilst in London he had spoken with the island's police chief and the biggest road haulier to arrange for the transport of the generators. However, whilst he had been at the airport, he had received a message from the police chief to say he had received instructions from the palace that the generators were not to be moved.

It had taken all of Marco's considerable negotiating skills, and the cool reminder that he was Niroli's future king, to persuade the police chief to change his mind and go against what he described to Marco almost fearfully as 'orders from the palace'.

Because of this Marco had decided to drive into the mountains himself to make sure that the generators were delivered safely. If his grandfather thought he could outmanoeuvre him, then he was going to have to learn the hard way that it was just not going to happen.

Marco's mouth compressed. As a successful entrepreneur whose views were respected he wasn't used to having his decisions questioned and countermanded. Had his grandfather really no idea of the potential damage he was inflicting on the island by his stubborn refusal to recognise that the world had changed and its people with it, and that it was no longer viable for a king as hugely wealthy as Niroli's to allow some of his subjects to live in conditions of severe poverty? Apart from anything else, there was the threat of civil unrest amongst the mountain-dwellers, which would be seized upon and further orchestrated by the Vialli gang that lived amongst them.

His step-grandmother had in part to be behind this, Marco decided grimly. Queen Eva was his grandfather's second wife, and it was Marco's personal opinion that she was and always had been hostile towards her predecessor's side of the family. That naturally included Marco and his two sisters. Given their step-grandmother's attitude, it was no wonder that Isabella rarely visited the palace, and that Rosa preferred not to live on the island, just as he hadn't, until recently...

EMILY HAD BEEN deeply engrossed in the notes she was making, but some sixth sense alerted her to Marco's presence, causing her to put down her pen and turn to look towards the entrance to the courtyard. Despite the sombreness of her earlier thoughts, the minute she saw Marco standing watching her all the feelings she had promised herself she would learn to control rushed through her. Pushing back her chair, she got up and hurried over to him.

As he watched her coming towards him Marco could feel the anger his morning had caused being eased from his body by the warmth of her welcome. He wanted to go to her and take hold of her, he wanted to take her to bed and lose himself and his problems within her. His need for her was so intense... He tensed once more. There it was again, that word need, that feeling he didn't want to have.

'What is it? What's wrong?' Emily asked him uncertainly when she saw his sudden tension.

'Nothing for you to worry about. An administrative problem I need to sort out,' he told her dismissively. 'I'll be gone for most of the afternoon.'

Emily did her best to hide her disappointment, but she knew she hadn't succeeded when she heard him exhaling irritably.

'Emily—' he began warningly.

'It's all right, I know. You're a king-in-waiting and you have far more important things to do than be with me,' she interrupted him briskly.

Marco looked at her downbent head.

'You can come with me if you wish, but it will mean a long, hot drive along dusty roads, followed by some boring delays whilst I speak with people. And since you haven't been feeling well...'

Emily wanted to tell him that being with him could never bore her, but she managed to stop herself just in time. Instead she assured him quickly, 'I'm feeling much better now. I've had a look round the villa and I could run some options by you in the car, unless…' She paused uncertainly, suddenly realising how very little she knew about what was expected of him in his new role. 'That is, will you be driving yourself, or…?'

'We aren't going on some kind of royal progress in a formal cavalcade, if that's what you mean, and, yes, I shall be driving myself,' Marco answered her. 'You'll need a hat to protect your head from the sun and a pair of sensible shoes for if you do get out of the car. Some of the villages we shall be going to are pretty remote and along single-track mountain roads. I don't want to delay too long though.' He didn't want the police chief getting cold feet and instructing the haulier to stop his fleet of lorries, or, worse, turn back.

Emily's eyes were shining as though he had offered her some kind of priceless gift, he reflected. He had a sudden impulse to take hold of her and draw her close to him, to kiss her slowly and tenderly. He shook the impulse away, not sure where it had come from or why, but knowing that it was dangerous…

CHAPTER TEN

'AM I ALLOWED to ask any questions?' Emily said lightly. It was nearly an hour since they had left the villa. Marco had driven them through the main town and then out and up into the hills. 'Or is this trip a state secret?'

'No secret, but it is certainly a contentious issue so far as my grandfather is concerned,' Marco told her.

'If it's private family business,' she began, but Marco stopped her, shaking his head.

'No. It's very much a public business, since it involves some of the poorest communities on the island. But instead of acknowledging their need and doing something about it, my grandfather prefers to ignore it, which is why I have decided to take matters into my own hands. The more remote parts of the island do not have the benefit of electricity,' he explained. 'Because of that, these people are denied modern comforts and communication, and their children are denied access to technology and education. My grandfather believes in his divine and royal right to impose his will and keep them living as peasants. He also believes he knows what is best for them and for Niroli. Because there has been a history of insurrection amongst our mountain population, led by the Viallis, in the past, he also fears that by encouraging them to become part of today's world he will be encouraging them to challenge the Crown's supremacy.'

'And you don't agree,' Emily guessed sympathetically.

'I believe that every child has the right to a good education, and that every parent has the right to want to provide their child with the best opportunities available. My grandfather feels that by educating our poorest citizens, we will encourage them to want much more than the simple lives they presently have. He fears that some will rise up, others will desert the land and maybe even the island. But I say it's wrong to imprison them in poverty and lack of opportunity. We have a duty to them, and for me that means giving them freedom of choice. You and I know what happens when young people are disenfranchised, Emily. We have already seen it in the urban ghettos of Europe: angry young men ganging up together and becoming feral, respecting only violence and greed, because that is all they have ever known. I don't want to see that happening here.

'I have tried to persuade my grandfather to invest some of the Crown's vast financial reserves in paying to install electricity in these remote areas, but he refuses to do so. Just as he refuses to see the potential trouble he is storing up for the island.'

Emily could hear the frustration in his voice. It had touched her immensely that Marco had connected the two of them together in their shared awareness of the downsides of keeping people impoverished and powerless.

'Perhaps, once you are King…' she suggested, but Marco shook his head again.

'My grandfather is very good at imposing conditions and I don't want to trap myself in a situation where my hands are tied. Plus, it seems to me that some of Niroli's youth are already beginning to resent my grandfather's rule, just as previous generations resisted the monarchy. I do not want to inherit that resentment along with the throne, so I have decided to act now to take the heat out of the situation.'

'But what can you do?' Emily asked him uncertainly.

'If your grandfather has refused to allow electricity to be supplied…'

'I can't insist that it is, no,' Marco agreed. 'But I can provide it by other means. Whilst I was in London, I bought what I hope will be enough generators to at least provide some electricity for the villages. My grandfather is furious, of course, but I am hoping that he will back down and accept what I have done as a way of allowing him to change his mind without losing face. He is an old man who has ruled autocratically all his life. It is hard for him, I know that, but the Crown has to change or risk having change forced upon it.'

'You think there will be some kind of uprising?' Emily was horrified, instantly thinking of the danger that would bring to Marco.

'Not immediately. But the seeds are there. And still my grandfather is so determined to hold absolute power.'

'You pretend not to do so, but in reality you understand him very well, and I think you feel a great deal of compassion for him, Marco,' Emily said gently.

'On the contrary, what I feel is a great deal of irritation and anger because he refuses to see the danger he is courting,' Marco corrected her. Her perceptiveness had startled him, making him feel that she knew him rather better than he had realised. 'There are so many changes I want to make, Emily, so much here for me to do, but my grandfather blocks me at every turn.'

'You've lived away from the island for a long time and you've grown used to making your own decisions without the need to consult others. Perhaps your grandfather is being difficult because he sees this and in some ways he fears it—and you. You said yourself that he's an old man— he obviously knows that he can't continue to be King, but my guess is that he doesn't want to acknowledge that publicly, and that a part of him wants to continue to rule Niroli through you. When you come up with your own plans and they are opposed to his, he tries to block you because he's afraid of losing his power to you.'

'I doubt you would ever get him to admit any of that.'

Emily could hear the frustration in Marco's voice and, with it, his hunger to right what he saw as wrongs. He would be a strong king morally, socially, politically and in all the other important ways, she recognised. Listening to him had brought home to her the reality of her own situation. Even if by some miracle he should return her love, there was no future for them. She could not be his queen, and she could never do anything that would prevent him from being Niroli's king. Not now, after hearing him speak so passionately about his country and his people. If Marco had a duty to his people, then she too had duties to him and her love for him; loving someone meant putting them first and their needs before one's own. Marco's great need was to fulfil his duty and he could not do that with her in his life. A small, sad shadow darkened her eyes—the ghost of her dreams. Seeing it, Marco frowned.

'I'm boring you,' he announced curtly.

'No,' Emily told him. 'No! I like listening to you talking about your plans. I just wish that you had told me who you were when we first met.' Had he done so, she would have been so much better armoured against her vulnerability to him, and she would certainly never have started dreaming they could have a permanent future together.

'It wasn't a deliberate deceit on my part,' Marco defended himself coolly.

'Maybe not, but you could have said something… warned me. Then, at least…' She stopped, shaking her head, not wanting to admit her own folly where he was concerned.

'In order to live the kind of life I wanted, to prove myself on my own terms, it was necessary for me to do it with anonymity and without the trappings of royalty.

'I grew up here as a renegade in my grandfather's eyes. I was his heir, but I refused to conform or let him turn on me and bully me the way he did my father.' Marco's expression changed, and Emily ached to reach out and comfort him when she saw that look in his eyes.

'My father was too gentle to stand up to my grandfather. As a child, I hated knowing that. As a form of compensation, I suppose, I rebelled against my grandfather's authority and I swore that I would prove to him, and to the world, that I had the capability to succeed as myself.'

'But while you were proving yourself, you missed the island and your family, your father?' Emily guessed tenderly.

Marco opened his mouth to reject her words and then admitted huskily, 'Yes. It was such a shock when he was killed in a freak accident off the island's coast. Something I'd never imagined happening…never considered.'

And along with his natural grief at the loss of his father, Marco had had to deal with the irreversible changes in his own circumstances that had followed, Emily acknowledged silently. It must have been so hard for him—a man used to taking control of every aspect of his personal life, to have to come to terms with the fact that, as King, a huge part of his life would now be beyond his control. Just listening to him was causing a change within her own thoughts, turning her angry bitterness and pain into compassionate understanding and acceptance. It altered everything for her. Did he recognise how very alone he was emotionally? Was that a deliberate choice, or an accidental one? If he knew about it, did he care, or did he simply accept it as part of the price he paid for his royal status?

'I would hate to be in your shoes.' The words had slipped out before she could stop them.

Marco looked searchingly at her.

'What do you mean?' he demanded.

'I can hear how important your people are to you, Marco, and how strongly you feel about helping them, but...' She paused and shook her head. 'I couldn't pay the price you're about to pay for being Niroli's king. On the one hand, yes, you will have enormous wealth and power, but on the other you won't have any personal freedom, any right to do what you want to do. Everything will have to be weighed against how it affects your people. That is such a tremendously heavy responsibility.' She gave a small sigh. 'I suppose it's different if you're born to it. I'm beginning to see why princes marry princesses,' she added ruefully. 'You really do have to be born royal to understand.'

'Not necessarily. You're doing a pretty good job of showing you have a strong grasp of what's involved,' Marco told her dryly. They had rarely spoken so openly to one another and it surprised him how much he valued what she had said to him. Impulsively, he slowed the car and reached for her hand, giving it a small squeeze that caused her to look at him in surprise. Such a small, tender gesture was so very unlike him.

'I'm glad you're here with me, Emily.'

Her heart was thumping and thudding with the sweetness of the emotions pouring through her. Marco brought the car briefly to a halt and leaned across and kissed her—a hard, swift kiss that contained a message she couldn't manage to decipher, but which sent a physical craving for him soaring through her body. She had never, ever known him exhibit such extraordinarily un-Marco behaviour before. Her heart felt as though it had wings, her own happiness dizzying her.

She mustn't let a casual moment out of time lead her into forgetting what she had just recognised, she warned herself. But, then, should she let what she knew to be their separate futures prevent her from enjoying their shared here and now? a different voice coaxed.

'At this stage of the game, when you've got so much to deal with, it's only natural that you need someone to bounce ideas off and confide in,' she told him, 'and…' She paused, unsure of just how much she dared say without giving herself away completely.

'And?' Marco probed as they bounced along the narrow track past a cluster of small houses.

'And I wouldn't want that someone to be anyone else but me,' Emily told him simply.

A young man, tall and gangly and outgrowing his clothes, was standing in the middle of the road in front of Marco's car waving his hands, his face alight with excitement.

Emily looked questioningly at Marco.

'Tomasso,' he informed her as he brought the car to a halt. 'He is the leader of a gang of young Vialli hotheads, and he is also the person I have chosen to be my representative in taking care of the generator and introducing his village to its benefits.'

The moment Marco opened the car door and got out, Tomasso bounded up to him exclaiming, 'Highness, Highness, it is here! The generator, just as you promised. We have built a special place for it. Let me show you…'

An elderly woman appeared from the nearest house, tutting and looking very disapproving as she came over to join them.

'What is this—where is your respect for our Crown?' she demanded. 'Highness, forgive my thoughtless grandson,' Emily could hear her saying as she curtseyed to Marco.

This was a side of him she had never seen, Emily thought to herself as Marco leaned forward and assisted the elderly woman to her feet, accepting her homage with easy grace, whilst maintaining a very specific formal dignity that Emily could see the elderly woman liked. As more villagers surrounded him, he was very much the future king, so much so that Emily's emotions blocked her throat. She felt so proud sitting in the car watching him and yet, at the same time, so painfully distanced from him. What she was witnessing was making her even more aware of how impossible it would be for them to sustain a long-term relationship. Already she could see the curious and even hostile glances being directed towards her, and she guessed when Marco turned to look at the car that he was being asked who she was.

She looked away, her gaze caught by an array of brightly painted and beaded leather purses spilling out of a basket, just outside the door to one of the houses. Her artist's eye could immediately see how, with some discreet direction, highly desirable objects could be made by adapting the leather and bead-work to cover boxes. She was constantly on the lookout for such accessories to dress her decorating schemes; they walked out of her shop faster than she could buy them. She made a mental note to ask Marco a bit more about the leather-work and those who produced it.

It was nearly half an hour before he returned to the car, having been pressed into going and viewing the generator in its new home. When he returned he was accompanied by a group of laughing young men, whilst Emily noticed the older people of the village held back a little, still eyeing her warily. One of them, a bearded and obviously very old man, went up to Marco and said something to him, shaking his head and pointing to the car. Emily saw the way Marco's expression hardened as he listened.

'What was that old man saying to you?' she asked him, once he was back in the car and they had driven out of the village.

'Nothing much.'

'Yes, he was. He was saying something about me, wasn't he?' Emily pressed him. 'He didn't like you taking me there.'

Marco looked at her. Rafael, the elder of the village, was very much his grandfather's man. He did not approve of the generator and had said so, and then, when he had seen Emily in the car, he had berated Marco for—as he had put it—'bringing such a woman to Niroli'. 'Where is her shame?' Rafael had demanded. 'She shows her face here as boldly as though she has none. In my day, such a woman would have known her place. It is an insult to us, the people of Niroli, that you have brought her here,' he had told Marco fiercely.

'Rafael has a reputation as someone with very strong views. He is even older than my grandfather and tends to think of himself as the guardian of the island's morals...'

'You mean he disapproves of me being here with you,' Emily guessed.

Marco was negotiating a tight bend, and Emily had to wait for him to answer her.

'What he thinks or feels is his business. What I choose to do is my own,' he told her grimly.

But the reality was that it wasn't, and that whatever Marco chose to do *was* the business of the people of Niroli.

In an attempt to change the subject, she asked him brightly, 'I saw a basket of leather purses...'

'Yes, the women of the villages make them. They sell them to tourists, if they can, although these days the visitors who come to Niroli would far rather have a designer piece than something fashioned out of home-made leather.'

'Mmm…I was thinking that, with a bit of time and effort, the leather could be used to cover trinket boxes, the bead ornamentation was so pretty, and I know from my own experience there is a huge market for that kind of thing. If, as you say, the villagers are short of money, then…'

'It's worth thinking about, but there's no way I want my people involved in any kind of exploitation.'

'It was only a thought.'

'And a good one. Leave it with me.'

When the time came for him to marry, Marco reflected, he would need a wife who would take on the role of helping him to help his people. Emily could easily fulfil that role. Somehow, that thought had slipped under his guard and into his head where it had no right to be. Just as he had no right to allow Emily into his heart. *Into his heart?* Now, *what* was he thinking? Just because Rafael's objection to her presence had made him feel so angry and protective of her, that didn't mean that she had found her way into his heart. Did it?

CHAPTER ELEVEN

EMILY SIGHED TO herself as she parked the car Marco had
hired for her to use whilst she was staying on Niroli outside
the island's elegant spa. Although he had made love to her
last night and it was at his suggestion that she was visiting the spa today, she knew that she would far rather have
had his company. Marco, though, was too busy with royal
affairs to spend time with her. His purchase and distribu-
tion of the generators had led to yet another row with his
grandfather, which had resulted in Emily asking Marco if
there wasn't someone within his family who could medi-
ate between the two of them.

'Someone, you mean, like my sister Isabella?' he had
replied. 'She claims that my grandfather doesn't value her
because she is female. No, Emily.' He had shaken his head.
'This is something I have to deal with myself.'

To Emily's relief, she had now gone three whole days
without being sick, although she had noticed that, despite
the fact that she wasn't eating very much, the waistline of
one of her favourite skirts was now uncomfortably tight,
and even more uncomfortable were her breasts, which felt
swollen and tender. It must be due to too-rapid a change of
climate, she had told herself this morning as she'd dressed.

Marco had told her that the spa was owned and run
by Natalia Carini, daughter of Giovanni, the Royal Vine-
keeper. Emily had been a bit hesitant about coming here
and putting herself forward for 'inspection' when she was

at her most vulnerable. But as she walked into the spa foyer she heard the pretty girl behind the reception desk saying to another client, 'I'm sorry, but Miss Carini isn't here today.'

Emily hadn't really been sure how she felt about meeting someone who might have known Marco when he was younger. Like any woman in love, she longed to know everything there was to know about him and yet, at the same time, the reality of her position in his life made her feel that she wanted to remain anonymous. In London, it might be acceptable for a couple to live together as lovers without any intention of making their relationship permanent, but she suspected that things were different here on Niroli—even if Marco weren't who he was and destined to be King and, no doubt, to make a dynastic marriage.

'May I help you?'

Emily returned the receptionist's smile. 'I don't have an appointment, but I was wondering if it was possible to have a treatment?'

'Since it isn't the height of the tourist season yet, we should be able to fit you in. What kind of treatment would you like? We specialise here in using natural substances, especially the island's own volcanic mud. It's very therapeutic, especially when we use it in conjunction with our specially designed massage treatments.

'Here's a list of the treatments we offer, and a medical questionnaire.' The girl smiled again. 'The owner of the spa takes her responsibility to our clients very seriously, and I should point out to you that some of the more vigorous massages are not suitable for women who are pregnant.'

Pregnant! Emily almost laughed. Well, she certainly wasn't. And then suddenly it hit her, her brain mentally registering the facts and assembling them: her sickness, her aching breasts, her growing waist… A wave of sickening shock and disbelief thundered through her, and she could hear the receptionist asking her anxiously if she was all right.

'I'm…fine…' she lied.

But of course she wasn't. She was anything but. How could she be 'fine', when the reason for the sickness she'd been suffering these last few weeks, and the fact that, oddly, her waist seemed to have expanded making her clothes feel tight, had suddenly been made blindingly obvious to her?

Was she right? Was she pregnant? She did some hasty mental calculations, whilst her heart banged anxiously against her ribs.

She needed very badly to sit down, but not here. Not anywhere where the truth might out and there could be any hint of a threat to her unborn child. It had only been seconds, minutes at the most, since she had realised the reality, but already she knew that there was nothing she would not do to protect the new life growing inside her. She would allow nothing or no one to imperil her child's safety and right to life!

EMILY STARED AT her own reflection in the bedroom mirror and tried not to panic. There was little to show that she was pregnant as yet, apart from that slight thickening of her waist, but how much longer would she have before Marco became suspicious? She couldn't afford to be still here on Niroli by then. Her throat went dry. Inside her head she could hear Marco's voice telling her, at the very beginning of their relationship, that there would be no accidents, and what he expected her to do if one occurred.

Of course, what he had meant and not said was that he didn't want any royal bastards.

But there was no way she could destroy her child. She would rather destroy herself.

However, logically, Emily knew that, even if Marco had not made it plain he did not want her to have his child, there would be no place here on Niroli for the future king's pregnant mistress, or his illegitimate baby! What on earth was she going to do? She had never felt more alone.

'AND NOW THE village elder says that his orders have been ignored, and that the generator-shed has been broken into and the generator itself stolen. You see what you have done, what trouble you have caused by your interference?'

Marco forced himself to count slowly to ten before responding to his grandfather's angry but also triumphant accusations.

'You say that Rafael gave orders that the shed housing the generator was to be boarded up for the safety of the villagers. What is that supposed to mean?'

One of his grandfather's aides bent his head close to the Royal Ear and murmured something in it.

'The peace of the village was being destroyed—by the noise of the generator and various electrical appliances. Several villagers had complained to him that it had put their hens off laying and stopped their cows producing milk.'

Marco didn't know whether to laugh or cry. 'And because of *that* he stopped the villagers using the generator?' he demanded incredulously. 'No wonder they decided to ignore him!'

'Rafael says that he has long had concerns about the rebellious Vialli tendencies amongst this group of young men. Now that they have stolen the generator and are refusing to say where it is, he has had no other option but to order that they are punished.'

'*What?*'

'Furthermore, Rafael has told me his village is on the

verge of anarchy, and that it will spread to other villages in the mountains.'

'This is crazy,' Marco told his grandfather. 'If anyone should be locked up, it's Rafael with his prehistoric views. Grandfather, you must see how foolish it was for him to have done this,' Marco implored. His grandfather was after all an educated, astute and wily man, whilst Rafael was a simple peasant.

'What I see is that you are the cause of this trouble with your reckless refusal to obey my commands.'

Marco didn't trust himself to stay and listen to any more, in case it provoked him into open warfare with his grandfather and his outdated ideas. Giving King Giorgio a small, formal half-bow, he then turned on his heel and strode out of the room.

In the corridors dust motes danced on the warm afternoon air. Emily would be back at the villa by now. An image of her slid into his head: she would be sitting in the shade, and when she saw him walking towards her she would look up at him and give him that welcoming smile. She would also look cool and calm, and just seeing her would take the edge off his own frustration. Right now, he admitted, he would give anything to share his experiences of the morning with her. Emily, with her understanding and her sympathetic ear—he needed both of those very badly.

He paused. There it was again, that word, 'need'. It suddenly struck him how very alone he would be feeling right now if Emily hadn't been here on Niroli with him. It was only since bringing her to the island that he had recognised how good she was with people, and at problem-solving, and how much it meant to him to have the safety valve of being able to talk openly to her about the situation with his grandfather. Increasingly he was beginning to feel that he didn't want her to leave either the island or his bed. But whilst he might flout the royal rules for the benefit of his people, where his personal life was concerned he couldn't do the same and succeed. The only way he could keep Emily on the island was by elevating her to the position of Royal Mistress, and to do that he would have to procure a suitably noble husband for her, one who understood the way in which these things were done. Whilst he knew he would be able to find such a husband, he also knew that Emily would refuse point-blank to enter that kind of marriage and, besides… Besides what? He didn't *want* her to have a husband…

He had no time to delve into the inner workings of his mind at the moment, he reminded himself; nor could he go back to the villa—and Emily—no matter how much he wanted to do so. First he must go up to Rafael's village and deal with the situation there before it got any worse. And what about his growing dependence on Emily? When was he going to deal with that—before it got worse?

'EMILY.'

She tensed as she heard Marco call out her name as he came out into the sheltered inner courtyard, where she was seated in the shade, one hand lying protectively against her stomach as she tried to come to terms with everything.

It was early evening and she could hear the sharp edge of something unfamiliar in his voice. What was it? Not tiredness or irritation, and certainly not anxiety, but somehow a *something* that made her heart ache for him, above and beyond her own pain and fear for herself and their child. Was it always going to be like this? Was she always going to have this instinctive need to give him the best of her love? How could she do so now?

'I would have been back earlier,' Marco told her, 'but I had to go up to Rafael's village to put an end to some trouble brewing there, as my grandfather informed me with great delight earlier.'

'What kind of trouble?' Emily asked anxiously.

Marco sat down next to her. She could smell the dusty heat of the day on him, but under it she was, as always, acutely conscious of the scent that was so sensually him. However, this evening, instead of filling her with desire, it filled her with a complex mix of emotions so intense that they clogged her throat with tears—tears for their baby, who would never know and recognise his father's scent, tears for herself because she would have to live without Marco. But, most of all, tears for Marco himself, because he could never share with her the unique feeling that came from knowing they had created a life together. Her child, their child, his first-born child. The huge tremor of emotion that seized her shook her whole body, overwhelming her with a flood of love and pain in equal proportions. She wanted this baby—his child—so very much. Its conception might have been wholly unplanned, but if she could go back and change things she knew that she would not do so. She was a modern woman, financially independent, with her own home and her own business, and more than enough love to give to her baby. A baby that would never know its father's love, she reminded herself as Marco answered her question, forcing her to focus on what he was saying and to put her own thoughts to one side.

'Rafael had tried to stop the villagers using the generator,' he explained. 'So Tomasso and some of his friends rebelled and hijacked it. Then Rafael—with my grandfather's approval—had the young fools punished. They were already antagonistic towards a way of life that traps them in the past and my grandfather's old-fashioned determination to enforce a way of life on them to their detriment.'

'It can't be good that they feel so disenfranchised,' Emily felt bound to comment.

'I know,' Marco acknowledged. 'If my grandfather was more reasonable, I could discuss with him my concern that these youngsters could, if handled the wrong way, become so disaffected that ultimately it could result in civil unrest and even violence. But the minute I tell him that, his reaction will be to have them imprisoned.'

'You need to find a way of getting them onside and opening a dialogue with them that allows them to feel their concerns are being addressed,' Emily offered.

'My views exactly,' Marco agreed. 'I've told them that it's an issue I intend to take on board once I take over from my grandfather and I've asked them to be patient until then. But I also know that the moment I start instituting any reforms, the old guard is going to react against them, because my grandfather has drip-fed them the fear that change means that they will lose out in some way.'

Emily listened sympathetically. She could see how passionately Marco felt about the situation. But she also sensed that the more angry and opposed to his grandfather Marco became, the less chance there was of them reaching a mutually acceptable solution.

'I don't have to tell you that your grandfather is an old man,' she replied. 'It may be that his pride won't allow him to admit that he has got things wrong and they've gone too far, or that the way the island is ruled needs to change. You might have to backtrack a little, Marco, and find a way to offer him a face-saving way of accepting your changes. Maybe you could handle them in such a way that he could feel they were his ideas—in public at least.' She could see from Marco's expression that he wasn't willing to take on board what she was saying. It seemed to her that he and his grandfather were two very proud and stubborn men and that neither was prepared to give in to the other.

'You haven't seen anything of the island yet,' he told her abruptly. 'We'll remedy that tomorrow.' For Emily's benefit, or for his own, because he needed to put some distance between himself and his grandfather?

CHAPTER TWELVE

'ARE YOU SURE you've got time to do this?' Emily queried as Marco held open the door of the car for her before they set off to see something of the island. The morning sunshine cast sharp patterns on the worn flagstones of the courtyard and Emily was glad of the welcome coolness of the air-conditioned car. Hadn't she read somewhere that pregnancy increased the blood flow and made one feel warmer? Pregnancy. She ached to be able to share her joy with Marco and yet, at the same time, she was also afraid of his reaction. If he should try to pressure her into having a termination it would break her heart, but, logically, what else could he do? Even if he was prepared to understand and accept that she wanted to have this baby and bring it up alone, she suspected that his grandfather would be totally opposed to the idea. The old king would surely put pressure on Marco to deal with her. She didn't want to put Marco in that position and she wanted to keep her child as far away as possible from what increasingly she felt was a very negative kind of environment. The Nirolian royal family might be the richest in the world, but so far as Emily was concerned they seemed to be as dysfunctional as they were wealthy. Money wasn't important to her, so long as she had enough for her needs. She wanted her child to grow up confident that he or she was rich in love rather than money. What she wanted, she admitted, was for her child to be raised somewhere very far away from Niroli and without the burden of being a royal bastard. So what was she going to do? Return to London without telling Marco she was having his child?

That was certainly her easiest option, Emily felt. But did she have the strength to do it? Could she walk away from Marco without telling him? She loved her child enough already to do whatever she had to do to protect him or her, including leaving the man she adored; she knew that, almost without having to think about it. However, did she also love Marco enough to spare him the necessity of having to take on board prospective fatherhood and the problems that would cause for him? Was she strong enough to deny her instinctive longing to share her news with him, even though she knew he couldn't, and wouldn't, share her growing joy at the prospect of having his baby?

It was an extraordinarily wonderful gift that fate was giving her: a child, and not just any child, but the seed of the man she loved. She could picture him now; somehow Emily already knew that her baby would be a boy. He would have Marco's features and perhaps a little of his arrogance. He would look at her with Marco's eyes and she would melt with love for him and the man who had fathered him. And, later, when he was old enough to demand his father's name? She would deal with that when it happened. For now, what concerned her most was her baby's health and whether she could leave Niroli without Marco suspecting anything. So how was she going to do that? She couldn't just tell him she didn't want him any more. He would never believe her.

Perhaps he would believe her if she told him she wasn't comfortable with her role in his life. She wasn't even his formally recognised mistress, and she felt it could reflect on her business reputation. Marco's own pride meant that he would be able to identify with that. Last night, when

they had made love, he hadn't questioned the way she had
encouraged him to gentle his possession of her, holding
her breath a little, caught as she was between her maternal
anxiety for her baby and the intense physical desire he always aroused in her. But Marco was a skilled and a sensual
lover, who knew every single one of her body's responses
and how to invoke them. There was no way he wouldn't
soon notice a new desire on her part to make his penetra-
tion of her less intense.

A small, sad semi-smile touched her lips. Marco didn't
know it yet, but the sightseeing journey they were taking
together today could well be the last they would make together. Now she was destined to set out on a new path,
which she would share with this gift he had given her.

'Seat belt,' Marco reminded her. He reached across to
secure the belt for her, before she could stop him. Immediately Emily breathed in, protectively. There was no bump
of any kind to betray her, but still she felt a sharp clutch
of anxiety for the vulnerability of her child. It would be
like this for the rest of her life, she recognised. No matter that one day this baby she had conceived so uninten-
tionally would be an adult; as a mother she would always
be fiercely protective. Though, of course, there would be
many things she could not protect her child from, foremost
amongst which would be the pain of knowing his father
hadn't wanted him.

'Emily?'

To her shock, Marco had placed his hand flat against
her belly. Fearfully she turned to look at him. Had he, by
some intuitive means, actually guessed?

'You're looking so much better than you did when you
first arrived here,' she heard him tell her. 'Niroli's sunshine
has done you good.'

Shakily, Emily released her pent-up breath. He hadn't

guessed; it was just her own anxiety that was making her think that he must have done.

'I don't think anyone wouldn't enjoy it. I know I haven't seen much of the island…'

'Today, we're going to see as much of it as we can,' Marco told her as he started the car, 'and my royal duties will just have to wait.'

Whatever else the future held for Marco's child, she was glad that it wouldn't be the dark shadow of duty that fell across Marco's life, Emily decided emotionally. The little boy might have to grow up not knowing his father, but he would be free of the burden Marco carried, and she was passionately grateful for that. Though, at the same time, almost overwhelmed by the intensity of her love for Marco, she reflected as he turned the car off the main road into a much narrower lane that ran close to the high, rocky coast-line where cliffs plunged down into the sea.

'This was one of my favourite places when I was a boy,' Marco confided as he stopped the car.

Emily could understand why. There was an elemental wildness about it; in some ways, the landscape matched the man.

'Come on, let's get out of the car.'

Emily wasn't sure she wanted to. The height of the cliffs gave her an uncomfortable feeling of vertigo. But she could see that Marco was determined and she didn't want to have to explain to him how she felt.

'I used to come here and gaze out to sea, and promise myself that one day I'd get away from here and from my grandfather. But, of course, even then I knew that ulti-mately I would have to come back,' Marco confessed, once they were standing a few feet back from the edge of the cliff-top. He bent down and picked up a handful of the thin, stony soil that lay at the roots of the weather-beaten gorse bushes that grew in such abundance along this part of the coast, and flung it as far out to sea as he could.

Watching him, Emily knew that this was a re-enactment of something he had done many times as a boy—as a way of releasing the anger inside him? It was an emotion he had partially dissipated by leaving the island and making a life for himself. But it would never really leave him so long as he and his grandfather struggled for supremacy one over the other. And whilst they were embroiled in that struggle, others would suffer. She could not allow her child to be one of them…

All of a sudden it hit her: she *had* to tell Marco that she intended to leave. She couldn't stop herself from reaching out to touch him and placed her hand on his bare forearm. Immediately he turned towards her.

'Marco,' she began tentatively, and then stopped. Unexpectedly he reached for her and took her in his arms, kissing her with such fiercely sweet passion that it made her eyes sting with tears.

Why was he doing this? Marco asked himself. He knew that it couldn't go on. Already, deep down inside, he knew he was becoming too dependent on her, and she was becoming too important to him. That couldn't be allowed to happen. There was no room in his life for that kind of relationship with her. He was Niroli's future king and he intended to devote every ounce of his mental and physical energy to his country and its people. He would break down the restrictions that centuries of royal rule had placed, he would open the door for Niroli's population to walk freely into the new century. There was no legitimate place in his life for the kind of relationship he had with Emily. He was reeling at the way he felt about her now, the intensity that was being demanded of him. It was only recently he had started to feel like this, to recognise there was within him this dangerous need to have her close, a need that went far beyond any kind of sexual desire. But such emotion could not be allowed to exist, it could not be given a name, or a place in his life.

He started to pull away from her and then stopped, smothering a savage groan before he tightened his hold on her and kissed her again.

Emily's mouth felt soft and giving beneath his own, her body warm, and he longed to possess her and fill her and lose himself in her and know the passion of loving her.

'Marco!' Emily objected, somehow managing to stem her own longing and drag her mouth from beneath his. She was trembling from head to foot, afraid not of him but of herself and the intensity of her feelings, and stumbling over the words in her desperation.

'There's no easy way to say this, but the truth is that I should never have come here. Niroli is different from London, and my role in your life has changed. I can't live like this, Marco, a semi-secret mistress, despised and ignored by the court, and forced to live in the shadows. I'm going back to the UK just as soon as it can be arranged. It will be best for both of us.'

She was only saying what he already knew to be true, and yet he felt as shocked as though his guts had been splintered with ice picks. She couldn't do this! He wasn't ready to let her go. He needed her here with him. He should, he knew, be feeling relieved, but instead he felt more as though he had suffered a mortal blow. Pain rolled over him in mind-numbing waves, crashing through him and drowning out reason, spreading its unbearable agony to every part of him. He could hardly think for it, do anything other than try somehow to survive its rapacious teeth as it savaged him and tormented him. How could this have happened? How could he be experiencing this? The thoughts and feelings that filled him were so new and unfamiliar that they made him feel as though he was suddenly a stranger to himself. He felt like a man possessed by…by what? He shook his head, unable to allow the word pulsing in his heart to form. He had wanted it to happen, he had wanted her to leave. But not like this… He'd wanted to be the one to tell her to go… But how? That he didn't want her here because he was afraid that she would come between him and his duty? His whole body shuddered as the pain savaged it once more.

Why didn't Marco say something, anything? Emily worried anxiously.

What could she say without risking betraying the truth?

'I loved the life we shared together in London, Marco. But things are different here. The time we're sharing together is borrowed time, stolen time, perhaps,' she told him sadly. 'It's better that I go now.'

Marco could feel the heavy drum of his heartbeat thudding out a requiem for their relationship as he heard the finality in her voice.

'There'll never be anyone else in my life like you, Marco, nor a relationship to match the one we've shared.'

The words felt as though they were being ripped from her like a layer of her skin, but she couldn't hold them back; they were after all the truth, even though she knew she was a fool for having said them.

But it didn't matter now that she was compounding that error by lifting her hand to his face, tears burning at the backs of her eyes as she felt the familiar texture that was hard with the beginnings of his beard against the softness of her palm.

'Emily.'

He had caught hold of her hand before she could stop him, lifting it to his lips and then dropping it when he felt her tremble, to pull her bodily into his arms and then plunder her mouth with his own. Not that she made any attempt to resist him. Instead, she gave him the sweetness he was demanding whilst she clung helplessly to him.

Few people visited this part of the island, and Marco realised that an irresistible need was flooding through him to know the intimacy of sex on this wild headland. He couldn't let her go without this one last time, a final memory he would have to make last a lifetime of days and nights once he was without her. There had been many many times when their pleasure had been more sensual and more sustained, when he had deliberately set himself the task of pleasing her. But no time had ever been more intense than this, or more emotional. Because this was the last time that finally he could give to himself what he had previously so rigidly denied, and that was the right to feel with his emotions what he was feeling with his flesh.

This was too much, Emily told herself. She just wasn't strong enough to endure this kind of passion. It was as though Marco had wrenched away, with his clothes, the barrier she had always sensed he kept raised against her.

As they lay together on the lavender-scented turf, the sun warming their naked bodies, the kisses he lavished on her body were hot and fierce with a desire that went beyond the merely physical. As though by shared consent, neither of them spoke. What words were there to say, after all? Emily wondered, with dry-eyed hurt. Words would only be lies, or, worse, create wounds. It was better this way, that their last memory of one another was one filled with a shared but unspoken awareness of what they'd shared and what they would never have again. It seemed to Emily as she touched him that she had never loved him more. Something within her, that was maybe both lover and prospective mother, swelled her heart with bitter-sweet emotion.

They kissed and touched, their lips clinging, their bodies urgent, trying desperately to hold onto every second of their pleasure. But, like sand, it could not be held, running swiftly through their fingers instead as Emily's cries of pleasure became soft sighs of contentment.

She would treasure her memories of this day for the rest of her life.

She smiled lazily up at Marco as he leaned over her.

'I don't want you to leave.'

Marco had no idea where the words had come from. No! That was lie. He knew exactly where they had come from and why. And even if he hadn't, the heavy pounding of his heart would have told him. What on earth was he doing, when he had already decided that she must go? What had happened to him to make him want to change his mind on the strength of a few minutes of good sex? he derided himself. But it wasn't the good sex he didn't want to lose—it was Emily herself.

Emily wondered if anything else in her life could ever be as poignant as this. Marco had never, ever asked her for anything, never mind pleaded with her so emotionally! She so wanted to fling herself into his arms and cover his face with passionately joyful kisses as she told him there was nothing she wanted more than to be with him. But how could she?

'Marco, I'm sorry. I can't.' Her voice was little more than an anguished whisper, but Marco heard it, releasing her abruptly and turning away from her. She knew how much it must have cost him to ask her to stay. Given his inbuilt sense of male arrogance and his pride, along with his background and upbringing, she could only marvel that he had.

She got to her feet and said his name unsteadily, but he was already heading back to the car.

'Marco!' she protested. 'Please listen to me…'

He stopped walking and turned around. She saw his chest lift as he breathed in sharply and the sadness that filled her was not just for herself, but for both of them. She knew what she had to do, where her responsibility now lay, but how could she walk away letting him think that she hadn't wanted to stay with him? She couldn't, she decided frantically. Yes, she had her baby to think of and, yes, she was afraid of Marco's reaction to the news that she was pregnant. But she loved Marco, too, and the knowledge that he wanted her enough to actually ask her to stay was too sweetly precious that she couldn't deny its tremendous effect on her.

She still had to leave, nothing could change that, but she knew she couldn't go away from him without telling him why it was so important that she went.

She took a deep breath; this was the most difficult thing she had ever had to do. 'I don't *want* to leave you, Marco. But I *have* to. You see, I'm having your child. I'm pregnant.'

What? Marco could feel her words exploding inside his skull as he battled with his own disbelief.

'I know you told me at the beginning of our relationship that there must not be any accidents,' Emily continued, carefully cutting into the tension of his complete silence, 'and…and of course I understand now why you said that. The future King of Niroli's bastard isn't the title I want for our baby.' She gave a small shrug. 'The truth is, I don't want him to have any title at all, and if there is one thing in all of this that I am grateful for, it's that our son won't ever have to live the kind of controlled and confined life you will have to live. What I want for him more than anything else is the kind of personal freedom that you don't have and that you can't give to your legitimate children. I want him to grow up in a home filled with love, where what matters most is that he finds his own sense of where his life lies

and how his talents should be used. I don't want his future
to be corrupted by wealth and position. I don't want him to
have to carry the burdens I can see you carrying, Marco.
I can't give him his father, but I can give him the right to
define his own life, and to me that heritage is of far more
value than anything your legitimate children will inherit.'

For a few seconds, Marco was too taken aback by what
she had said to speak. From the moment of his birth he
had been brought up to be aware of the tremendous importance of his role and his family. The thought that someone was not awed and impressed by it was something he
found hard to take in. But he could see that Emily meant
what she'd said. Senses of isolation and aloneness, of having lost something he could never regain, an awareness that
somehow, somewhere, he had turned his back on something
precious stabbed through him. With it came the drift of
painful memories: of himself as a young boy longing passionately for the freedom to be himself. He could see his
father's struggles and his mother's anguish and, of course,
his grandfather's anger. He could also hear the echo of his
own childishly piping voice stating defiantly, 'When I am
grown up and I can do what I want, I won't be a prince!'
But with a kick like an iron-tipped boot, slowly but surely
his position and its claims on him had reshaped him. He
pictured two small boys, both dark-haired and sturdy, one
of them grubby and laughing as he played happily with
his friends. The other was sad-eyed and alone, held at a
respectful distance by his peers, protected by privilege, or
was he imprisoned by it?

What folly was this? Marco forced back the memories,
refusing to acknowledge them any more, letting his pride
take over instead. 'You are being naïve. No one else will
share your views, Emily. In fact, they will think you a fool.
And, besides, being King of Niroli is about more than any

of those things,' he retaliated sharply. 'It's about making a
difference to my people, it's about leading them to a better future. Do you really think our son, my son, will thank
you for denying him his birthright?'

'He has no birthright here on Niroli. I am your mistress,
and he will be illegitimate.'

'He has the birthright I choose to give him.'

'By recognising him and making him face the world
as less than your children born within royal wedlock? By
making him grow up in an environment where he will always be beneath them—in their eyes and, ultimately, in
his own?'

'He will be a member of the Niroli royal family, how can
you think of denying him that? Do you really think he will
thank you when he is old enough to know what he has lost?'

In the space of a few heated sentences, they had become
opponents, Emily recognised.

'It doesn't matter how much we argue about our own
feelings,' she told him. 'You are not yet King Marco, and I
doubt that your grandfather would welcome the birth of an
illegitimate child to a woman of such lowly status as me.'

There was just enough edge to her voice to warn Marco
that, at some stage, she had learned of his grandfather's
opinion of her.

'The fact that I am his father automatically gives him
his own status,' Marco retaliated, and then realised his
words had added to Emily's fury rather than softened it.

'Yes, as your bastard—a royal bastard, I know. But he
will still be your bastard. I won't let him suffer that, Marco.
I'm going home.'

'Niroli is my child's home, and this is where you and
he are staying. When did you find out—about the child?'
he demanded abruptly.

'Very recently. I had no idea...' Emily looked away from

Marco, remembering how shocked she had been. 'I would never have agreed to come here with you, if I'd known.'

'So how would you have informed me that I'd become a father? Via a birth notice in *The Times?*'

Emily flinched as she heard the savagery in his voice. 'That wouldn't happen,' she told him quietly. It had been foolish of her to give in to her urge to comfort him, because now she had created a new set of problems. Why had she told him? Because secretly she had been hoping—what? That he would sweep her up into his arms and say that he was thrilled she was expecting their child?

'I'm sorry if I've given you a shock. I was stunned myself when I realised. But I didn't want you to think I was leaving because...' The words 'because I don't love you' formed a tight knot that blocked her throat. How could she say them when she knew he didn't want her love? 'I wanted you to know that I have a valid reason for leaving the island,' she amended, her voice growing firmer as she underlined, 'a reason that matters to both of us. We already knew that one day we would have to part. The fact that I have accidentally conceived your child only makes that parting all the more essential. We both know that. I will not be your pregnant mistress, Marco.'

Emily was having his child, their child! A complex mixture of unfamiliar emotions were curling their fingers into his heart and tugging hard on it.

'How far advanced is this pregnancy?' he asked her brusquely.

Emily felt as though her whole body had been plunged into ice-cold water. This was what she had dreaded. An argument with him, in which he would try to demand that she terminate her pregnancy—something she had absolutely no intention of doing.

'I'm not sure,' she admitted honestly. 'I think that pos-

sibly it could have happened when I had that stomach bug.
I remember reading somewhere that that kind of thing can
neutralise the effect of the contraceptive pill. I should have
thought about that at the time, but I didn't.' She lifted her
head and told him firmly, '*You* needn't worry about the
consequences, though, Marco. I am fully prepared to take
sole responsibility for my child.'

'My child.' Marco stopped her ruthlessly. 'The child is
my child, Emily.'

She looked at him uncertainly. It hadn't occurred to her
that he would react like this. He sounded almost as though
he felt as possessive about the baby as she did herself.

'I don't want to discuss it any more, Marco. There's no
point. I can't stay here now.'

THE MORNING SUN was slanting across the courtyard. The
coffee Maria had brought him half an hour earlier had
grown cold as Marco sat deep in thought. He was not going
to let Emily leave. And he was not going to allow his child
to grow up anywhere other than here on Niroli. Both were
unassailable and unchangeable tenets of what he felt about
his role as king-in-waiting and as the father of Emily's expected baby. It wasn't any longer a matter of what he did or
didn't want; it was a matter of his royal duty, to his pride,
to his name and to his first-born.

It was ridiculous of Emily to suggest that their child
would have benefits that his so-called legitimate children
would not, folly for her to claim that he would one day
thank her for denying him his royal status. Marco might
have enjoyed the freedom of his time in London, but he had
also never forgotten who and what he was. Having royal
blood and being able to lay claim to it, even if one was born
on the wrong side of the blanket, was a life-enhancing benefit that couldn't be ignored. His son, growing up here on

Niroli as his accepted child, could look forward to the best of everything and, when grown, a position of authority at his father's court. He would be revered and respected, he would wield power and he would be on hand to support his legitimate half-sibling when finally he became King. Would he be imprisoned by his royal status, as Marco had sometimes felt he had been? No!

All of that and more could be made possible for this child, provided that Emily was prepared to see sense. She didn't have the status of a proper royal mistress, that was true. But his grandfather, for all his faults and stubbornness, also had a strong sense of duty and family. He, too, would want his great-grandchild to remain on Niroli. There was a way in which it could be made possible for her to stay and be elevated to a position in which she and their baby would have the respect of the people.

He swung round as he heard Emily come out into the courtyard. The sun had brushed her skin a warm gold, driving away its London pallor. She wasn't showing any visible sign of her pregnancy yet, but there was a rich glow about her, somehow, a sense of ripeness to come. Watching her, Marco experienced a swift surge of possessive determination not to let her go. She was having his child; whether by accident and not by design, that did not alter his paternal responsibilities or that a baby of royal blood was to be born. Who other than he could tell that child about his heritage and where better a place to do that than here on Niroli?

'I've just seen Maria and she's going to bring out some fresh coffee for you.' How domestic and comfortable that sounded, Emily thought tiredly as she sat down on the chair Marco had pulled out for her. She had hardly slept, her thoughts circling helplessly and tumultuously.

'I'm not prepared to let you leave the island, Emily. You, and my child, are going to stay here where both of you belong. It seems to me that marriage is the best way to secure our son's future and your position at court.'

Marriage! Emily almost dropped the glass of water she had been drinking. Marco wanted to marry her? She was shaking from head to foot with the intensity of her joy. Emotional tears filled her eyes. She put down the glass, and protested shakily, 'Marco! You can't mean that. How can you marry me?'

She realised immediately from his expression that something was wrong.

'I can't marry you,' he told her flatly. 'You know that. What on earth made you think that I could?' Why did he feel this dragging weight wrapping itself around him? He couldn't marry Emily, and he was surprised that she had thought he might. And, yet, just for a moment, seeing the joy in her eyes, he had felt… He had felt *what?* A reciprocal surge of joy within himself? That was ridiculous.

'You need a husband, Emily, and a position at court. There is within European royal families a tradition whereby noblemen close to the throne marry royal mistresses. This kind of marriage is rather like a business arrangement, in that it benefits all parties and, in the eyes of the world, bestows respectability on the mistress and any children she may bear. The nobleman in question is of course rewarded for his role and—'

'Stop it. Stop it. I have heard enough!' Emily had pushed back her chair and got to her feet. She could hardly breathe but she struggled to speak. 'I thought I knew you, Marco. I even felt sorry for you, because of the heavy responsibility your duty to the Crown lays upon you! But now I realise that I never really knew you. The man I thought I knew would never in a thousand years have allowed himself to become so corrupted by power and pride that he would suggest what you have just suggested to me!'

'What I propose is a traditional solution to a uniquely royal problem,' Marco persisted curtly. 'You are overreacting.' Her outburst had made him feel as though he were doing something wrong, instead of recommending a logical solution to their problem. A logical solution of the kind his grandfather would have suggested? Was the pressure of becoming King turning him into a man like his grandfather, the kind of man he had once sworn he would never allow himself to be? His critical inner voice would not be silenced, and its contempt echoed uncomfortably inside him.

'Am I? Take a look at yourself, Marco, and try seeing yourself through my eyes, and then repeat what you have just offered as a solution. You want to bribe another man to marry me so that—so that *what?* You can have your child here, conveniently legitimised by a convenient marriage between two strangers, though I'm sure that won't stop the gossip. But what about me? Am I expected to be a dutiful bride to this noble husband you're going to find for me? Am I supposed to submit willingly to having sex with him, bear his children, be his wife in all senses of the word?'

'No, there will be no question of that.' The harshness of his own immediate denial caught Marco off guard. But he couldn't retract his words, nor deny the feeling of fierce possessiveness that had gripped him at the thought of Emily in another man's bed.

'What kind of man are you, Marco, if you think that I would be willing to sell myself into such an arrangement? But then I was forgetting: you aren't a mere man, are you? You are a king! I'm not staying on the island a minute longer than I have to. Everything you've just said underlines all the reasons why I don't want my son growing up here. Your proximity to the throne has corrupted you, but I don't intend to let it corrupt my child.'

'And I don't intend to let you leave Niroli.'

They had been the closest of lovers, but now they were enemies locked in a battle to the bitter end for the right to decide the future of their child.

CHAPTER THIRTEEN

THE PLANE HAD taken off, but Emily was holding her breath, half expecting that, somehow, Marco still could prevent her from leaving Niroli.

She'd hated having to appeal to Marco's grandfather for help behind his back. At first, the king had refused to see her when she'd made her secret visit to the palace. She had been expecting his rejection, though, and so had lifted her chin and told the stiff-faced, uniformed equerry who had told her that the king would not receive her, 'Please tell His Majesty that the favour I want to ask him will benefit both of us and the throne of Niroli.'

She had been made to wait over an hour before she had finally been shown into the royal presence. It had shocked her to see how very like the king Marco was, traces of Marco's stunning good looks still visible in the older man's profile.

She had chosen her moment with care, waiting until she knew that Marco had gone up to the mountains to see Rafael before she visited the palace.

'I want to leave Niroli,' she told King Giorgio. 'But Marco does not wish me to leave. He has said he will do everything in his power to stop me and to keep me here.' She didn't tell the king about her pregnancy, just in case he echoed Marco's insistence that her child be brought up under the cover of an arranged marriage between herself and a nobleman.

'Only you have the authority to enable me to leave without Marco knowing.'

'Why should I do that?' the king challenged her.

Emily was ready for that. 'Because you do not want me here,' she replied. 'You do not consider me good enough to be Marco's mistress.'

'He is not the man I thought if he cannot provide sufficient inducement to keep you in his bed, if that is where he wants you.'

'Marco is more than man enough for any woman,' Emily defended. 'But I am too much of a woman to be prepared to share him with the throne and everything else that entails.'

She thought she saw a glimmer of grudging respect in the king's eyes before he gave a stiff nod of his head. 'Very well. I will help you. A royal flight will be made ready for you, and I shall ensure that Marco is kept out of the way until it has taken off.'

The king had kept his promise to her, and now she was on her way home. She closed her eyes against the acid burn of her tears and pressed her hand against her body as though in mute apology to her baby for what she was doing. 'You may not understand it now, but I'm doing this for you and for your future,' she whispered to him.

'How DARE YOU do this?' White-faced with rage, Marco towered over his grandfather, royal protocol forgotten in his fury. Now he knew why Rafael had kept him at the village for so long with his endless complaints against young Tomasso and his friends.

When he had returned to the villa to find Emily missing, he had summoned Maria, and she had been the one who had told him that a car bearing the royal crest had arrived for her.

He had gone straight to the palace, demanding to see his grandfather.

'Emily applied to me for aid, because she feared you would force her to remain here on Niroli against her will. Naturally, I helped her.'

'Naturally,' Marco agreed grimly, registering even more grimly that her departure had elevated Emily from being a floozy to someone his grandfather was prepared to speak of with far more intimacy. 'After all, you never wanted her here.'

'Whatever role she might have played in your life in London, there is no place for her here on Niroli. She herself accepts this and, in doing so, she shows far more sense and awareness of the importance of your future role than you do, Marco. I confess that she impressed me with her grasp of your responsibility. She fully understands what will entail when you become Niroli's king.'

'She also fully understands that she is to be the mother of my child,' Marco told his grandfather sharply. 'That is why she has left—but I don't expect she told you that, did she?'

'She is having your child?'

'Yes,' Marco confirmed unashamedly.

The king was frowning imperiously. 'But that alters everything. Why did you not say something to me about this? She must be brought back, and at once! What if this child she is carrying should be a son? It is unthinkable that he should be brought up anywhere but here. Sons are a precious commodity, Marco, even if they are illegitimate. It is important that this child grows up on Niroli knowing his duty and his responsibility to the Crown. That knowledge cannot be instilled in him too early. When is the birth expected? There is much to do—the royal nursery will have to be prepared, and a suitable household established to take charge of him. The mother can stay in London if she wishes, in fact it would be better if she did,' the king continued dismissively.

His grandfather was only painting a picture that was similar to the one he himself had put before Emily. But instead of feeling vindicated, Marco could feel a cold heaviness seeping through him, as though leaden weights had been tied to his hands so that he was effectively imprisoned.

'You will order the woman to return, and when you do you will inform her that it is against the law of Niroli for anyone to remove a child of royal blood from the island, on penalty of death.'

Marco shook his head.

'Don't be ridiculous, Grandfather. Once in some mediaeval age it might have been possible to make such a threat, but I can tell you now that the British courts will take a dim view of it, and that Emily is totally within her rights to want to keep her child with her. I would certainly support her in that. I want my child to grow up here, yes, but I also want his mother to be here for him, as well.'

'Ridiculous sentimentality. I blame your mother for it. And your father. He should have insisted that she followed tradition and handed you over to those appointed to be responsible for your care as a future king, instead of meddling in matters that did not concern her. It is thanks to her that you developed this stubborn streak that puts you at odds with your duty.'

Marco forced himself not to say anything. Instead he focused on his childhood. He could see himself playing, running and his mother chasing him, and he could see too the disapproving looks of the elderly courtiers his grandfather had insisted were to be responsible for his upbringing and formation. His mother, had she still been alive, would have supported Emily and helped her. They would have got on well. His father had struggled to oppose the king's insistence that Marco was brought up to be a prince, rather than as a member of a warm and loving family. His grandfather would try to impose his will on his great-grandchild, Marco knew. He frowned, suddenly sharply aware of his own desire to protect his child from the cold discipline and royal training he had known in his own childhood. He was not his father, he reminded himself. He was more than strong enough to ensure that his son was not subjected to the misery of his boyhood.

'Whilst you are here,' his grandfather was continuing imperiously, 'I have decided that the generators will have to be removed from the island completely. They are causing too much conflict between our peoples. It is just as I had thought, these young dissidents in the mountains have been encouraged by the Viallis to band together and challenge the authority of their village elders. And the blame for that can be laid at our door, Marco. By publicly going against my wishes, you have turned yourself into a figurehead for their rebellion. Various informants have told me of their concern that they are only waiting until you are on the throne to force your hand and make demands that can never be granted. If there is any more trouble, I shall impose a curfew—that will teach them to respect the law and the Crown.'

'If these youngsters are angry and filled with resentment, who can blame them?' Marco demanded. 'They need the controls on their lives relaxing, not tightening to the point where there is bound to be increased conflict. By imposing a curfew, all you will be doing is driving their feelings underground and alienating them further. What we need is to establish a forum in which they feel they can be heard and their views properly addressed.'

'What, reward them for their rebelliousness and their disrespect? They need teaching a lesson, not to be indulged.' \

'Have a care, Grandfather,' Marco warned. 'Feed their sense of injustice by imposing your royal will, and in the end we will all pay a heavy price.'

'Bah…! You are too soft, too much the modern liberal. You cannot rule Niroli like that, Marco. You rule it like this!' The old king closed his fist and banged it down hard on the table in front of him. 'By letting them know what it is to fear your anger.'

As he had learned to fear his grandfather's anger as a child? As his son would be forced to learn to fear it? Marco was filled with a sense of revulsion. He had returned to Niroli committed to working to improve things for its people, but now he was beginning to question his ability to do that. With his grandfather so opposed to the changes he wanted to make, and his own views so diametrically opposed to the king's, weren't they more likely to tear Niroli apart between them than anything else? Perhaps Emily was right to refuse to allow their child to be brought up here?

Marco closed his eyes, deep in thought. No, his son should be here because he, his father, was here. Emily would have to accept his determination to play his royal role, whether she liked it or not…

CHAPTER FOURTEEN

EMILY SAT HUDDLED in the squashy, cream-ticking-covered chair in the pretty sitting room of her Chelsea home, staring numbly at the letter she was holding. Not that she needed to read it again. She knew its every word off by heart, she had read it so many times since it had arrived two days ago: the consultant at the hospital where she had been for her twenty-week pregnancy scan wanted her to return, so that they could do a further test.

She had of course rung the hospital the moment she had received the summons, and the nurse she had spoken to had assured her that there was no need for her to worry. But Emily was very worried. In fact, she was worried sick, reliving over and over again that tell-tale moment during the ultrasound when the young operative had suddenly hesitated and then looked uncertainly at Emily before carrying on. Nothing had been said; she knew the scan had shown that her baby had all the right number of fingers and toes, and had even confirmed her belief that she was carrying Marco's son. If she hadn't received the letter requesting her to go back, she suspected she would never have given the girl's hesitation another thought. Why had she hesitated? Was there something wrong with her baby? Oh, please, God, don't let there be! Was she being punished because of what she had done? Because she had left Niroli? Because she was deliberately planning to lock Marco out of their son's life?

But that was to protect the baby, not punish Marco, she protested to herself.

The sound of someone ringing her doorbell brought her out of her painful thoughts: it would be Jemma. The shock of being requested to return for a second scan had brought home to her how alone in the world she was, and upset her so much that she had unburdened herself to her friend and assistant. As a result, Jemma had started to adopt an almost maternal attitude towards her and had insisted she would accompany her to her repeat scan. Smoothing down the skirt of the loose linen dress she was wearing, Emily got up to answer the door. Whilst she had been on Niroli a heatwave had come to the city and, at first, when she opened the door the light pouring in from the fashionable London street outside dazzled her so much that she thought she must be imagining things: it couldn't possibly be Marco who was standing on her immaculate doorstep, the formality of his dark business suit a perfect foil for the bright red of the geraniums that filled the elegant containers that flanked the entrance.

But it *was* Marco, and he was stepping into her hallway and closing the door behind him, looking just as impressive against the interior's old-English-white walls as he had done outside.

For a while after her return from Niroli, she had barely slept for fear that he would come after her and demand she go back. But there had been no sign of him. Then, the arrival of the letter had given her something much more worrying to keep her awake at night. Her heart was thumping in jerky uncoordinated beats; he had brought with him in the hallway, not just his presence, but also his scent. Helpless tears of longing pricked in her eyes, blurring her vision.

'Is this what you're planning to take to the hospital?' Without waiting for her response, Marco leaned down to pick up the pale straw basket into which she had packed everything she thought she might need.

'The hospital?' Her voice faltered. She was shocked by those words, her face nearly as pale as her hall walls.

'I've just been round to the shop. Jemma told me about the scan. I've got a cab waiting. Where are your keys?'

'Marco, there's no need for this. Jemma's coming with me.'

'No, she's not. *I* am going with you—there is every need for me to do so. This is my child you are carrying, Emily. Are you ready?'

She shouldn't be letting him take charge like this, Emily told herself, but the stress of the last few days was telling on her and she simply felt too weak and drained to argue with him. And, besides…if she was honest, wasn't there something comfortingly bitter-sweet about having him here with her…with them… Her hand went to her tummy as inwardly she whispered comforting words to her baby, promising it that, no matter what the scan showed, no matter what anyone said, he would have life and she would love him.

The stress of worrying about the baby had stolen from Emily the bloom she had gained whilst she'd been on Niroli, Marco recognised as he took hold of her arm and guided her to the waiting taxi.

Marco gave the driver the name of a private hospital, ignoring Emily's small start of surprise. It hadn't been difficult getting Jemma to tell him what had happened. In fact she had been so relieved to see him that she had told him everything he needed to know without him having to probe. He had come to London with the sole intention of taking Emily back to Niroli with him, and of telling her that their child would be born on the island and would remain there; whether or not she chose to do the same was up to her. Since he had last seen her, his feelings towards

Emily had turned both angry and hostile. She had gone behind his back to his grandfather; she had walked out on him, she had insulted him. She'd given him, for no good reason whatsoever, sleepless nights analysing what she'd said and what she hadn't, trying to find ways he could fit together the pieces of the jigsaw his life now was, working out what would make it possible for him to have her living on Niroli with him—and willingly. And then going over everything he had already analysed once more, to double-check that the reason he wanted her there was only because of his child. Because, somehow, though he found it hard to admit, deep down inside, a suspicion still lurked that he wanted *Emily*.

But the news Jemma had given him about Emily being called back for a second scan had caused a seismic emotional shift within him, so that all he could think about now, all that concerned him and occupied his thoughts, was Emily and their baby.

The hospital was one of London's most exclusive and private and Emily's obstetrician had been likely recommended to her. He was a charming middle-aged man, with a reassuring smile and a taste for bow ties. In his letter, he had stated that he would be on hand once Emily had had her repeat scan to discuss the results. It made her feel sickly cold inside every time she thought about the underlying hint that there might be some kind of problem.

'Has anyone said why you are having to have a second scan?' Marco asked her as the taxi pulled up outside the hospital.

Emily shook her head.

'But you have asked?'

'I rang Mr Bryant-Jones, my obstetrician, and he said that sometimes a repeat scan was needed.'

'But he didn't explain why?'

'No,' Emily admitted shakily. Marco's terse words, along with his grim expression, were increasing her fear.

Marco paid the taxi driver and, still carrying her basket, put his free hand under her elbow, for all the world as protective as though he were a committed husband. But he wasn't, and Emily knew she must not give in to her longing to turn to him and get him to reassure her that she had no need to worry, and that everything was going to be all right.

The hospital's reception area could well have been that of an expensive hotel, Emily recognised, looking at the two receptionists who were stunningly attractive and very smartly dressed.

It was Marco, and not she, who stepped forward and gave her name. But any thought she had of objecting to his high-handed manner or to his taking charge disappeared when she heard him telling the receptionist very firmly, 'Please inform Emily's obstetrician, Mr Bryant-Jones, that we are here.'

'My appointment with him isn't until after I've had my scan,' Emily reminded Marco. She could see that he was about to say something, but before he could do so a smiling nurse came up to them, asking, 'Emily? We're ready for you now, if you'd like to come this way.'

'I shall be coming with her,' Marco informed the nurse imperiously.

'Yes, of course. It's this way,' the nurse replied pleasantly.

'This isn't where I had my last scan,' Emily commented anxiously.

'No. Mr Bryant-Jones has requested a three-D scan this time.'

'A three-D scan—what's that?' Emily asked apprehensively.

'Nothing to worry about,' the nurse reassured her cheerfully. 'It's just a special imaging process that gives us a clearer, more in-depth picture of the baby, that's all.'

'But why…I mean, why do you need that?'

Emily wasn't aware that she had stopped walking until she felt Marco reach out and take hold of her hand. Anxiously she looked up at him, mutely telling him that she didn't feel able to go any further.

'Here we are,' the nurse announced, opening a door several yards up the corridor and holding it open, waiting for Marco and Emily to catch up with her. 'I'll hand you over to Merle, now,' she told Emily as another nurse came forward to direct her over to the waiting bed.

'Once you've put on your gown, the ultrasonographer will start the scan. I'll be putting some gel on your tummy, like the last time,' she told Emily kindly.

'You don't need to be here for this, Marco,' Emily told Marco firmly as she pulled the curtains round the bed and got undressed. For once, the thought of the potential indignity of wearing the universal hospital gown, with its open back fastening, didn't bother her. All she could think about was her baby. Why wouldn't anyone tell her anything? Part of her was relieved that Marco was ignoring her request and not making any move to leave, but another part of her felt even more anxious. If there was something wrong with their baby, Marco's pride… It didn't matter what Marco thought. She would have her baby, no matter what.

When Emily had changed into her gown and she drew back the curtains, she looked both vulnerable and afraid. Just looking at her caused a sensation in Marco that felt like a giant fist squeezing his heart and wringing from it an emotion so concentrated that it burned his soul.

The nurse helped Emily lie down on the bed next to the scanner and covered her legs with a blanket, then she started applying the necessary gel.

Given she was around twenty weeks pregnant, her stomach was only gently rounded. Emily held her breath anxiously as the ultrasonographer, a very professional-looking young woman passed the probe over her bump, whilst studying the resulting images on the screen in front of her.

'Why am I having to have this kind of scan?' Emily asked her.

'See—look, your baby is yawning.' The ultrasonographer smiled, ignoring her questions. Emily stared at the screen, her heart giving a fierce kick of awed joy as she stared avidly at the small but perfect form.

'Maybe he's not a he, but a she.'

Emily had been so engrossed in watching the screen that she hadn't realised that Marco had come to stand behind her and was looking over her head at the image of their baby.

'Oh, I think we can safely say that he is a he,' the girl told him with a broad smile and pointing, before suddenly going silent as she moved the scanner further up the baby's body. Then her smile gave way to a frown of concentration.

Why wasn't she saying anything? Emily worried. Why was she staring at the screen so intently? Her heart thumped with fear.

'What is it?' Emily asked anxiously. 'Is something wrong?'

'I'm almost finished and then you'll be able to go and get dressed,' the girl told her smoothly. 'You've got an appointment to see Mr Bryant-Jones, I think?'

'Yes,' Emily confirmed. 'Look, if there's something wrong with my baby...'

'Mr Bryant-Jones will discuss the scan with you.' The girl was using her professional mask to hold her at a distance, Emily recognised shakily. She looked at Marco. She could see in his eyes that he too was aware of the heavy weight of what the girl had not said hanging in the room. What was it? What was wrong? The tiny being she'd seen on the scan had been yawning and stretching—to her eye, he looked completely perfect. Maybe she was worrying unnecessarily. Maybe this *was* just a routine check.

Her fingers trembled as she re-dressed herself. On the other side of the curtain, she could hear Merle, the nurse, telling Marco that as soon as Emily was ready she would escort them down to see the obstetrician…

CHAPTER FIFTEEN

EMILY COULD FEEL her anxiety bathing her skin in perspiration as they were shown into the obstetrician's office. Mr Bryant-Jones was smiling, but not as widely as he had done the first time she had seen him.

'Ah, Emily, good. Good.' He was looking past her towards Marco, but before Emily could introduce him Marco stepped forward, extending his hand and saying curtly, 'Prince Marco of Niroli. I am the baby's father.'

'Ah. Yes… Excellent.'

'Mr Bryant-Jones, why have I had to have another scan?' Emily demanded, unable to wait any longer. 'And this three-D scan, what is that—? Why…?'

'Please sit down, both of you.' The obstetrician wasn't smiling any more. He was looking at the scanned images he had on his desk, moving them around. 'I'm sorry to have to tell you this, but it looks as though your baby may have a heart defect.'

'A heart defect? What exactly does that mean? Will my baby—?' Emily couldn't get any further; her pent-up emotions were bursting out and making it impossible for her to speak.

'The baby will have to be between twenty-two to twenty-four weeks before we can make a full diagnosis. At this stage, all we can tell from the scans is that there is a likelihood that your baby could have a foetal heart abnormality.'

'You said there *could* be a heart abnormality.'

Marco's voice seemed to be reaching Emily from over a great distance, as though she weren't really here and taking part in this dreadful, dreadful scene, as though she and her baby had gone away somewhere private and safe where nothing bad could touch them.

'What exactly does that mean?' Marco questioned the obstetrician.

'It means that the baby's heart does not seem to be forming as it should. Now, this can be a small problem, or it can be a far more serious one. We cannot tell which, as yet. That is why you will need to see a cardiac specialist. There is a very good one here in this hospital, who collaborates with our specialist neo-natal unit. My recommendation would be that we arrange for you to visit him as soon as it can be arranged.'

'Is…is my baby going to die?' Emily's voice shook with fear.

'No,' the obstetrician assured her. 'But depending on how severe the abnormality is, there could be a series of operations throughout his childhood and teenage years and, maybe, if things are extreme, there will be the necessity for a heart transplant at some stage. Severe heart malfunctions do limit the kind of life the sufferer can live. If this is the case, your son will need dedicated care; boys like to run and play vigorous games, but it might be a possibility that he'll not be able to do that.'

Her child could be a boy who might not be able to run and play like other children, a boy who could be subjected to operation after operation to keep him alive! But he would have a life, and she would give every hour, every second, of her life to him and his needs, Emily vowed fiercely.

Marco looked across at Emily; he could see the devastation in her eyes. He wanted, he realised, to take her in his arms and hold her there. He wanted to tell her that there was nothing to fear and that he would keep both of them safe, her and their child. He wanted to tell her that he was there for them whatever happened and he always would be, and that they were the most, the only, important things in his life. The news they had just received had at a stroke filled him with an emotion so complex and yet so simple that it could not be denied.

Love…

What he was feeling for Emily right now was love: a man's love for his woman, the mother of his child, for his companion and soul mate, without whom his life would never be complete.

Earlier, while watching the scan take place, he had experienced the most extraordinary sense of enlightenment, of knowing that he had to be part of his son's life. Now had come the knowledge that nothing could ever be more important to him than guarding this precious, growing life and the woman who was carrying it.

Not power, not wealth, nothing; not even the throne of Niroli.

Marco knew that others would not understand; he barely understood what he was experiencing himself. But, somehow, it wasn't necessary for him to understand, or to be able to analyse; it was simply enough for him to know. Maybe he had been travelling towards this place, this crossroads in his life, for longer than he realised; maybe there had been many signposts along the journey that he had not seen. However, now, not only had the crossroads been reached, they had been traversed simply and easily, without any kind of hesitation or doubt. He could not be Niroli's king *and* his child's father—certainly not this child's father, whose young life might always hang precariously on a thread, and who should never be subjected to the rigours of kingship. This boy would need his father's loving presence. And he would have it. Singularly, neither he nor Emily was strong enough for their child, but together they would be.

'I HAVE TO return to Niroli.'

They were back home in Emily's kitchen. The necessary appointment had been made with the cardiac specialist, and now Emily inclined her head slightly as she listened to Marco.

'Yes, of course,' she agreed. She had been expecting him to say this, and she knew, too, that there would be no demands from him now that she should return with him so that his son could grow up on the island. The royal family of Niroli were arrogant and proud, too arrogant and proud to want to accept that one of their bloodline could be anything less than perfect. No, Marco would not want a sickly, ailing child around to remind him of that. She could feel the pain of the rejection on behalf of her baby, but she stifled it. It was Marco who was not worthy of their child, not the other way around. Not worthy of her child and not worthy of her love.

Marco desperately wanted to tell Emily how he felt—but this was not the right time. Unfortunately, he had a duty to inform his grandfather first of his intentions. Once he had done that, then he could tell Emily how much he loved her. Did she love him? His heart felt as though there were a knife twisting inside it. But even if she didn't love him, he still intended to be a full-time father to his son.

'I'll be back in time for the appointment with the cardiac specialist.'

Emily bowed her head. She mustn't let her own feelings swamp her. She had to be strong—for her son. Was it something she had done, or not done, that had caused his heart defect? she had asked the obstetrician.

No, Mr Bryant-Jones had told her, sometimes the condition ran in families, but sometimes it 'just happened', without there being any reason.

'WHAT DO YOU mean you no longer wish to succeed to the throne?'

'I mean, Grandfather, that I am abdicating my claim to the Crown. I intend to make a formal speech to that effect, but I wanted you to be the first to know,' Marco told his grandfather calmly.

'You are giving up the throne of Niroli for the sake of a woman and her child.'

Marco could hear the disbelief in his grandfather's voice.

'*My* woman and *my* child. And, yes, I am giving up the throne for them. For them, and for our people.'

'What do you mean by that?'

'It would never have worked, Grandfather. I could never step into your shoes.' Marco saw that the old man was looking slightly gratified.

'For me, they would be constraining, too limiting,' he finished firmly. 'We have done nothing but argue since I first arrived. You block every attempt I make to make reforms—'

'Because they are not right for our people.'

'No, because they are not right for you.'

'What you want to do would cause a schism that would split the island.'

'If you continued to oppose me, then, yes, there is that possibility. Niroli needs a king who will bring it into the twenty-first century—I firmly believe that. But I also believe now that Niroli's king can never be me. That does not mean that I don't care about my homeland and my people, I do—passionately—but I now know that I can do more for it and for them by working from outside its hierarchy.'

'By spreading anarchy, you mean?'

'By setting up a charitable trust to help those who most need it,' Marco corrected him evenly.

THERE WAS A certain irony in the fact that, whilst he had refused to wear the heavily decorated formal uniform his grandfather had had made for him on his arrival in Niroli, he was wearing it now to take his formal leave, Marco admitted as he waited for the king's equally elderly valet to finish fastening him into the jacket with its heavy gold braid. But somehow it seemed fitting that, on this one occasion, he should defer to tradition.

The world's media had been alerted to the fact that he intended to make a public speech; TV and radio crews had already arrived and the square below the palace balcony, from which he had chosen to address the people, was already full.

How different he felt now, compared with the way he had felt when he had first returned. Then, he had been filled with a fierce determination to fulfil his destiny; it had ridden him and possessed him.

This morning he had woken up with a sense of release, a sense of having gained back a part of himself he was only just becoming aware he had been denying.

The valet handed him his plumed hat. He could hear the shrill sound of trumpets. Walking slowly and majestically, he headed for the balcony, timing his entrance to when the military band broke into the Nirolian national anthem. Then he stepped forward...

CHAPTER SIXTEEN

EMILY STOPPED OUTSIDE A shop window to look at her reflection and push her hair off her face. It was a sullenly hot day and her back was aching. She had been to see a client, but had hardly been able to focus on what the man had been saying to her because of her dread of what the cardiac specialist might say. Part of her wanted to rush the appointment and the specialist's opinion of her baby's future forward, whilst another part of her wanted to push it away. She was standing outside an electrical store that sold televisions. Its windows were filled with a variety of large screens. She glanced absently at them and then froze in disbelief when she realised she was looking at Marco. A camera homed in on his face, and then panned to the crowd in the square beneath him.

What was happening? Emily could think of only one thing: Marco must already be formally taking his position as the new King of Niroli. She wanted to ignore the screens and walk on past the shop, but instead she found that she was going inside.

'This is a most extraordinary event,' she could hear a TV news commentator saying excitedly. 'The royal family of Niroli is one of the richest in the world. They live according to their own set of rules. Of course the current King of Niroli is Giorgio. However, there have been rumours for some time that he is about to step down in favour of his grandson, Prince Marco. Now we have learned that

Prince Marco has said that there is something he wants to tell his people. It can only mean one thing. What a change this will be for the island. There are already mutterings that Prince Marco wants to make too many changes too quickly, and that these could stir up unrest…'

Whilst the commentator talked over the last notes of the Nirolian national anthem, Emily focused feverishly on Marco's face. This could be the last time she would ever see him.

'People of Niroli…' he said in Italian. Tears stung Emily's eyes as she read the English subtitles at the bottom of the screen. She could hear the strength of purpose in Marco's voice as he went on, 'What I have to tell you today causes me great joy and also great sadness. Great joy, because when I leave you I shall be making the most important commitment a man ever can make, a commitment to the future through the next generation. Great sadness, because, in order to do that, I must abdicate my responsibility to you, the people of Niroli—'

Emily could almost feel the ripple of shock surging through the listening crowd. Her own thoughts were in turmoil. What was Marco doing? What was he saying? He was Niroli's future king and nothing could or should change that… She had listened to his passionate diatribes against his grandfather and she had known his fierce longing to do something to help his people. And yet now he was saying…

Marco was still speaking, so she moved closer to the screen.

'It is my belief that Niroli and its people need a ruler with a different mindset from my own, a ruler who can combine the best of the old ways with a new path into the twenty-first century. I am not that man, as both my grandfather and I have agreed. King Giorgio needs an heir to step into his shoes whom he can trust to preserve all that is good in our traditions. Niroli also needs a new king who can take it forward into the future. With the best will in the world, I cannot be that king.'

A low murmur of objection filled the air accompanied by younger male voices shouting angrily and declaring, according to the TV commentator, that Marco was the king they wanted. Tomasso and his friends, Emily guessed.

'Do not think, though, my people, that I am deserting you, for I am not. I am soon to be the father of a child, and that knowledge has taught me how important the bond is between parent and child, between generation and generation, between a ruler and his people. My love for my child fills me and humbles me, and reinforces in me my love for the people of Niroli. It is out of this love—both for my child and for you, my people—that I am stepping down from the succession line to the throne, but never think that I am deserting you. I intend to set up a charity which will make available funds to help those citizens of Niroli who are most in need. It will provide the opportunity for our young people to be educated and to travel abroad, to broaden their horizons and then bring back to Niroli the gift of what they have learned so that they may share it. It is my passionate belief that this island needs a better system for encouraging its young to reach their full potential. I can do this best from outside the hierarchy of kingship and all that goes with it. At the same time, I shall remain at all times supportive of my grandfather and whoever he chooses to take the throne after him.

'I ask for your blessing, people of Niroli, and your understanding that sometimes it is more important for a man to be just that, than for him to be a king...'

'Excuse me, love, only we're about to close the store.' Her gaze blurred with her tears, Emily looked at the young man who was addressing her. Marco had left the balcony. The young man was looking impatient. Reluctantly, she nodded her head and headed for the exit.

It wasn't a long walk from the shops back to her house, but it was long enough for Emily to mentally question what Marco had done. He had told his people that he was giving up the throne because of his child—her child. Why? Marco was arrogant and proud, a perfectionist; did he—or his grandfather—fear the existence of a child who was not perfect might somehow damage the power of the Nirolian royal family? Had his grandfather pressured Marco into stepping down, or had his own resolve spurred his abdication? Either way, she had no wish to be a party to depriving Niroli of its future king, and nor did she want her son growing up carrying the burden and the blame for his father's decision to deny himself a role Emily knew he had been eager to take on.

She turned the corner into her street and then stopped, her heart hammering against her ribs as she saw Marco standing outside the front door of her house. Ridiculously, her first impulse was to turn and walk away, but he had already seen her and he was walking towards her.

'What are you doing here?' she demanded when he reached her. 'I've only just seen you on television! Marco, you can't give up the Crown. Why have you? It isn't—'

'It isn't your decision,' Marco told her calmly. 'It was mine, and as for you seeing me on TV, well, it must have been on a rolling news programme rounding up the day's events. I made my resignation speech at eleven a.m. this morning, Nirolian time. I had a private jet standing by, another personal decision, before you ask,' he added dryly.

'It isn't fair of you to do this and to say publicly that it's because of my baby,' she told him passionately. 'Isn't he going to have enough to cope with, without the added blame of being responsible for—'

'We can't discuss this out here,' Marco interrupted her. 'Where are your keys?'

Helplessly, Emily handed them over and let him open the door for her.

The small house smelled of Emily's delicate scent, Marco recognised, also realising how much he had missed her. Soon, no doubt, the air around her would be filled with the scent of baby powder. With every mile that had brought him closer to her, his conviction that he had made the right decision had grown and, now, recognising how much he was looking forward to being part of the family unit they would form with their child was like one door closing behind him on an old habitat that no longer had any relevance to his life and another opening that had everything to do with it.

'There was no need for you to abdicate, Marco,' Emily burst out as soon as they were inside. 'I know how much you wanted to be King, so why?'

'If you had heard my speech in its entirety, then you would have known why I decided to step down, and why it was necessary for me to abdicate.'

'Because of our baby? Because he might not be perfect? Because you're ashamed of him, and you and your grandfather don't want him associated with Niroli?'

'What? Ashamed of him? You couldn't be more wrong. If there's anyone I'm ashamed of, it's myself for taking so long to recognise what really matters to me. Or perhaps I did recognise it, but tried to pretend that I didn't. Emily, when you were having your scan and I saw our baby, I knew beyond any kind of doubt that you and he are the most important things in the world to me, and that nothing could ever or would ever matter more. Actually, I think I knew a little of that when I first came to Niroli and I missed you so much I had to come back for you. I certainly knew it when you told me you were pregnant and all I could think of was finding a way to keep you with me. I couldn't and wouldn't accept that it wasn't possible for me to be King and to have you and our child. And then you told me why you were pleased that our child would never be King, and it was as though you had unlocked a door inside me. Behind it lay the memories of my own childhood, my parents' constant battles with my grandfather to provide me with a normal childhood, my own sense of aloneness because of what I was, and I knew unequivocally that you were right not to want that for our child.'

'But you wanted to be King! You had so many plans, there was so much you wanted to do—you can't give that up.'

'I don't intend to. I can still do all those things without being King. In fact I can do them more easily. My grandfather would never really release the reins of government to me, and the hostility between us and the constant fight for supremacy would not aid our people. I can do far more outside the constraints of kingship, and I can do those things with you at my side. I love you, Emily.'

There was so much she wanted to say, so many questions, so many reminders to him of times when he had not seemed to love her at all. But, somehow, she was in his arms and he was kissing her with a fierce, demanding passion that said more clearly than any amount of words what he truly felt.

'I STILL CAN'T believe this is happening,' Emily whispered to Marco half an hour later. She was still in his arms, only now they were upstairs in her bedroom, lying side by side in her bed. The way Marco had controlled his need to possess her, been gentle to protect their child, had brought emotional tears to her eyes and flooded her heart with the love for him she had dammed up for so long.

'You want me to convince you?' Marco teased her suggestively, his hand cupping her breast.

'Maybe,' she agreed mock-demurely.

His, 'Right, come on then, let's get dressed,' wasn't the response she had been expecting and her chagrin showed, making him laugh.

'We're going shopping,' he told her. 'For a wedding ring and a marriage licence.'

When her eyes rounded, he pointed out, 'You said you wanted me to convince you. I can't think of a better way to do that than marrying you, just as soon as we can arrange it.'

'Oh, Marco... Shouldn't we wait to make plans until after the scan?'

'Why? The potential severity of our baby's heart defect doesn't make any difference to my feelings for you or for him. You suggested earlier that I might be ashamed of our baby for not being perfect. That could never happen. He will be perfect to me, Emily, because he is ours, perfect in every way, no matter what.'

'Oh, don't,' Emily protested. 'You'll make me cry all over again.'

'And then I'll have to kiss you all over again,' Marco said, pretending to give a weary sigh, but smiling whilst he did so.

'WELL, THEN, LET'S have a look. It's been a few weeks since we did your last scan, and that will have given your baby a chance to grow and us the chance to get a better idea of what's going on. As I told you at your first consultation with me, these days, in-utero surgery means that we can do so very much more than we once could. Even with the most severe cases.'

Emily felt Marco squeezing her hand, but she dared not look at him just in case she broke down.

These last weeks since their initial appointment with the neo-natal heart consultant had seemed so long, despite the fact that they had managed to squeeze getting married into them, along with a flying visit to Niroli, where Marco's grandfather had very graciously welcomed her formally into the family. Marco had also brought his grandfather up to date with his plans to establish the charity he had promised during his abdication speech.

New scans had been done, and now they were waiting anxiously for the specialist's opinion.

'However, in the case of your baby, I don't consider that an operation would be appropriate.'

Emily gave a small moan of despair. Was he saying there was no hope? 'What exactly is our baby's prognosis?' Marco's voice wasn't quite as level as normal, and Emily could hear the uncertainty in it.

'Very good. Excellent, in fact,' the specialist told them, smiling. 'There is a small area that we shall need to keep an eye on, but if anything it seems to be healing itself— something we do see with this condition. Sometimes babies will grow in stops and starts, and this leads us to make di-agnoses we later have to amend. That is what has happened here. Initially, it did look as though your baby's heart might not be developing properly, but these latest scans show that everything is just as it should be.'

'Are you sure?' Emily asked anxiously. 'I mean, should I have another scan in a week or two? What if—?'

'I am perfectly sure. In fact, I was pretty sure when you first came to see me, but I wanted to wait and see how things went before I said anything, which is why I wanted to do this last scan. Of course, I am going to recommend that we continue to monitor the situation, just to be on the safe side, but my view is that there is nothing for you to worry about. Your baby is perfectly healthy and developing normally.'

OUTSIDE ON THE street, oblivious to the amused looks of passers-by, Marco held Emily close and tenderly kissed the tears from her face.

'I can't believe it,' she whispered to him. 'Oh, Marco… It's like a miracle.'

'You are my miracle, Emily,' Marco told her softly. 'You and our child, and the future we are going to share.'

'HOW HAS THE king taken things?'

'Not as badly as we might have feared.' The senior courtier was well versed in tact and diplomacy, and he had no intention of telling the junior aide anything about the extraordinary scene he had just witnessed in the Royal Chamber, when the king had stopped in mid-rant about the stupidity of his grandson and heir to stare at the report he had just been handed, about an Australian surgeon who was pioneering a new treatment for the heart condition from which the king himself suffered.

On the face of it, there had been nothing in the grainy photograph and short biography of the young Australian to cause such a reaction. But the senior courtier had been in service at the palace for a very long time and when the king had handed the report to him in an expectant silence he, too, had seen the same thing that the king had seen.

'I want that young man brought here, and I want him brought here now,' the king had instructed.…

* * * * *

A ROYAL BRIDE
AT THE SHEIKH'S
COMMAND

PROLOGUE

SHE WAS IN total shock.

She needed very badly to sit down, but of course she couldn't. For one thing she was still in the Royal Presence Chamber, and, whilst she was a modern go-getting woman, her Nirolian ancestry within her reminded her that she was alone in the presence of Niroli's King.

And for another... Well, she told herself grimly, the king wasn't going to welcome seeing any kind of weakness being shown by the bride he had selected for this newly discovered heir. So newly discovered, in fact, that she, the bride-to-be in question, had been sworn to absolute secrecy about the whole thing.

It was of course a story that would attract every member of the paparazzi like blood in the water attracted sharks, and one that could be just as potentially perilous to any-one who obstructed King Giorgio's plans. She had just learned that these plans required her, as a dutiful subject, to marry this Prince Kadir Zafar, the King's previously 'secret' illegitimate son, for the sake of the island she loved so passionately.

CHAPTER ONE

Venice

SHE MIGHT BE passionately attached to Niroli, but there was
no doubt that Venice had a very special place in her heart,
Natalia acknowledged, lifting her hand to try to stop the
breeze from playing with the heavy weight of her thick
dark curls. She was waiting for the water taxi to take her
to her destination, and was totally oblivious to the admiring male looks she was attracting. When one man proved
bold enough to murmur, *'Bella, bella,'* caressingly as he
stopped to stand and stare openly at her, she couldn't help
but laugh, her marine blue eyes sparkling with the rich
colour of the lido in the sunshine. Just having her sombre
mood lightened for a few seconds was a much needed relief at the moment.

It was all very well having sleepless nights and worrying herself half a stone thinner over whether or not she had
made the right decision, but what she ought to be asking
herself surely was why on earth had she ever agreed to do
it in the first place.

The water taxi arrived and she picked up her small
weekend bag and stepped into the taxi with ease and elegance. She was a tall woman of close to six feet who wore
her height with calm pride.

'Via Venetii? The Buchesetti Spa Hotel,' she asked the
vaporetto driver.

'Sì,' he agreed, with open admiration in his gaze.

The tranquil ride to her destination made Natalia reflect ruefully on the uncomfortable speed with which the direction of her life had suddenly changed. Increasingly she was waking up in the morning feeling as though she had stepped on board a train that had then suddenly picked up speed to such an extent that she was beginning to feel that it was running away with her.

So why had she allowed it to happen in the first place? After all no one had forced her.

No? When your king appealed to you personally for your help to save the future of your country, a country you loved, you didn't just turn round and say no, did you? At least not if you were a Carini.

The trouble was that, since she had said yes, the list of reasons why in her own interests she would have been better off saying no had begun to grow by the day.

'Via Venetii,' the *vaporetto* driver pointed out to her, interrupting her thoughts. 'The hotel, she is not far now. Is a very beautiful hotel. You go there before?'

'Yes,' Natalia told him. She could see from the expression on his face that the answer had sounded more curt than she had intended. But how could she explain to him how she felt about the fact that she had been obliged to sell her beloved spa hotel on Niroli to this one in Venice?

True, the choice of whom she should sell to had been her own. True, too, that she knew that the new owners, Maya and Howard, would uphold her own high standards, now that they had officially added her spa to their portfolio, but that still did not mean that she was not allowed to grieve for her much cherished and loved 'baby', did it?

So why give it up in the first place? Why give up the life she had worked so hard to build for herself to enter into an arranged marriage of state? So that she could be a princess?

Natalia almost laughed out loud, the white flash of her even white teeth contrasting with the full warmth of her soft red lips making the driver of the *vaporetto* sigh in a way that caused Natalia to look away to conceal her amusement.

At twenty-nine she had had ample time to get used to her effect on the opposite sex.

To get used to her effect on the opposite sex, but never to fall in love. And now with her forthcoming marriage to the newly discovered heir to the Nirolian throne she was giving up the chance to do so for ever, wasn't she? After all, she wasn't foolish enough to think that a marriage arranged between two strangers by a king whose only thought was to secure the future of his kingdom could by some miracle turn into a passionately intense and lifelong love affair, was she? Not when she had never, ever fallen in love; not when her sole reason for agreeing to this marriage had been her passionate love, not for a man, but for a country, *her* country, just as her husband-to-be's desire was directed towards the throne of Niroli and not towards her. Could it work? Was she as mad as she was beginning to think to have agreed to marry Prince Kadir just so that she would be there at his side to ensure that he ruled her beloved country with wisdom and love? If only there were someone she could turn to for advice, but there wasn't. The king had forbidden her to discuss the matter with anyone.

The elegant and exclusive spa hotel that was her destination had its own landing stage. As she saw it approaching Natalia turned to pick up her bag. As she did so a man striding impatiently across the small square to the side of the hotel caught her eye, as much for any other reason as for his height. At almost six feet herself, she was appreciative of the visual impact of men who were taller than her, and this man was certainly that, taller, and broad shouldered, with surprisingly hard-packed muscles, too, for a man who looked as though he was closer to forty than thirty. Thick dark hair that just brushed the collar of his jacket gleamed with good health under the brilliant sunlight. His skin was warmly olive and although he was too far away for Natalia to see the colour of his eyes she could see the hard, precision hewn perfection of his facial bone structure with its high cheekbones and strong jaw. Here was a man, she acknowledged.

As though by some alchemic means he had somehow sensed her interest and paused, turning his head to look directly at her. She still could not see the colour of his eyes, but she could see that he was even more stunningly handsome face on than he had been in profile. It had to be the sun that was making her feel slightly dizzy and not the fact that he was looking at her... Had been looking at her, she recognised to her relief as he turned away and resumed his progress across the square. As the *vaporetto* pulled into the landing stage she admitted to herself that her brief interest in this man was not the wisest of things in a woman soon to enter into a dynastic marriage. How was she going to go on in that marriage if she was experiencing sexual desire for another man now? Sexual desire? That was ridiculous. She had simply been looking at him, that was all, and anyway he had gone now, and she was hardly likely to ever see him again, was she?

WHEN NATALIA ARRIVED in the lobby, Maya hurried forward to hug her exuberantly. 'This is so good of you to come and help us with the transition of ownership. We wanted it to go smoothly and there's still so much to learn about your Nirolian spa. We had not dared to hope that you would be generous enough to come back to Venice so quickly.'

Natalia returned the hug a bit guiltily. It was impossible of course for her to tell her that the main reason she was back in Venice was because King Giorgio had wanted her out of the way until the newly discovered heir to the throne of Niroli had arrived on the island. Then she would be allowed to return and they would be presented, with full pomp and dignity, to the people of Niroli, along with the announcement of their marriage.

'But why can't I remain here?' she had questioned the king. 'After all I shall have to make arrangements for the future of the business.'

'You are a woman and I cannot permit you to remain where you could be tempted to break the vow of secrecy I have sworn you to.'

She had of course been tempted to object to the use of that contemptuous 'you are a woman' but, knowing King Giorgio as she did, she had decided that there wasn't very much point, and then she had received the frantic plea to return to Venice to discuss the handover of the business with Maya and Howard. They had expressed their wish to buy some of her special formulae for the oils she used.

The truth was that, much as his old-fashioned attitudes often infuriated her, on this occasion, and perhaps against her own best interests, she had actually felt slightly sorry for the king when he had approached her with his unexpected proposition. He had run through each and every one of his potential male heirs in turn and been forced to reject them. Loving Niroli every bit as much as he did, she had fully understood his contrasting feelings of joy at the discovery that he had fathered an illegitimate son during a brief affair over forty years ago with an Arabian princess, and anxiety about offering this son the throne in case his son's Arabian upbringing meant that his ideas on how to rule were not suited to Niroli. And, yes, if she was honest it had been flattering—very flattering—to be told by King Giorgio that he had picked her out of all his single

female subjects to become the wife of Niroli's future King
because he had seen in her certain strengths and virtues
that reminded him of his beloved first wife, Queen Sophia.

Everyone knew how much the people of Niroli had loved
and revered King Giorgio's first wife and how much she
had done for Niroli. As a little girl Natalia had woven foolish daydreams as children did of somehow going back in
time to meet Queen Sophia and 'helping' her with her work.
Now she had been given that opportunity in reality, or at
least an opportunity to continue the work Queen Sophia
had begun. At the time, filled with euphoria at the thought
of her coming role in the future of her country, she hadn't
thought marriage to a stranger too much of a price to pay.
After all she had never been in love and had no expectation
of being in love; she liked to think of herself as practically
minded and she had embraced the idea of taking a marriage between two people with a common goal and making it work. Of course, even then she had had some doubts
and concerns. Marriage to a future king meant producing that future king's heirs and spares, and that of course
meant having sex with him. But King Giorgio had been too
thrilled not to mention the fact that his secret son looked
very like him, and since the king, even now in his old age,
was a very good-looking man Natalia was assuming that
her future husband was reasonably physically attractive.

What about his personality, though? she wondered and
worried now. What if he was the kind of man she just could
not grow to like or respect? If he was, she wouldn't want
to abandon her country to him, would she? No, she would
want to do what she could to offset those faults in him as
his wife. Those who thought they knew her as a forward-
thinking, successful businesswoman would, of course, be
stunned and disbelieving when the news did break, and
would no doubt question why she had not immediately re-

fused to have anything whatsoever to do with the king's grand plan.

But then that was the trouble, wasn't it? Whilst on the surface she might appear to be all modern, she herself was something of an anomaly in that deep down inside her there was something else. That 'something' was her passionate and deep-rooted love for her country, for its past and its present but most of all for its future. Or rather the future it could have in the right hands. Because Niroli, like so much of the rest of the world, was at a crisis point where traditional values were clashing badly with modernity; where those on and off the island like herself, who wanted to see Niroli move forward into a future that guarded and protected its unique geographical benefits rather than wasted and abused them, were often in conflict with those who could see no reason not to squander Niroli's natural assets, or even worse those who sought to strip the island of its unique heritage in the name of progress by turning it into one huge tourist attraction.

What Natalia favoured was a different way, an ecologically and Nirolian friendly way that would preserve the best of their traditions as well as move them forward into a prosperous future. She had never made any secret of her feelings about this. Her commitment to her other work, as an apothecary using natural oils and holistic treatments in the spa she had set up, was well known. However, as Natalia Carini she could only do so much and her sphere of influence was limited to those who for the most part shared her views. As Niroli's Queen she would be in a far, far more influential position to make very real and worthwhile changes. Certainly far more so than she did as the granddaughter of the island's acknowledged expert vintner.

'I'd be very happy to give you exclusive rights to some

of my special oil recipes,' she told Maya now, switching her thoughts.

'We have been using the samples you were kind enough to give us during the negotiations for the purchase of your spa,' the sweet round faced Italian said, 'and our clients have raved about them. The deep muscle replenisher you have created for sportsmen has found particular favour and we have a growing client list of sportsmen already using our spas—skiers, football and polo players mainly— who come to us by word-of-mouth recommendation, and Howard has been panicking that we would soon run out of your oil.'

Natalia laughed. She was as responsive to flattery when it was genuine and given for the right reasons as anyone else, and it always delighted her when people reported favourably on her therapeutic oils.

'Then it is just as well perhaps that I took Howard's hint when he phoned last week and brought you a fresh supply with me,' she told Maya. Whilst she knew she could hardly continue to run a business once she was married to Prince Kadir, one thing Natalia did intend to stick out for was her own private space where she could continue to use her 'nose' as a perfumier—not to create new perfumes so much as to use the ingredients that went into them in a more therapeutic way. Just as music and now colour were both recognised as having healing properties, increasingly people were beginning to accept that scents also possessed the power to heal the body, the mind and the heart when blended and used properly. It was one of her dreams to create a range of scents that would do this, and now she had added to that a new dream of using her position as Niroli's Queen to set up a charity to distribute them to those in need.

'You will dine with us later this evening, I hope, but

for now we thought you might welcome some free time to enjoy Venice, before we sit down together to talk over the mechanics of the purchase of your oil recipes.'

'That would suit me perfectly,' Natalia confirmed.

She laughed when Maya hugged her again and said emotionally, 'Oh, Natalia, I am so glad that you are willing to do this for us.'

As she returned Maya's grateful hug, Natalia acknowledged that she had been hoping to have a bit of time for herself, because there was one place in particular that she really wanted to go.

THE LATE AFTERNOON autumn mist stealing from the canals and swirling round the squares and streets created an atmosphere within the city that for her, whilst concealing it in the material sense, revealed it very sharply in an emotional sense. With the mist came a sombreness and a melancholy that she felt somehow truly reflected the deep hidden heart of the city, stripping from it the carnival mask it wore so easily for those it did not want to know its secrets. Natalia, though, had been coming here for many years, drawn back to it time after time, and there was no hesitation in her long-legged stride as she made her way to the *vaporetto* stop from which the water taxi would take her to the small glass-making factory she had discovered years ago on her first visit here. She had been awed and entranced then by the beauty of the perfume bottles she had watched being blown, and on each return trip she had revisited it, choosing for herself a bottle that reflected in its unique colours something of her mood of that visit. What would catch her eye on this visit? she wondered. It was part of the game not to anticipate what she would choose, but simply to let it happen.

As she crossed the square she had seen earlier she realised that she was following in the footsteps of the man she had watched from the water taxi. Now what had brought him into her thoughts? Not some ridiculous idea that she might see him again? After the dismissive look he had given her? When she was almost on the eve of getting married? Fantasizing about tall, handsome men glimpsed in the street hadn't been a folly she had indulged in even when she was a teenager. Why was she doing it now?

That was Venice for you, Natalia told herself ruefully. It played tricks on the imagination and the eye, and in more ways than one.

'SIGNORINA, IT IS you. Ah, you grow more lovely with every visit.'

Old Mario, the head of the family, gave her a gummy smile as he welcomed her.

'And you grow more silver-tongued, Mario.' She laughed, already looking past him towards the inner sanctum where they kept their special one-off creations, like a small child anticipating Christmas, and salivating almost at the prospect of being allowed to choose just what she wanted.

Mario was turning away from her and she made to follow him, but his son stopped her.

'Please, we have something special for you this time. My father has made it himself. He said that he had this thought of you and that he felt he must do this thing…'

Natalia tried not to look as disappointed as she was feeling. She was strong-minded and independent enough to want to choose her own perfume bottle, but sensitively she didn't want to offend the old man.

He had disappeared into the back room and it seemed an age before he returned, carrying a battered cardboard box from which she could see tissue paper sticking out.

'Here,' he told her, proffering her the box.

Forcing a wide smile, Natalia took it, carefully unwrapping the tissue paper until she had revealed the small perfume bottle that lay within it. At first all she could see was every colour of the rainbow spliced with silver and gold and every nuance of beautiful colour and shade the human eye could imagine. It defeated her ability to rationalise what colour it actually was.

'Hold it in your hand,' the old man urged her.

A little hesitantly Natalia removed the bottle, and held it.

'Now look,' the shop owner commanded.

Natalia gasped as she stared at the bottle. It seemed to shimmer and glow as though it were still molten and not solid; as though it had a life force of its own that pulsated within it and, absurdly, she felt afraid to touch it, in case she harmed it.

'What…what is it?' she asked in an awed whisper.

'It is diamond glass, a very special and old recipe—we don't use it any more because it is not easily possible to come by the ingredients, and they have to be ground down and heated in such a way that makes it dangerous to the creator and the creation. Legend has it that only the Doge was allowed to own glassware made from this recipe, which was stolen from one of the great Caliphs of the East,' the younger boy explained wryly to her.

'It's so beautiful…'

'It is unique—possibly the last of its kind ever to be made and my father has made it for you. It is said that when the pure of heart hold the bottle it glows as it did just then for you, but when those who are motivated by darkness and evil touch the glass it grows dull and cold so that its colour vanishes.' He laughed. 'As yet we have not been able to confirm whether or not that is true, although my father swears that it is.'

The older man said something huskily in Venetian, which his son translated for Natalia even though she was able to do so herself.

'My father says that whenever you touch this bottle you will be reminded of the purity of your heart and the true beauty that comes from within. May it lift your spirits and warm your heart throughout your life.'

Tears filled Natalia's eyes. Increasingly she was beginning to worry that she might need raw warmth from outside her marriage to sustain her through it, and yet again she questioned whether she had made the right decision.

It was later than she had planned when Natalia finally left the factory and as she glanced at her watch she recognised that she was only just going to make it back to the spa hotel in time to join Maya and Howard for the pre-dinner drink they had offered her.

However, the minute she stepped into their private suite she realised that they had more to worry about than her being late for drinks. Maya was seated on one of the large room's three plain cream leather sofas, her right hand heavily bandaged and her arm in a sling.

'She slipped and dropped a glass bowl and then cut her hand on it,' Howard explained.

'And now we are in the most dreadful fix.' Maya sighed miserably. 'We had a phone call earlier, before I fell, from an unexpected client who is in between flights and who wanted to book in for the night. He plays polo and has an old injury that occasionally flares up. He requested the massage you showed me, Natalia, you know the one? The deep muscle massage you devised for sports injuries?'

Natalia nodded her head. The massage in question was one of her spa's specialities.

'When he was here last month I recommended it to him,' Maya continued, 'and he said it was most beneficial. Apparently these days he spends more time behind a desk than he does on the polo field and so this old injury occasionally flares up. Naturally I took the booking, and now he is expecting his massage in half an hour's time. He has taken our best suite, so he is not someone we would want to offend. Now I can't do the massage, and Gina, the only other masseuse we have who could do it, is on holiday. I can't tell you how cross with myself I am for doing something so stupid as dropping that wretched bowl.'

Natalia sympathised with her. She could tell that Maya was like her in that she set herself very exacting standards and she knew just how she would be feeling in her shoes. 'Couldn't I do the massage for you?' she offered impulsively.

'Would you?' Immediately Maya was all relieved and grateful smiles. 'We *were* hoping you might offer,' she admitted honestly, adding, only half jokingly, 'Natalia, are you sure you would not like a partnership with us? Only you would be the most wonderful asset to the business.'

Don't tempt me, was Natalia's immediate private reaction as she smiled and shook her head. The explanation she had given the other couple for her decision to sell the spa had been her wish to focus on developing her skills as a perfumier. Another lie, but a necessary one, according to King Giorgio.

'What time is he booked in for?' she asked Maya quietly, slipping into her professional persona.

'Half past. You've got twenty minutes to get ready. I've already brought up a uniform for you. His name is Leon Perez. Since his injury is a polo injury I imagine he must be South American. He's requested the massage in his suite, by the way, but there's nothing untoward in that, as you will know. We do offer that facility. However, if for any reason his behaviour *should* become unacceptable, just press the buzzer at the side of the bed. We've had them in-stalled in all of the rooms just in case. We intend to keep a list of those guests who mistake our services for those of a very different kind, so that we can make sure they don't repeat their mistake.'

'A wise precaution,' Natalia agreed. 'I did the same thing, although fortunately they haven't been used as yet.'

'When you've finished, we'll have drinks and dinner and continue our business discussions then,' Maya said as she handed Natalia a spa uniform.

The spa's uniform was a simple cap-sleeved, high-necked linen-mix A-line shift dress in plain white. The fabric was thick and heavy enough not to reveal what its wearer might be wearing underneath, Natalia noted approv-ingly. She liked the fact that Maya respected her employ-ees enough not to give them a uniform that was in any way provocative. There was just about enough time for her to go to her own suite to shower, plait her hair to keep it out of the way and change into the uniform. It was rather shorter perhaps than she would have liked, and a bit tighter, but that was a problem one became accustomed to when one was tall and had a voluptuously curved hourglass figure. She gathered together everything Maya had given her that she would need before making her way to the guest's suite.

NATALIA HAD GIVEN clients massages a hundred thousand times and more so there was no reason at all for that funny little sensation to curl its way through her stomach as she pressed the bell and then stood outside the suite waiting to be let in.

The suite door was being opened. A man was standing just inside it, wearing the ubiquitous white hotel bathrobe.

As she looked at him Natalia found that she was blink-ing dizzily in much the same way she had done when she'd first looked at the perfume bottle. It was *him*. Leon Perez was the man she had seen earlier, crossing the square. That it should be him was surely against all the laws of reason and logic, and yet there was no mistake. It was him. Her senses were telling her that very loudly and clearly. Her *senses*. What right had they to get themselves involved in what was after all a purely professional matter? This was dreadful. And what was worse, far worse, was that everything she had just told herself about there being no need for her to feel anxious had just been blown totally out of the water by the force of one single look from those impossibly long-lashed jade green eyes.

Her heart swung crazily through her chest as though suspended from a pendulum and then stopped dead. She felt as though she were drowning in the depths of his eyes; as though she were being sucked under by some powerful sensual undertow come out of nowhere to possess her. Through the clamouring tumult of her senses she could think only one clear thought. And that was how very, very badly she wanted him.

CHAPTER TWO

WHAT *WAS* THIS…THIS lightning dart of pure volcanic sexual desire shooting up inside Natalia to spill past the long-closed gates of her own restraint, melting them into nothing?

Leave! Leave now, an inner voice was urging her. You can't afford this. Just turn around and go…because if you don't…

'You booked a massage?'

Too late…too late. *Why* hadn't she done what that inner voice had urged her? she wondered shakily as she stepped into the warm womb of semi-darkness that was the dimly lit foyer of the suite. Her 'nose', so sensitive always, too much sometimes, went into overdrive. She was being overwhelmed by the flood of scents washing over her, the new decorations smell of paint and carpet and fibres all mingled together. The scent of the lilies in the hallway, overlaying the special signature perfume she had created for herself and always wore, a special recipe based on roses, with a hint of musk sharpened with the unique oil she had produced by blending grapes as they ripened, and vines as they thrust out new growth, maturity blended with the raw, powerful surge of new life. Normally it pleased and soothed her, but now was distorted perhaps by the smell of her own fear and she discovered that she was fighting against its unfamiliar demanding sensuality.

But most powerful of all was the scent of *him*. Images

flashed inside her head; heat; the scent of something alien and unknown to her carried on a hot wind, the scent of male power both physical and mental; a rawness and vitality merging into something so intimate that she felt almost as though he had physically imprisoned her. Something dangerous and very unwanted was happening to her, Natalia admitted, grand slamming her senses, rushing over her and through her, forcing her to surrender to it.

'This way.'

With a tremendous effort Natalia forced herself to ignore what she was feeling. For a moment she had wanted him. So what? That was probably just a knee-jerk reaction to her own knowledge that her unplanned years of celibacy were shortly to be brought to an end via her marriage. There was perhaps nothing like recognising that something was about to be taken 'off the menu' for it suddenly to be extraordinarily desirable. As for that dizzy, soft-boned feeling sliding through her like warmed precious oils, *that* was probably caused by the unfamiliar act of having to tilt her head back to look up at him, instead of him being on her own eye level as most men were. How tall was he, exactly?

King Giorgio had not offered her any information as to the physical make-up of his illegitimate son, other than his very proud boast that he was 'obviously his son'. All she knew about him was that he was forty years old, had never been married, and had been brought up as a sheikh-in-waiting, but that on being offered the throne of Niroli he had handed over the rulership of Hadiya to his younger half brother.

There had been days since she had agreed to the king's proposition when it had been a hard call *not* picturing someone squat, plump and wearing too much gold, especially in his teeth, despite King Giorgio's obvious admiration for him.

In contrast, this man was six feet three at least, power-fully muscled without an ounce of excess weight and, as for his teeth, well, that small chip in one of the front pair suggested that despite their excellent shape and colour they were all his own. It would be wonderful to dance with a man whose height was so perfectly devised by nature to physically match her own. Just to dance, what about...? She tensed her body against what she was thinking. It was tilt-ing her head that was responsible for her out-of-character response to him, she told herself feverishly. After all, at that angle the flow of blood to the brain would be dimin-ished and that alone would be enough to induce...to induce what? Mind blowing images of such sensory sensuality that her nerve endings felt stripped of their protective covering.

For such a tall and powerfully built man he moved very lightly and easily—and very confidently, walking ahead of her, leaving her to follow in his wake like some harem woman following her master? Now where on earth had that idea come from? This man was South American, Maya had told her.

MAYA AND HOWARD had chosen to renovate the interior of the small palazzo they had transformed into their spa hotel in a way that was naturally holistic and an example of pared-down minimalism. The luxurious comfort of its rooms and décor came from the quality of the natural fur-nishings and fabrics they had used. This suite, the most exclusive of all the rooms, had plain off-white walls to off-set its marble floors. All the rooms had specially designed massage tables in addition to their huge king-sized beds.

'You booked one of the spa's special neck and back massages,' Natalia checked as they approached the mas-sage table.

'Yes. And let me warn you, you had better know what you are doing.'

He sounded almost antagonistic towards her, something that Natalia wasn't used to either as a woman or as a professional, and somehow, instead of dampening down the unwanted feverish intensity of her reaction to him, it only seemed to inflame it. Was she really so immature? Wanting what she couldn't have because she couldn't have it? That was ridiculous. She just wasn't that kind of person.

Perhaps now wasn't the time to tell him that she was the one responsible for creating the massage in the first place, Natalia admitted, even if his attitude towards her had put her on her mettle. She knew without vanity that she was an excellent masseuse—it was a gift and an instinct she had known she possessed virtually from childhood, this power to soothe and heal with the touch of her hands. Had she been doing this in her own spa she would have been talking with her clients, drawing them out about themselves whilst she assessed which of her own specially blended oils would suit their needs best. She had no intention of trying that with this man though. She had no idea why she should feel this instinctive awareness of a need to protect herself from him.

Don't you? an inner voice taunted her. Take a good look at him—that should tell you. No woman with red blood in her veins could fail to be affected by his maleness, especially not one who has just agreed to a passionless dynastic marriage.

Was that it? Was her unexpected and definitely unwanted reaction to him solely some unfamiliar last-minute and reckless desire to rebel against her own decision; a reminder by her senses of just what she would be giving up? She had never been promiscuous, she reminded herself, so why on earth should her senses suddenly have her physically yearning for an unknown man now? Physically yearning? She was doing no such thing! Yes, you are, her senses responded smartly. Determinedly Natalia fought to subdue them. She was here to work, nothing else. Just to work.

He had his back to her now and was stripping off the spa's robe, letting it drop to the floor. Natalia held her breath. If he was nude, beneath the robe—and he certainly had the kind of male confidence that would mean that he could quite easily be. But he wasn't. And she wasn't prepared to let herself know whether she was pleased or disappointed to see that he had a small towel wrapped around his hips. Far better from a masseur's point of view than underwear, it showed her that he was familiar with this kind of experience. How many other foolish women had felt as she was feeling right now? Had he looked at them as indifferently as he was looking at her or had they seen desire for them in those dark green eyes? From out of nowhere like a fierce tornado, jealousy gripped hold of her. The shock of it made her hands tremble as she waited for him to lie face down on the table.

She was, Natalia discovered, holding in her breath, and no wonder, when she saw the way those superbly defined muscles rippled with pure male strength. Yes, he was obviously a horseman, she acknowledged—those thighs certainly indicated that. And as for him being a polo player—he certainly had the requisite muscle structure, and the wealth if the understated but still discreetly logoed expensive watch and the fact that he was in this suite were anything to go by. His flesh shone a subtle warm bronze in the room's lights, moving sleekly over the heavy padding of his muscles. He moved like a hunting cheetah, light on his feet, swift, silent and deadly. If she had not known he was South American she suspected that she might have put him down as Italian, although there was something within the devastatingly hard-boned masculinity of his face that hinted at a cultural legacy she could not quite define, something alien—and challenging to her as a woman? Ignore it, she warned herself speedily, trying to focus on other aspects of her client. His manner was certainly European, and yet it was also not. Because he was South American? Irritatingly that something 'other' for some reason was nagging at her subconscious, trying to tell her something, though she didn't know what. More out of habit than anything she turned away whilst he settled himself on the massage table.

An important part of this particular form of massage was the mood music and lighting that accompanied it. Maya had instructed her how to activate the sound and light systems, both pretty similar to her own, although she preferred whenever possible to open the windows and have the simple sounds of nature as the only auditory accompaniment to her massage. But then of course she also used her oils and she was a great believer in not overloading the senses with too many strong stimuli at once.

She poured a small amount of oil into the waiting bowl and warmed it over a tea light and then poured a very small amount into her own cupped palm.

'This massage is designed to work on tensions and blocks within the deep muscle structure,' she explained calmly. 'You may find that it gives rise to the occasional uncontrollable movement of one or other of those muscles depending on the degree of stress they are under, but that's completely normal.'

The sound of him exhaling conveyed his impatience far more effectively than any words could have done—and his desire for her to keep her distance from him by not talking. Well, that certainly suited her.

She started to sweep her hands over his skin, assessing

the tone and texture of the muscles beneath it, breathing evenly and slowly as she let herself sink down into and be absorbed into her gift for her work. So many things could be learned by this silent communication of touch and flesh, so many secrets withdrawn—he, for instance, was tensing himself against her even though he might be pretending with his steady, even breathing not to be doing so. At some stage in his life he had fallen heavily on his left hip, possibly from a horse. Polo again? There was no obvious damage but she could feel the muscle's sensitive flutter as it whispered to her of its secret trauma. Automatically she responded to its need, stroking first reassurance and then, once it had accepted her touch, using a deeper, more searching kneading technique to send strength back into it, giving it power and confidence, telling it with her touch that it need not fear, that it could trust itself.

His hair, thick and dark—darker than her own, in fact— would, as she already knew, brush his collar when he was dressed. Now it felt sweetly soft against her fingertips as she swept up over his back and searched out the tensions in his neck muscles. She had been working for nearly fifteen minutes and her own muscles were beginning to ache slightly. Beneath the A-line shift all she was wearing was a pair of boy shorts, a practical decision, she had thought, but one she was regretting now as the movements required by the massage had brought her nipples into the kind of contact with the shift dress that was making them swell and ache. At least she assumed it was the fabric of her uniform.

She had never seen, never mind touched, a man with such a perfect body. She wanted to go on stroking and learning his flesh for ever. The feel of it intoxicated and delighted her whilst the scent of his massage-warmed skin was surely the scent of sensuality and sex itself, distilled to perfection. It possessed her 'nose' as physically and completely as though he had actually taken possession of her, causing a weakening of her own muscles and a corresponding ache deep within her belly, a sense of mingling heat and need that flowed up through her, affecting her like alcohol might do a drinker, melting bonds of her inhibitions and taking from her her ability to make rational decisions or to think rational thoughts. Her fingertips traced the long length of his spine, delicately tracing each vertebra. No wonder he stood so tall and proud. She had reached the edge of the towel wrapped low on his hips now. Since his request had been for a deep-textured neck and upper back massage there was no reason for her to be touching his body here. No reason other than her own need to indulge herself. All bodies had their strengths and their weaknesses, their good and their bad, but this body, his body, was so perfectly constructed that the pleasure of touching it was acting on her like a drug. Automatically her fingertips eased down the towel and sought the small indents either side of his spine just above the covered curve of his buttocks. She breathed in slowly and closed her eyes, stroking and circling, savouring the rush of pleasure surging through her as she caressed him.

'What the hell...?'

The angry curse with which he rejected her unplanned intimacy made her step back, exhaling shakily as her face started to burn at her own lack of professionalism, and then stand completely still as though transfixed. When he had moved away from her he had started to turn over. As he had done so the towel had slipped from his body allowing her to see that, no matter what that angry curse might have been intended to convey, the real evidence of the effect of her touch on him was there for her to see in the thick, strong erection he had inadvertently revealed.

Natalia couldn't take her gaze off it. He wasn't the first

client with a hard-on she had ever seen, of course; it was
a natural and automatic male reaction to female touch,
after all, she reminded herself. But this was the first time
she had reacted like this to a client. Massage was a form
of therapy and healing; she did not use it as an aid to turning herself on. By rights she should apologise, but what
was there for her to say? That she had loved the feel of his
flesh so much she had wanted to have more of it? Hardly.
She bent down, intending to pick up his robe and hand it
to him. Out of the corner of her eye she could see that he
was getting up off the massage table. Would he complain
about her to Maya and Howard?

How embarrassing would that be, given the true nature of her business relationship with them? She held out
the robe to him, determined not to look at him, but some
power greater than her own was obviously at work because against all logic she was reaching out and running
her fingertip down the dark line of hair that would take
her in only one direction.

She felt him contract his stomach muscles. Against her
touch or against his reaction to it?

'Look,' she heard him saying bitingly, 'I don't want…'
And then abruptly he stopped speaking and swung his legs
to the floor, reaching for her as he did so.

The shock of feeling his hands on her flesh beneath her
shift sliding up her bare thighs, and then further until his
fingers were massaging the rounded curves of her buttocks beneath her underwear, jolted through her, making
her shudder in violent mindless pleasure. She could smell
as well as feel her own arousal, with its familiar sleek
wetness and softly swollen flesh. She had thought she had
gone beyond the hyper-sexuality of those late teenage years
when learning about her body and its reactions, along with
learning about her own desires, had been safely in a haven

of deliberately chosen abstinence, where not experiencing sexual desire had been something she had accepted and preferred. But now she was having the security of that comfort wrenched from her, leaving her naked and exposed to what she was feeling. And as to what she was feeling...

Natalia was fighting hard to suppress her unwanted and unacceptable desire, but already she could feel the gathering tightness presaging an orgasm. As though a switch had been thrown inside that part of her mind that regulated how she thought and felt, suddenly she wasn't sensible, respectable Natalia Carini, bride-to-be of Prince Kadir, but a far more pagan Natalia, who was all hedonistic, sensual woman. Instinctively she struggled to hold back her body's response—not now out of rejection of her orgasm, but instead because, shockingly, this other Natalia actively wanted to prolong each millisecond of pleasure for as long as she could. Everything about Leon Perez dominated her senses, in a way that flooded past her defences. She had nothing within her experience to hold up to herself as a pattern card of what she could do to stop what she was feeling, because quite simply she had never, ever felt like this before. She longed, not just to touch him, but to taste him as well, to hear the sound of his breathing in the last seconds before he lost control, ragged and tortured in his need to possess her. She wanted to smell the hot, aroused male scent of him as it mingled with her own scent, creating a new fragrance that was unique to them, as potent and alive in its own way as though between them they had created a new life.

But most of all she wanted the experience of feeling him within her, her flesh sheathing his and holding it, her muscles stroking the most pleasurable of all pleasures into his, drawing the essence of life itself from him as sweetly and perfectly as she knew how to draw the essence of its per-

fume from a flower. It bemused her that she, who prided
herself on her mature restraint, should not only feel this
depth of passion, but actively relish giving in to it. Why?
Because she was about to get married? Because she had
not had sex in such a long, long time? Because of him, the
man himself?

Of the three options the one she preferred was the second, but wilfully her brain refused to accept her offer of it.
The warning of the closed door brought about by her marriage, then? It had to be that. It could not be him, this man.
It must not be, she told herself determinedly, knowing she
could not allow herself to accept what that might mean.

'Who are you? What are you…?' she could hear him
demanding thickly as he slid the shift from her body. 'Or
need I ask? No, don't tell me,' he answered his own question. 'Because we both know the answer. You are what your
sex knows so well how to be, deceit, full of promises and
tricks, all things to all men, for so long as it pleases you to
be.' There was a hard contempt in his voice matched with
bitterness and anger, but Natalia was oblivious to its warning and had no sensual space left to hear it, anyway. She
was totally lost in the dark surf like curl of pleasure she
was riding. Her soft, husky purr of approval at their intimacy swelled into the soft notes of the music and became
part of it. Never once had her thoughts ever even come
close to conjuring up a fulfilment for her as all consuming as the one her senses told her she would have with this
magnificent male. It felt so right to want him as completely
as she did. They were standing body to body, the aching
pressure between her legs growing with every breath she
took. She leaned forward, breathing in the scent of his
flesh, and then, placing her lips against it, she stroked her
hands down over him.

'No!'

The harshness of his rejection shocked through her. Her heart was thudding in uneven beats.

'You may have stolen from the other men you have shared your body with their right to be in control of your pleasure, but you will not do so with me,' he warned her. 'Where I come from it is the man who leads and the woman who follows, not the other way around. It is the man who takes and the woman who gives.' His hands were on her body, stroking far too slowly upwards towards her breasts, causing her breathing to become an uneven, jagged sound of repressed need.

Her breasts had become so engorged with arousal that the ache of her tightly stretched nipples had almost become a physical pain. When he touched one, cupping her breast and rubbing the pad of his thumb-tip over it, she cried out in raw need.

'Your flesh is the colour of almond milk brushed with sunset and gold. It demands the homage of a man's touch and it seeks to enslave him. But I will not be enslaved.'

Natalia could barely focus on his poetic words. She was on fire with the intensity of her own aching need. She reached up and placed her hands either side of his face, drawing him down towards her body, driven by her longing to feel his mouth against her flesh, and already ready to cry out with disappointment when he refused her.

And then to her disbelief he did something she had never in her wildest dreams imagined any man doing. He picked her up bodily in his arms and carried her over to the bed. She was just under six feet, and, whilst narrow-waisted, she was voluptuously curved and yet he was carrying her as though she were a size 00 and skin and bones. It was ridiculous to feel so thrilled and awed by such a basic display of masculinity, but yet she still was.

'Now,' he told her as he placed her on the bed and leaned

over her. 'Now I shall take from you what you are so willing to give me, even though my intellect tells me that it is a worthless offering worn thin by the hands of all the others who have possessed you before me.'

He was insulting her, but she was too aroused to check him and to retaliate that of the two of them she suspected his tally of past intimate partners would be far greater than hers. He was an adult male, after all, nearing forty, she suspected. A very sexual adult male, whereas she was a woman who had been celibate for what she now knew to be dangerously too long. Instead she arched up in obedience to the touch of the male hands shaping her, learning her, and then whilst she cried out and moved urgently against him he knew her with their touch, stroking open the secret places of her sex with the art a skilled perfumier might bring to drawing the most precious essence from deep within the heart of a rose. Somehow it was as though by his touch he were in some elemental way taking her apart and rebuilding her to fit his own desire, a sensual alchemist using the dark power of his sexuality to transmute her flesh into his creature. And she knew she would not have had it any differently. Her senses revelled in every small nuance of her own arousal and response, the lips of her sex swelling and opening eagerly to give him the glistening sweetness of her pleasure. Through just the touch of his fingertip he drew from her the sweet agony with ecstasy she had tried to hold at bay, earlier.

'No,' he commanded thickly, 'don't close your eyes.'

Obediently she gave him the eye contact he was demanding, holding nothing back as she allowed him to look past her barriers and share with her all that she was experiencing. Never, ever had she known such a powerful sense of being possessed. It consumed her utterly, leaving only the shell of her previous sexual self.

Her gaze heavy with her retreating pleasure, she watched as he parted her legs and positioned himself between them.

From somewhere he had produced the necessary means of protection, the rustle of its packaging striking a distant note of reassurance, even whilst a part of her still mourned the accompanying loss of the sensory pleasure of skin-to-skin, flesh-to-flesh intimacy with him.

From his first thrust within her Natalia knew what she had not wanted to let herself imagine; that this man was so perfectly physically formed for her that every particle of her responded to that knowledge. Her body opened softly and moistly for him, still sensitised by the pleasure he had already given it, holding him and gripping him, glorying in the width and the strength of him, tiny quivers of pre-orgasmic pleasure rippling through her as she lifted her hips and wrapped her toned body around him, wanting to draw him as deep within herself as she could. She could hear the thunder of their mutual heartbeat, shaking both their bodies; she could taste the warmth of his breath, smell the aroused heat of his flesh as it mingled with her own scent. With each thrust he took her deeper and higher, and with each counter movement she urged him on until there was no more climbing to be done, only that final leap together into eternity itself.

NATALIA DREW A shuddering breath of shocked disbelief. From the bathroom she could hear the sound of the shower running. She slid from the bed, pulling on her underwear and her shift with clumsy fingers. What had she done? No one must ever know about this. No one! Her anger against herself clawed at the back of her throat. How could she have been so reckless and so foolish? And for what? To have sex with a stranger? How sleazy that sounded. How against everything she believed about her own respect for herself.

The shower was still running. She had to get out of here before he came back. She was dressed now and, with no reason to stay and any number not to do so, why was she delaying?

Go, go now, she urged herself, before he comes back and humiliates you even more. Even *more*? Could there be any deeper humiliation than those words he had said to her as the final surges of her pleasure had subsided.

'Right,' he had told her tersely, as he had withdrawn from her and got up off the bed. 'You've had what you wanted, now go.'

What *she* had wanted! He had wanted it—*her*—too, hadn't he? Of course he had. But she had initiated it, hadn't she? And that was certainly something she had never done before.

She opened the door into the corridor, relieved to see that it was empty, and then hurried towards the lift that would take her down to her own room on the floor below. Thank God Maya had said he was leaving first thing in the morning. What had happened between them was a secret she would keep to herself for the rest of her life. For her own sake and for Niroli's. And thank God, too, for that safety-ensuring rustle she could hear echoing inside her head. At least that meant that the only repercussions from her uncharacteristic behaviour would be her ones she would carry within her senses and her conscience in secret.

How could she not feel conscience-stricken? After all, she wasn't just feeling guilty and suffused with shame because her behaviour went against her own personal moral code. There was also her awareness of her additional responsibility to the role she was about to play and the fact that she was about to become the wife of Niroli's future King. How could she have been so lost to all sense of what was right and proper and responsible as to have transgressed against the code she knew her agreement to marry Prince Kadir automatically enforced on her? As a royal bride, a royal wife, it would be of paramount importance that she was seen to be beyond any kind of moral reproach. She knew that King Giorgio would more than likely have had discreet enquiries made into her sexual past and had no doubt been reassured by her long-standing period of celibacy.

She must not dwell on what had happened. She must put it right out of her mind now. Either that or she must go to King Giorgio and tell him that she could not marry Prince Kadir. The surge of emotion that gripped her appalled her. So what if she was free? That did not mean that he…this Leon Perez would want her again. No, what she was thinking was crazy. So crazy that it scared her. And besides, she had her duty to think of, her already-given commitment. No, her mind was made up, her future decided, and it would not be a future filled with the sickness of longing for a man who had already made it plain just how he felt about her.

Like someone fearing drowning, Natalia clung to the knowledge that she was committed to marrying Prince Kadir. What she had done was dreadful, unforgivable, appalling—a form of madness. She must learn to accept and then forget it as some last-minute form of prenuptial panic that her senses had sprung on her. Something that was now over and done with and in the past, whilst she must look towards her already-planned future.

CHAPTER THREE

KADIR LOOKED GRIMLY round the now-empty bedroom. She had gone. Good. The music she had left playing was still on and the dimmed lights were far too evocative a reminder of what had happened, but nowhere near as compelling as the scent of her, which seemed to cling to his own flesh despite his shower. It was an unusual blend of sensual warmth spiced with something he couldn't name, and it had insinuated itself into his awareness in a way that infuriated him.

What was he doing wasting time thinking about her? She was nothing to him. Nothing, just a woman who was a sexual opportunist. He wouldn't have gone near her if it hadn't been for the fact that a near deathbed promise wrung from him by his dying mother that he end his relationship with his mistress had resulted in a period of celibacy far longer than he was used to. That was the only reason for what had happened, the only explanation there could be.

After all, it hardly suited the new roles he was about to take on, of both King-in-waiting and newly married man, for him to be having sex with a stranger; a masseuse, for heaven's sake. What had happened to his self-control? He normally found it easy to control his sexual appetite. She hadn't even been his type—he liked petite women, not sensual Amazons with lush curves and demanding sexual appetites. Yet he had allowed his loins to rule his head.

Well, it certainly must not happen again—not with any woman.

Kadir had no intention of being one of those rulers who pretended to have a certain moral stance in public whilst freely indulging in the most salacious of habits in private. There had never been a time in his life when sensual promiscuity had appealed to him. There had been women, yes, especially during his years on the professional polo circuit, but those were long behind him now and the only women to share his bed these last years had been a modest succession of discreet mistresses, of which Zahra had been the latest.

He had known her for many years, but they had only become lovers after her husband's death. From his point of view it had been a very convenient and practical arrangement. Kadir liked such arrangements; emotions weren't something he wanted to bring into his relationships, and an over-emotional mistress was the last thing he wanted. Or had been. Surely now the last thing he wanted was an emotional new wife.

It had been some financial business connected with his late mother's estate that had brought him to Venice, and he was glad now that he had without thinking booked into the hotel using his alias from his polo-playing days.

From what he had learned about King Giorgio his father might have enjoyed a pretty varied sex life himself, but he had very strict views on the conduct of current members of the Nirolian royal family, especially his own heir.

Kadir's frown deepened. Should she discover who he was and try to make use of that information, he might be forced to defend his behaviour to his father and the thought of that was totally unpalatable. How could he have put himself in such a situation? And with such a woman; the very antithesis of everything he personally wanted to see in a woman—especially one who shared his bed.

It was lucky that he had had the means of protection to

hand, otherwise… Otherwise he would have stopped; there was no question of that. How could there be? He had a responsibility, after all, not just to himself, but to the woman he was committed to marrying. Was he really so sure that he could have stopped? Kadir swore inwardly as he ground the taunting inner voice into silence.

It was too late now to wish that he hadn't come to Venice. His mother had loved the city. 'It is like a miracle to those of us born of the desert to live in a city of water,' she had once told him.

Kadir's mouth hardened with bitterness. He had thought he had known his mother; had believed he shared a special closeness with her, but he had been deceiving himself just as she had deceived him. The last thing he had expected in those final days before she had finally succumbed to the fatal illness that had stalked her all summer was to hear her tell him that the man he had always thought of as his father had been no such thing and that, instead, he was the result of a youthful affair she had had with a European. And not just any European, but King Giorgio of Niroli, the head of what was reputed to be Europe's richest royal family. Not that money was of any primary concern to him. Kadir had turned the million-plus inheritance he had received from his maternal grandfather into a billion-figure empire before he had reached his thirtieth birthday, thanks to his own financial and entrepreneurial skills. No, he had no need of King Giorgio's wealth, and no real need either of the title he would inherit from him, but what he did need was to find out if this new persona his mother's revelations had given him fitted him more comfortably than the one he had always previously worn. And if didn't? If he felt as alien and apart from those he lived amongst as King Giorgio's son and heir as he had done as Hadiya's sheikh, then what? Then he would just have to live with it. He was forty now, after all, not an untried boy who knew nothing of himself. Niroli would give him the chance to stretch himself, to prove himself in many ways that ruling Hadiya could not. Besides, it was too late now for him to change his mind. He had given his commitment to his brother, Ahmed, to support his claim to become Hadiya's new sheikh and he had also given his commitment to his as yet unmet father to become Niroli's next King.

But whilst the outcome of his mother's revelations might ultimately be to his benefit, Kadir could not overcome his sense of betrayal that his mother could have kept something so important to him a secret.

She had begged him to understand and to forgive her, telling him that she had already been promised in marriage to her husband when she had met King Giorgio. She'd stopped off on the island of Niroli on her way home to Hadiya. According to her, theirs had been an intensely passionate and equally intensely brief affair, and her marriage to her husband had taken place before she had realised she was carrying King Giorgio's child.

'So why tell me now,' he had demanded angrily, 'since you have not seen fit to do so before?'

'Before I was afraid for you,' she had told him. 'Everyone assumed that you were the legitimate heir to the sheikdom and I could not bear to be responsible for taking that from you. But now…I am close to death, my son, and I have watched you these last weeks since your uncle died. For all that you are ready to assume your responsibilities to Hadiya I can see that you do not have the heart to do so. You have always yearned to be free of the restrictions our small kingdom has imposed on you. Where your brother is content to go and count the revenues from Hadiya's oil wells and listen to the state advisers, you could never exist beneath the yoke of another's rule.

'There is something I want you to do for me, Kadir.'

That was when she had produced the small gold amulet, worn and thin and decorated with ancient writing.

'King Giorgio gave me this. I want you to return it to him for me—and in person. I have kept an interest in his world over the years and I understand that King Giorgio is in despair because he does not have a direct male heir to inherit the throne from him. You are his son, Kadir. Your rightful place is on the throne of Niroli, not here in Hadiya where I have always known you have never quite felt at home. Oh, you have tried, but I have seen your impatience with our ways, and your desire to live a different kind of life. You have learned the subtleties of the way we in the East do business, but I have seen in your eyes that you are impatient of it and that you yearn for the directness of your European heritage.'

'If by that you mean that I resent the paying of large bribes to already wealthy men when the poorest of our world go without, then, yes, I do grow impatient,' he had agreed tersely.

She had died three days after making her confession to him, and Kadir knew that his gentle brother had been shocked by his inability to shed any tears for her.

Women! What sane man would ever trust one? He had learned young about their duplicity. He had been just eighteen when he had discovered that the bride chosen for him by his family was far from being the innocent sweet virgin she was supposed to be and had in fact been having an affair with a married cousin for over a year. It wouldn't be true to say that the discovery of her deceit had broken his heart. He had broken off the betrothal—it had been an arranged marriage, after all—but it had certainly taught him to mistrust the female sex. They lied when it suited them to do so, with their kisses and their protestations of love, and far more importantly they lied about their fidelity. He had learned that much the hard way. What infuriated him now, though, was that, knowing what he did, he had still given way too easily to his own physical desire for the woman who had just left him. Why? Why? Because his need to possess her had been stronger than anything he had ever experienced. That was rubbish, he denied his inner voice angrily. Total rubbish. She had been the one who had come on to him, after all. And he had been the one who had taken her, so filled with need for her that he couldn't stop himself. A moment's aberration, that was all…a nothing…to be obliterated as though it had never been, like an empty Bedouin camp covered by the desert sands.

He looked down at the amulet he was holding. It had still been warm from her own flesh when his mother had handed it to him and sometimes when he held it in his hand and closed his eyes he could almost convince himself that he could still feel the echo of an imprint of that warmth on it. As a boy he had thought his mother the most beautiful and wonderful woman in the whole world, and she in turn had adored him. Adored him but kept from him the truth about his parentage.

When she had given him the amulet she might have had some romantic idea of him turning up on Niroli barefoot and ragged from some solitary and arduous odyssey spent journeying to claim his birthright and being welcomed by his father with tears of joy. But modern life wasn't like that.

Far from travelling like some would be Ulysses he had initially simply and discreetly let it be known through the right diplomatic channels that he and the King of Niroli needed to make personal contact with one another.

The result had been a flurry of letters and telephone calls interspersed with terse emails from the king's more IT-savvy advisers, and a DNA test to establish the truth of his mother's claim, all without he and King Giorgio ever speaking personally to one another, never mind setting eyes on one another.

Cynically he was inclined to suspect that it was the result of the DNA test that had ultimately led to King Giorgio's formal offer to him of the throne of Niroli.

Further negotiations had followed once he had been able to establish that his brother was willing to step in and rule Hadiya in his place. Negotiations during which he had raised his own concerns about the willingness of the people of Niroli to accept him as their absolute ruler. King Giorgio's response to his concern had been to suggest that a diplomatic marriage should be arranged for him with a Nirolian woman who would be welcomed as their queen by the people.

Historically in Arab society there was no right of primogeniture—a man made his way within his extended family by his own skills and strengths and he married where he could achieve the best bargain for himself in terms of the benefits the marriage would bring. And therefore Kadir had no issues with the fact that his wife-to-be was the granddaughter of the island's most senior vintner. What she was bringing to the marriage bargain would be of far more value to him that any supposed blue blood.

With everything organised for him to fly direct from Hadiya to Niroli at the end of the week, this matter of his mother's still-outstanding Venetian bank account and business interests had needed resolving, and so he had flown here *en route,* reawakening an old polo injury ache in doing so, hence his decision to book into the spa, which he knew was one favoured by top sportsmen and women.

In the morning he was leaving by private jet for Niroli. The king had been quite specific that he did not want his people to know of their relationship until he himself presented him to them as his son and their new King-to-be, followed by an immediate announcement of his marriage to Natalia Carini, and, being the man he was, Kadir had thought that it made good sense to arrive ahead of schedule just to see how his father would react. From what he had heard of him King Giorgio was an autocratic ruler who refused to delegate, or allow his country to change.

Kadir intended to make it plain to him that if *he* was to rule then he fully intended to rule alone and on his own terms.

He looked at the door again. Where had she gone? To another man's bed? His fist closed round the amulet, and then he made a sound of angry self-disgust as he turned on his heel and picked up his laptop. He had more important things to do than think about a promiscuous pleasure-giver whom he would never see again—nor would ever want to see again.

As SHE WALKED across the square Natalia was oblivious to the admiring looks she was attracting from passers-by. Yesterday's mist had turned into a soft drizzly rain that lay like diamond drops on the darkness of her hair, causing its soft waves to turn into rebellious curls. She wasn't doing this in the hope of seeing Leon Perez and she certainly hadn't humiliated herself by checking the register to see if he had actually checked out this morning. No, she was crossing the square because she needed some fresh air, some space inside her head in which to come to terms with her own horror at what she had done. The only saving grace of the whole incident, if it could be called such, was the fact that he Leon Perez thankfully—mercifully—had used protection, so she need have no concerns about there being any repercussions of any kind from their intimacy. It made her feel physically sick to think of the potential consequences if he hadn't done. How could she have been so lost to everything to have taken such a risk—to her own health, to the trust King Giorgio had placed in her, to her husband-to-be's right to expect her to come to him free of any kind of taint from another relationship?

She could see a coffee shop up ahead of her and she ducked into its crowded warmth. Her mobile started to ring. She put down her cappuccino so that she could answer the call.

'The king wishes you to return to Niroli immediately,' she heard the voice of the king's most senior minister informing her tersely.

'Immediately? But why?'

'I cannot tell you any more.'

'But my flight back is booked for the day after tomorrow, and I don't know if I can—'

'A private flight has been arranged for you. All you need to do is present yourself at the special check-in desk at the airport.'

'But why? What is going on?' Natalia started to demand but it was too late; the King's Chief Minister had already ended the call.

'Have you finished with the table?'

'What? Oh, yes,' she confirmed, getting up to let the two young women take over the table.

Outside it was still drizzling. Niroli had a warm and sunny climate all year round, rather like that of the Canaries, albeit with seasonal fluctuations, and the drizzle and its accompanying grey skies made her shiver.

What was behind the urgent summons of her to return ahead of schedule?

Had the new heir changed his mind about their marriage and, if so, how did she feel about that? Natalia wondered just over a couple of hours later when she had been escorted on board her private flight to Niroli.

'What would you like to drink?' the smiling steward was asking her. 'We have champagne?'

Natalia could feel the movement of the sleek modern jet as it started to roll down the runway. A feeling of panic gripped her but she swiftly controlled it. This was it, she was on her way—not just home, but to her future and her future husband. 'No…no champagne, thank you,' she told the steward hollowly. 'Just water, please.'

CHAPTER FOUR

'BUT THIS IS ridiculous,' Natalia objected to the driver of the imposing chauffeur-driven car that had been waiting for her right on the runway the moment her plane touched down. 'I don't want to go to the palace; I want you to take me home.'

'I'm sorry, but my orders are to take you to the palace,' the driver told her woodenly.

Natalia stared out of the blacked-out windows in frustrated silence. This was crazy. What on earth was going on? Why on earth hadn't an official from the palace been waiting in the car for her to explain everything?

The sky had turned clear blue-green, and was now shading into midnight-blue velvet as darkness fell and the car sped along the modern ceremonial highway linking the palace and the main town to the airport.

Up ahead of them Natalia could see the lights of the town itself, crowned by the familiar sight of the royal palace.

The driver took an unexpected detour, skirting the town, and taking her off guard as he drove down a very narrow road that led to the back of the castle.

So, Natalia decided wryly, whilst her presence was commanded and so important apparently that she had been flown home in a private jet, her person was still unimportant enough to have to enter the palace via what looked very like much a tradesman's entrance to judge from its gateway—so narrow that she sucked in her breath fearing that the car was too wide to fit through it. Beyond the gateway lay a dank, unlit courtyard, the windows overlooking it were shuttered and the whole atmosphere was inhospitable and unwelcoming.

The chauffer had brought the car to a halt and was getting out to open the door for her. Despite her irritation, Natalia still managed to find a warm smile for him. He was after all merely following instructions.

This cloak-and-dagger type of thing was in many ways typical of the way King Giorgio ran his court, she thought ruefully. It wasn't unknown for those who knew him best to exclaim in irritated exasperation that Machiavelli ought to have been King Giorgio's middle name. The old king loved playing people off against one another, and always had done, Natalia acknowledged, but she admitted that she had come to feel a certain amount of sympathy for him as one after the other the candidates for his heir had had to be rejected. He might be arrogant and proud, but he was also old, and she suspected he had begun to feel real fear about what would happen to Niroli if he died without appointing his own successor. For all his faults, and she wasn't going to deny that they were many, no one could ever doubt his fierce love for his country. A love that she of course shared, as he well knew. He had surprised her once by telling her that she reminded him a little of his first wife, Queen Sophia, and that she had the same elegance and spirit. Natalia had been touched and flattered by his words, knowing how well thought of his first queen had been by the people of Niroli and those who knew her more closely. She suspected that it was in part because of this likeness to Queen Sophia that King Giorgio had initially conceived the idea of her marrying his newfound son.

A door was opening, a man coming towards her, although because of the lack of proper lighting she didn't realise that it was the King's Chief Minister until he reached her.

'Why all the urgency and secrecy? What on earth is going on?' she demanded.

'Come this way. I'll explain everything to you as I escort you to your apartment.'

Natalia, who had been on the point of walking into the palace, stopped and turned to look at him.

'My what?'

'Since you are about to be proclaimed as the official fiancée of King Giorgio's successor, it is only fitting that you should have your own apartments within the palace.'

'But I have my own home…'

'That is no longer suitable. Countess Ficino has been appointed as your personal lady-in-waiting. She will be responsible for the day-to-day organisation of your diary, and all matters relating to your wardrobe and your official duties. She will also be on hand to instruct you in matters of royal protocol.

'It is a pity that His Highness Prince Kadir has chosen to arrive ahead of schedule.'

'Prince Kadir is here? But I thought…'

'Exactly. However, it seems His Highness was so eager to make the acquaintance of his father and fulfil the promise he made to his mother on her deathbed that he gave into the impulse to arrive early.'

At any other time the stiff disapproval in the Chief Minister's voice would have amused her. The whole court operated under a routine so regimented and rigid that it was centuries out of date. Any hint of spontaneity was not merely discouraged, but actively stifled, and the prince would very quickly have been made aware of his crime in deviating from the agreed arrangements. Right now, though, she felt too irritated by the way her own life had suddenly been taken over to feel amused.

'The king fears that it will not be possible to keep his son's presence confidential for very long and for that reason he has brought forward both the official announcement of their relationship and of your betrothal.

'The palace's press officer has already alerted the media to the fact that a very important announcement is about to be made. That is one of the reasons why you were brought into the palace in the way that you were. Men are already working in the courtyard square in front of the palace decorating it ahead of tomorrow's speech from the king to present Prince Kadir to the people.'

'Tomorrow?'

The Chief Minister paused to direct her down a long corridor hung with gloomy portraits of past Nirolian heads of state. At the end a flight of marble stairs swept coldly upwards. At the top of them Natalia could see the familiar figure of the elderly countess waiting for her, her hands folded in front of her.

Natalia's brain was pulsing with questions but she knew there was no point in expecting answers from the elderly courtiers now flanking her. They were too steeped in the traditions of their roles to unbend enough to tell her for instance just what her husband-to-be looked like, and what kind of nature he might have.

Not that it sounded as though she was going to have to wait very long to find out herself, she admitted as she was handed over into the 'care' of the countess, who then escorted her up another flight of stairs and down another corridor to a pair of double doors.

'You will present yourself in the Royal Chamber tomorrow morning at eleven a.m. exactly. From there you witness the king making his official introduction of Prince

Kadir to the people of Niroli from the salon adjoining the balcony. You will then wait fifteen minutes exactly before joining them on the balcony, where you will be introduced to Prince Kadir, and where you will both receive the king's royal blessing on your betrothal and forthcoming marriage.'

She pushed open the doors to the 'apartment' inviting Natalia into the large salon that lay beyond them. Natalia's heart sank as she surveyed the heavy old-fashioned décor of the room. Three young women were standing with bowed heads, each of them dipping a curtsey in turn as the countess introduced them as her personal maids.

Natalia was used to managing her own staff, and she greeted each girl warmly in turn, asking them for their Christian names. She could see that the countess did not approve of this informality but she ignored her disapproval. It was high time that the fresh air of modern life blew away some of the restrictions of court life.

'It is late, and you will of course wish to sleep ready for tomorrow, but first, it is my duty to tell you that the king has provided you with a new wardrobe to suit your new role, and I have given instructions to your maids as to which outfit you are to wear tomorrow for the official announcement of your betrothal.

'Additionally, I shall come to you just prior to you making your way to the Royal Chamber to ensure that everything is in order. I should warn you that whilst you are on the balcony the king intends to bestow on you some of the royal jewels that belonged to Queen Sophia. You will of course wear them as well during the formal reception that will follow the balcony announcements, but they are to be returned to me afterwards so that they may be put safely under lock and key.'

A new wardrobe; royal jewels. She should have anticipated something like this, but somehow she had not done so, Natalia admitted. It all seemed so outdated and ridiculous. She had seen the jewels worn by the king's second wife and she shuddered with horror at the thought of having to be weighed down with anything similar. It went against everything she believed in about the duty to help those less fortunate than herself to allow herself to be used as a display for so much wealth. It was one of her dreams that in time she might be able to influence her husband enough to persuade him to share at least some of the Nirolian royal family's fabled wealth with, not just Niroli's people, but all those people throughout the world who were in need. A charity to explore ways to develop better health care for everyone was just one of the things she would like to establish. It was things such as this that would be her reward for becoming Queen, not rows of diamond necklaces.

'I shall leave you now to prepare yourself for the morning.'

The countess made it sound as though she were about to go to the guillotine, Natalia decided ruefully, and perhaps in some ways she was. After all, her marriage to Prince Kadir would mark a very sharp slicing-off point between her old life and her new and it would certainly sever her from the sexual freedoms that belonged to a modern-day single woman. Why was she thinking that now? Not because of last night, Natalia hoped.

'If there is anything you should wish for,' the countess was saying, 'something to eat, a book to read perhaps, then one of your personal maids will be on hand to bring them to you.'

To *bring* them to her? What was wrong with her nipping out into the city and getting them herself? Natalia wondered independently as she thanked the countess and waited for her to leave. After all, for now at least she was still merely Natalia Carini and as such free surely to enjoy the anonymity of being just that.

The three anxious-looking young maids looked as relieved to be dismissed as she was to dismiss then, she thought wryly ten minutes after they had gone and she had her new apartment to herself.

Who had used these rooms last? she wondered. Although the beautiful inlaid wooden furniture was polished and dust-free and every surface sparkled under the huge chandeliers, the salon still had an air of disuse and melancholy about it. Huge swathes of silk brocade covered the windows blotting out the light, and the same fabric had been used to cover the baroque-style gilded chairs and sofas scattered around the room. The colour of the fabric at least she could admire, since its sea-green-blue colour, under the light of the chandeliers, was only a few shades lighter than the colour of her own eyes. Natalia suspected it would originally have been chosen to reflect the colour of the sea, which this side of the palace would look out over.

A carpet replicated the intricate plasterwork design on the ceiling. A huge gilt-framed mirror hung above the fireplace reflecting the elegant proportions of the room with its matching pairs of double doors at either side of the opposite wall. One pair as she already knew led into the corridor, the other pair must therefore take her towards her bedroom.

Beautiful though this room was, it was quite simply not 'her'. She liked modern, pared-down décor, and simple natural fibres. She was fussy about what she bought, choosing only 'green' products, and just as fussy about sourcing them to make sure that the workers who produced them had not been exploited.

The small anteroom into which she had walked had another pair of double doors in it which as she had expected opened into her bedroom.

Her heart sank the minute she stepped into it. The décor echoed, indeed complemented, that in the salon. A huge ornate French rococo-style bed was draped and swathed in the same silk, two further sets of double doors opened off it, both of them open. Through one lay a large bathroom with an enormous claw-footed bath, whilst the other pair led into a large wardrobed dressing room, which, as Natalia discovered when she walked into it, also had a door leading into the bathroom.

Someone had already opened and unpacked the suitcase she had brought with her from Venice. Behind these wardrobe doors lay the new clothes the king was providing her with for her new role. Trying to quell the horrible sinking sensation invading her stomach, she took a deep breath and opened the first pair of wardrobe doors. And then closed them again after one appalled look at the row of stiff satin evening 'gowns' and formally tailored silk suits—clothes far more suited surely to Queen Eva then they ever would be to her. Puce, jade-green, peacock-blue were not colours she favoured or that suited her, just as stiff tailoring was not her style. She thought longingly and rather angrily of her own clothes, soft, unstructured clothes in natural fabrics and colours that flowed round her body instead of constricting it.

She couldn't offend the king by refusing to wear what amounted to a gift from him, although she had no doubt that these garments had been chosen more with the dignity and image of the crown in mind than her feelings.

Those couture clothes with their intricate stitching and beading surely epitomised everything that she so passionately wanted to see changed about the monarchy and its relationship with the people of Niroli. In these modern times true respect surely came from having a monarchy that could be truly respected for the way the members of it lived their lives and cared for their people rather than being feared and admired for the power of their wealth and status.

CHAPTER FIVE

'MY SON…' KING Giorgio murmured emotionally as he reached out to place his hand over Kadir's and shook his head in wonderment.

'Even now I still cannot believe it. It is like a miracle…' His expression changed, becoming harsh and stern. 'Your mother had no right to conceal your existence from me. But then that is women for you—enchanting creatures though they can be, they are not to be trusted to think or behave logically. It is a poor apology for a man, in my opinion, who allows a woman to rule him. But you, I can see, are not such a man, Kadir.'

Kadir could see the old king's emotions threatening to overwhelm him as he blinked and shook his head.

'To think that all this time when I had begun to despair of ever finding someone of my blood who was fit to rule Niroli after me, you should be there, the best and most suitable of all. My son…my son,' he repeated, clasping Kadir's arm firmly.

'Your mother did us both a great disservice in not revealing your true paternity earlier.'

His father's angry bitterness reflected his own feelings, Kadir admitted. In that as in so many other things—he was quickly coming to discover that he and the man who had fathered him were very alike. However, from the moment he had arrived at the palace, ahead of schedule, and not because of anything whatsoever to do with the woman who had so enflamed his desire in Venice, he had fought against picturing his mother here, a young virgin on her way to her marriage succumbing to the experienced sensual charm of the island's powerful King. These were not the mental images of his mother he wished to have, and so, like his unwanted memories of Venice, Kadir firmly refused to allow them space inside his head.

'Your mother would have deprived you of a truly great future if she had not acknowledged your true paternity,' the king was boasting.

'There are those who consider that becoming Ruler of Hadiya is a great future,' Kadir pointed out.

'Hadiya…' The king gave a dismissive shrug. 'How can ruling a few square kilometres of desert compare with ruling Niroli?'

'It is what lies beneath Hadiya's desert that gives it its wealth,' Kadir told him dryly. 'And there are many so-called rich Western nations who would sacrifice their pretty views for Hadiya's sands—and its oil.'

Kadir could tell that the king didn't like what he was saying, but he had no intention of allowing his newfound father to bully him. The late sheikh, his father, had been a powerful and autocratic ruler and one who commanded and indeed demanded obedience from all around him. Whilst his younger brother had accepted this easily and good-naturedly, Kadir had always fought against it and fought too to establish his own independence of spirit and outlook. He was not about to allow another autocrat to think he could rule him now at this stage of his life, even if that autocrat was his father, and, despite all his efforts to conceal it, growing tired and vulnerable.

'Here on Niroli when its crown is placed on your head you will be inheriting more than mere wealth,' the old king told him. 'You will be inheriting your true birthright.'

At forty he was surely old enough not to be swayed by such blatant emotional manipulation, Kadir told himself wryly, but there was a suspicious sheen of moisture in his father's eyes and a small tremor in his voice that threatened to undermine his own cynicism. Despite the king's outer shell of arrogance and disdain and his apparent lack of regard for those he considered to be of lower status than himself, especially the female sex, there was hidden within him some emotional vulnerability. Kadir was not easily swayed by the emotions of others, though. He had spent too many years concealing and even denying his own emotions to feel sympathy with emotional vulnerability in others. The truth was that he had spent far too long learning to protect himself by remaining 'apart' from society to abandon that defence system now.

It was in King Giorgio's interests, after all, to make him feel welcome and wanted. That did not mean the older man really felt like a father towards him. For the same reason Kadir did not allow himself to believe now that simply because King Giorgio was his natural father that meant that the people of Niroli would accept him with the same emotional delight as the king. Or that he himself would be able to feel the same sense of commitment and belonging that his father felt for his country. After all, he had not grown up here; as yet he felt no sense of kinship with it or with those who had.

What he did have, though, was the strong belief that here on Niroli he could put into practice the skills of government and diplomacy and leadership in his own way. His hope was that Niroli would give him the opportunity to stretch himself politically in the mainstream of the world arena in all the ways that Hadiya never could. And that in doing so he would find the inner peace and sense of himself that had previously always eluded him.

'Our people are already gathering in the square, crowding into it now according to the Chief Minister. They will welcome you, Kadir, because I, their King, am welcoming you, just as they will recognise you as their future King. All the more so, of course, when they learn that you are to marry Natalia Carini. I personally have chosen her to be your bride. She comes from an old Nirolian family, much respected on the island. Natalia lives and breathes Niroli; she will teach you all that you will need to know about the ways of the people. She is close to them and understands them.'

The picture his father was painting of his bride-to-be was not exactly one to stir a man to desire, Kadir thought cynically. Not that it mattered whether or not he desired her, just so long as he fathered a son on her. Those were the rules of the game as he had grown up knowing it to be played and it did not concern him that he might not find Natalia Carini physically attractive. That was what a man who had to make a dynastic marriage accepted. He did, however, think it ominous that this father had not made any attempt to introduce them to one another prior to the imminent public announcement of their betrothal.

'I do not know how much time I may have left and for that reason, if no other, I have decided that your marriage to Natalia will take place in ten days' time,' the king told him. 'The arrangements for it are already in hand.'

Kadir frowned. He might have grown up in a royal household and indeed expected to succeed to its throne, but he was still not used to having such an important part of his life arranged for him in this autocratic manner, without being consulted beforehand. In Hadiya he would have had his own choice of bride, and not had one forced upon him.

'Won't the people find it somewhat suspicious that we rush into such a swift union?'

'If by suspicious you mean they might think you have already got her with child, then surely that would be all to the good. I know my people. There is nothing that will make them embrace you as their future King more eagerly than the birth of your son to a Nirolian wife.'

First marriage and now fatherhood, Kadir frowned.

'I still have certain duties I must perform in Hadiya, duties connected with the official handover of power to my younger brother, and which require my presence there.'

'That is easily dealt with. As soon as you are married you and Natalia can travel to Hadiya on honeymoon.'

Their conversation was interrupted as the Chief Minister came hurrying into the room.

'Your Highness,' he addressed the king, 'it is almost time. The people are already gathering, and Prince Kadir needs to change into the formal robes of state ready to be proclaimed your heir.'

'YOU DON'T REALLY expect me to wear that!' Natalia stared in revulsion at the satin corset with its heavy-jewelled beading. It looked more like an instrument of torture than an article of clothing.

'The king specifically desires that you wear it. It is a copy of the gown worn by his first wife at her own betrothal,' the countess told Natalia stiffly. 'It is his belief that the sight of you in it will remind the people of their love for Queen Sophia and that they will transfer that love to you.'

And, of course King Giorgio, being the man he was, would never let slip an opportunity to trade on the loyalty of his people for his own ends, Natalia acknowledged disapprovingly, although in this instance she was obliged to admit that serving his own ends would also benefit his people.

The bodice of the gown had to be laced up so tightly

that she could hardly breathe and then the straight, elegant column of its skirt attached to it. She had already endured an hour with a hairdresser summoned to put her hair up in a stiffly regal style and now as she looked at herself in the mirror the only familiar part of herself she felt she had to comfort her was the subtlety of her own specially blended scent.

There was a knock on the outer doors to her apartment and then they were opened to reveal the small phalanx of traditionally costumed palace guards.

It was time for her to go.

Once she walked through these doors she would be leaving Natalia Carini behind for ever.

When she walked back through them in her place would be the betrothed fiancée, soon-to-be wife, of Crown Prince Kadir of Niroli.

KADIR COULD HEAR the excited buzz of the crowd outside in the large courtyard below them. This room with its balcony onto the courtyard, according to his father, had been traditionally the place from which past kings had always addressed their people, giving them news both good and bad.

The doors to the balcony were hung with the Nirolian flag and the coat of arms of his father's family and that too of his mother's, and now those doors were flung open to a shrill fanfare of trumpets. As they stepped forward onto the balcony Kadir saw the rainbow-coloured ribbons of flowers and confetti being hurled into the air as the band in the square played the national anthem. The gaudy brilliance of the celebratory colours matched the excitement in the crowd as they yelled and cheered their joy.

He barely knew his father as a father; they were meeting now as two mature men both with their own agendas to promote. A fierce surge of unexpected emotion stabbed painfully through him, catching him off guard. He was forty years old, for heaven's sake, far too old and too self-aware to start mourning some sentimentalised vision of a non-existent father-and-son relationship.

King Giorgio stepped forward holding up his hands for silence.

'My people,' he announced. 'I give you my son.'

NATALIA COULD HEAR the frenzied roar of the crowd as she stood in the shadows of the balcony room, waiting for her summons to join the king and her future husband. Down there amongst them would be her grandfather and other members of her extended family. No matter what other past quarrels might lie between them, her grandfather and King Giorgio were united in their love for Niroli.

Through the open doors she could hear the king's voice, trembling slightly now. With age? With emotion? His stirring words had certainly elicited a roar of approval from the listening crowd.

'We must always remember that there is a purpose in all things,' the king was saying. 'When one after another my heirs disqualified themselves from the right to follow me onto the throne, I was filled with despair, for you, my people, and for my country, not knowing then as I know now that fate had already chosen the one who will come after me; the son I did not know I had.

'A chance meeting many years ago led to his conception, hidden from me and kept hidden until his mother relented and confessed to him on her deathbed that I had fathered him. Prince Kadir has given up his right to rule the Kingdom of Hadiya to take on the mantle of his duty to his blood, my blood, your blood, people of Niroli. He will need help if he is to rule you as you deserve to be ruled and to that end it is my pleasure to inform you that my son, and your future King, Prince Kadir, will in ten days be married to Natalia Carini, daughter of Niroli.'

As the roars of approval surged upwards from the crowd Natalia felt the countess give her a small push. Automatically she took a step forward, and then another, her heart thudding frantically inside her chest cavity.

The brilliant sunlight after the shadows of the salon momentarily blinded her as she stepped out onto the balcony, trying not to wince at the shrillness of the trumpeters.

The king was standing in the middle of the balcony. She dropped him a small stiff curtsey and felt her bodice corset digging into her flesh as she did so. Behind her the court dignitaries were filing onto the balcony; below her the crowd was cheering and calling out her name exuberantly, 'Natalia. Natalia… You are a true Princess of Niroli.' The air was filled with the scent of the bombs of flower petals being thrown by the revellers, some of whom were already dancing to the impromptu burst of music from a lone musician.

'Daughter of Niroli,' she could hear the king saying firmly, 'give me your hand so that I in turn may symbolically unite it, and thus you, here in front of our people with the hand and the person of our chosen heir, my son Prince Kadir.'

The king was reaching for her hand, and for the first time Natalia was able to look past King Giorgio and at her future husband.

The world swung dizzily around her as though she had been scooped up and were being swung from a funfair wheel. *Him! The man from Venice!* Leon Perez! Surely there was some mistake, and she was just imagining…but, no…it was quite definitely him! Prince Kadir, her husband-to-be, was Leon Perez, and the man she had made love with in Venice. It couldn't possibly be, but it was!

The shock struck right through to her heart, pinioning her with disbelief, sucking the air from her lungs and turning the bright sunshine dark. The sound of the crowd became a dull roar reaching her from a distant place. From that place she was only vaguely aware of the laughing excitement of the crowd being checked and then becoming a low-voiced sound of confused anxiety as they saw her sway and then semi stumble.

Natalia was oblivious to their concern. All she could see was the man who was to be her husband. He might be dressed in the historical dress uniform of the Commander-in-Chief of Niroli's Armed Forces, a cloak of dark green velvet lined with ermine slung from one shoulder, and the Nirolian Seal of State ring very evident on his ring finger, but none of that could mask the reality of the fact that he was the same man she had had sex with in Venice.

A hard hand gripped her by the elbow keeping her upright as she swayed, a too well remembered male scent shocking her senses. The murderous look he was giving her was enough to have her stomach lurching without his for-her-ears-only, 'Pull yourself together,' mouthed against her ear as he made a pretence of showing concern for her.

Somehow she managed to force herself to turn to the crowd and smile as the king placed her now-icy-cold hand on that of his son and heir, Niroli's future King and her future husband.

'My people,' King Giorgio announced emotionally. 'I give you my son and his betrothed, your future King and Queen. May their lives together be spent in joyful service to our country and may they be blessed with the gift of children to carry on our traditions after them. I ask you to pledge to them your loyalty and love, as they pledge theirs to you. My people, will you accept Prince Kadir as your future King and his wife-to-be Natalia Carini as your future Queen?'

'We will…' the crowd roared as though with one voice.

THEIR ACCEPTANCE SEEMED to reverberate throughout the square as though sending its message to every part of the island, Natalia thought as she was overwhelmed by her own feeling of kinship with the people down below her in the crowd. She was a part of them and they of her in a way that the king and even less his son could ever be. She had been born amongst them and had grown up with them. She would, she promised silently, from now on dedicate herself to her service to them and to her country.

The crowd was now going wild with joy, some of the younger and bolder onlookers calling up to the balcony, 'Kiss her, Your Highness. Kiss your bride-to-be.' It was all Natalia could do to struggle to assimilate the true enormity of what was happening. How could this be? How could the man she had given herself to so ill advisedly in Venice be her future husband? She felt feverish and yet also cold, numb and yet acutely sensitive.

As though in obedience to the wishes of the crowd Kadir was leaning toward her. Instinctively she pulled back, as alarmed as though she were sixteen and a virgin and not twenty-nine and a mature woman. The hand clasping hers tightened its grip to an almost bone-crushingly punishing intensity, the green eyes sent her a message of warning and fury, and then the hard-cut male mouth was brushing hers to put a cold seal on the prison she herself had willingly walked into.

'One more thing,' King Giorgio was saying, as he had to raise his voice to make himself heard about the exultant roar of delight. 'In recognition of how much pleasure it gives us that Natalia should become the wife of our son, we wish to publicly make this gift to her.'

Somehow both the countess and the Chief Minister had managed to make their way to the front of the balcony carrying the leather-covered jewellery case, which they were now opening for the king.

The glitter from the sunlight reflecting on the diamonds inside it was so brilliant that it made Natalia's eyes hurt to look at them.

'These diamonds were my gift to my beloved first wife, Queen Sophia,' the king said emotionally. 'Since her death I have kept them locked away, unable to countenance seeing anyone else wearing them. Until now. Now it is my belief that it is fitting and right that they should now be worn by my son's betrothed, Natalia.'

Obediently she bent her head, shivering as she felt the cold, heavy weight of the diamond necklace lying against her skin.

'Kadir.' King Giorgio motioned to his son, indicating the enormous diamond ring that lay with the bracelets and tiara in the box.

As he picked up the ring Kadir looked at her again, his green eyes so hard with dislike and rejection that Natalia felt as if it were a physical blow.

'Let him give you the ring,' the countess snapped in her ear. 'The people will want to see you wearing it.'

Wrenching her gaze from Kadir's, Natalia held out her hand. Her fingers, long and slender, looked unfamiliarly delicate against the width of his palm and the length of his hand whilst the ring, held between his fingers, seemed to glitter malevolently at her. She was trembling so much that her hand brushed against him. Immediately he closed his fingers into a fist as though in rejection of the physical contact with her. Natalia's face burned. She longed for the courage to simply turn and walk away. But it was already too late. He was sliding the ring onto her ring finger, and holding up her hand to show the crowd.

The noise of their roared approval was almost deafening. King Giorgio was looking triumphant but she dared not look at Kadir to see how he might be feeling. Her heart felt heavy with the weight of what she feared lay ahead of her. But it was too late for her to have regrets now, she told herself sickly, before rallying to remind herself that she hadn't been alone in what she had done. But she had no explanation for what had happened; no rational means of making it seem more palatable. Unless she told him the truth. What truth? The truth that she had been so overwhelmed with desire for him that nothing else had mattered. Surely as her husband to be he would welcome that news.

CHAPTER SIX

WHEN WAS IT going to end? Natalia wondered tiredly. She had not imagined, when the countess had told her that there was to be a formal reception after the announcements on the balcony, that she would have to stand at the side of her husband-to-be under such devastatingly untenable circumstances. Her head was throbbing and she could hardly move thanks to the constriction of her gown and the weight of the king's gift to her. It would have been bad enough if they had simply been the strangers they should have been and not…not what they really were.

There was no need for Kadir to tell her what he thought of her, those hostile looks he had been giving her had made it mercilessly plain, and yet what right did he have to judge her? What after all had she done that he had not? There was no point in her even thinking about trying to wave the equal-rights flag in this situation, though. In a marriage such as theirs there was all the difference in the world between the moral laws applying to the woman and those applying to the man. Historically men of power and position married virgins on the assumption that way they would be guaranteed that the child born hopefully nine months after the consummation of the marriage would be theirs. The all-important first-born son. Despite the changes in the world over the last fifty years, the old beliefs were too deeply ingrained in some men to ever be erased or even softened. Kadir's heritage from his mother's people would

mean that even more than most his pride would demand
that the woman to whom he gave his name and his seed
would be his alone. Natalia could sense that about him as
clearly as though he had said the words to her himself. Her
mistake was not so much what she had done, but that she
had not thought more deeply about the expectations and
mind-set of the man who would be Niroli's next King before allowing herself to be carried away on a wave of emotional loyalty to her country.

Theirs would not, she realised now, be a prosaic marriage of convenience between two people who understand
one another's goals and beliefs. Even without Venice she
would never have been the kind of woman Kadir would
want as his wife. Her lip curled slightly in womanly contempt for a man she now saw as inwardly weak in all
the ways that mattered the most to her, for all his raw
masculinity and sexuality; a man who was so steeped in
old-fashioned beliefs that he automatically considered it
beneath him to take as his wife a woman who had been
'used' by another man.

She, on the other hand, was proud of everything that
she was, of all that she had learned and all the ways in
which she had grown from girlhood to womanhood by
making her own choices and learning from them. Until
Venice there had never been a relationship she had regret-
ted or felt shamed by. She was a mature woman, morally
the only judge she believed she needed, perfectly capable
of policing her own sexual behaviour, instinctively knowing what was right for her and what was not. She had always believed that to deny her sexuality as she matured
would have been as much of a sin as being promiscuous.
And she wasn't promiscuous. How could she be when she
had been celibate for so many years? The only time she
had broken her own self-imposed moral rules—the only

time she had ever wanted to, in fact—had been that one night with Kadir, but how could she make him understand and believe that, as she must—for the sake of their marriage and Niroli?

Here they were standing side by side as they greeted the guests invited to meet them, joined together by the king's own hand and by the heavy weight of the ring she was wearing, by the expectations of the Nirolian people, and yet in reality already divided by suspicion, deceit, mistrust and attitudes to life that were worlds apart.

KADIR COULD FEEL the stiff gold braid embossed collar of the uniform jacket he was wearing pressing against his flesh. It felt alien and constricting after the more familiar softness of the Arab robes he wore on formal court occasions in Hadiya, and more than that he felt almost as though he were dressed up to take part in a play, with a role imposed on him by the expectations of others, rather than living through a vitally important part of his own future life.

The research he had done on Niroli after his mother's devastating revelations had shown him an island with the potential to play a vitally important role on the world stage. Geographically alone, its position was unique. The world was changing; old powers giving way to new; men with minds sharp enough, perceptive enough, forward-thinking enough to encompass what could be achieved were in a unique position to guide that world through its rebirth. He had learned so much from studying the history of his own country and the Middle East in general. He wanted his future sphere of influence and that of his sons to reach far beyond Niroli, and to that end he had decided that he needed a wife who understood this, a wife who would dutifully provide him with children he knew would be his, not a woman who would casually give herself to any man who happened to stir her to lust—a woman who could be stirred to that lust as easily as a bitch on heat.

Kadir could feel fresh fury raging through him as he re-lived the moment on the balcony when his wife-to-be had stepped out to show herself. His wife-to-be was a whore... worse than a whore: *she* gave herself for nothing other than her own pleasure; a whore at least put a price on her virtue or lack of it. Every time he thought of the casual contempt with which she had disregarded their marriage to throw herself at him he wanted to turn to her and rip the diamonds from her neck and the ring from her finger, the clothes from her body, to reveal her as she really was.

How many times had she slipped away from Niroli to pose as she had done with him in a role that allowed her access to men? Ten times? A hundred? A thousand? How long had she planned to wait after their marriage before doing so again? A year...a month?

It was of course unthinkable that his father knew the truth about her. He had seen in King Giorgio's eyes the same arrogant pride he knew burned within himself. His father would never have considered her as a potential bride if he had known. The last thing he wanted to do was marry her, but the potential complications if he refused now were too great to be contemplated. He was the one who was the outsider here; the one who had to prove himself and win the acceptance of the island's people. To reject one of their 'daughters' would be seen as an insult, here just as it would be in Hadiya, no matter how justified his reason. No, he was stuck with the marriage if he wanted Niroli. And Kadir knew that he did.

THE LAST OF the guests were finally being persuaded to leave by the courtiers discreetly walking them towards the exit.

Kadir, deep in conversation with his father, was ignoring her. Deliberately? Did she need to ask herself that? The longer the reception had lasted, the more time she had had to think and to assess the stark reality of her future, and how impossible it was going to be for her to live it. She could see the countess coming towards her, no doubt about to suggest that it was time for her to 'retire', Natalia thought wryly.

Nirolian court etiquette remained firmly fixed in the habits of the early nineteenth century, where the men had to wait to 'let their hair down', as it were, until after the women had 'retired'. To judge from those left in the ornate grande salon now, with its décor and mirrors so very much in the style of the mirrored ballroom at Versailles the conversation amongst them would be very much on the future political strength of Niroli and its ruling Royal Family.

The countess had reached her and was waiting.

'What should I do about these?' Natalia asked her, briefly touching her diamond necklace.

'The king has made it plain that it is now your personal property,' the countess answered her briskly. 'It will make a good start for the jewellery collection you will need as Prince Kadir's wife. Of course, once he ascends the throne you will have access to the Crown Jewels of Niroli, and I dare say when he takes you to Hadiya with him after your marriage he will make a gift to you of his late mother's personal jewellery. Of course you can also expect to receive gifts of jewellery from the heads of other states and countries on your marriage, but for now, if you are ready to retire...'

Natalia nodded her head and then waited for the countess to escort her over to the king, so that she could go through the court formality of requesting his permission to leave.

He had just given this and to her relief turned his back to her, thus enabling her to turn round herself instead of having to back out of his presence, when Kadir broke off his conversation with his father to say curtly, 'I would like to have a few minutes' private conversation with my wife-to-be.'

'Highness, provision has already been written into to-morrow's schedule for you and Natalia to spend an hour walking together in public,' the king's Chief Minister began, but Kadir stopped him shaking his head.

'There are matters I wish to discuss with my betrothed that are for her ears only. With my father's permission I shall escort her to her apartment?'

King Giorgio actually laughed and gripped Kadir's arm, telling him jovially, 'You are a man after my own heart and indeed my son. I too would have wanted some time alone with my wife-to-be, in your shoes.'

'Your Highness, Natalia is still wearing Queen Sophia's jewels. She—'

'My son is hardly likely to steal them, Countess,' the king dismissed the countess's anxious reminder sharply. 'You have our permission to escort Natalia to her apartments, Kadir.'

The king had misunderstood the reason for the count-ess's comment, Natalia suspected, but then he had not had to wear the heavy jewellery and nor was he laced into a bodice so tight that Natalia suspected her ribs would be bruised when she was finally released from it. From the looks being exchanged by the remaining courtiers, it looked as though they and the king thought that Kadir planned to indulge in some pre-marriage intimacies, but of course Natalia knew better. Even so she didn't allow herself to betray her thoughts as she placed her fingertips on the

arm Kadir extended to her, and allowed him to lead her
towards the exit.

Already she was beginning to get used to the fact that
her new role meant virtually always being surrounded by
other people. Two uniformed guards snapped to attention
as they left the grande salon, whilst a formally liveried at-
tendant flattened himself against the wall of the corridor
as they walked past him.

'My maids will be waiting for me in my room to help
me to undress,' she told Kadir without turning her head
to look at him. 'So whatever it is you wish to say to me,
if you want to do so in private you had better speak now.'

'*Whatever* I wish to say to you? Isn't it obvious what
I might want to say, or rather the explanation I might demand you give?'

'My behaviour before we met today as a couple about
to enter into an arranged marriage has no bearing on that
marriage,' Natalia told him quietly, hoping he wouldn't be
able to guess that inwardly she was nowhere near as confident as she was trying to appear and was in fact feeling
sick with guilt. 'You have no right to demand an explanation for it and neither do I intend to give one. I am mistress
of my own life.'

'Mistress. You use *that* word with good reason. No wonder it slips so familiarly from your tongue. As easily as the
lies you must have told over the years to conceal your true
lack of morality. Had I known what you were…'

He wasn't making any attempt to conceal either his
anger or his contempt and Natalia's body reacted to it,
stiffening as she stopped walking and tried to pull away
from him. Immediately his right hand clamped down on
hers where it lay on his uniformed arm, imprisoning her as
he turned towards her. She could feel his anger as though
it had a life force of its own. His antagonism towards her

filled the air around them, pressing down on her. They were alone in the corridor, no man had ever made her feel so physically vulnerable and *small*.

'What I am now is what I have always been, openly and honestly. My body is mine to gift as I see fit. My sole error, as I see it, was not in my desire but in my lack of judgement in my choice of partner,' Natalia burst out passionately.

'Of course you would have behaved differently if you'd known who I was.'

'That was not what I said and it certainly isn't what I feel. My lack of judgement was not realising how unworthy of me you are. You want me to feel shame, to allow you to blame me for some imagined crime against you that you consider I have committed. My crime, if there is one, is against myself, for not recognising how impossible it is for a woman of my outlook and independence to have any kind of relationship with a man like you.'

'You dare to speak so of me? You who have behaved as no woman with morals would ever behave.'

'No woman of morals? What do you know of a woman's morals? Nothing. All you know, all you want to know, of a woman is her obedience and her submission. A woman's morals are the pact she makes—the vow she takes for herself, with herself—and they rest in her alone. Only she knows where the defining lines lie for her and only she has the right to know. In the past my sexuality was mine to claim—for myself and for those I have chosen to share it. Our betrothal marks a point in my life where my "morals" compel me to consider my own desires in tandem with the restrictions placed on me by my soon-to-be public role as the wife of the future King of Niroli. In that role I have a duty to the people of Niroli and its Crown, and it has been my choice to accept that duty and those restrictions.'

'If you are trying to tell me that what I witnessed in

Venice was a final fling, a sickening sexual binge intended to stifle your appetite for the rest of our marriage, then let me tell you now that I don't believe you. And even if I did, for me there would be no excuse—a woman who behaves as you did can never be a satisfactory wife or mother,' he told Natalia arrogantly.

It was too much.

'How very typical that you stand in sexual judgement of me. A woman's ability to experience sexual desire has no direct bearing on her ability to be a good wife and mother, far from it, and if you were half the man you obviously like to think you are you would know that for yourself.

'King Giorgio told me that you wanted to rule Niroli because you felt you could not in all conscience rule the people of Hadiya as you would have been expected to rule them. He said you wanted to embrace a more modern form of leadership. He said that you were ready to learn from me what it means to be Nirolian, but obviously none of that is true. And yet you have the gall to stand there and accuse me of deceit.'

In the shadows of the corridor she could see the warning angry colour seeping up under the taut flesh of his jaw.

'You dare to accuse me—'

'I dare to do whatever I have to do for my country. That is after all the only reason I am marrying you.' Natalia almost threw the words at him in defence of herself.

The look he gave her made her burn and now it was her turn to feel the hot surge of angry blood burning up under her skin.

'The only reason? What about the couture gown you are wearing, the diamonds around your neck?'

'You think I want those? Well, I do not. They mean nothing to me. No, that isn't true. What they represent to me is the way in which the poor are forced to work for a pittance so that the rich can adorn themselves. You talk of me deceiving you—well, I could make the same accusation of you. You are not the man I believed I would be marrying, the man I believed would be worthy of fathering my children.'

Natalia gave a small gasp as he took hold of her arm and wrenched her round into the light so that he could look down into her unprotected face.

'You dare to talk to me of the fathering of a child? Before this marriage of ours is consummated I shall require you to provide me with evidence that you are not carrying the child of another man.'

'That would be impossible since the last man, the only man in fact for a very long time, that I have been intimate with is you.'

'You expect me to believe that?'

'Why not when it is the truth? You are very quick to demand that I give you an explanation for my behaviour but you are just as culpable.' Natalia could see how little he liked her reminder. She was feeling so tired now and so emotionally vulnerable. A part of her was longing to be able to take hold of his hand and tell him how much she longed right now for the luxury of being able to be honest with him, and of being able to tell him that it was his own devastating effect on her that had led to her totally uncharacteristic need of him. Could she do that? Could she take that risk and beg him to give them both the chance of a fresh start, and one in which as his wife-to-be she was free to say openly how physically desirable she found him? They were to be man and wife, after all. Hope filled her. Surely it was worth her lowering her pride to ask him and to be honest with him…

'I am a man; it is several weeks now since I last spent any time with my mistress…'

He had a mistress. Natalia felt as though she had been plunged into a vat of icy cold water and held there until every bit of her burned with the pain of what she was being forced to endure. He had a mistress. Of course, he would. Of course he did! Why, why had she not thought of that simple explanation for his fierce possession of her for herself, instead of being foolish enough to imagine that he had wanted her for herself?

As though someone else had taken her over she heard her own voice saying with brittle emphasis, 'Really? Well, I am sure she will be delighted to learn that you haven't allowed yourself to suffer any sexual frustration whilst you've been apart from her.'

Kadir cursed himself under his breath. Why had he allowed her to infuriate him into saying anything about Zahra, especially when their relationship was already over? Kadir had his own self-imposed personal moral code and it did not include having sex with a mistress when he was a newly married man. Somewhere at the back of his mind there had been the intention of establishing at least a working sexual relationship with his bride, even whilst he had also realistically acknowledged that it was all too likely that there would not be any real passion or desire between them.

How fate must be laughing at him for the trick it had pulled on him. There was no way he could establish a comfortable sexual relationship with this woman, whilst when it came to passion and desire... He did not feel passion or desire for her. Logically speaking it was all too likely that he had been driven to possess her in the way that he had because he had been living a celibate life. That was all. Nothing more. Nothing personal... Nothing that meant that he had actually wanted her so much that that need had overridden everything else.

That intense, unbearable pain inside her couldn't really

be because Kadir had told her he had a mistress, could it? It mustn't be. Not now that she knew what he really thought of her. She could not, would not, endure a marriage in which she wanted a man who felt only contempt for her. She could not take the risk that that might happen and there was only one way she could ensure that it did not. A quick slicing shaft of swift agony now to separate her from him for ever and it would be over, leaving her free to make her own life, if necessary away from Niroli. That would bring more pain—she loved her country so much—but she must not think of that now. Natalia took a deep breath.

'Look, why don't I save us both from a situation neither of us want?' she told Kadir briskly. 'I've changed my mind, Kadir, and I do not intend to marry you. I shall tell the countess in the morning and ask her to inform—'

'No!' The vehemence of his own denial shocked through him. 'No,' he repeated. 'You will do no such thing. You will marry me and you will do as I say.' Not because he wanted her. Never that. No, it was for Niroli and the future that she had to be his wife. King Giorgio had rejected many heirs already; Kadir wasn't about to give him a reason to reject him.

'This is Niroli, not Hadiya,' Natalia told him angrily. 'You may have been proclaimed as Niroli's Crown Prince, but there is no rule of absolute royal law here. Niroli is a democracy; we have laws that protect the rights of the people. Enforced marriage does not happen here.'

'You will marry me.' Kadir continued as though she hadn't spoken, 'because if you don't, I shall tell the world that I am the one who is refusing to marry you because of your behaviour.'

She was trapped, Natalia acknowledged bitterly. She might not care what he told the world for her own sake, but she did care for her grandfather's. He would be shocked

and hurt and, not just that, he would feel publicly humiliated, as well.

'You will marry me and from now until the day you conceive my child I do not intend to let you out of my sight. I
will make sure you are watched day and night to make sure
that you are never given the opportunity to foist someone
else's bastard on me. Since it is necessary for me to have
heirs, you had best hope that you conceive as quickly as
possible—once our month of abstinence is up, that is. I
need to make sure you aren't carrying someone's bastard.'
He released her so abruptly that she almost staggered into
the corridor wall, her arm throbbing where the blood was
returning to it.

CHAPTER SEVEN

NATALIA LOOKED UNHAPPILY round her bedroom. Later on today Kadir would make his formal oath of allegiance to Niroli and King Giorgio and in return the king would proclaim him Crown Prince. Tomorrow morning she would be married to Kadir in Niroli's cathedral, and then the next day they would board the private jet taking them on their honeymoon journey to Hadiya.

Tonight, as on every night since their engagement had been announced nine days ago, two guards would be on duty outside both exits from her apartment. It was a formality Kadir had somehow or other managed to persuade the countess was necessary. During the daytime there was never a minute when she was left alone. Either the countess, or one of her maids or, even worse, Kadir himself was at her side. The countess had told her that Kadir was concerned that her new duties might prove too onerous for her and so had asked the countess to be on hand at all times to help her. The maids seemed to think that without them in attendance she would not be able to manage the lavish couture outfits Kadir had insisted he wanted to see her wearing in preference to her casual clothes, clothes which in their way were as constricting and imprisoning as any lock and key. And then there were those worst of all times when Kadir would put his arm through hers, the gesture of a devoted tender fiancé asking her to walk in the palace gardens with him so that she could acquaint him with the history of the Nirolian people.

Part of her, the weak part that she privately despised, longed for her to get pregnant as soon as possible so that she could escape this constant stifling monitoring but another part of her, the real, stronger part of her, hated the thought of her bringing a vulnerable child into the world under such circumstances, and longed to find a way to escape from her marriage.

On their return from their honeymoon they would be sharing the royal apartments traditionally made available to the Crown Prince, and in a few minutes' time she was due to make a tour of them with Kadir and the Comptroller of the Royal Household. Was this what she had given up her freedom for? This marriage based on suspicion and mistrust to a man she now felt she despised as much as if not more than he so obviously despised her, and certainly far more than she had ever wanted him? How foolish the high-minded ideals that had motivated her to agree to marry Kadir seemed now. How empty the promises she had made to herself of what she would do for her husband and their people.

'SO WHEN WAS the last time these rooms were decorated?'

It surprised Natalia that Kadir should ask such a question. It seemed out of character for him to concern himself with something so trivial.

'They were last decorated for occupation by the king's late son and his family.'

Did that explain the air of sadness that seemed to haunt the now-empty rooms? Natalia wondered. The king's first-born heir, Queen Sophia's son, had after all died in tragic circumstances and prior to that there had been the trauma of the kidnap of one of his twin sons.

The remaining twin, Prince Marco, might be happy now married to his English wife, Emily, but he had freely admitted that his childhood had been shadowed and difficult and that he had as an adult felt alienated from his birthright. So much so in fact that he had rejected the throne. She had no wish for her children to suffer the same fate. The burden of royal birth could be a heavy one if it was not lightened by love and the closeness of a shared family life and sense of purpose. She wanted her children to grow up in the sunshine of Niroli's future with their hearts attuned to that future and the way in which they would share it with the people of their country.

The room they were in had windows that opened out onto a private inner courtyard garden on one side, and the sea on the other. Impetuously Natalia turned to the comptroller, addressing him directly for the first time.

'Are there no rooms we could have that have windows overlooking the city?'

The comptroller was frowning. 'There are such rooms, yes, but traditionally members of the royal family have preferred an outlook that gives them privacy.'

'What is it you have in mind?' she heard Kadir demanding, as though impatient of her input.

'Our children will one day be the ones to take Niroli forward into the future,' Natalia informed them both. 'How can they do that if they grow up turning their faces away from our people? How will they understand and appreciate what it means to be of Niroli if they never see how our people live? As a child I roamed the city freely, exploring it, making it my own, binding it to me as it bound me to it. I could find my way through its streets blindfolded, I know now every nuance of its scents, all the places where the most precious flowers and herbs grow. Loving a country is something a child learns from its parents. Understanding it, knowing it and its people is something they can only learn by experience.'

She had said too much, been too outspoken, Natalia recognised, and in doing so would of course have antagonised Kadir and harmed her cause.

'It is for His Highness to approve or disapprove our apartment,' she told the comptroller tiredly. 'I must be guided by what he says.'

'My wife-to-be is right. I myself know now little as yet of my new country. A man who looks only inward learns much of himself but little of others. A king who would rule others must learn to study them as well as himself. If there are rooms available with windows that overlook the town…'

Natalia stared at the comptroller in disbelief. Kadir was agreeing with her, supporting her. A seed of something fragile but, oh, so precious was opening inside her heart beneath the warmth of her pleasure in his reaction, and putting out small quivering tendrils of hope. She turned to look at Kadir, but he was looking away from her.

'It is also my wish that my wife and I share a bed instead of occupying separate rooms,' Kadir was telling the comptroller in a businesslike voice. 'After all, we have a duty to provide Niroli with the next generation of heirs.'

'THE STATE OF marriage is so approved by God as to be the foundation of family life where children are born…'

Natalia tensed under the heavy weight of her ornate wedding gown and long veil. The Valenciennes lace overdress of her gown had originally been made for Queen Sophia's wedding dress. Softly cream with age, it looked magnificent over the shimmering gold dress beneath it.

It had always been Natalia's intention not to wear a white gown. She was a woman not a girl, a woman proud of all that she was. And if Kadir was not man enough to accept that, if he had felt it necessary to turn to her and give her a look of comprehensive cynicism when she had joined him at the altar, then that was his choice. Her conscience was clear.

Was it? If she should have conceived in Venice... *If* she should have, but how could she have done so when Kadir had used protection?

Kadir's white uniform with its gold braid, instead of looking faintly ridiculous, actually brought home to her the reality of what it had meant in previous centuries for a king and his heirs to ride out into battle for their country at the head of their armies. All too easily she could see Kadir in such a role. Not that Hadiya or Niroli had been at war during Natalia's lifetime, and nor would she want that. In fact she hoped that she and Kadir and then through him their children would play a strong role in promoting world peace. So why did she find it so stirring to visualise him in a combatory role? Women were drawn to the alpha men their instincts told them could protect them and, more importantly, their young, Natalia reminded herself as she forced herself to look forward instead of towards him.

'I pronounce you man and wife...'

Natalia was shocked to discover that she was having to blink away emotional tears as the notes of 'Ave Maria' soared from the choir to fill the ancient cathedral and Kadir raised her fingertips to his lips.

It was done. She was his wife. Her commitment to her country and its future must now come before everything else.

NATALIA WAS NOW his wife. This woman whom his intellect told him to despise and revile but whom his body ached for in the dark, empty hours of the night. Where had that admission come from? Kadir wondered grimly. So there might have been one night, possibly two when he had woken up like many another man with his body aching for a woman—that hardly meant that he desired Natalia Carini. Not Natalia Carini any more but Crown Princess Natalia, he reminded himself. His wife, his partner in this new venture he had committed himself to, a decision he'd probably made to avoid acknowledging his difficult relationship with his father.

How old had he been when he had first realised that the man he had believed to be his father did not love him, and that nothing he could do would ever draw the praise from him that he so willingly gave to Kadir's younger brother? Eight? Six? Younger? Old enough to recognise he was being rejected certainly and at the same time still young enough for that to hurt, and for him not to have known how to put in place any defences against that pain. How could his father have turned away from him, his eyes cold and his manner aloof, whilst they had lit up with warmth the minute his gaze had rested on Kadir's younger brother, his manner changing to become paternally indulgent?

He could still mentally see and sense his mother's anxiety as she had stood watchfully in the shadows of the courtyard where he and his brother played. The minute his father had entered the courtyard a word from his mother had brought a maid to his own side, a firm hand on his shoulder as he had been led away, leaving his parents alone with his brother.

His protests had always been met by some rational explanation: he was the elder, and had his schoolwork to do; his brother was just a baby. And he had struggled harder to win his father's attention and approval whilst his mother had in turn worked harder to keep them apart.

'I did it for your sake,' she had told him. 'To protect you

because I was afraid that he might look at you and see as I could see so clearly that you were not his child.'

All lies of course. She had not done it to protect him but to hide her shame and protect herself. But as he had come to learn, that was what women did. They lied to protect themselves and then added insult to injury by pretending that their motivation had been altruistic. A man did not allow women to undermine him. He certainly had no intention of allowing Natalia to undermine the position he intended to claim for himself here in Niroli. It was all too easy now for him to understand why his father had so often, and unfairly, he had believed at the time, questioned Kadir's own allegiance to Hadiya and his ability to rule it well. His mother had sworn to him that her husband had never known he was not his son, but Kadir was not convinced. The sheikh might not have been able to prove he hadn't fathered him, but Kadir felt sure that he had had his suspicions. He had seen by example what happened between man and child when that man did not accept his paternity of that child. That was not going to happen to him. No child growing up with his name would ever have cause to doubt his love or his complete belief that he had fathered him.

THEY WERE TO spend the first night of their marriage in their palace apartment before flying to Hadiya in the morning, and Natalia stood stiffly still and silent in the middle of her large dressing room whilst her maids removed her ornate gown. Whatever the circumstances she would have felt some natural apprehension about what lay ahead tonight. She might be old enough not to be sentimental about human sexual relationships, but she would be lying if she tried to pretend to herself that there wasn't still a tiny part of her that foolishly longed to experience the close intimacy of a loving sexual relationship in which the two parties concerned were totally committed to one another, and that it hurt knowing that she would never have that.

Despite that she had determinedly refused to think of herself as a daydreamer or an idealist, but now she knew that her biggest mistake had been in believing that she and Kadir would bond over what she had believed would be their shared commitment to Niroli. Taking due care to make their relationship work would surely mirror the care they would take to work for the higher good of the island. That mind-set seemed risible now in view of what had happened. She thanked her maids as she stepped out of her gown and then scooped it up, acknowledging how bitterly disappointed she was and how bitterly angry with herself—and Kadir—she felt.

Beyond her dressing room lay her private bathroom just as on the other side of their shared bedroom lay Kadir's dressing room and his private bathroom. She really didn't want to think about the preparations he might be making for this, their first night together as the future King and Queen of Niroli. Was he still determined to wait a full month after Venice to consummate their marriage? Surely he would come to her on their wedding night?

She was under no illusions and knew that he had meant what he had said about having her watched night and day until she had conceived his child. How bitterly ironic it was considering her long years of celibacy. A celibacy broken only by her overwhelming desire for one man— Kadir himself.

She had already made it plain to her maids that she preferred to bathe alone, and her eyebrows rose when she walked into her bathroom and saw the champagne chilling in a bucket of ice. To calm her bridal nerves? Whose idea had that been? She would have preferred a glass of Niroli's organic white wine, given the choice.

She showered quickly and efficiently instead of luxuriating in the huge round bath, drying herself and then pulling on a towelling robe to make her way to the bedroom.

Someone had been in to turn down the bed and switch on the bedside lamps, and another ice bucket had been placed close to the bed.

She stared at the empty bed and then took a deep breath and pulled back the covers to get into it and wait for her husband.

TWO HOURS LATER she was still waiting. She had heard sounds from Kadir's dressing room, the murmur of voices, probably his valets, she guessed, and then silence, and now as she released her muscles from their bonds of tension she acknowledged the unwantedly unpalatable truth. Kadir did not intend to spend the night with her and she would not be spending her wedding night with her new husband, but on her own.

Had she been nineteen his behaviour might have reduced her to a tearful, quivering, shamed wreck of rejection. But she wasn't nineteen and she certainly didn't intend to let Kadir play mind games with her and win. And that ache deep down inside her? What ache? She refused to allow there to be any ache, she decided proudly.

CHAPTER EIGHT

NATALIA HAD THOUGHT she knew heat, but Niroli's heat was nothing compared to the hot blast of air that had greeted them on their arrival in Hadiya. It had been like standing in front of an open oven door with a fan blowing.

Here though, at least, in the private apartments she had been assigned in the women's quarters of the Hadiya Royal Palace, the architecture made the most of what breeze there was, especially in the beautiful courtyard garden.

She had woken this morning breathing in the scent of the roses from that courtyard, whilst her ears were filled with the gentle sound of falling water and the fan of the whirring wings of doves. Every aspect of the apartment was designed to fill the senses with delight, right down to the coffee she was now drinking as she sat admiring her surroundings and considering everything that had happened following their arrival in Hadiya the previous night.

If she was honest it had shocked her to see just how very Eastern in its customs Hadiya actually was. There had been no question of her attending the formal reception that was given to welcome Kadir home as the Crown Prince of Niroli. Instead she had had to watch the proceedings from behind the delicate grill work that separated the women's area from the public 'divan' Kadir's brother was holding.

It had also seemed strange to her that Hadiya's subjects were in theory free to attend such a 'divan' and ask questions of their ruler. The young woman who had been appointed as her guide in matters of Hadiya protocol had carefully explained to her that in these modern times all those wanting to approach the sheikh were carefully vetted first. It was a custom much like that of the traditional 'laying on of hands' common amongst European monarchs.

It was certainly potentially a very democratic process, making the ruler approachable and accessible to his subjects from all walks of life. And one from which Niroli might benefit?

A slightly wry smile touched Natalia's mouth now. She doubted that many brides of two days' duration would be spending their time thinking about matters of political domestic policy, especially not when they were married to a man as outwardly physically sexually attractive as Kadir. But then not many new brides would have spent all those nights sleeping alone.

It certainly wasn't a part of Hadiya protocol for newly married couples to sleep alone and apart. Basima had already discreetly let her know that it was considered perfectly proper and indeed expected for a bridegroom to visit his bride in those rooms set aside for her.

'It was the sheikh's wish that you should be given the apartment of his mother, the sheikha,' she had explained that first evening, and for a few minutes Natalia had thought she was telling her that it had been Kadir who had requested his mother's rooms for her, but then she had realised that Basima was telling her that it had been Kadir's brother, the kind and jolly new sheikh, who had requested that the rooms be prepared for her.

And what of the haughty and arrogant woman who had been introduced to her as the daughter of a prominent Hadiyan—Zahra Rafiq? What a wonderful thing the female instinct was. Natalia had disliked her intensely even before the other woman had let her know very unsubtly that she was Kadir's mistress. Was? Zahra had certainly made it plain that she wanted that relationship to continue, but Zahra lived here in Hadiya and, as Kadir had already made clear to Natalia albeit in a very different context, he considered his future role as Niroli's King of first and foremost importance to him, above and beyond everything and everyone else.

Had Kadir spent last night with Zahra? Her hand shook, making her put down the glass perfume bottle she had been given in Venice and which some impulse had made her bring with her to Hadiya.

She had watched whilst Zahra had prowled her room, picking it up herself. Somehow it had not surprised Natalia to see the way the beautiful glass had dulled the moment Zahra's fingers had tightened around it. No wonder Zahra had replaced it so swiftly, looking at it with scorn. She on the other hand loved the way it glowed at her touch, giving off a warmth that seemed to heal the sore places of her heart, reaffirming for her that she was the worthwhile human being she knew herself to be. Now she put the bottle down.

Logically speaking, why after all should it bother her if Kadir had a mistress and that mistress was Zahra? But a person's emotions weren't always subject to logic, were they? Was she just a jealous wife resenting another woman's role in her husband's life? Since when had her *emotions* had any role to play in her marriage? They didn't, and they must not, Natalia told herself fiercely. Just because she had felt physical desire for Kadir that did not mean that emotion was involved. Right now she was going to forget that she had ever had this time-wasting conversation with herself, and focus instead on her new role as consort to Niroli's Crown Prince.

This morning, for instance, she was going to be given a

tour of Hadiya's new technical college for girls, an innovative step towards modernisation set in motion by Kadir's mother, where young women could learn modern business skills. The outer door to the room opened and, as though her thoughts had had the power to produce her like a genie from a bottle, Zahra herself stalked in. The lushly curved socialite with her dyed blonde hair was the kind of woman instantly recognisable to other women as cold and calculating and yet somehow perceived by men as being sweetly feminine and desirable.

'I have told Basima that I shall accompany you on your formal visit this morning,' she announced. 'There are matters I wish to discuss with you that will be of benefit to you in your marriage to Kadir.'

Natalia gave her a long thoughtful look, and then reminded herself of the decision she had just made.

'I doubt it,' she told her calmly. 'A mistress's experience of a man rarely has any bearing on his wife's experience of him. The role of a wife after all encompasses so much more than merely spending a few hours in his bed giving him pleasure.'

Natalia could see from the flash in Zahra's hard brown eyes that her own deliberately pointed comments had hit their mark.

'Kadir is right. You are not the kind of woman he would have married had he remained here,' Zahra returned with a falsely sweet smile. 'But of course we all know that the only reason *you* have been elevated to such a position is because of the folly of Kadir's mother. Had she not compounded her sin of betraying her husband by keeping the truth of Kadir's paternity to herself then there would have been time for Kadir to make more suitable arrangements for his marriage.'

'I am not surprised that Princess Amira found it necessary to keep her secret, given the lack of understanding she was likely to have found,' Natalia retaliated quietly. 'But if by more suitable you are thinking of yourself...'

Natalia could tell from Zahra's swift and audible intake of breath that she hadn't been prepared for her to be so outspoken.

'I am far too modest to dare to dream of such an honour,' Zahra told her, sounding anything but modest. 'It is enough for me that Kadir is generous to bestow his loving desire on me.'

Just so long as it came with a huge helping of expensive gifts and public recognition of the importance of his mistress's unofficial role, Natalia decided cynically.

'For me Kadir's happiness is far more important than my own,' Zahra continued unconvincingly, 'and that is why I am forcing myself to put aside my natural feelings in an effort to help you to become the kind of wife Kadir needs.'

Zahra was clever, Natalia admitted. Zahra wanted a fight and she certainly knew how to provoke one, there was no doubt about it. With those few well-chosen words she had well and truly ignited the slow burning fuse of Natalia's own sensitive temper.

'Look,' she told her curtly. 'Let's not waste one another's time. Why don't I be blunt? Kadir has chosen to accept an offer put to him from the King of Niroli, *my* country, not Kadir's and certainly not yours, to become its next King; a role which he is only eligible to play through the mother you seem to despise so much. King Giorgio has chosen *me* to be Kadir's wife because, whilst I may know now nothing of the customs of Hadiya, I do know the hearts and the minds of the people of Niroli. I know what matters to them, how they think and how they feel, what they want in their new King and what they don't, because I am one of them. That is why King Giorgio asked me if I would consider giving up my personal freedoms as a single woman to become the wife of Niroli's future King. It is out of love for my country and my duty to its future that I agreed. A large part of that duty as Kadir's wife is to make sure that he is kept aware of the needs and beliefs of his adopted people.'

Let Zahra think about that! She was not going to allow Zahra or anyone else, but most of all Kadir himself, get away with thinking she was some docile obedient fool, dazzled by the false glitter of a royal title; someone so shallow and lacking in substance that she could be bribed with it into accepting the bullying of her husband's mistress. Natalia had her own agenda for her future as a royal wife, and it certainly wasn't for the royal title that she had agreed to marry Kadir.

'I don't need you to tell me that his marriage to you was not of Kadir's choosing,' Zahra interrupted her angrily. 'Do you really think I do not know why Kadir did not come to you last night?'

Now it was Natalia's turn to suck in a breath as sharply as though she had sucked on the fruit of one of the lemons growing on the trees outside in the courtyard.

'You talk very cleverly about the practicalities of your arranged marriage, but you cannot deceive me. I can see into your heart and what you want to conceal there. You want Kadir as a man.'

Natalia felt the words as though they were physical blows. They weren't true. They couldn't possibly be! She wasn't going to let them be. Kadir meant nothing to her. *No? Then why had she behaved the way she had in Venice?*

That had had nothing to do with wanting Kadir. She had just…

She had just what—just wanted sex?

Yes!

No! Because if that were true then why had she been

able to spend so long living her freely chosen celibate life so comfortably?

She had been celibate for too long, that was all. Kadir could have been anyone.

Liar—isn't it the truth that the moment you saw him you felt...

I felt nothing, she denied furiously. Nothing. And she continued to feel nothing for him now despite what Zahra was trying to say.

'Did you really think I would not know?' Zahra continued to taunt her. 'Kadir and I have laughed about it. Kadir has his duty to perform, of course, but it is to me that he gives his true passion. I am the one who will sit beside him when ultimately he rules both Niroli and Hadiya. It is my destiny to be with Kadir, not yours. Kadir is mine and I will never let him go. Nor will I ever let anyone or anything come between us, and you had better remember that. It is our destiny to be together,' she repeated, 'and nothing can stand in the way of that destiny.'

How had it happened that suddenly their argument had veered off the apparently straight road at such a sharp angle that it had completely thrown her? The conversation had taken a completely new and disturbing direction, Natalia realised, remembering the intensity she could hear in Zahra's voice.

Listening to Zahra, Natalia was suddenly struck how very similar in attitude Zahra seemed to be to the kind of woman the press delighted in labelling a 'stalker'. But maybe she was being unfair and jumping to the wrong conclusions. Maybe that was the way a passionate Middle Eastern woman spoke? If so it certainly contrasted with her own far more pragmatic approach to life, Natalia admitted. Zahra must of course know that there was no way Kadir would ever succeed to the Hadiyan throne. After all

Kadir had already renounced the throne of Hadiya. Zahra was something of a bully, Natalia guessed, and no doubt used to frightening others into giving way to her. Well, she was going to have to learn—and Kadir with her—that she was not bullied so easily. Far from it.

'You are beyond foolish if you think that Kadir does not see as I do that for all your pretence not to, you yearn to give your heart to him.' Zahra astounded Natalia by throwing the accusation at her, and in doing so changing tack yet again. 'How predictable you are to fall in love with him as you have done. I told him it would be so. How indeed could it not be with a man such as Kadir? But he does not want your love; he does not want anything of you. Why should he when he has me, and when he will always have me? I am the one he loves and he will never give me up... never.' Zahra moved closer to Natalia and then unexpectedly grabbed hold of her arm before Natalia could move out of the way. Her nails were long and lacquered a blood dark red. 'Do you understand that?' Very determinedly Natalia stood up, ignoring Zahra's hold on her.

'I understand that if I don't get ready now I shall be late for my formal duties,' she answered her as lightly as she could.

What nonsense Zahra had talked. As though she would be foolish enough to fall in love with Kadir. She was a mature woman, not some foolish young girl with daydreams. If she believed in romantic love, and Natalia was not sure that she did, then she still felt that a couple needed far more to build a life together on than merely 'falling in love'. They needed shared beliefs, and shared interests, a shared sense of commitment and dedication; they needed of course the passion that came with mutual sexual desire to truly have the foundations of a long-term relationship, but sexual desire could not be relied upon to last and was surely the least important of all those 'must haves'.

'I WANT TO talk to you.'

'Well, I do not want to talk to you,' Natalia snapped back smartly at Kadir as he followed her into her rooms dismissing the waiting maids with a curt inclination of his head.

'That is something you have already made more than evident today,' Kadir retaliated sharply as the maids melted away leaving him to slam the door enclosing the two of them in the dimly lit room.

In the time it had taken them to walk through the palace from the cars, darkness had fallen. They had just come from the final formal event of that day, the opening of a new shopping centre, attended by not just the two of them but also Kadir's brother and his wife and family. The glass doors to the courtyard were still open and Natalia went to stand in front of them to breathe in the rose-scented air. The car in which she had travelled had reeked of the strong Arabian perfume favoured by Zahra. Natalia could smell it coming off Kadir now.

'What was there for me to say?' she challenged him. 'Your mistress pre-empted every attempt I made to speak.' She wasn't going to let him see how angry and then humiliated she had felt at the way in which Zahra had upstaged her or how foolishly hurt she had been about the fact that she had not had the opportunity to use the few words of Arabic she had so carefully learned and rehearsed so that she could greet the children in their own language. To do so would make her seem petty, and reinforce Zahra's accusation that she was emotionally vulnerable to Kadir, which she wasn't; not in the least! Not now and not ever. Zahra was welcome to him in that respect. In *that* respect maybe, but Natalia, in her role of consort to the Crown Prince of Niroli, did not intend to continue to allow herself to be humiliated the way Zahra had done, for the sake of Niroli itself.

'Why bring Zahra into this?' Kadir demanded angrily. 'She has nothing to do with it.' It had thrown Kadir completely on his return to Hadiya with his wife to find Zahra insisting on behaving as though they were still lovers. He fully intended to discuss her behaviour with her and remind her that their relationship was over.

'She has *everything* to do with it,' she contradicted him. 'You may think that by foisting your mistress off on me as my official Hadiyan female companion it is only me who is insulted, but you are wrong. What you did insults the Throne of Niroli as well because it elevates your mistress to a superior position than me, your wife. This is not what King Giorgio had in mind when he agreed that I should accompany you here.'

'You dare to lecture me on my behaviour? You dare to question my decisions on matters of protocol and diplomacy?' Kadir was practically incandescent with fury, Natalia recognised. '*If* Zahra *is* my mistress.'

'*If?* There is no "if" about it, is there, Kadir? She told me herself this morning exactly what she is to you. Your mistress may feel she has the right to pass on to me her expertise on the subject of how best to act as your consort so as to make the best impression on you and the people of Hadiya. However, you are not becoming King of Hadiya, but King of Niroli, and it seems to me that she is in danger of making the same mistake as you and that is in believing that Niroli is some kind of extension of Hadiya, simply because you want it to be. Your word is not law, Kadir, and my guess is that you have already found that out here, but because you cannot accept it you have blamed your mother for your own inability to adapt to become the ruler Hadiya needs. If you aren't careful you will repeat that mistake on Niroli. The more I learn about your mother, the more I wish I had met her. How brave she must have been and how saddened and disappointed that you, the son she did so much to nurture and protect, should be so lacking in vision and so filled with self-delusion and bitterness that you cannot see her for the wonderful loving and giving person that she was.'

'Why, you—'

Kadir was looking at her as though he wanted to lock his hands round her neck and choke the life out of her, Natalia recognised, but she didn't care. If he hadn't had the decency to protect their marriage and his new wife from the venom of his mistress, then he could take the consequences. She looked across at him. The lamplight revealed Kadir's features quite clearly. She could see the harsh down-turned curl of his mouth and the cold glitter of anger in his eyes.

'You hate this, don't you?' she challenged him before he could finish. 'You hate being married to me. Well, you only have yourself to blame.' She saw the flash of temper igniting the jade-green darkness of his eyes.

'I am to blame for your immorality?'

He was as adept as his mistress about changing the direction of a conversation to suit his own ends, Natalia acknowledged, but she was not going to give in to those tactics.

'The fact that you have chosen to think me immoral does not make me so. And what you are to blame for is insisting on marrying me when you have already judged me to be not good enough to be your wife. You are angry with me, but in reality your anger should be for yourself.'

'How typical of a woman that you use words with the same deceit with which you use your body.'

'There is no deceit apart from in your imagination,' Natalia rejected his accusation.

'Have you forgotten the wanton way in which you, a woman on the brink of marriage, gave yourself to me?'

'My physical desire for you had no bearing on my commitment to this marriage. As a single woman, which I was, I had the right to own my own body and my own desires, and besides...'

Just in time Natalia managed to stop herself from admitting that he was the only man she had given herself to in a very long time.

'And as your husband-to-be, I had the right to expect you to bring yourself to our marriage bed free of any evidence of another man's possession of you. I will not be cuckolded in the way that my mother—'

'But there isn't another man! And it always comes back to what happened with your mother, doesn't it?' Natalia retorted. 'You can't move forward into the future, Kadir, because you will not let go of the past. Your mother was eighteen,' she told him grimly, already protective of the young girl who must have suffered dreadfully and been so afraid. A true man, a loving son, surely would have compassion for her and understand how she must have felt. But it was not Kadir's mother she wanted to discuss. 'You talk of my supposed immorality. That is so hypocritical when you yourself have a mistress. And by the way,' she added cuttingly, 'the next time you feel like discussing my failings as a wife with that mistress, I suggest you at least tell her that you've already had sex with me.'

'What do you mean the next time I feel like discussing you with my mistress? What are you talking about? Tell me!'

'Tell you? Yes, I will! Zahra couldn't wait to let me know that she knew I spent last night alone. You're a fine one to talk to me about morality. And, no, I didn't descend to her level and spoil the fun she was having letting me know how wonderful you think she is in bed by telling her that I already know that by my standards her idea of fun isn't anything to write home about.'

'You must have misunderstood her,' Kadir stopped her curtly. 'I did not spend last night with Zahra.' Kadir could hardly believe what he was admitting, and he certainly did not know why he was admitting it.

'Oh, come on, you don't really expect me to believe that, do you?'

Ignoring her, Kadir continued coldly, 'I spent last night in the desert. My brother had made arrangements for us to visit the tomb of our mother together.' His voice had become clipped. 'It was her wish that she was buried with her parents. We spent the night there together in prayer.'

Something—shame, perhaps; regret maybe—fierce and scalding burned its way through her, but she couldn't let it sway her.

'You cannot deny that she's your mistress, though.'

Kadir's eyebrows rose. 'You sound more like an emotionally jealous and possessive traditional wife than someone taking part in an acknowledged dynastic marriage.'

Kadir's criticisms were so close to what Zahra had said to her—so close that it was obvious to Natalia that they had shared a discussion about her and her supposed 'feelings' for him. What had they said? And where? In the intimacy of their shared bed? And no doubt when Kadir made love to Zahra he... The pain seized her out of nowhere shocking her rigid; leaving her unable to either fight it or deny it. If she had any sense she would abandon this discussion and now before it got totally out of hand, a warning voice inside Natalia's head urged her, but she refused to listen to it. Her pride was hurt and demanding recompense for the wound inflicted on it.

'My concerns are exactly the same as your own,' she

told Kadir furiously. 'On health grounds alone, you must see that you can't expect me to share your bed when you are having sex with another woman.'

She saw from the faint widening of his eyes that she had caught him off guard, but he recovered very quickly, telling her coldly, 'I wasn't aware that I *had* asked you to share my bed.'

'Good, because although Zahra may consider you to be a good lover...' she began insultingly.

'You do not?'

How had he managed to get so close to her without her noticing him moving? Too close, she recognised uneasily. 'No, I do not! But then of course my experience of you as a lover can hardly compare to Zahra's, can it?'

What was she doing? What was she saying? She might as well throw herself off the top of one of Niroli's cliffs, her behaviour had become so self-destructive, Natalia recognised.

'If that is meant as a request for me to remedy that disparity—' Kadir began.

'No, it is not.' Now look what she had done, fool, fool that she was!

'Of course a woman like you will not be able to go very long without hungering for the feel of a man between her legs.'

She did not deserve so cruel and cutting an insult. 'A woman like me?' Natalia's eyes flashed a stormy petrol-blue-green.

'You know nothing about women like me. How could you? Zahra is your image of what a woman should be; everything about her is fake, from her dyed hair, through her faked submissiveness, to her no doubt faked orgasms,' she threw at him passionately, and then stopped as something in his silence told her that she had gone too far.

'Keep away from me,' she protested apprehensively, backing away from him. 'Don't touch me.'

'I am your husband. I have the right,' Kadir reminded her silkily.

'Keep away from me,' Natalia repeated. 'You...you stink of her scent,' she told him wildly. 'It makes me feel sick.'

'With what? With jealousy?'

There it was again; that accusation that made her heart jump around so painfully inside her chest.

'No! Why should I be jealous of a relationship I would not want, and will never want, even if you went down on bended knee and offered it to me? I am your wife and it is my duty to have sex with you.'

'Your duty? You mean like it was your duty in Venice,' he taunted her.

He was circling her like a hawk circling its prey, Natalia acknowledged. Even the unmoving air in the room felt heavy and weighted with the promise of implacable determination to make her back down. She had pushed him too far, Natalia admitted, dangerously too far, and for what reason? Because Zahra had got under her skin?

'So let us see then—again—just how good you are at separating duty from desire, shall we?' Kadir told her softly.

No woman had ever aroused him to such passion and fury, to such a fierce, consuming need to make her take back the lies with which she had ripped apart his pride. Right now the only thing that would salve his wounds would be her tears of regret and shame as she begged him to forgive her. And then begged him to possess her?

'You will take back each and every one of those insults before tonight is over,' he told her savagely as he reached for her.

CHAPTER NINE

NATALIA LAY STILL on the wide bed, her heart thumping visibly heavily within her naked body. She would not demean herself by trying to resist. Physically his strength was the greater, and all that she wanted now was for him to leave her alone, even if to have that she had to allow him to inflict his hunger for punishment on her first.

Kadir could feel his heart hammering against his ribs. In the lamp light her skin was the colour of clear warm honey. Just seeing her was awakening an unsteady mental flash of jumbled images of the last time he had seen her this intimately; images he had had no idea until now that his brain had even recorded, never mind put to a sound track of his own arousal and spliced with the scent and the feel of her until the images sprang to unwanted three-dimensional life inside his head in a way that undermined his self-control and fed his hunger for her.

She had challenged his maleness in a way he could not leave unanswered. And that was the reason he was doing this. The only reason. There was no other. She herself meant nothing to him.

Kadir's hands shaped her body, mercilessly seeking to expose its weaknesses, Natalia sensed. His touch was light and gentle and far too knowing. It skimmed her throat and then her breastbone, the curve of her waist, the shallow dip of her belly and then began again. She badly wanted

to draw in a huge lungful of air, but she dared not let him
see that need in case he took it as a sign of weakness. His
fingertips stroked the delicate flesh just behind her ear.
A shudder racked through her body. Because of the chilling night air coming in from the courtyard, Natalia assured herself, nothing more. And that heavy, expectant
weight of sensual awareness mushrooming low within her
body? It was nothing. Nothing at all. Less than nothing. She
could quite easily pretend she couldn't feel it. Quite easily.
Couldn't she? She could feel his mouth against her skin,
the tip of his tongue sliding expertly against the sensitive
ridges of her ears. Why did he have to do that to her? How
did he know…? Her whole body shuddered as though it
had been electrified as she tried to fight her own pleasure
and failed. She put out her hands to push him away, but he
caught hold of them, forcing them back onto the bed, his
fingers locked around her wrists, leaving his mouth free
to torment her agonised flesh as he trailed slow, fiery ribbons of unbearably erotic stimulation from one sensitive
point to the next and then the next, each tug on those ribbons drawing the ache between her legs tighter.

When his tongue-tip flicked against the tight heart of
her nipple she cried out like someone in mortal agony, begging him to stop.

'Are you sure? Wouldn't you rather I did this?' he tormented her, brushing her nipple with his lips, releasing
her wrists so that he could cup her breasts and then tug
rhythmically on her flesh making her whole body respond
to that rhythm.

Tears of disbelief and despair stung her eyes. How could
she have let this happen so easily? She wasn't a girl to be
overawed by her own body's needs. She had felt like this
before.

Had she? Had she, or was the truth that she had never

known anything like this, or anyone like this? No! She would not let herself think like that.

If it was the truth then she could not and wouldn't admit it, and never wanted to know it again, Natalia told herself as she fought desperately to stave off her own defeat. Never!

HE SHOULD BE celebrating winning; he should be exulting in his victory over his ability to bind Natalia physically to his will, Kadir knew as he felt her losing her self-control and being forced to submit to her desire for him. Only he wasn't celebrating, Kadir acknowledged; he could not do so because with every touch, every stroke, every kiss, every breath of his body, his senses were playing out too much of the reel of his own self-control. He was no longer controlling her sexual desire, instead it was controlling him. As if they were two finely opposed and equally balanced powers, all that was supporting the edifice he had built out of her desire and his own fury was the counter weight between them; if that broke he would be plunged into the abyss of his own desire for her. He must stop now, withdraw from the field, leaving her punishment for her offence incomplete even if that meant that he had to go without the full taste of her complete surrender on his lips as she begged him for his possession of her—and he withheld it. She must never know he felt like this, ached like this and needed like this. It broke all the rules of what he was, so carefully constructed to protect him. The rules he'd created as he'd grown up with a father who had rejected him and a mother who had seemed not to care, a first young love to whom he had given his trust and his infatuated adoration and who in turn had betrayed him; they had taught him not to be ruled by his emotions and not to trust those who tried to touch those emotions.

Now unexpectedly all that was in danger of being undermined by a woman who had the power to move him to such anger, to excite him to such desire, to wound him to such depths that all of him that was male clamoured within him to compel her to sacrifice herself to him in payment for that sin in every way that there was. But somehow things had rebounded on him.

He would stop now before it was too late. Now, after just one more touch, just one more kiss, just one more heartbeat imagining the shuddering, gut-wrenching pleasure of her hands on his body, and then…

Natalia clung to him, her nails biting into the smooth warm flesh of his upper arms, her head falling backwards as she arched up in sensual sacrifice.

The scent of her would live with him for ever, ever constant and yet ever changing with each breath she took, one minute cool and aloof, another hot and charged with her arousal. It filled his senses colouring even the taste of her when he folded back the swollen lips of her sex to draw from her the fierce pulse that lay within the moist heat of her body. Now of its own accord that hard bead of flesh pulsed and throbbed, her body eagerly opening to the stroke of his fingers. He could do it now, stop and walk away letting her know the price she must pay for what she had said. He *could* do it, but the feverish movements of her body were more than his own could bear. The ache he had thought controlled had become a raging, savage, primal male call he couldn't silence or ignore.

HAD IT BEEN like this before? If so she couldn't remember it, Natalia thought feverishly as her clitoris quivered with orgasmic shudders of moist urgency and the muscles within her flexed helplessly against their own emptiness. She had never wanted like this before; must never, ever want like this again. It was killing her, destroying her, taking her down to a dark place she was afraid she might never come back from out of fear for what it was doing to her and what it might turn her into. She heard a raw moan. Her own?

No. It was Kadir's male voice savage with a need that her own senses recognised as he moved over her and stroked into her, full and hard, momentarily satisfying the greedy contracting of her muscles as they clung avidly to him, relaxing into helpless pleasured obedience when he commanded their movement. The pleasure running swiftly through her was now gathering pace, climbing swiftly, mounting the plateau and going way way, beyond it, taking her with it.

Kadir's breathing was a harsh litany of command and demand against the ear, her body tightened fiercely around him in a series of sharp contractions. She could feel him starting to withdraw, instinctively she clung to him, until she could feel the hot, wet pulse of him inside her.

Too late…too late! He had left it too late, but Kadir couldn't see any sign of triumph in the glazed darkness of Natalia's open-eyed gaze as he looked down into her eyes.

CHAPTER TEN

THERE WAS NO denying the fact that Natalia had a way with her that people responded to, Kadir admitted as he watched from a distance whilst she thanked the suddenly shy school children who had gathered in the square outside the palace of Niroli to welcome them back. He had seen it in Hadiya when she had talked to the women there, communicating with them despite their inability to speak one another's language. Somehow she had reached out to them and made them laugh and respond to her, just as the children were doing now. His mother had had the same gift. His mother!

Kadir withdrew from his own thought as though it had physically burned him. Natalia had had no right to speak to him about his mother as she had done. She knew nothing of their relationship or of his childhood. And as for her gibe about him wanting to prove himself to his mother's husband, the sheikh—that was so much rubbish. What did he have to prove? He had chosen voluntarily to hand Hadiya into his brother's care after all.

He had not slept with Natalia for the last two nights they had spent in Hadiya. To punish her or to prove to himself that he controlled his desire for her and not the other way around?

'My son—I have missed you! It is good to have you back.' King Giorgio's greeting was warmly emotional as he welcomed Kadir with these private words during the formal reception ceremony to welcome them back. Was it his imagination or was his father's handshake really not quite as strong as it had been? Kadir felt an unexpected pang of emotion grip his heart as he looked at the older man. There was nothing to link them together other than their blood; no shared past, no shared history, and yet his father's words touched a place deep within his heart.

'We have so many years to catch up on,' the king was saying. 'May God grant me enough time. What I wish for more than anything else now, Kadir, is to hold your son in my arms; the next generation. Niroli's future King, born here of my blood and of the blood of the island through Natalia.'

The king looked across to where Natalia was still talking to the children. 'Kings cannot always marry where they wish, but in Natalia you have a wife perfectly suited to her role. When I look at her I see both my gentle first wife Queen Sophia and your own mother, she has qualities that belonged to both of them.'

One of the smallest of the children surrounding Natalia was accidentally jostled by some of the others and started to lose his balance. Kadir watched as Natalia saw what was happening and acted promptly, scooping the little boy up to give him a cuddle whilst exchanging a few words with his mother. Immediately the child's threatening tears turned to shy smiles, and it was obvious to Kadir how at home he felt in Natalia's arms, and how easily she had diffused what could have been a difficult situation. But it wasn't her unintentional display of her skills as his future consort that was causing that sharp shaft of pain to lance through his heart, was it? A sense of something breaking open inside him under intense pressure filled his body and his senses. It was a physical pain accompanied by a surge of melan-

choly; a feeling of loss and aloneness and angry antagonism and a profound sense of longing.

He had no need to ask himself what was happening to
him. He knew all too well that the protective shield he had
thrown around his emotions had cracked apart. Because
of Natalia? Because she was making him both see and feel
things about his own behaviour and his own reactions that
he couldn't ignore? He didn't want this. He didn't need it
and somehow or other he was going to make sure he found
a way not to let it happen.

'Now,' he could hear the king saying, 'whilst you have
been in Hadiya our Chief Minister has been putting in hand
the arrangements for your formal ascension to the throne.
There is much we need to discuss.'

Although she was refusing to look at him, Natalia knew
the minute Kadir left the square with his father. She could
almost feel the empty space where he had been just as she
could feel the emptiness beside her in bed at night where
he should have been. Had he shared Zahra's bed in Hadiya
when he had left her alone in hers? The violence of her own
jealousy filled her throat with nauseous bile.

What was happening to her? This was not the way
things were supposed to be. She and Kadir were supposed
to have a calm, adult, businesslike relationship based on
mutual respect and awareness, on a shared desire to work
towards an acknowledged logical goal, a relationship
within which there was trust in their commitment to that
goal, and trust too in their mutual awareness that nothing
outside their relationship should prejudice it. Their marriage was supposed to be one where both of them retained
the right to their own emotions and ultimately to their own
freedom sexually—so long as they were discreet—where
they wished. So how had this happened, how had she been
turned into a seething mass of furious female jealousy at

the mere thought of Kadir so much as looking with desire at another woman? Was Zahra's accusation true? Had she fallen in love with him? If so, no wonder she was feeling so sick and dizzy.

'AND THE FUNDS we receive from the charitable trust set up by Prince Marco and his wife enable us to provide the very best kind of neonatal care, and to attract top experts in their field to our hospital.'

The young Chief Administrator was beaming with pride as he showed Kadir and Natalia over the newly opened wing of Niroli's maternity hospital, which they were visiting.

As she listened to the administrator Natalia risked a brief glance at Kadir, wondering how he was reacting to this mention of King Giorgio's eldest grandson whom he had not as yet met and who should have been the one to step onto the throne when the old King stepped down. She could not, though, see any hostility in Kadir's concentrated expression of interest as he listened attentively to the young administrator. No, it was more *her* sex—or at least certain members of it—that aroused him to anger, she acknowledged as she stifled a small yawn. Not because she was bored, but rather because she was feeling so unusually tired for some reason.

'Thanks to the charity donations, we have been able to acquire for our maternity unit two of the world's most up-to-date foetal scanners. These machines are capable of taking three-dimensional pictures of the unborn child—thus enabling doctors to pinpoint any potential problems far earlier than was previously possible.' The administrator showed them some example images.

Natalia was reluctantly being forced to admit that Kadir was handling his new role with far more sensitivity and diplomacy than she had expected. At no time during the last few hectic days of tours around government institutions, factories, vineyards and the like had he ever by so much as the flicker of an eyebrow displayed anything other than complete understanding of and respect for the obvious pride of his new subjects in their country; never once had he mentioned Hadiya or offered any comparisons between the two countries, never once had he risked offending the pride of the old guard, whose stiff formality on first being introduced to him had quickly melted into open respect for him once he had listened to them. And yet he still showed them what kind of King he was going to be with informed questions, and crisp forthright answers to those questions they put to him once he had broken down the natural barrier of their reserve towards him as a stranger.

'He is King Giorgio all over again and more,' Natalia had heard one of the village headmen saying approvingly. 'He is a true man and not afraid to say what he thinks. Mark my words, he will rule Niroli as it should be ruled.'

'AND THE YOUNG people of Niroli are saying that it will be a true new beginning for them and that we shall no longer be left in the past when our new King takes the throne. King Giorgio has been a good king, but he is the king of our grandfathers and our great-grandfathers, he's getting old and he no longer goes out amongst the people as Prince Kadir is doing, talking to them and learning how they feel,' one of her young maids was telling Natalia excitedly as she helped her to remove the heavy formal gown she had worn for the evening's reception to introduce Kadir to the most influential of Niroli's citizens and some from the international community of the very rich who owned property on Niroli, along with the resident diplomats from other countries.

Kadir needed no help from her in speaking with such people nor in subtly using his skills in diplomacy to persuade them that the future of Niroli was one they would be privileged to both invest and share in, Natalia had recognised. She felt a small pang of regret as she felt her own role was diminishing in a direct ratio to Kadir displaying his leadership skills. After all, the whole purpose of her agreeing to marry Kadir had been her belief that she was doing so for the benefit of her country. Now it seemed that Kadir might not need her help as much as she had believed, and that he was perfectly capable of winning the love and the respect of the people by himself.

And, as though that weren't enough, to judge from the snatches of conversation she had overheard, the evening's event had secured a large number of pledges from the super wealthy to assist Kadir in his plans to take the island into the kind of future that would benefit, not just those who invested money in this, but also the people of Niroli themselves.

'The greatest investment of all will not be the money you pledge to the island, but rather the investment made by the people of Niroli when they return your investment to you tenfold with the skills our young people will be able to learn with your financial support and co-operation.'

Natalia was not surprised that Kadir had received a standing ovation for his speech.

'Everyone is saying how fortunate we are to have such a handsome Crown Prince,' her maid confided as she removed Natalia's heavily beaded gown. 'They say that you will make very beautiful children together.'

The Crown Prince might be handsome, but what she longed for was a true marriage. Her new life might be busy, but right now it was leaving her feeling hemmed in and restless, she admitted as she thanked her maid and dismissed her. Because she envied Kadir the many challenges that lay ahead of him? Because tonight she had seen so clearly the breadth of the vision he had described so well to those listening, and she had longed so fiercely to be his true partner in that vision? His true partner in every single way?

That could have been, perhaps if only he had not judged her as he had. Now of course he saw her as a person he could not trust. They could have had so much together, worked so closely together. Natalia blinked away the pain given tears clouding her eyes and went into her bathroom.

Tonight, as he had done every night since their return to Niroli, Kadir would emerge from his own dressing room to share their huge bed with her, but he would not touch her. Not now. Not until she told him whether or not the intimacy they had shared had resulted in a child. Natalia placed her hand to her still flat stomach. She had first suspected the truth the morning of their return flight from Hadiya, but she had had to wait until she had gained the privacy of her grandfather's home and the services of the old family doctor who was her grandfather's close personal friend and sworn to secrecy to confirm those suspicions. The telltale line in the pregnancy-testing kit the doctor had given her had confirmed what she had suspected—she had conceived Kadir's child. The dates also confirmed that this child, this son or daughter, had *not* been conceived after their marriage in Hadiya, but in Venice. But how, when he had used a condom? It was hardly a question she could ask her family doctor. All she could do was assume that the condom had failed as she now remembered reading somewhere that they weren't a hundred per cent effective.

Perhaps because of the concern of her own thoughts she had lingered longer in her bathroom than she had intended with the result that Kadir was already in bed when she returned to the bedroom.

Kadir slept naked, and she knew it was that knowledge that caused her heart to jerk sharply as she tried not to see the way the light from the bedside lamp played on the smooth olive tautness of his shoulders and chest as he lay propped up against the pillows reading a document, and not the fact that she was concealing from him something he had every right to know.

Kadir watched Natalia approach the bed. She was wearing a thin silky robe that, whilst concealing the feminine curves of her body, somehow still drew mental images for him of a highly sensual and intimate nature.

'I have to thank you for the role you played in the success of tonight's reception,' he told her as she sat down on the edge of the bed with her back to him, discreetly slipping out of the robe before getting into the bed.

'I was only doing my duty,' Natalia told him woodenly.

Immediately his mouth thinned and he put down the papers he was holding.

'I would strongly advise you against adopting the role of a martyr,' he told her. 'It does not suit you. You are an extremely intelligent woman well versed in world affairs, with an important role to play in the future of Niroli.'

Natalia stared at him, astonished that he should compliment her.

KADIR WAS A proud man, it wasn't easy for him to admit that he had made any kind of error of judgement, never mind a huge misjudgement, but he was also a formidably fair and honest man. He had watched Natalia today interacting with their guests during the formal reception. He'd seen just how valuable an asset she was going to be to him and to the future of Niroli. He had been surprised and impressed today at the ease with which their separate roles had harmonised, thanks to Natalia. He had watched her speaking on a one-to-one basis to several of their male guests and at no time had her body language been anything less than confidently professional. She had not flirted, or teased; she had not used the obvious sensuality of her body or her beauty to focus their attention on her. Instead she had held them captive with her intelligence, winning their respect with that air of calmly regal distance he had watched her adopt in public. That they were charmed by her was not in doubt, that they would envy him such a wife so openly and obviously, he had always known, but that she should by her manner know exactly how to ensure that she was treated with the respect her role demanded had surprised him. Even if no one had introduced her to anyone within that room today as Niroli's future Queen, everyone there would have guessed it from her dignified warmth. Natalia possessed that rare ability to be both genuinely herself and what others expected of her. He looked across at her as she lay next to him all too aware of the now-familiar ache that wanting her brought to his body. They were married, their future lay together, he wanted her, and he knew he could arouse her to desire for him. Maybe these were the things he should concentrate on instead of focusing on her sexual past?

Natalia reached out to switch off her own bedside light, tensing a little when Kadir did the same.

'Don't let me stop you from reading your papers,' she said lightly.

'They can wait. Right now I have far more pleasant duties I prefer to perform,' Kadir told her smokily, catching her off guard as he reached over to her.

Wasn't it poor, unloved Catherine de Medici who had desperately refused to tell her husband that she was already

pregnant because she longed so much to be intimate with
him and to keep him in her bed and out of that of his mistress? Natalia thought guiltily as she felt her body flooding
with response to the deliberate intimacy of Kadir's actions.

'Perhaps I should be grateful that fate has given me a
wife so easily stirred to passion,' he murmured.

The trouble was that it was no longer merely physical
passion he aroused in her, Natalia admitted as she shivered with pleasure beneath the sensual play of his fingertips against her naked flesh.

'Natalia…'

It shocked her to feel the warmth of his breath so close to
her lips, and it shocked her even more to recognise that he
was going to kiss her. The intimacy of shared kisses had not
after all been something that had played a role in their relationship. The sweetness of eager, hungry kisses belonged to
lovers and they were not and never could be that. And yet
her lips were parting on a small exhaled breath, and then
softening beneath the persuasive hard warmth of Kadir's.
How easy it was to wrap her arms around him now and to
pretend that this was a new beginning for them, a chance
to start again. How easy and how very foolish and yet she
couldn't stop herself from doing so as she melted into his
hold as the intimacy of his kiss deepened from slow, masterful exploration to a fierce possession that had her heart
thudding against her chest wall.

'Natalia… My wife…' Kadir whispered softly against
her lips as he threaded his fingers through her hair and
held her still beneath him.

'My wife… My Queen…' He kissed her slowly and lin-
geringly, making her shudder with female longing for what
was to come. He kissed the corners of her mouth and then
traced its outline with his tongue tip.

'Your perfume is as permanently etched into my senses

as the perfume of life itself. I breathe it in with every breath until I am constantly filled with the memory of you, but tonight you are not a memory, you are a reality…' His tongue thrust against the frail barrier of her lips, deliberately taking possession of the inner sweetness that lay beyond them, stroking against her own tongue until he had seduced it into begging to reciprocate his intimacy.

Natalia could feel her head spinning. This was like no intimacy, no kiss she had ever known before. It was unique, overwhelming, possessing her…branding her as his for all time.

'There were many at the reception today who let it be known that they expected us to make haste to fill the palace nurseries and provide Niroli with a new heir, but none of them are quite so persuasive as my father,' Kadir told her. 'He reminded me only the other day that he may not have much time left to him…'

Natalia went cold as she listened to Kadir and realised just why he had initiated this intimacy.

Of course he was only making love to her because it was his duty to do so, and she was a fool if she had thought anything different. If? Why was she bothering to try to deceive herself? She had responded to him, welcomed him in her arms as a woman welcoming the man she loved. Had Zahra been right after all? Could she have seen what Natalia herself had not wanted to see?

'What is it?' Kadir was asking her. 'What's wrong?'

She couldn't bear to have him guess the truth and realise what a fool she had been. Bearing his contempt was hard enough; she didn't want to have to bear the burden of his pity as well.

'Nothing,' she told him lightly. 'I am sure that King Giorgio would admire your dedication to your duty.'

She was mocking him, Kadir realised angrily. Had she

guessed that just now when he had touched and held her that the only kind of duty he had been obeying had been his duty to show her just how much he desired her? Just as other men had desired her and possessed her before him. Men whom she had loved? Did she think of one of them when he held her in his arms just as his mother had thought of her lover and not her husband, secretly longing for that lover whilst obeying the 'rules' imposed on her by her royal marriage? Did every prince with a kingdom to inherit share this bitterness he felt at the thought of being tolerated, endured by the woman to whom he was married because of what he was? And what was it exactly that he wanted? He was forty, not a boy—he had long ago become cynical about the reality of 'love'.

Why was he experiencing these contradictory feelings that were pulling him in two such completely opposite directions? It wasn't necessary for him to share any kind of emotional intimacy with Natalia, and therefore it wasn't necessary for him to be feeling what he was feeling right now. Maybe not, but he must have absolute loyalty and fidelity in his wife. He must be able to trust her moral stature, knowing the pressures their position would put on her, and he was a fool if he didn't recognise that a woman who had so easily given herself to him on a mere whim did not have that moral stature, no matter how much he might wish to convince himself that she did. It wasn't for his own sake he must remember this, it was for the sake of his role as Niroli's future King. If he knew that Natalia could be not trusted, then he knew also that she must be morally policed to ensure that she did not bring disgrace on the crown and a bastard child into the royal nursery. Giving in to his desire was not policing those morals, it was indulging himself. Trying to convince himself that he might have been wrong about her was the worst kind of

self-indulgence there could be for a man in his position, and
he must not do it. He must not let her think that he had any
weakness for her. Angrily he crushed the unwanted and
unnecessary tender feelings that had come from nowhere
to challenge the reality of their relationship.

'I can assure you that no one will be happier to abandon that dedication than I,' he told Natalia harshly. 'You
cannot surely think that I have any real personal desire to
possess you.'

His words cut into her like a razor and in the agony of
her emotional pain Natalia didn't think of the consequences
of what she was saying when she told him recklessly, 'Well,
you may as well abandon it right now, then.'

There was a small ominous silence and then Kadir was
reaching up and switching on his bedside lamp so that he
could look down at her.

'And what exactly does that mean?' he demanded.

'It means that I am pregnant,' she told him quietly. It
was too late now to wish that she had been more cautious.

Kadir started to frown. 'That is good news, of course,'
he told her formally, 'but isn't it too soon for you to be
sure…?' Here thankfully was a way out of his impasse, at
least for the duration of her pregnancy.

Here was her opportunity to backtrack and lie by de-
fault by accepting the get-out he was unwittingly offering
her. What difference would it make, after all? She knew
that this child she was carrying was his. A baby born a
matter of about two weeks short of nine months would not
cause any undue comment, and there was surely no point
in risking what she knew she would be risking if she told
Kadir the truth.

But how could she lie to him feeling about him the way
she now knew that she did? She already knew how little he
trusted her sex; she was not his mother, a young girl forced

by fear and circumstances to foist her lover's child on her husband; this baby was after all Kadir's. She did not want the baby or their marriage to be shadowed by the burden of any kind of deceit. Who knew what the future might hold or how close to one another the years might one day bring them? It was perhaps foolish of her to have such dreams, but she did have them and she could not bear to prejudice them by building into the foundation of their future now a deliberate lie.

As though her silence had alerted him to the truth, Kadir's frown deepened. 'When?' he demanded curtly. 'When was this baby conceived?'

Natalia took a deep breath.

'In Venice,' she answered him. 'I conceived in Venice.'

To her shock he thrust back the bedclothes and got out of the bed.

'Kadir!' Natalia protested.

Her admission coming so closely on the heels of his own private thoughts felt almost as though they had been some kind of warning omen. If so it was one that he could not afford to ignore.

'That is impossible. We used protection, as you very well know.'

'I know you did, but condoms aren't always infallible,' Natalia pointed out. 'They do occasionally fail.'

'How convenient for you, but I don't accept your argument, not having had firsthand experience of your promiscuity. What happened, Natalia? Did you allow a lover to be over-enthusiastic and then decide that you had better ensure that you had sex with me, as well, just in case you might be carrying his child? Did you deliberately seek me out in Venice, knowing perfectly well who I was? After all, I have used my polo playing alias for many years now.'

Natalia gave a gasp of shocked disbelief.

'That's ridiculous,' she told him shakily. 'I had no idea who you were and there was certainly no previous lover. I don't—'

'You don't what? Have sex with strangers?'

Natalia could feel her face starting to burn. There was no way she could defend herself from that charge.

'Nothing you can say to me will convince me that the child you are carrying is mine,' Kadir told her coldly. He had picked up her scent bottle and was holding it in the palm of his hand; almost absently Natalia watched it start to glow with growing brilliance. Kadir could make the glass shine with his purity of heart and his goodness? There must surely be some mistake.

'I will not allow you to foist this child off on me,' he repeated savagely, replacing the bottle on her dressing table before turning away from her.

Kadir could hardly bear to look at Natalia. So much indeed for those feelings, those hopes he had begun to allow himself to acknowledge he was experiencing, those cautious, vulnerable tendrils of the beginnings of a need within himself to forget the past and allow himself to believe that here on Niroli he could put aside the ghosts of his childhood and build a true future with Natalia and the children she would give him.

His own bitterness tasted sour on his tongue where so recently it had known the sweetness of Natalia's kiss. What sweetness? he challenged himself savagely. That so-called sweetness had masked acid-sharp poison. Did she really think he had become so vulnerable to her that she could openly foist another man's bastard on him without him challenging her? And running behind the violence of his justifiably angry thoughts was the pride-scouring knowledge that a part of him actually wished that she had not answered his question truthfully and that instead she had…

that she had lied to him? Allowed him to believe that the child she carried was his?

Natalia waited until Kadir had left her to shut himself in his dressing room before daring to give way to her tears.

CHAPTER ELEVEN

SHE WAS NOT going to let them see how she felt, not now not ever, Natalia thought to herself as she watched the way Zahra clung to Kadir's arm as she laughed up flirtatiously at him.

Did anyone believe for one single minute that the other woman had really come to Niroli because she was interested in using some of the fortune left to her by her elderly late husband to finance a hotel and spa complex at a desert oasis some miles from the capital city of Hadiya, and thus wanted to know more about the success of Niroli's own resort? Or could they see right through what was so obviously a blatant plan on Kadir's part to bring his mistress to Niroli, even if publicly Zahra appeared to have arrived here under her own steam and on her own whim. To stay here permanently? Was it really only three months ago that the thought of her as-then-unmet husband having a mistress had been one she had accepted with calm equanimity? Natalia was forced to ask herself. How naïve she had been, and how very foolish.

King Giorgio was beckoning her over to join him. Forcing herself to smile as serenely as she could, Natalia made her way across the salon, dropping the king a deep formal curtsey before taking the seat he had waved her into.

'It is good that Kadir intends to maintain good relations with Hadiya. As two nations we have much to offer one another and much to learn from one another.'

'Prince Kadir is bound to feel a strong sense of allegiance towards the country of his birth, Your Highness,' Natalia responded calmly.

'That is indeed so, but Kadir's home is here now, our customs his customs. I understand you met Zahra Rafiq on your honeymoon visit to Hadiya—is that so?'

'Yes,' Natalia agreed woodenly.

To her astonishment the king reached for her hand and squeezed it gently. 'You are a good girl, Natalia, and I can see in your eyes and hear in your voice the pride you feel. That is only natural and right, of course, however—' the king paused '—over the course of my lifetime I have perhaps made more than my fair share of mistakes, errors of judgement that my pride would not allow me to admit at the time, but which I now bear on my conscience even though it is not my habit to admit as much to others. Kadir is a very proud man. How could he not be when he is my son? As Niroli's future King he will be all the things that I want him to be for Niroli, but even at my time of life, Natalia, there are surprises and unexpected discoveries. I had not thought, for instance, that I should love him so immediately and so very dearly. It is as though he has been a part of my heart from the beginning. It is through that love I bear him that I say to you now that I do not want him to suffer the unhappiness my own pride has sometimes caused me to suffer. I have seen the look in your eyes when you look at him when you think no one else is watching and I have seen too the way Kadir looks at you.'

Natalia could guess what the king was about to say.

'Sir, you need have no fear that either of us will let you down,' she assured him vehemently. 'We are both committed to our duty to Niroli. I…I cannot speak, of course, for Kadir's most private feelings but…' oh, how it tore at her heart to say that knowing those private feelings were given

to Zahra '…but I know he will not allow them to come between him and that duty.'

Through his words, King Giorgio was making it clear
that even he could see how much Kadir wished that he
could have made Zahra his wife. It was more than Natalia
could bear. Barely able to control her voice, she bowed her
head and begged huskily, 'Sir, if I might have your permission to retire…'

'YOUR WIFE IS leaving,' Zahra told Kadir with obvious triumph. She smiled up at him provocatively and stroked the
sleeve of his jacket with her fingertips.

'Zahra, you should not have come here to Niroli,' Kadir
told her wryly.

'How can you say that when I can see how much you
need me?' she reproached him.

Kadir shook his head reprovingly. He had not been at
all pleased when Zahra had presented herself at the palace
claiming to officials that they were close friends, and insisting to him that all she wanted to do was to make use of
the new trade opportunities opening up between the two
countries. She'd said she'd wanted to remain his friend, but
when he had taxed her with it Zahra had been so sweetly
insistent that she fully understood that their relationship
was over, whilst begging him not to be cruel to her and
send her away, that Kadir had felt reluctantly compelled
to allow her to stay, at least until her business negotiations
were completed.

'I know now I should find someone else, Kadir,' she
was telling him softly now. 'But how can I when you are
the only man I want, and the only man I could ever want?
I could never be your Queen, I know that now, but foolishly my heart can't help hoping that you might find a small
place in your life for me, even if it is only that of a trusted

and discreet friend with whom you can spend a few precious hours relaxing.'

'This is foolish talk, Zahra, and you know it.' Kadir had to stop her. 'I am a married man now with a country to rule and an example to set to my people.'

'But you need me, Kadir. We are destined to be together. We would be together if it wasn't for the meddling of your mother. It was only when that fool, your mother, revealed her lies to you that you put me to one side. Until then—'

'Enough! I will not hear you speak of my mother so. You forget that she was your Queen.' He was not going to let Zahra make him feel guilty about ending their relationship. He had hardly been her first lover, after all, and he'd always made the boundaries of their relationship clear. It had surprised him that his mother should have disliked her so intensely.

'Your mother betrayed her husband; she was not fit to be Queen.'

'That is enough!'

'She claimed the sheikh as your father when he was not,' Zahra continued, ignoring him.

'You forget that she was little more than a child when she made the decision to conceal my conception from her husband.' What was he doing defending his mother, and, worse, echoing Natalia's passionate arguments to him? Kadir didn't know. All he did know was that Zahra's unexpectedly venomously angry criticism of his mother had filled him with a desire to protect his mother from her.

'Kadir, why are we quarrelling like this when we could be doing something so much more pleasurable?'

This was the Zahra Kadir knew, a wickedly provocative, wholly sensual woman, who knew very well how to please a man in bed.

But who left him cold emotionally?

Kadir shook both thoughts away. No matter what their relationship might have been in the past, there was no place here in his present or his future for it, and he had made that plain to Zahra from the moment he'd known he wanted to take up his father's offer to succeed him to the throne of Niroli.

'You should not have come here,' he repeated firmly. 'You must return to Hadiya; I think you already know that.'

She was looking away from him so that Kadir did not see the flash of fury in her eyes as she bent her head and said submissively, 'Of course, as you wish, Kadir.'

It was unthinkable that Kadir should break with protocol here in the palace at this semi formal gathering of court officials and cause unwanted gossip by openly rejecting Zahra in front of everyone, but he still couldn't stop himself from removing her hand from his arm and stepping away from her.

Why had Natalia almost run from the room like that? He had seen her talking with the king. Had his father said something to her to upset her? Had he perhaps asked her when he might look forward to hearing the news he so longed to hear?

'You cannot deceive me, Kadir,' Zahra was saying. 'I know that it is me who you want. Let me be the one to give you your first child, not her, that nobody you have married. Let me give you your first son…come to me tonight and we can—'

'Zahra, you are talking nonsense and you know it,' Kadir checked her firmly. 'Besides, it's already too late,' he told her curtly. Natalia was already carrying a child she claimed was his, but which he knew quite simply could not be. After all, he had used a condom. It was far too convenient for her to suggest that the condom might have been flawed.

Like her? Like the feelings for her he did not want to admit to? He shook the thought of Natalia away and tried to focus on Zahra instead. What on earth had got into her? She knew it was out of the question that they should restart their relationship, never mind that she should have his child, and he couldn't understand why on earth she should be saying such nonsense. He hoped that letting her know that Natalia was already pregnant would underline those facts and bring her to her senses.

THE DOOR FROM their bedroom to Kadir's dressing room stood open, the space beyond it dark and empty. Wherever Kadir was he was not here in their private apartments. Wherever he was, Natalia taunted herself bitterly. It was three o' clock in the morning. Where else could he be other than in the bed of his mistress? No wonder he had been so adamant that Zahra should not stay at the palace, but should instead have the use of a small private villa close by for the duration of her visit. Her visit or her permanent residence?

To her shock the outer door to the bedroom suddenly opened. Through the shadows Natalia could see Kadir look across to the bed where she lay.

'What's wrong? Did you decide it might not be a good idea to spend the night with your mistress after all?'

Why had she said that? She had promised herself she would not humiliate herself by descending to that kind of revealing sarcasm, but, as Natalia was beginning to discover, her emotions were far stronger than her logic.

'And what exactly is that supposed to mean?'

Natalia could hear something beyond anger in Kadir's voice that could have been exhaustion, but she did not want to listen to it.

'You know exactly what I mean, Kadir. Zahra is your mistress; she made that plain enough to me in Hadiya. You invited her to come here and tonight you made it plain to everyone just what your relationship with her is.'

'I did not send for Zahra.' He had dropped down onto his own side of the bed and was sitting there with his back to her, Natalia saw as she switched on her own bedside light.

'You don't really expect me to believe that, do you?' she threw at him scornfully.

'Yes, as a matter of fact I do,' he told her angrily. 'You see, unlike you I do not lie and use deceit.'

'Unlike me! You criticise me as freely as though you know everything there is to know about me, Kadir. And yet the truth is you know nothing about me, because if you did you would know that whilst, yes, I understand and enjoy my sexuality—what woman of my age does not unless she has serious issues on both counts—but that does not mean that I abuse it. In fact it may interest you to know that prior to my folly in Venice in giving in to…to what we did, I had been celibate for well over five years—and by choice. You, of course, will not believe that because you would much rather believe the worst you can of me because that reinforces your decision to think badly of your mother and you have to do that otherwise you might—just might,' she told him bitterly, 'find yourself having to admit that you misjudged her. And that would mean that she died longing for your forgiveness and being refused it—'

'No…'

His tormented denial shamed her back to reality. No matter how unhappy she was, that did not give her the right to try to hurt him, and, besides, the truth was that in reality she loved him too much to want to do so. Loved him! How that knowledge tore at her vulnerable heart, and how she wished it were not so.

A terse apology quivered on the tip of her tongue but before she could offer it he repeated, 'No…you are wrong.

I did…that is… No matter what I thought privately I could not let her die thinking… Of course I told her that I understood. How could I not? She was my mother…'

There was a huge lump in Natalia's throat. 'I'm… I'm sorry,' she told him huskily. 'I should not have said that.'

'No, you shouldn't have,' Kadir agreed tiredly. 'And as for your accusation that Zahra is my mistress, yes, once that was true, but it ceased to be true with my mother's death. Zahra's decision to come here had nothing to do with me and I have made it clear to her that there is no place here for her, and certainly not in my life or my bed.'

Could that be true, and, if it were, perhaps this sudden mood of admittedly somewhat hostile exchange of confidences between them could lead to a better understanding between them? Perhaps that might mean that in time… What? That in time he would love her?

'So if you haven't been with her, then where have you been?' she challenged him.

'Driving…and then walking.' Abruptly he changed the subject. 'You say you were celibate before Venice. I am not a fool, Natalia. I've seen just what a woman will do to protect the child she carries. My mother told me that it was not out of love for King Giorgio that she allowed her husband to believe he was my father, it was out of love for me, her child. She told me that when a woman conceives a child, no matter what her feelings or her moral stance was before, from the moment she knows of the new life she carries within her, protecting that life becomes her prime concern. In many ways you remind me of my mother. You share the same concern for others and the same strength of purpose and spirit.'

'And because of that you believe that I would lie to you about the paternity of your child—is that what you are saying?' Natalia asked him.

It seemed incredible that they should be having a conversation of such intimacy when less than an hour ago she had believed him to be holding another woman in his arms. How odd and unfair it was that she should be able to accept his words as the truth when he could not do the same with hers. But then she did not have his experience with his mother to contend with.

'You are lying to me. I know that.'

'That is not true. I am telling you the truth. This baby is your baby.

'Perhaps I shouldn't have told you I was pregnant,' Natalia burst out miserably when he made no response. 'Perhaps I should have held back the truth and let you think I had conceived after we were married,' she told him. 'Only, you see, I didn't want to think that the future relationship I hoped we might have together had been built on a lie.' She put her hand on her stomach. 'This *is* your child, Kadir. If you can't believe that—or me—then there are always DNA tests,' she reminded him, hating herself for being so weak as to offer him this instead of insisting that he accept her word. 'Although they cannot be done until after the baby is born.'

'Do you think I'm completely stupid? We used protection—this child cannot be mine and so there is only one way the situation can be resolved.'

'And that is?' Natalia demanded shakily.

'A document must be drawn up which you will sign stating that this child is not mine and therefore cannot be my heir nor ascend to the throne of Niroli on my death.'

Natalia stared at his unbowed back. 'I don't understand what you are saying,' she told him, but she was horribly, sickeningly afraid that she did. 'Do you really expect me to sign away my child—our child's rights to its paternity? Do you really think I would do that to our baby?'

'Your baby,' Kadir corrected her coldly. 'This child is none of my doing, Natalia, and I will never accept it as such. So either you agree to sign such a document or I will have to go to King Giorgio and tell him that the marriage will have to be put aside and why.'

'You can't do that,' Natalia whispered.

How could she tell him after what he had just said that she had truly come to believe that, somehow or other, il-logical and fantastical though it seemed, something deep within her *had* somehow recognised in Venice all that he would come to mean to her, and that as a result fate had willed that she would conceive his child.

'I don't want to,' he surprised her by admitting. 'I have my father's feelings to think of. He personally chose you to be my wife. He is a very proud man, and to learn what you are would humiliate him. Plus, your lack of sexual morals aside, rather surprisingly in the short time in which we have been married I have come to recognise how well equipped in other ways you are to be Niroli's Queen, and how much the island will benefit from having you as their Queen,' he told her sombrely. 'Together we can work to give this island and its people all that they deserve to have, but I cannot and will not allow this bastard child to claim me as its father. You will do well to keep the child out of my way because it will for ever remind me of all the rea-sons why I have learned to doubt and mistrust your sex.'

Kadir thought about the hours he had just spent battling with himself, with what he truly believed was right. He had forced himself to admit how much she had already come to mean to him, and how much he wanted her by his side, but he could not overcome his fury that she continued to try to force on him a child he knew could not be his.

'The choice is yours,' he told her as he got up off the bed.

'And if I refuse?' Natalia asked him, dry-mouthed. But

of course she already knew the answer. 'Kadir, please, this is your own child you are talking about,' she begged him. 'The condom must have perished. The baby can have DNA tests and I promise you this is your child. You can monitor them yourself. Kadir, you grew up with a father who turned his back on you. You know how much that hurts and the pain it causes a child.'

'Don't ask me to lie to you, Natalia, because I won't. I'm afraid I can't see how this can be my child. I will sleep in my dressing room tonight.'

Natalia lay back against her pillows after he had gone.

He was offering her so much that she wanted, but at such a dreadful price. She could not and would not allow him to deny their child its right to his or her true paternity, but she could not force him to give the baby his love any more than she could force him to give it to her. Why, why, why had this had to happen? If only she had not gone to Venice, if only she had not met him until their wedding day... But why say that, why not ask herself why Kadir could not accept her word, why could he not accept the gift of herself she had already given him and the gift of his child that came from that night? But she knew the answer to that, didn't she? Kadir's inability to trust the female sex was very deeply rooted indeed.

Well, she would not let him punish their child because of what he himself had suffered in his own childhood. If he rejected it, then she would find a way of providing it with loving male influences from within her own family. She would protect and love their baby no matter what Kadir said, and even if it meant closing the door for ever on the love she had so longed to see grow between them.

CHAPTER TWELVE

NIROLI WAS EXPERIENCING one of its fortunately rare periods of bad weather, with fierce winds lashing the coast and whipping up the waves; grey skies had replaced the normal sunny blue and the outlook from the window of the salon in their private apartments looked dauntingly bleak. But nowhere near as bleak as her own future and the future of the child she was carrying, Natalia acknowledged.

She had planned to spend the morning working on her notes for a series of talks she'd been invited to give to Niroli's young women, the mothers-to-be of the next generation. She had planned to talk to them of the many opportunities she hoped would be available, not just for their unborn children, but for them, as well, but now the words of hope and encouragement and excitement simply would not flow. All she could think of was the poor child growing within her body and the fact that it would not have the opportunity to be loved by its father, the opportunity to grow up confidently and happily in a loving atmosphere, secure in its knowledge of its place in the world. Maybe these were the issues she should be addressing in her speech; the sadness of children born without love, unwanted, their chances of human fulfilment in all its most important senses pitifully crushed before they even drew breath. What did her vision of a new wonderful Niroli have to offer these children? Natalia pushed back the laptop on which she had been working and stood up. Today, because there'd been no formal engagements, unlike Kadir who was due to go on a tour of the island's vineyards, she had dressed in her own clothes, a soft off-white fine wool long sleeved top worn loosely beneath a tunic top in pale grey, worn over a gently flowing black shirt. It was one of her favourite outfits, designed by a talented young local designer. It was one of Natalia's dreams to be able to establish the kind of art college on Niroli that ultimately would attract tutors and students from all over the world.

She heard the door to the salon opening and turned round to see who it was, her heart sinking when she saw Zahra closing the door and standing between her and it.

The last person she felt like being with right now was her husband's mistress; her husband's ex-mistress, she corrected herself.

Kadir had after all sworn that that was the truth, and if she expected him to accept her own words as the truth then she could do no less for him.

'Is it true that you are to have Kadir's child?' Zahra demanded without preamble.

Her bluntness took Natalia slightly aback, but more importantly and more hurtfully was the knowledge that the only way Zahra could know about her pregnancy was because Kadir had told her about it himself. So much then for there not being any intimacy between Kadir and Zahra. After all, it was hardly the kind of information one would just throw into a conversation with one's supposedly ex-mistress, was it?

And when had he told her? Last night after she had finally drifted into an exhausted and unhappy sleep? Had he gone then to his mistress seeking solace with her because of his feelings about their child?

'Is it?' Zahra pressed her.

There was an almost fevered look about her, Natalia noticed uneasily, a wildness about her eyes and her manner, her movements uncoordinated and slightly jerky as though she was not fully in control of herself.

'Whether or not I am to have a child is surely a private matter,' Natalia answered with quiet dignity.

Zahra ignored her attempt to apply discretion to the situation by telling her passionately, 'Kadir has no secrets from me. He tells me everything. Everything,' she repeated fiercely. 'Do you understand? I know you are to have his child, but of course he doesn't want it. How could he?'

Natalia felt a wave of sickness surge through her, draining her strength. Until she had heard those last few telling words she had tried to convince herself that Zahra was exaggerating the extent of the intimacy she shared with Kadir, but now with that damning 'he does not want it' she was forced to accept the truth. Kadir had called *her* a liar, but he was the one who was obviously lying. No, she could not bear to go there. She must not let Zahra see how much she had upset her; she must think of her child instead.

'You say nothing, but I know it is true. Your very silence gives you away,' she could hear Zahra raging. 'You think you've won, don't you?' she told Natalia furiously. 'You think that just because Kadir has impregnated you he is yours, but he is not and he never will be. You may have conceived but you have yet to give birth. A king needs sons, heirs, live children…and you will never bear those.'

Something was going dreadfully wrong. She could sense it, taste and smell it almost in the air that separated her from Zahra. The other woman's words now surely had turned away from those of a jealous, vengeful mistress determined to stake her claim in a shared man and had instead become a direct threat to Natalia herself. The first tiny tendrils of fear began to unfurl coldly inside Natalia's stomach.

Where were her maids and the countess? It was too late

now to regret insisting that she preferred to be left alone unless she sent for them. Zahra was standing between her and the main doors into the public corridor. The other doors in the room, which were further away, led towards the rest of the apartment, which was empty.

Surely, though, she was being overly dramatic, something that perhaps all newly pregnant women were inclined to be when it came to the safety of their unborn child, Natalia reasoned, but no sooner had she offered herself the comfort of this thought, Zahra began to rant.

'Do you really think I will let you take Kadir from me? Do you really think that just because you tell him that you are to have a child that he will choose you above me? If so you are a fool. Because he won't. I won't let that happen. Not ever. I am the one he loves and wants. I am the one who is destined to stand by his side. Kadir is mine. Our sons will be his male heirs, and not yours. He can never be yours.'

Suddenly the tone of Zahra's voice had dropped to a chilling hiss that brought up the hairs at the back of Natalia's neck in warning.

'I will kill you first! You and your child. I will slit your throat and then tear the child you carry from your belly before I let you take Kadir from me.'

Zahra was mad. Completely and totally insane, Natalia recognised in a rush of shocked horror. Insane and dangerous, she admitted, icy cold fear gripping her as Zahra's words sank in. Instinctively Natalia looked towards the door. Quick as lightning Zahra intercepted and correctly interpreted her look.

'It is no use. You cannot escape.'

She must do something to try to calm her down, Natalia recognised. She must not panic and make an already dangerous situation even worse by playing into Zahra's hands. Someone would come, they were bound to do so. Desperately she tried to force herself to think past her panic and her instinctive and urgent need to protect her baby, to use logic, calming measures to diffuse the situation.

'There's no need for this, Zahra,' she told her, trying to keep her voice calm and steady. 'I don't want to take Kadir from you.' If she could just skirt round Zahra and get to the inner corridor doors she could escape into the corridor and lock herself in her bedroom until she could summon help.

'You're lying. You love him and you want him for yourself. I have seen it in your eyes. You have told him that you are carrying his child in an attempt to keep him, but it will not work, because you will not be carrying it for much longer.'

To Natalia's horror Zahra suddenly reached within the flowing sleeve of the long gown she was wearing and produced a wickedly sharp-looking curved and pointed dagger.

There was no doubt now that Zahra *was* totally insane, Natalia recognised numbly. There was no point in her trying to reason with her because wherever Zahra was it was somewhere way beyond listening to any kind of logical reasoning.

'First it was that mother of his who stopped him from marrying me,' she panted as she started to move towards Natalia. 'She did not approve of me. She did not think I was good enough for Kadir. And now because of her and her lies there is you, a European nobody who Kadir has been forced to marry. But he doesn't want you. He wants me. And I want him. Only you stand between us and our happiness. It is my duty to kill you, because it is my duty to make Kadir happy, and I am the only one who can give him true happiness.'

She had to reach those inner doors, Natalia knew, because if she didn't Zahra would try to harm her baby and try to kill her. She was the taller of the two of them and the more athletic, but she had no knowledge of how to use a knife or how to defend herself from one and from the slashing stabbing movements Zahra was making as she stalked her. Zahra was well versed in handling the murderous-looking weapon she was holding.

Even if she turned and ran for the doors, they were heavy and not easy to open and Zahra would be on her before she could do so, bringing that dagger down to rip and tear at her flesh.

Oh, what was she to do? Natalia found that she was praying silently for strength and help, begging God or anyone who was nearby to please help her and, more importantly, her baby.

THE VINES WERE in their resting period, row upon row of immaculately tended brown stems. As he watched and listened to Giovanni Carini, Natalia's grandfather, as he lovingly described their virtues and their vices to him it was as though he were talking about his children, Kadir recognised. Each vine was known to him and cherished for its individuality.

'And these are the new vines that were the gift to us of Rosa Fierezza,' Giovanni told him proudly. 'Their strength grafted onto our own vines will produce our best wines yet.'

'You obviously love them as though they were Nirolian born,' Kadir teased him gently.

'Surely it is every man's duty to cherish that which is a gift of love as much if not more than that which he has created himself?' Gioivanni told him steadfastly.

Suddenly, out of nowhere, inside his head Kadir could see an image of his mother as she had been in her last weeks, frail in body but the strength of her spirit shining through as she begged him to be proud of his true paternity.

'Niroli will benefit from all that you bring to ruling it, Kadir, just as Hadiya would have done had you chosen to take up your inheritance there. Your brother is a good administrator, and a fair and kind man, but you are the one who has the vision and the passion that is needed by a true leader and those are your gifts from your natural father. I beg you, do not turn aside from them or scorn them.'

His mother… How she would have loved Natalia. And the child Natalia was carrying? As clearly as though she had been standing at his side he could hear his mother's voice telling him softly, 'Do not deny your child, Kadir; do not turn away this precious gift, out of fear.'

Was *that* it? Was his refusal to accept that he was the father of the child Natalia was carrying based on fear? He knew perfectly well, despite having denied it to Natalia, that condoms were not always reliable; what man did not? In every other way Natalia had proved to him over and over again her honesty and her strong moral code through the things she said and did. Was it therefore so very unlikely that she would not tell him the truth about this child…? This child… His child. And he wanted to believe her, didn't he? He wanted her to be truly his wife, his partner, his, totally and completely. Again he felt that sharp stab of fear. The fear of a man deeply in love so lacking in true strength that he feared he was not able to win and hold the love of the woman he loved so deeply, because in the past he had felt unloved?

Kadir had never imagined that he would ever be called upon to look so deeply within himself and question his own motivations. But when a man fell deeply in love, the way he looked at everything changed.

Deeply in love? Him? With Natalia? Well, wasn't he? Wasn't that what this was all about? Was he really not man enough to accept her word that this child was his? What if their positions were reversed? What if he was being accused of having fathered a child who was not his, for instance, and she refused to believe him? How would he feel? All at once Kadir knew he needed to see Natalia and talk to her, honestly and openly, to lay before her his own insecurities and his love for her. He had been the first man, the only man she had slept with in many years, she had told him. How did accepting the truth of that admission make him feel? Didn't it make him ache to wrap his arms around her and tell her just what it did to him to know that her immediate and overwhelming desire for him had led her to break her own rules and show him how she felt? He looked discreetly at his watch. The tour was only half over, it would be several hours yet before he could return to the palace.

A sudden powerful surge of wind bent the vines to the ground, whistling as it ripped through the air around them, followed by the splatter of heavy rain.

'It is the notorious Niroli storm,' Giovanni told them. 'They come out of nowhere from the sea, blessedly infrequently, but when they do come…' He was looking anxiously at his precious vines and Kadir could see that he was impatient to do what he could to protect them.

'Your Highness, we should perhaps head back to the palace,' one of his aides was suggesting, 'at least until the storm blows over.' He was having to raise his voice so that Kadir could hear him above the increasing howl of the gale now battering them.

Kadir nodded his head, thinking ruefully that, whilst he wished the vines of Niroli no harm, he couldn't help but be pleased that the storm was giving him an excuse to be with Natalia.

Natalia! The urgency of his desire to be with her was pounding inside his head and his heart, driving him, and for once in his life he was determined to follow his instincts and his heart and not his head and logic.

THE FIRST PERSON Kadir saw as he walked into the palace was the countess.

'My wife?' he asked her. 'Is she…?'

'She is in your apartments, Your Highness. She asked not to be disturbed, but if you wish me to tell her that you—'

'No, there is no need, I will go myself,' Kadir said, thanking her.

'YOU CANNOT ESCAPE, you know that, don't you?' Zahra told Natalia. 'Even if you scream and someone hears you, by the time they get here it will be far too late.'

Natalia was struggling to accept what was happening. She knew that inwardly she had likened the previous intensity of Zahra's manner to that of a potential stalker, and she had, too, felt irritated by Kadir's typical male inability to see beyond the adoring, soft-as-butter, man-pleasing façade Zahra put up whenever she saw him, but it had never occurred to her that Zahra might physically attack her. The very idea seemed outlandish and like something out of a bad film. But it wasn't a film and it was happening to her.

'Zahra, you need to think about this and about what your own future will be if you go ahead,' Natalia urged her, striving desperately to bring down the tension by talking matter of factly about what was happening. 'You won't be able to escape. You will go to prison and how can you be with Kadir then?'

Zahra, though, was refusing to be sidetracked. 'Kadir will protect me,' she insisted. 'He is beyond the law and so I will be, too. Besides, why would anyone mourn you? You are nothing…and once I have given Kadir his first son no one will remember that you ever existed, but first of course I have to destroy the child you are carrying and you with it.'

How could she sound so casual? Surely only some kind of mental disorder could be responsible for such behaviour? And that surely meant that there was no point in trying to reason with Zahra. She had to try to get to those doors, Natalia recognised. There was no other chance of escape from her. With every deadly word Zahra uttered her madness became more clear. There was no point in trying to reason with her.

Natalia tried to judge the distance she would have to run; if she feinted and pretended to make for the far set of doors that might draw Zahra off and allow her to get behind her to the main set.

She took a deep breath and said a small prayer to her guardian angel, if she had one, and to her child for its forgiveness if they didn't make it.

She must focus on the doors, on getting them open and getting out. Abruptly the main door to the suite opened, causing both women to turn towards them.

'Kadir…' Natalia sobbed his name in sick relief as she saw her husband standing there. Whilst he might have encouraged Zahra to come here to be with him, Natalia did not believe for one minute that he could have known of her obviously hidden precarious mental state.

'What the—?'

Kadir took in the scene with one brief glance around the room. 'Zahra,' he began but she didn't let him continue.

Without taking her eyes off Natalia, she said with mad glee, 'It is all right, Kadir. Soon she will not come between us any more because I shall have killed her and the brat she carries.'

'Guards. *Guards!*' Kadir called out urgently into the

corridor as Zahra made a swift lunge towards Natalia, ripping the sleeve of Natalia's top with the downward plunge of her dagger as Natalia dodged her and started to run for the now-open doors. Natalia was fast, but Zahra's madness had obviously given her even greater speed. Natalia could hear the sound of her breathing behind her, she felt the sharp, biting sting of the blade as it sliced into the flesh of her shoulder and then, incredibly, unbelievably and surely impossibly, just as she thought there would be no escape for her after all, Kadir, who must have moved at the speed of light, threw himself protectively in between them to shield her and to take the full force of Zahra's savage stab towards his heart.

The last thing Natalia heard before she fainted was the soft, low grunt of pain Kadir gave as he fell forwards onto her.

'YOUR HIGHNESS, THE woman Zahra Rafiq was intercepted on her way to the airport. She has refused to undergo a medical examination here in Niroli. We have therefore as you instructed been in contact with the necessary authorities in Hadiya and they have given permission for her to be escorted there to undergo a medical assessment and receive treatment.'

Kadir's mouth compressed. He knew he would never cease to blame himself for not realising the dark truth Zahra had been concealing behind her mask of apparent sanity. Natalia, saint that she was, might have urged him to think compassionately of her and to understand that her behaviour sprang from an undiagnosed mental condition, but for the moment Kadir was finding that hard to do. The true guilt, of course, was his own for not realising the truth about Zahra himself, and he doubted he would ever forgive himself for that.

Having thanked the minister for his report he turned to
the palace aide waiting anxiously to talk with him. 'King
Giorgio is most anxious to see you, Highness,' he told
Kadir. 'The news of the dreadful attack on you and the
Crown Princess could not be kept from him and he is be-
side himself with anxiety.'

'Please tell my father that I am well and that I shall be
with him as soon as I have spoken with the Crown Princess's consultant.'

Not even to reassure his father did Kadir intend to leave
the hospital until he had spoken with Natalia and told her
what he had to say.

He knew that from now until his dying day he would
never, ever forget the emotions that had seized him when
he had thrust open the doors to the apartment and seen
what had been happening. The reality of her own imminent death had already been shadowing Natalia's eyes, her
hands clasped across her body to protect her, *his* child,
and in that moment all he had known, his single and only
thought, had been his need to protect them both. Not just
Natalia, but the child she carried as well, for he had known
instinctively then, when it was almost too late, that the baby
could not have been fathered by anyone other than himself.
He had felt protective of the baby and he'd been filled with
the most tender love for him or her. Who would protect
them both if he did not do so, who had more responsibility, more right to stand between them and whatever harm
might threaten them? His wife… His child…

His last thought as he had begun to lose consciousness
had been that he loved them both almost beyond bearing.

It had therefore been a shock to arrive at the hospital,
still barely conscious himself from his loss of blood, to be
told there was a grave danger that Natalia might lose the
baby—all the more so because of his own only just discov-

ered feelings. 'You must save the baby,' he had told them as they had worked to cleanse his wound—not, fortunately, as deep as it had first looked and not having damaged any vital organs despite the flow of blood.

'We will do our best,' they had assured him, not knowing his concern was not because the child was his heir, but because he knew how distraught Natalia would be if she were to lose it, and how he couldn't bear it if neither she nor the baby ever got to know how wrong he had been and how much he loved them both.

In her hospital bed, Natalia stared anxiously up at the consultant.

'My husband—how is he?' she asked him, realising even now when she was still in shock that, as Niroli's Crown Prince, Kadir's safety was paramount for his people and she surely must remember that.

'The Crown Prince is fine apart from a small flesh wound,' the consultant assured her. 'He is waiting outside to see you now.'

Natalia nodded her head, and then looked at him. 'You are sure…about…about the baby?' she pleaded with him, tears filling her eyes. They had already removed the drip they had used to replace fluids and she'd also been mildly sedated to keep her calm whilst they fought to prevent her from losing her child. 'There's no mistake…?' she begged him.

'No, there is no mistake,' the consultant confirmed tiredly. It had been a long night and they had been anxious to save the Crown Prince, the Princess and their baby.

The door to her room was opening. The consultant gave Kadir a small bow, before leaving them alone together.

'Thank you for…for saving my life.'

Kadir grimaced. He looked tired and drained. The

blood-soaked shirt he'd been wearing had been replaced by a clean one; the wound Zahra had inflicted was now cleaned and dressed.

'If I saved you, then it was only right that I should have done so since I was the one who put you both at risk in the first place. I had no idea about Zahra…she never showed any signs… When I told her that there was no point in her trying to remain here on Niroli, and reinforced that by reminding her that you are my wife and that you were to have a child, I never imagined for one moment…'

Something in the obvious sincerity of his shocked and earnest demeanour broke through Natalia's protective distance. She wanted to reach out and touch him, tell him, but how could she now when she knew what he must be thinking about the baby? He probably would have wanted her to lose it, even if he was not prepared to admit as much to her. She knew that. How could she not after the way he had refused to accept that the baby was his? 'You weren't to know. I expect she wasn't even aware that she was suffering from a mental illness herself. It's sad really…poor woman…' Natalia told him emotionlessly. 'But there's no reason for you to blame yourself.'

'On the contrary, there is every reason. You are my wife, it is my duty to protect you, I should have realised…'

'Have they told you yet about…about the baby?' Natalia asked him in a low voice.

Kadir nodded his head.

'I expect you think that it would also have been for the best if I had lost it, as they feared I would.'

She could not bring herself to look at him. Throughout the long hours when she had lain sedated whilst her baby had fought so hard to hold onto life she had known that Kadir must have been hoping equally hard that it would not. That hurt her far more than anything that Zahra had done to her.

'Natalia…'

The door to her room opened and an aide stood there. 'Your Highness,' he began, obviously flustered. 'The king…King Giorgio is here. He will not accept that you are alive and well until he has seen you for himself…'

The king was here? The king who never left his palace and who expected others always to dance to his will? Natalia's eyes widened. She had seen for herself the way in which his love for Kadir had softened the king's arrogance and warmed his heart, but this was evidence indeed of how much Kadir had come to mean to him.

'You must go to him,' she told Kadir quickly, reminding him, 'He is an old man, Kadir, and he must have been badly frightened.'

Kadir inclined his head. 'Very well,' he told her, 'but I shall return as soon as I can.'

No sooner had Kadir gone than the consultant returned carrying an envelope.

'These are copies of the scans we did of the baby,' he told her with a small smile. 'As you know, we do not advocate the use of our wonderful new scanner merely as a means of detecting a child's sex before its birth so that the parents can know what colour to decorate the nursery, but, since we had to do these scans to check that the baby was okay, I wondered if you might wish to have them?'

Smiling through the sudden emotion of her tears, Natalia took them from him.

'I did ask the Crown Prince if he would like to see them but he refused…'

'Yes,' Natalia agreed quietly. 'He would.'

'He said that you should be the first to see them,' the consultant told her, oblivious to the true meaning of her quiet and very sad words. 'You might not want to see them if you don't want to find out the sex of the baby—it is quite clear from these images.'

'No, that's okay, I'd love to know.'

'But, either way, it is good to know that the future King of Niroli values a daughter as much as a son. When I offered him the chance to discover the sex of the child you are carrying he said that its sex did not matter, only that it should live.'

Natalia stiffened in disbelief. 'I can't imagine…that is… he didn't really want…'

As though he had guessed some of what she was feeling and could not say, the consultant told her gently, 'The whole of Niroli knows that your marriage is a matter of state, but no one seeing the Crown Prince with you during these last worrying hours could doubt that, whatever might have been, he is now a man very much in love with and devoted to his wife. You were his first concern when you were all brought here. He begged us to attend to you first and he has remained here outside your room throughout the night. In fact at one time my nurse was forced to report to me that he had disobeyed my instructions and that she had found him sitting here with you watching over you whilst you were unconscious. Now, please promise me that you will accept that you need have no more fears for the safety of your baby. I do assure you that all is well and the crisis safely past.'

Natalia nodded her head. Kadir had said that to the consultant? He couldn't have meant it though—could he? She stifled a sleepy yawn. The consultant had warned her that she would feel tired for several days after all that she had been through and that her body would compel her to sleep to give both her and her baby a chance to recuperate fully. She looked at the envelope the consultant had left for her and then opened it slowly, studying the three-dimensional images inside it, her tears blurring her gaze as she saw her beautiful baby looking back at her. The baby she could so easily have lost…the baby she could so easily never have conceived in the first place.

NATALIA WAS ASLEEP when Kadir returned to her room and settled himself on the chair beside her bed. He looked down at the smooth bedclothes covering her still-flat body. His father's emotions as he had held him and reassured himself that he was truly alive had touched a well spring of responsive emotion within himself. He reached out and placed his hand on Natalia's body. He didn't need to struggle to recall how he had felt during the long hours of the night fearing with every heartbeat that she might lose the child she was carrying. That memory would remain with him for ever.

'I have prayed for you, little one,' he murmured softly, 'and my prayers have been answered. Be assured that you shall have my love for always and that I shall be a true father to you, just as you are already a true son to me, the son of my heart, as well as of my body, loved and held in my heart for always. You and your mother shall have the greatest gift I can give you and that is the gift of my love for the whole of your lives.'

'Kadir.' Natalia's voice was thick with tears. She had heard him come in but she had not opened her eyes, not realising that he would think she was still asleep.

'I mean it,' he told her, reaching out for her hand and clasping it between his own. 'I do mean it, Natalia. I love you. You, Natalia Carini, you, the bold, exciting woman who showed me her pride in her sexuality and shamed my own foolish blindness to the real reason I fought so hard against my love for you. Fear is a terrible thing, all the more so when that fear belongs to a man who refuses to accept that he can feel it, and gives it other names instead. Natalia, my wife, my love, my life, you are my love, even if I have refused until now to fully recognise that love.' He took a deep raw breath of air. 'When I saw Zahra with that knife and realised what she was going to do, it wasn't just your life I knew I had to protect, it was the child's, as well. You need have no fear that this child, this son, who I now freely accept as being my own child, will not suffer as I did. He *shall* be my son and I shall be his father, my first-born son, I love him as that already.'

'Your son?' Natalia asked him softly. She could barely keep the smile back from her lips or out of her voice. Her happiness was welling up inside her like champagne bubbles.

'Well, I don't want to disappoint you, Kadir, but actually this son you plan to love is going to be a daughter…' Still smiling, she handed him the scan pictures.

She might know now that Kadir was prepared to accept that their child was his, but somehow she knew that Kadir would fall totally and besottedly in love with his daughter in a way he would not have done with a son. Later, fate willing she would present him and the people of Niroli with a male heir, but for now to know she carried this precious wonderful gift of a daughter was almost more happiness than she could bear.

'A daughter…' Kadir marvelled as he looked at the images, his eyes bright with emotion.

'I thought we might name her for your mother…' Natalia suggested hesitantly. 'I…I thought about her when I was afraid and alone with Zahra and I prayed…'

Kadir's hand covered hers. 'I, too,' he told her thickly. Silently they looked at one another and then Kadir leaned towards her. 'Oh, my love, my dearest, dearest love. If I should have lost you.'

'But you didn't and you won't,' Natalia assured him as she lifted her face for his kiss.

A nurse coming to check on Natalia opened the door and then quickly withdrew. Who would have thought that a royal couple could behave like that—just like everyone else, holding one another and kissing so passionately that they were oblivious to her unwitting interruption?

'You know, I really think that she does have a look of my mother,' Kadir told Natalia judiciously later as they studied the scans together for the umpteenth time.

'No, she definitely has your nose,' Natalia corrected him firmly.

EPILOGUE

'THE FIEREZZA GENES are astonishingly vigorous,' Natalia heard Emily Fierezza, the wife of Prince Marco, saying laughingly to the women of the family gathered in the courtyard. They were preparing to leave for the cathedral where Kadir was to be formally crowned and anointed as Niroli's new King.

'I've lost count of how many new babies have arrived or are about to arrive. You will tell me if you start feeling tired, won't you?' Emily pressed Natalia. 'Only Kadir made me swear that I would watch over you like a hawk.'

'You and the countess and pretty much the rest of the royal household.' Natalia laughed as she waited to enter her carriage, one of several that would form the coronation procession that would escort Kadir to the cathedral as Niroli's Crown Prince and then back again as its new King.

'I can't get over the change in King Giorgio. I never thought I'd see him looking so happy and relaxed. Marco says it's like discovering a grandfather he never knew he had, and it's all thanks to you and Kadir. Marco says that, between you, you've humanised him.'

'I haven't done anything,' Natalia protested. 'I think it's more that King Giorgio has come to realise how important a loving family is and that one has to give love in order to receive it.'

'Kadir will make Niroli a wonderful King, Natalia,' Emily told her warmly. 'We all think so.'

Tears pricked at Natalia's eyes. 'You know how much it means to Kadir to have so much family support.'

'He and Marco have such a lot in common. They are both very determined and independent, true Fierezza men.'

They certainly were, and her own Fierezza man had that extra something very special that came to him via his mother's blood, Natalia acknowledged. A small secret smile curled the corners of her mouth, her gaze hazing with sensual memories. Initially Kadir had insisted on reining in his passionate desire for her because of their baby, but last night he had been swept away by her on the full tide of her own longing for him, and her assurances that it was perfectly safe. He had loved her with tenderness and intimate sensuality, in such a way that her body still ached a little from their shared pleasure. Her skin still remembered the heat of the kisses he had lavished on it, every sensitive place visited and then revisited until she had not been able to stop herself from crying out to him in hot, sweet arousal. He was so very much a man. Her man, and, as she had whispered to him last night as she had revoyaged over that territory she had explored the first time she had touched him, she truly did believe that something in her at some deep, little understood level had recognised him as her soul mate.

'Once I would not have believed you,' he told her in turn. 'But now, how can I deny it when every breath I take is witness to my love for you? I am so very blessed, Natalia,' he told her as he kissed her throat and then her jaw, his deliberate slowness making her ache for the feel of his mouth on her own. 'I have you, and our child…a father who loves me, a country that, with you at my side to guide me, has taken me into their hearts. Truly I am indeed blessed.'

And then he kissed her and Natalia knew that nothing

in the world could possibly ever mean more to her than this man and the child he had given her. Just thinking about last night was making her body ache with longing for Kadir. But now that ache was edged with the delicious eroticism of anticipation instead of the pain of doubt. Tonight she would hold him and touch him and show him…

'Princess, it is time,' the countess announced importantly, bringing her out of her secret sensual daydream by gesturing to the waiting maids to pick up the train of Natalia's coronation gown.

THERE HAD NOT been such an occasion in the whole lifetime of many of the people gathered in the square and along the streets, lining the way to the cathedral, and Natalia could hear their cheers of encouragement and delight as the old fashioned horse-drawn coaches bowled past them.

She would merely be an observer at this, the formal handing-over of the crown by King Giorgio to Kadir, but later she and Kadir planned to renew their vows to one another, in front of their people.

The cathedral was packed, its lofty spires reaching up into the bright blue sky, the hum of excited voices filling its cavernous interior.

But there was still, too, that quiet sense of spirit and belief; that awareness of times past and vows made, Natalia recognised as she joined the procession entering the cathedral.

At its head was King Giorgio escorting Kadir, but they were too far away for Natalia to be able to see Kadir's face, even though she could see the royal-blue velvet of his ceremonial cloak and the dark sheen of his bared head.

The sound of choir voices filled the air, rising on it like the most perfect notes of the most perfect scent. Today Kadir was wearing her special gift to him, a cologne she had made for him combining the most rare and special of ingredients to reflect the depths of her love for him and the beyond-price gift that he was giving to the people of Niroli in committing himself to them.

The king and Kadir had reached the two thrones waiting for them.

Natalia joined the other close members of the family in their designated pews.

The Archbishop of Niroli began the service of dedication. The ebb and flow of the solemn words of the ritual filled the ancient building, the reverence and awe of what was happening reflected in the radiance shining from the faces of the people as they said a respectful farewell to the king who had served them for so long and then turned with hope and confidence to the son who would, with his blessing, take his place.

'May you be blessed with many years in which to enjoy the fruits of your labours, King Giorgio,' the Archbishop prayed.

'And no doubt many years to interfere in the lives of the fruits of his loins,' Emily whispered ruefully to Natalia with fond affection.

They had grown especially close since it was the generosity of Marco, Emily's husband, and the worrisome health at one stage of their own now perfectly healthy child, that had led them to give the scanner to Niroli's maternity wing.

'He has grown very tired these last months,' Natalia whispered back, 'and, although he is far too proud to admit it, I think he would have been in despair if he still hadn't found an heir.'

They both fell silent as the choir stopped singing and King Giorgio rose from his throne to take the crown and place it on Kadir's head.

A hush filled the cathedral as though everyone there

held their breath, and not just those inside the cathedral, but those outside in the square who were watching the ceremony on the giant TV screens that had been erected there.

The old king's hands trembled visibly but the crown held fast. There was a collective release of breath as the archbishop began the prayer of ordination and then asked Kadir the three requisite times if he accepted the Crown of Niroli.

His final firm assent had barely died away when the old king clasped Kadir's shoulders and spoke emotionally as though unable to hold back the words.

'My son.'

Natalia suspected she wasn't the only one with tears in her eyes when Kadir replied equally informally and emotionally, 'My father.' When they embraced the roar of approval from the crowd rolled in from the city gathering force as it filled the cathedral until the building echoed with the joy of a people welcoming their future.

'I COULD NOT do this without you by my side, Natalia.'

'You could, but I am so glad that I am the one to share that future with you, Kadir.'

They were standing on the now-shadowed balcony, safely hidden from the sight of the stalwart revellers still celebrating in the square beneath them.

'Did you ever think we would be here like this that first time we stood on this balcony together?' she asked him.

'Never,' Kadir admitted, 'but I had much to learn then; much that you have taught me and taught me well.'

'The people of Niroli love you already.'

'I hope so, but they cannot love me anywhere near so much as I love you, and will continue to love you—you and our children, this child and the others I hope will come after her. You are my life, Natalia.'

'And you mine, Kadir.'

* * * * *

REQUEST YOUR
FREE BOOKS!

PASSION
GUARANTEED
SEDUCTION

2 FREE NOVELS PLUS
2 FREE GIFTS!

YES! Please send me 2 FREE Harlequin Presents® novels and my 2 FREE gifts (gifts are worth about $10). After receiving them, if I don't wish to receive any more books, I can return the shipping statement marked "cancel." If I don't cancel, I will receive 6 brand-new novels every month and be billed just $4.30 per book in the U.S. or $4.99 per book in Canada. That's a saving of at least 14% off the cover price! It's quite a bargain! Shipping and handling is just 50¢ per book in the U.S. and 75¢ per book in Canada.* I understand that accepting the 2 free books and gifts places me under no obligation to buy anything. I can always return a shipment and cancel at any time. Even if I never buy another book, the two free books and gifts are mine to keep forever.   106/306 HDN FERQ

Name _____ (PLEASE PRINT) _____

Address _____ Apt. # _____

City _____ State/Prov. _____ Zip/Postal Code _____

Signature (if under 18, a parent or guardian must sign)

Mail to the **Reader Service:**
IN U.S.A.: P.O. Box 1867, Buffalo, NY 14240-1867
IN CANADA: P.O. Box 609, Fort Erie, Ontario L2A 5X3

Not valid for current subscribers to Harlequin Presents books.

**Are you a current subscriber to Harlequin Presents books
and want to receive the larger-print edition?
Call 1-800-873-8635 or visit www.ReaderService.com.**

* Terms and prices subject to change without notice. Prices do not include applicable taxes. Sales tax applicable in N.Y. Canadian residents will be charged applicable taxes. Offer not valid in Quebec. This offer is limited to one order per household. All orders subject to credit approval. Credit or debit balances in a customer's account(s) may be offset by any other outstanding balance owed by or to the customer. Please allow 4 to 6 weeks for delivery. Offer available while quantities last.

Your Privacy—The Reader Service is committed to protecting your privacy. Our Privacy Policy is available online at www.ReaderService.com or upon request from the Reader Service.

We make a portion of our mailing list available to reputable third parties that offer products we believe may interest you. If you prefer that we not exchange your name with third parties, or if you wish to clarify or modify your communication preferences, please visit us at www.ReaderService.com/consumerschoice or write to us at Reader Service Preference Service, P.O. Box 9062, Buffalo, NY 14269. Include your complete name and address.

One unbreakable legacy divides two powerful kingdoms....

Read on for a sneak peek at
BEHOLDEN TO THE THRONE by USA TODAY
bestselling author Carol Marinelli.

* * *

"LET'S go now to the tent and make love...." Emir's mind stilled when he tasted her lips; the pleasure he had forgone he now remembered. Except this was different, for he tasted not a woman, but Amy. He liked the still of her breath as his mouth shocked her, liked the fight for control beneath his hands, for her mouth was still but her body was succumbing. He felt her pause momentarily, and then she gave in to him. But there was something unexpected, an emotion he had never tasted in a woman before—all the anger she had held in check was delivered to him in her response. A savage kiss met him now, a different kiss than one he was used to. The gentle lovemaking he had intended, the tender seduction he had pictured, changed as she kissed him back.

"Please..." The word spilled from her lips. It sounded like begging. "Take me back...."

Except he wanted her now. His hands were at the buttons of her robe, pulling it down over her shoulders, their kisses frantic, their want building.

She grappled with his robe, felt the leather that held his sword and the power of the man who was about to make love to her. She was kissing a king and it terrified her, but still it was delicious, still it inflamed as his words attempted to soothe.

"The people will come to accept…" he said, kissing her neck, moving down to her exposed skin so that she ached for his mouth to soothe there, ached to give in to his mastery, but her mind struggled to fathom his words.

"The people…?"

"When I take you as my bride."

"Bride!" He might as well have pushed her into the water. She felt the plunge into confusion and struggled to come up for air, felt the horror as history repeated—for it was happening again.

"Emir, no…"

"Yes." He must know she was overwhelmed by his offer, but he didn't seem to recognize that she was dying in his arms as his mouth moved back to take her again, to calm her. But as she spoke he froze.

"I can't have children…."

* * *

Can Amy stop at one night only with the enigmatic emir? Especially when this ruler drives a hard bargain— one that's nonnegotiable…?

Pick up
BEHOLDEN TO THE THRONE
by Carol Marinelli on December 18, 2012,
from Harlequin® Presents®.

*They're Wilde by name,
unashamedly wild by nature!*

Discover a deliciously sexy new
Wilde Brothers family dynasty tale
from *USA TODAY* bestselling author

Sandra Marton

Caleb Wilde, infamous attorney, has a merciless
streak and a razor-sharp mind…until one New York
night changes everything. Now, he's haunted by the
memory of tangled sheets, unrivalled passion and
one woman—Sage Dalton. But when he learns of
the consequences of their night together, Caleb will
stop at nothing to claim what's his!

THE RUTHLESS
CALEB WILDE

Available December 18, 2012.

Bound by blood, separated by secrets...

USA TODAY bestselling author

Kate Hewitt

introduces *The Bryants: Powerful & Proud,*
a stunning new trilogy.

Architect Chase Bryant has spent years appreciating
beautiful structures, and Millie Lang has all the right
angles! A passionate affair on a desert island is just
what he needs. As long as they keep their hands on
each other and off messy emotions, all will be fine.
But are they prepared for the Pandora's Box
of emotions that their intense passion unleashes?

Find out in

BENEATH THE VEIL
OF PARADISE

Available December 18, 2012.

www.Harlequin.com

HP13117

Rediscover the Harlequin series section starting December 18!